Pableaux Johnson

NATHANIEL RICH is the author of two previous novels: *Odds Against Tomorrow* and *The Mayor's Tongue*. His short stories have appeared in *McSweeney's*, *Vice*, and the *Virginia Quarterly Review*, which awarded him the 2017 Emily Clark Balch Prize for Fiction. He is a writer-at-large for *The New York Times Magazine* and a regular contributor to *The Atlantic* and *The New York Review of Books*. He lives in New Orleans.

ALSO BY NATHANIEL RICH

FICTION

Odds Against Tomorrow

The Mayor's Tongue

NONFICTION

San Francisco Noir: The City in Film Noir from 1940 to the Present

Additional Praise for

KING·ZENO

"Rich tells a complicated story with great skill and style, sketching the mental lives of a dozen major characters and bringing a vanished era to colorful and realistic life." —*The Wall Street Journal*

"Meticulously timed and plotted . . . [with] unforgettable characters . . . It takes time to learn a city, to love it, to make a mark on it, and Rich has done that in *King Zeno*."

—Susan Larson, *The New Orleans Advocate*

"[A] dark, panoramic thriller . . . Rich excels at character development, painting vivid, interior portraits." —*The Seattle Times*

"*King Zeno* is a great detective novel, a fitting tribute to the Crescent City." —Jeffery Gleaves, *The Paris Review* (Staff Pick)

"Action packed . . . Rich has a feel for New Orleans life."

—Dan Cryer, *San Francisco Chronicle*

"Rich uses music, race, and historical details in ways that will likely spark comparisons to E. L. Doctorow's multifaceted *Ragtime*. It's a nicely paced detective thriller, clever on corporate corruption and police procedure . . . marked by offbeat humor and up-tempo writing." —*Kirkus Reviews* (starred review)

"*King Zeno* is the New Orleans novel we've been waiting for . . . It reminded this reviewer of John Dos Passos's U.S.A. trilogy, with its clever melding of real and fictional events, its snippets of newspaper articles and astonishingly memorable characters."

—Arlene McKanic, *BookPage*

"Wildly imaginative . . . With an artful blend of humor, suspense, and noir, Rich folds facts into a work of fiction that evokes the historical novels of E. L. Doctorow."

—*The National Book Review* (Hot Book of the Week)

"In this deft historical thriller, Rich seamlessly blends fact with fiction as three characters attempt to secure their legacies in the shadow of a gruesome murder, with post–World War I New Orleans as the backdrop . . . The period details—most taken directly from the historical record—are expertly deployed."

—Michael Pucci, *Library Journal*

"The fates of those characters interweave in a tragic yet funny way to highlight the social and economic disparities in a city attempting to regain its faded glory . . . Rich knows well the city, its people, and the racial hierarchies that underpin their life and this story. His offbeat humor and lively writing make *King Zeno* a good read on both levels."

—Chris Smith, *Winnipeg Free Press*

"Rich brings multiple themes together in this roiling genre-blender set in New Orleans in 1918 . . . It's a rich gumbo of ingredients, and Rich stirs them effectively, combining a lyrical, impressionistic style with a sure-handed grasp of the historical moment . . . A heady mix of literary thriller and high-end historical fiction."

—*Booklist*

"Rich's spirited third novel contrasts the luminous early years of jazz with a number of particularly American darknesses . . . [He] excels at immersing the reader in the narrative."

—*Publishers Weekly*

"Those who have studied jazz history will find themselves right at home in Nathaniel Rich's new novel, *King Zeno* . . . Rich, who lives in New Orleans, has given his city yet another reason for local celebration." —Robert Fulford, *National Post* (Canada)

"Fans of historical crime fiction: Look no further than *King Zeno* . . . With its memorable cast of characters and historical flourishes, *King Zeno* is a winner." —*Bookish*

KING • ZENO

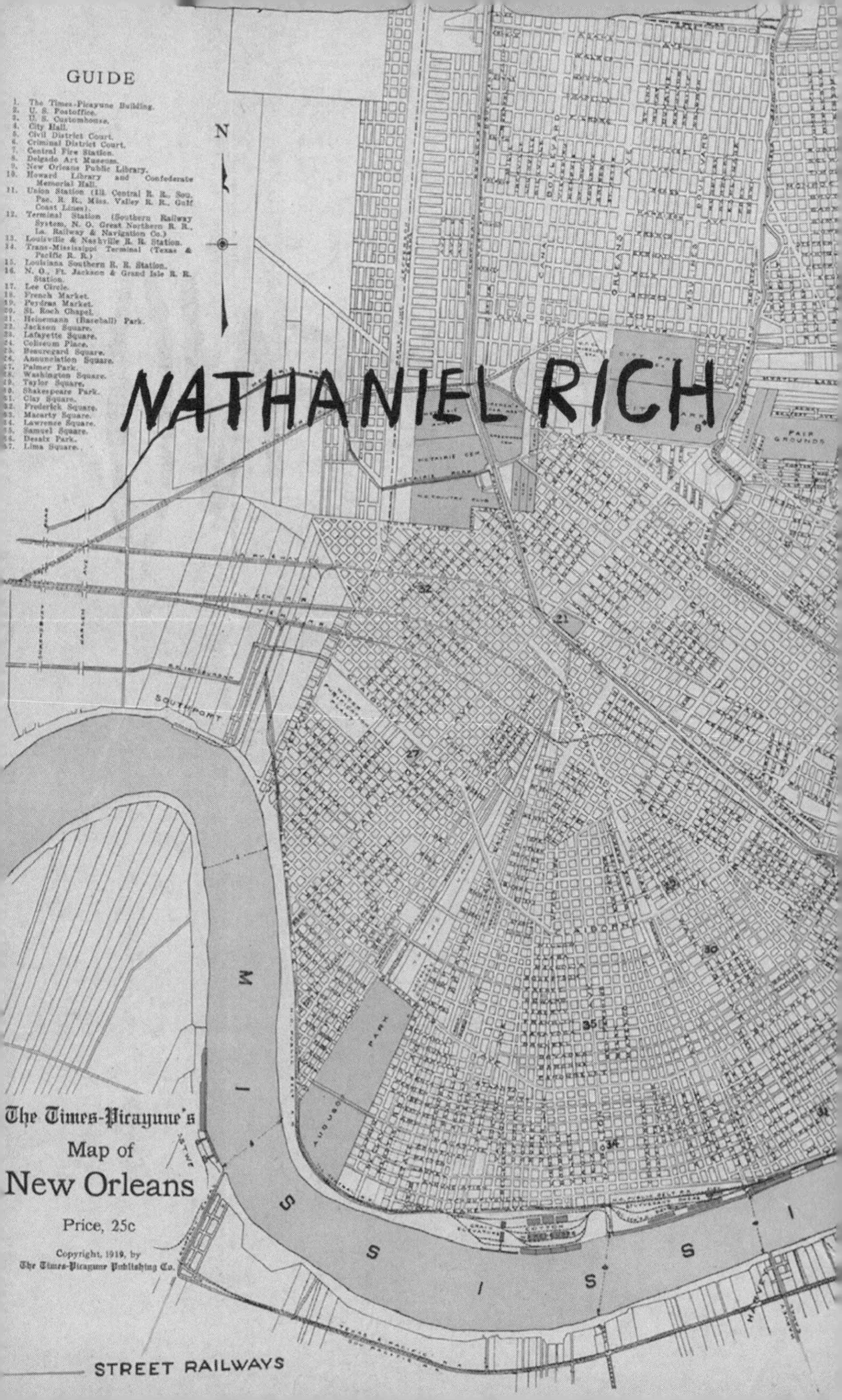

NATHANIEL RICH
GUIDE
1. The Times-Picayune Building.
2. U. S. Postoffice.
3. U. S. Customhouse.
4. City Hall.
5. Civil District Court.
6. Criminal District Court.
7. Central Fire Station.
8. Delgado Art Museum.
9. New Orleans Public Library.
10. Howard Library and Confederate Memorial Hall.
11. Union Station (Ill. Central R. R., Sou. Pac. R. R., Miss. Valley R. R., Gulf Coast Lines).
12. Terminal Station (Southern Railway System, N. O. Great Northern R. R., La. Railway & Navigation Co.)
13. Louisville & Nashville R. R. Station.
14. Trans-Mississippi Terminal (Texas & Pacific R. R.)
15. Louisiana Southern R. R. Station.
16. N. O., Ft. Jackson & Grand Isle R. R. Station.
17. Lee Circle.
18. French Market.
19. Poydras Market.
20. St. Roch Chapel.
21. Heinemann (Baseball) Park.
22. Jackson Square.
23. Lafayette Square.
24. Coliseum Place.
25. Beauregard Square.
26. Annunciation Square.
27. Palmer Park.
28. Washington Square.
29. Taylor Square.
30. Shakespeare Park.
31. Clay Square.
32. Frederick Square.
33. Macarty Square.
34. Lawrence Square.
35. Samuel Square.
36. Desaix Park.
37. Lima Square.
N
SOUTHPORT
FAIR GROUNDS
AUDUBON PARK
M I S S I S S I
The Times-Picayune's
Map of
New Orleans
Price, 25c
Copyright, 1919, by
The Times-Picayune Publishing Co.
STREET RAILWAYS

KING • ZENO

PICADOR
MCD
FARRAR, STRAUS AND GIROUX
NEW YORK

This is a work of fiction. All of the characters, organizations, and events portrayed in this novel are either products of the author's imagination or are used fictitiously.

Printed in the United States of America. For information, address Picador, 175 Fifth Avenue, New York, N.Y. 10010.

picadorusa.com • instagram.com/picador
twitter.com/picadorusa • facebook.com/picadorusa

Picador® is a U.S. registered trademark and is used by Macmillan Publishing Group, LLC, under license from Pan Books Limited.

For book club information, please visit facebook.com/picadorbookclub or email marketing@picadorusa.com.

The *Times-Picayune*'s map of New Orleans appears courtesy of the Norman B. Leventhal Map Center at the Boston Public Library.

Articles and quotations from the *New Orleans Item*, the *New Orleans States*, and the *Times-Picayune* appear as originally published, with cuts made for syntactical consistency and concision.

The quotation from Dante's *Inferno* on page 124 comes from John D. Sinclair's translation.

Invaluable assistance with primary source material was provided by the Historic New Orleans Collection's Williams Research Center, the New Orleans Public Library, the Louisiana Research Collection at Tulane University, Alexandra Milsom, Thomas Schwank, and Richard Campanella.

This novel would not have been possible without the generous and wise contributions of Sean McDonald, Elyse Cheney, Sam Freilich, and, most of all, Meredith Angelson.

Designed by Abby Kagan

The Library of Congress has cataloged the Farrar, Straus and Giroux edition as follows:

Names: Rich, Nathaniel, 1980– author.
Title: King Zeno / Nathaniel Rich.
Description: First edition. | New York : MCD / Farrar, Straus and Giroux, 2018.
Identifiers: LCCN 2017034573 | ISBN 9780374181314 (hardcover) | ISBN 9780374716318 (ebook)
Subjects: LCSH: New Orleans (La.)—Social life and customs—20th century—Fiction. | New Orleans (La.)—History—20th century—Fiction. | Serial murderers—Fiction. | New Orleans (La.)—Fiction. | GSAFD: Historical fiction. | Mystery fiction.
Classification: LCC PS3618.I3334 K56 2018 | DDC 813/.6—dc23
LC record available at https://lccn.loc.gov/2017034573

Picador Paperback ISBN 978-1-250-31034-7

First published by Farrar, Straus and Giroux

First Picador Edition: January 2019

10 9 8 7 6 5 4 3 2 1

This is for Meredith

PART ONE

GLYPTODONT

New Orleans Item, 5/23/18:

COUPLE HACKED TO DEATH WITH AX IN SLEEP

Joseph Maggio and Wife Slain in Grocery Home During Night

BROTHER OF MAN IN NEXT ROOM HEARD GROANS

For the last six years Joseph Maggio, a native of Sicily, has run a small grocery at 4901 Magnolia street, corner of Upperline.

It was a typical establishment of its kind—the grocery in the front and the rooms of Maggio and his wife in the rear. In one of them there also lived Maggio's brother, Andrew, a barber.

The grocery served a small and mixed clientele, half black and half white. Its receipts were not enormous, but they were sufficient to keep Maggio and his wife in comfort.

HAD NO KNOWN ENEMIES

So far as is known they had no enemies. Born of a farming class, they had attained the distinction of owning a small business—the ambition of nine out of ten immigrants. They had been married fifteen years. Altogether a commonplace, contented couple, with a long and peaceful life ahead of them.

At 5:30 o'clock Thursday morning the police received a telephone call from Andrew Maggio. They should come to Upperline and Magnolia at once. His brother and sister-in-law had been killed.

A squad found the bodies of Maggio and his wife lying in bed, throats and heads cut open by repeated blows from an ax. The story of a wholly murderous intent was told by the fact that, of the dozen blows struck, all but one or two would have been sufficient to kill. But the murderer had wanted to make sure . . .

New Orleans States, 5/24/18:

TERROR:
FOUR MEN FALL VICTIM TO BANDITS;
ONE LOSES HIS SHOES

The waylaying of four early-morning pedestrians in three separate holdups in the upper-rear section of the city Friday brought the negro highwaymen but scant returns. For hours a squad of men was busy rounding up negro suspects.

The victims of Friday morning's holdups are: Charles Lowe, ticket agent at the Union Station; Florin Bodemuller, 16, of 1748 Jackson avenue; Joseph Tolozzio, banana packer for the United Fruit Company; and Richard Boland, newsdealer at Canal and Royal streets.

Lowe had gone to a bakery shop at Clio and Liberty streets, where he purchased two loaves of bread at 2:30 o'clock Friday morning. While waiting for a streetcar, he was approached by a negro, who forced him to throw up his hands at the point of a revolver. The negro took from Lowe thirty cents and compelled him to give up his blue worsted coat.

Bodemuller was returning from a dance at 1 o'clock when a negro held him up with a revolver at Jackson avenue and Brainard street. After taking a Waltham watch and ribbon fob, valued at $30, Bodemuller was forced to remove his shoes, valued at $4.50. The youth was compelled to walk home in his stockings.

Tolozzio and Boland got out of a streetcar at Howard avenue and Carondelet street and were confronted by a negro with a revolver, who forced them to throw up their hands. From Tolozzio the highwayman secured $1.50 and from Boland twenty cents in pennies. Tolozzio and Boland set up cries for help and the highwayman fired a shot at them as he fled.

New Orleans Item, 5/25/18:

BAKERY DRIVER WOUNDED BY NEGRO HIGHWAYMAN

Victim of a negro highwayman's bullet, received at 2 o'clock Saturday morning, Theodore Blaum, driver of wa bakery wagon, is in Charity Hospital in a critical condition. Chances of recovery are said to be slight. He was shot in the left breast, the bullet just missing his heart.

Blaum was fired upon without warning as he emerged from an alley in the rear of 1813 Baronne street, where he was delivering bread. After shooting him, says Blaum, the negro took $3 from his clothing. Blaum climbed back on his wagon and drove to the hospital. The negro escaped.

Hours earlier, Charlton R. Beattie, former U.S. district attorney, residing in the De Soto Hotel, was fired upon by a negro highwayman at Coliseum, near First street. He was not injured. Henry Baldwin, president of A. Baldwin & Co., who witnessed the assault from the gallery of his home, was fired upon when he yelled at the footpad. Mr. Baldwin was not hurt. The negro got nothing.

The police believe the man who held up Mr. Beattie is the one who shot Blaum. The descriptions tally. The highwayman is said to be about 25 years old, 5 feet 8 inches, and 135 pounds. He wore a brown shirt and black pants.

The holdups Saturday morning made five "highway jobs" in 48 hours. In all cases the assailant was a negro.

Although the negro held a revolver to his head, Beattie refused to comply.

"I'll not do it," he told the robber, when ordered to throw up his hands.

The negro's loud talk attracted Mr. Baldwin.

"As I came out on the upstairs gallery to investigate the loud talking," Mr. Baldwin told the police, "I saw a negro pointing a gun to the head of a white man. I hollered to the negro and he backed away and fired two shots."

Mr. Blaum is married.

New Orleans Times-Picayune, 5/26/18:

AX MURDER SUSPECT RELEASED

Withstands Grilling by Police Chief

Andrew Maggio, held since Thursday in connection with the murder of his brother and sister-in-law, keepers of a grocery store at Magnolia street, was released from custody by Superintendent Mooney Saturday night.

"It is terrible that I should be accused of killing my brother when I am innocent," said Maggio. "I may say something at another time, but I can't talk about it tonight."

New Orleans States, 5/26/18:

NEAR DEATH AS BANDIT FIRES IN SIXTH HOLDUP

Saturday night was no exception to the rule applying to the nightly holdups since Wednesday, during which time six holdups of citizens occurred. In every case the highwayman was a negro who held his victim at bay with a revolver.

The latest highway victim was J. E. Ragan, supervisor for the Illinois Central Railroad at the Union Station.

Mr. Ragan was on his way home shortly after 11 o'clock. When he reached Baudin and Rendon streets, a negro jumped out from a hiding place and commanded Ragan to throw up his hands. Instead of complying, Mr. Ragan leaped forward and grabbed the hand which held the revolver. A struggle followed, during which shots were fired. Fortunately they all went wild. The negro escaped. He secured nothing.

POLICE SQUAD ON SCENE

Armed with riot guns, and led by Senior Captain Capo, a squad of policemen scoured the neighborhood in a vain search.

The highwayman Saturday night did not escape without leaving telltale evidence behind. The police are in possession of a dark slouch hat which remained in the grip of Mr. Ragan, who tried desperately to hold on to the negro until assistance could reach him.

New Orleans Times-Picayune, 5/26/18:

HIGHWAYMAN TAKES CLOTHES

Another holdup in the series of highway robberies of white persons by armed negroes was reported to the police early Sunday morning. Richard Bray, 17, was relieved of $1.40 and a bundle of clothes, at Banks and Clark streets.

The negro answers the description of the one who, earlier in the night, held up and shot at J. E. Ragan. As in the earlier robbery, the highwayman left his hat in making his getaway.

MAY 26, 1918—THE IRISH CHANNEL

Navies called it instinct. Not sense, skill, talent—*instinct*. If it wasn't in you, you couldn't fake it. How to hear the truth in a lie. How to spot the shark in a crowded streetcar. How to persuade a mother to betray her son. How to locate the trigger that would make a man talk: A full revolution of the wrist? A poke to the baby skin behind the knee? A potato sack cinched around the neck? Most critical: how to figure when a person was lying to your face. In that category he was gallingly deficient. Particularly when the person of interest was a woman. Particularly when the woman was his wife. No, that wasn't fair—Maze had never lied to him. At least so far as he knew. If Maze *had* lied to him, he wouldn't have been able to tell, so what difference did it make? This was how his brain worked, in closed circuits, always questioning itself, questioning itself questioning itself, questioning itself questioning itself questioning itself.

Two police skills Bill did have: observation and memory. They came to him conjoined like the two-headed boy, grinning from both mouths. They were loyal old companions, observation and memory, and had never abandoned him, though in the last year they had been less blessing than curse. Nineteen minutes had passed since he and Charlie Breaux had split from Obitz and Dodson, and he could remember, with photographic clarity, every person he had seen since. On Clio an emaciated bald man driving a peanut wagon, most likely asleep, bent like a tree in a storm. Two women of high school age, though assuredly unenrolled, floated across the intersection at Erato in silk gowns that brushed the rubble. Around the lakeside corner at Thalia loped an ursine man, about thirty, in a long trench coat and dark homburg. And near Terpsichore an unconscious drunk blocked the sidewalk, belly down, his cheek caked with mud. On a typical night the drunk would prompt a call to the butcher wagon. But this was no typical night, for a maniac highwayman was loose.

The stillness of the street was a rebuke. But what did Bill expect? Citizens' groups on patrol? A marching band? The families in this back-of-town neighborhood, stuck between the rock of the Irish Channel and the whirlpool of Storyville, many of them recently arrived on steamers from Naples or Queenstown, barricaded themselves inside at night, ceding the streets to the drunks, the blackguards, the thieves. Electric streetlamps supervised the major intersections but most of the bulbs had died. It was madness: the city was spending six million dollars on the excavation of a gargantuan canal to connect the Mississippi River to Lake Pontchartrain and it couldn't bother to maintain its streetlamps? But even when the lamps worked they gave little benefit, as the blocks were long and for great lengths suffocated by night.

Charlie's bad leg scuffed on the gravel, creating a clumsy percussion that announced their presence to the rows of darkened houses. Step-*scuff*, step-*scuff*, step-*scuff*.

"I don't like this, Billy," said Charlie. "It's hinky."

"Too quiet? Too dark?"

"Too hinky."

It was three in the morning. Bill had traveled a full day's distance from his last sleep. He'd awoken early to provide security at a breakfast rally at City Hall for war bonds; at noon he was summoned to Annunciation and Second Street, where a six-year-old girl had been struck by a streetcar; at five, after registering the girl in Charity Hospital, he reported to the station for a briefing on the all-night patrol for the negro highwayman. That meeting was delayed by three hours, however, because Superintendent Mooney was busy interrogating Andrew Maggio, the brother of the butchered Italian grocer. Mooney made a habit of presiding over the flashiest cases, and before the highwayman spree that meant the Maggio murders. The only suspect was Andrew Maggio, a barber, who claimed to have overheard the slaughter, but he did not break and Mooney had to release him. It was nine before Mooney gave the men their details. Bill and Charlie had patrolled six hours without relief.

"I'm tired," said Charlie. "My feet are singing."

"Tired. I don't remember what that's like. Tired."

"It's like being thirsty in your brain."

"I moved past tired a long time ago."

"It is like your feet belong to a stranger."

Bill felt mainly a panicked restlessness. The knowledge of the lurking fanatic had whittled his senses to a fine point. In the queasy silence of Baronne Street the creaking of Charlie's bum knee and the ghostly scuffing of his foot and the muddy squelch of Bill's own trench boots screamed in his ears.

So when the gun fired it was like a thunderstroke.

Another police instinct: run toward gunshots. Bill never had the instinct and even used to puzzle at its existence, but since returning to New Orleans he thirsted for violence and its baptismal promise. Here was his first real chance at it. He followed George downtown, their legs pistoning, ribbons of green slime leaping onto their pants, toward the explosions.

Near the corner of Calliope they came upon two men hugging. The men were sprawled across the step of a shotgun cottage. The larger one—six feet, two hundred pounds—lay on top, his posterior extruding unnaturally. His cap had fallen off and the moon illuminated his bright yellow hair and the gold buttons of his navy jacket. The smaller man was nearly invisible beneath him. Bill realized at once that it was Harry Dodson, being smothered by Teddy Obitz.

"*Offa* me." Dodson's voice was a deflating balloon.

Charlie stopped midstride, an automaton that had lost its electrical charge. "That you, Harry?"

"Get 'em *offa* me!"

They pulled the large man's shoulders but Big Blond wouldn't budge. Harry wheezed terribly.

"Whatsa matter, Big Blond?" said Charlie. "You're hurting Harry." The poor bastard was always feebleminded, but when he was scared, he became borderline moronic.

"Teddy's shot, Charlie."

"Big Blond is shot?"

They tried again, tugging on Obitz's stiff giant shoulders. With a grotesque peeling sound, Obitz fell back, his head cracking against the porch column like an ax striking a tree, the sound reverberating in the empty street. Obitz's blond hair was wet. His eyes were open, staring in disbelief. His chest was sticky with black mess. As was Harry's.

"You shot too?" said Charlie.

Harry shook his head. He gulped the night deeply and crossed his hands over his ribs, as if to protect them from further insult. "It's Teddy's," he said. "It's his insides."

"The man did this," said Bill. "Where is he?"

Harry coughed, a wet, mucousy cough. He was breathing strangely. He wheezed something that sounded like "telephone."

"Which telephone?" asked Charlie.

"Down *Baronne*. Toward the Battlefield."

That's all Charlie had to hear. He was off in a sprint—a bow-legged, herky-jerky sprint. That was instinct for you.

With his two comrades sitting on the porch, staring at him—one gasping like a fish, the other dead—Bill knew he should say something, something reassuring. He tried to remember what you were supposed to say but the violence was pulling him. "I promise," he began. "I promise."

"Get!" shouted Harry.

Charlie was nearly a block ahead. Bill ran after him and almost immediately stumbled on a broken paving stone, twisting hard to the ground. When he rose, Charlie was gone. This stretch of Baronne had no cuts—the cottages were jammed tight against one another—but when he reached the corner, the intersection was empty. The only sign of life was a cur with a deformed front paw. It walked in a repeating loop, its head bent, its jaw working furiously. To the right, beyond the dog, was Lee Circle. To the left, Union Station Plaza and behind it the Battlefield. Bill stopped, listening. He heard only the cur's low plaintive whimper. *Toward the Battlefield*, Harry had said. Bill's instinct was to go right, toward the sick dog, away from the Battlefield, so he ran left.

Five rows of palm trees ran the length of the grassy plaza in front of Union Station. Electric globes stood on tall black stanchions around its perimeter. The palms cast shadows like long fingers across the lawn. It was an obvious place to hide, within the alleys of the tree-lined plaza, among the broad palm fronds that were like gigantic splayed hands protecting a secret.

Bill waded between the palms, the stiff leaves raking over his cap. A sharp pain shot through his wrist—he was squeezing his revolver too tightly. He transferred the weapon to his left hand and flexed until feeling returned. In his mind he saw Teddy Obitz, sprawled on the cottage porch, staring into infinity. Detective Obitz: the city's shrewdest investigator, a mentor to Bill before the war, kind, loyal, shrewd, strong. If the violence could claim a man as strong as Obitz, it could claim anyone, and there was no resisting its dark lullaby. It helped to remind himself of that.

He burst into the first alley, gun ready, and swiveled—left, right. Nothing but a smooth rectangular lawn followed by another row of palm trees. He listened for rustling, but the grass muted everything and the silence was a Klaxon in his ears.

He dashed across the lane and into the next line of palms. The gigantic hands parted to admit him. *There*: across the next alley, a movement. He froze. One of the shadows bent like a beckoning finger. Someone stood not fifteen feet away, screened by a pair of low-hanging fronds. The light from the electric globes barely reached the center of the plaza and Bill squinted into the darkness. It had become very cold. The sky was ashy, the palms blackish green, the grass blue. The fronds across the alley waved again, as if taken by a breeze, but there was no breeze.

"New Orleans Police!" Bill felt cowardly even as he yelled, for he was still hidden behind his own scrum of leaves. But only part of him was here, in the plaza in the middle of New Orleans. The other part of him was in a dark linden forest near the Alsatian border, the branches scratching his face, the burrs sticking in his socks, the blood gavotting in his brain.

The leaves trembled.

"You can't see me," said Bill. "But I see you. I am aiming a revolver."

The frond hands flapped loudly together, applauding. The night was momentarily still. There came another burst of activity and out rushed a black hog.

It was a big bastard, three hundred pounds, its tusks flaring in the moonlight. The flank was banded by harsh silver bristles, the flat forehead was like the back of a shovel, and from the wide, clownish mouth, the jaws extended nearly to its ears. But the hog had no interest in Detective William J. Bastrop. It grunted, a sound like an air horn, as if to underline the point. It hurtled down the aisle toward Baronne. Bill watched it hop over the curb, its rump falling and rising as it trotted away. He placed his hand on his chest and pulled it away, as from a blazing panhandle, when he felt the hammer of his heart. He decided he would like to sit in the soft grass below the palm tree, to lean against the trunk and sleep until it was tomorrow. He wanted to sleep there very much.

"Bill!"

The voice was distant but clear. It came from downtown. One navy instinct he did have: when his partner called out, he ran to him. Bill sprinted down the alley to the back of the plaza. He broke right, down Rampart.

"Bill!" Charlie's voice was still faint—at least a block away.

He came to the terminus of the New Orleans Canal. He was fully exposed here, but could see nothing. He continued down Rampart, past the Texas Gas Station on Julia Street, and came to a work yard that occupied a full square block. The sign said LOUISIANA DEMOLISHING COMPANY, HECTOR SCHMITZ, PROP. The gate was open. Beyond it stood a huge pile of amputated cypress trees, each trunk easily seventy feet long.

Behind this great wall of lumber came an agonized shriek.

"He's loose!" screamed Charlie.

Bill prepared himself. He squatted slightly to lower his center of gravity, raised his weapon, and prayed wildly in his mind.

In a frenzied flurry a form whirled into view from behind the wall of trees, mewling incoherently, and for a moment Bill wondered whether it wasn't again the snorting hog attacking him, eyes wide and crazed. The silence became very loud in his ears, the Klaxon revving up until Bill suspected he had gone deaf.

Bill noticed that the right part of the highwayman's face had fallen off. The man stumbled and raised one arm. His hand rotated as if unscrewing an invisible lightbulb. The revving grew even louder, climaxing in a series of detonations.

Everything went still.

Charlie's disembodied voice came from behind the lumber. "You get 'im?"

Bill tried to form words.

Charlie crept into view. "He must've got nervous when he heard you," he said, approaching tentatively. "He was sleeping when I found him."

"He was asleep?"

"He's sure sleeping now."

There were footsteps behind Bill.

"New Orleans Police Department!" someone shouted. "Yay! NOPD!"

"It's us, Harry." Charlie raised his hands. "Bastrop and Breaux." Charlie gestured at Bill to lower his revolver.

He saw that he was still pointing it at the body on the ground.

Bill turned to find Harry Dodson's silhouette edging through the gate, followed by Harry himself. Harry looked minuscule in the wide factory entrance. He had shed his bloody jacket but still wore his cap. That's funny, Bill thought. A tiny navy in his undershirt with a cap but no uniform. That's a funny sight.

Harry approached, relaxed by the sound of Charlie's voice. But he lurched violently when he saw the corpse. He bent over it, tentative. He knelt. He peered into what remained of its face. He seemed baffled.

"That's him, right?" said Bill.

Harry Dodson, his mouth contorted in a jagged rictus, turned to look up at Bill.

"Harry? That's *him*, isn't it? The guy shot Big Blond?"

It wasn't confusion on Harry's face, Bill realized. It was horror.

"That's him, Harry—isn't it?"

"Billy," said Charlie.

Bill ignored him. He wished Harry would speak.

"*Harry?*" said Bill, louder. "Isn't that him? The highwayman?"

His own voice sounded strange in his ears, as if it were coming from another person. *Was* it coming from another person? From the body on the ground? The more he thought about it, the more certain he became. Yes, the body spoke to him. While Charlie gaped idiotically and Harry, solemn now, stared at Bill, the dead man screamed out of the half of his mouth that remained. He pleaded through his bloodied broken teeth, screaming, "That's him—isn't it, Harry? That's the highwayman who shot Big Blond. Isn't that right, Harry? *Harry?*"

MAY 26, 1918—UPTOWN

A fat red-haired fellow stood at the entrance to the alley. His bearing—stooped posture, smug arms crossed over the swollen chest, a smirk, just visible in the streetlamp's pale gumdrop light—exuded a cool self-assurance, as if he and Isadore had made a plan to meet right here, next to the garbage barrels in the middle of the 2100 block of St. Charles Avenue, at exactly 4:09 a.m., and he was mightily looking forward to their parley. Isadore flashed the palms of his hands, the palest skin on his body. They were trembling; he jammed them into his pockets. He gave a silent prayer in gratitude for having been spotted from a hundred yards away and not surprising the man by coming up behind him. Isadore concentrated on maintaining an even stride, holding eye contact, and resisting the urge to run. As he stepped into the streetlamp's penumbra he forced a large, supplicatory smile.

"Sir." Isadore nodded, two stiffs passing each other on the way to work.

"I don't know you." The Paddy seemed very pleased with himself, as a toddler might be pleased at forming a full sentence.

"I can see what you're thinking," said Isadore. St. Charles was so silent that he could hear the vibration of the iron streetcar tracks against the gravel, though the streetcar itself was not yet in sight. "You're wondering if I'm up to something."

"Something." He was almost exactly the same diameter as the garbage barrels beside him. "There's been some business with a Negro highwayman. Maybe you heard."

"I stay right here," lied Isadore. "Down the block."

"That so."

"I'm puzzled," he said daringly, "that I haven't seen you around yet." He wondered where Bailey was. He hoped Bailey had been smart enough to go home when they parted, at the first sight of the police, that he hadn't kept chasing down bakery-truck drivers like a stray dog. "I've been staying here nearly a week."

"At whose pleasure?"

"My old lady works for some gentlefolks here."

"Which folks?"

Isadore laughed—too loudly perhaps, but the laughter was the only channel for his rage. It often went like that with him, the terror, unexpected and sudden, slipping into rage. It was enraging to be scared all the time. Enraging and also exhausting, being perpetually alert to mortal threats that might be triggered by the crime of walking on the wrong street, looking at the wrong person, saying the wrong thing or saying the right thing with the wrong inflection. Not to mention being the wrong color, or no color, not quite white enough to pass, not dark enough to be invisible. But in those moments when he came face-to-face with his fear—face-to-face with a red-faced Paddy on a dark night on New Orleans's whitest street, who had legal sanction to kill him—he felt something close to relief. Nothing bad could happen anymore. It was already happening. The awareness soothed his fear, which is to say his rage, and his mind focused.

He could not reveal that he was visiting his wife because if the Tiltons found out they would fire her. He could not run because the watchman would shoot. He could not head back to the Battlefield, into the dragnet, nor continue blindly into the night, now that he'd said he stayed down the block. He could not do anything. It was a familiar feeling.

He imitated the watchman, crossing his arms over *his* chest, to create the impression that he was in no rush either—that he wouldn't mind chatting until sunup. With his right hand, concealed beneath his left elbow, he felt through his jacket for the butt of his revolver, tucked into the rolled-up waistband of his trousers. Its heft reassured him and he told his next lie.

"I call them Sir and Missus, to be honest." Isadore gave his voice a singsongy lilt and despised himself for it, picturing a shoeblack executing a buck-and-wing. "That is," he said, "when I have the chance. I keep unfriendly hours, on account of my trade."

The watchman nodded. "What's that?"

"Sir?" Isadore snuck a glance at the alley. It wasn't ten yards away. Halfway down the alley was the back entrance to the Tiltons' house.

"You work nights."

"I play the honky-tonks, sir." Isadore recognized his mistake as soon as he heard himself say it. Most of the tonks were in the District or the Battlefield. He might as well have said he ran prostitutes, played cotch, cut cocaine. He might as well have said he was an accomplice to the highwayman.

The Paddy's grin stayed frozen but his eyes sharpened, a photograph developing in a chemical bath.

"When I'm not working my regular gigs, at least," said Isadore. The sound of his own voice made him want to vomit. "The New Orleans Country Club," he lied. "Economy Hall. On the weekends you can find me at Spanish Fort, playing at the gentlefolks' picnics. Cornet man, myself. Just about blowed my brains out tonight."

"Jass." The man spat. "'S'not music."

"No, sir. But it's a living."

"Where's your instrument?"

Now that was a good question. The watchman's ghastly grin stretched a bit wider, the streetlamp notching shadows in the creases of his cheeks. The streetcar tracks hummed louder. Isadore made a show of looking down at his arms, as if surprised to realize that he wasn't holding his horn. The weight of the Webley & Scott tugged on his hip.

"Mr. Webley, at the Country Club?" he said blindly, crazily. "Mr. Webley holds our instruments overnight so we don't have to carry them home." Isadore was speaking quickly—too quickly, perhaps—and might have kept going had the watchman not poked a stubby forefinger into his own eye. He dug around the socket, as if trying to carve out the eyeball.

"I got something in here," mumbled the Paddy. "Something what won't get out." Isadore tried to master his disgust while the man dug deeper into his skull with his filthy finger. "Doctor prescribed silver nitrate. But with the salary I draw from the neighborhood association . . ." He kept digging. The tracks rumbled; the next streetcar couldn't be five blocks away. Undoubtedly navies would be on the streetcar. The police were fanning wide tonight.

"Sir, how much does the medicine cost?"

"Oh?" said the Paddy, removing his finger. Isadore could swear the finger was covered with a waxy residue. "I expect it'll take about a dollar."

It was a trick. If Isadore took out a bill, he would renew the man's suspicion.

"Would you allow me to make a donation to the eyeball fund?" Isadore reached into his pocket, past his roll, and scooped out the coins. "Here's seventy-two cents. It's everything I got."

The watchman gave an irritated grunt but accepted the money. "C'mon. I'll see you home."

"I know the way. I'll let you continue with your rounds."

"Don't be ridiculous. It's a dangerous night. You said you lived on this block?" He paused. "Or are you down the alley?"

The men stared at each other for some time.

"Down the alley."

With a magnanimous gesture, the Paddy indicated that Isadore should lead.

The alley, which ran between the delivery entrances of grand houses, was littered with broken things: a cracked cistern, a dismantled pram, a splintered palette stamped RIZZO'S GROC. He saw his lifeless body lying facedown in the alley, another broken, discarded thing. The Tiltons' door was the fourth down, maybe twenty paces away. Isadore gripped hard the barrel of the revolver. In the moonlight, puddles of sewage, swarming with mosquitoes, glowed green. A rat glanced up from a nest of chicken bones, rubbing its paws like a wino before a fire. If the watchman struck him down, would the rats find his body before Orly did? The Paddy was so close behind him that Isadore could smell the gin on his stubble. He could hear the man's watery exhalations. Without thought Isadore twisted and swung the gun barrel into the watchman's rheumy eye. There was a loud pop and the watchman fell sideways to the ground. He didn't move. Panic electrified Isadore. It told him: *Move.*

Within a heartbeat he was at the small back door to the Tiltons' manor. He glanced once behind him—the watchman remained motionless on his back—and swung the door open. His wife's amazed face stared back at him. She stood wrapped in a thick brown muslin bathrobe cinched at the waist with a lanyard.

"Izzy!"

"Don't speak." He closed the door behind him. "Does this lock?"

"It don't lock," she whispered. "What are you doing here?"

In the middle of the tiny room a copper lantern stood on a doll-size table covered with green oilcloth. The lantern cast onto the walls the roiling waves of a black ocean.

"Turn off the light," he said.

"Why are we whispering?"

"I came to surprise you. A night watchman saw me, got suspicious."

"Mr. Boyle. Where is he?"

Isadore snuffed the lantern and returned to the door, listening for movement. He heard nothing but his own shallow breathing. In the moonlight he took in Orly's room for the first time—he had dropped her off before, using the alley, but had never dared to enter. The ceiling wasn't seven feet high. A narrow bed lay against one wall, the sheets rumpled. A tiny brown oval rug covered the remaining floor space. Despite its size, the room was meticulously clean. At the back, between the doll table and the bed, a door connected to the main part of the Tiltons' house. He was touched to see that Orly had mounted above her mattress a torn print of Saint Peter Claver, parrots on his shoulders and an infant in his arms.

"We're clear," Isadore said finally. Even if the man, Boyle, came to, he'd have no idea where Isadore had gone. He'd have to assume that Isadore ran out the other side of the alley.

"Why did you come here?"

"I wanted to see you."

Orly gave him a serious look.

"I guess I was excited after the show. We were on it tonight. I tell you, it was getting Spanish in there. Real Spanish talkers, the bunch of us."

Orly slapped his mouth.

"How stupid do you got to be?" She caught herself raising her voice and repeated herself in a whisper. *"How stupid do you got to be?"*

Isadore rubbed his mouth. A wave of exhaustion overtook him. He leaned back on the table for support.

"You almost died." She said it matter-of-factly. Her brown eyes—normally so open, warm, erotic—narrowed to slits. "Mr. Boyle is a savage."

"Come."

She gestured behind her, presumably toward the nursery, where the two Tilton children slept. "You know how easily I can get fired?" He noticed that, despite her anger, she was trembling. She never trembled. She sat heavily on the bed. "I love you, Izzy, but you're bringing evil home with you."

"The watchman doesn't know I'm here."

"Forget Boyle. It's not hard to find someone to wash children's behinds. If the Tiltons come to suspect I have a man coming around, even if he is my *husband*—"

He sighed. Lately she had begun to place emphasis on that word. Whether conscious or not, it conveyed a subtle indictment, to the effect that he wasn't holding up his marital duties: bringing home sufficient money to support his family, to be precise. "It was a long night at Savocca's," he said, "and the streets being so wild—"

She shot him a wrinkled, pinching look. "You were at Joe Savocca's tonk?"

"—with the highwayman on the loose, but I don't worry about that so much as the navies, there're more of them than termites tonight, fanned out looking for any black son of a bitch they see walking the streets."

"This morning you said Ferrantelli's."

"Savocca's. Anyway, you should've seen Sore Dick . . ."

She let him talk himself out of breath. She had been looking forward to bawling him out all right and she was going to take her time with it. But he wasn't about to make it easy for her. He reminded himself, halfheartedly, that he had done nothing wrong. At least nothing wrong to Orly. He had taken up with Bailey for her, after all. Not that he could tell her that.

"I figured it'd be stupid to walk through the Battlefield. Besides, I didn't want to scare your mother coming home so late. Besides, I wanted to see you."

She nodded patiently, languorously—no doubt the same gesture she used with the Tilton kids when they made excuses for their cretinism. "You were playing at Savocca's," she said in a reasonable voice.

"That's what I said."

"Where's your horn?"

"Funny, that's what the Paddy said."

"What's that?" She sniffed—a bit melodramatically, it seemed to Isadore. "Smells like the gutter."

It wasn't the gutter, but she was close. It was fear—similar to sweat but stiffer, like a toxic mushroom.

She shook her head. "Get out."

"What?"

"Go out the other end of the alley."

"What about the watchman?"

"You said it. He's either passed out or he's gone." She rubbed her stomach absently. That was another new habit she'd been developing. It made her look as if she were hungry all the time. "This job's the only steady money we have."

"Dick agreed to take my horn. He lives across from Savocca's. The cornet's with Dick."

She paused, trying to read him. "All right," she said at last, her tone softening. She rose from the bed. "Give me your jacket."

"Thank you, baby." He removed the jacket and handed it over. He unbuttoned his shirt. He really did feel exhausted. He could have slept standing up, leaning against the wall. Given the size of her bed, that might be the only place for him. "We were Spanish tonight, I'm telling you. Just a bunch of regular Spaniards. We stormed. We thundered and lightninged. We tornadoed. I'm telling you, people are starting to understand."

When he glanced up she was holding his roll. She had tossed the jacket onto the bed. The pockets were turned inside out.

"It must have been a hurricane if you made eleven dollars in tips."

"Orly."

"I know you play better than anyone in this town. But eleven dollars?"

"We raised Cain."

"You're bringing some bad business home with you. Home to *us*."

"Baby—"

She pointed to the door.

"To go where?"

"To my mother's house. Or anywhere else you go. I'm tired."

He wondered what she would do if he just fell onto the ground and started to snore. Probably she would beat on his head until he woke up.

She stuffed the wad back into the pocket and held the jacket out as if it were a garbage bag containing a dead rodent. He slumped toward her but she sidestepped him, dropping the jacket onto his shoulder. He bent for a kiss and she jerked her face away. Her eye was wet.

"I suppose you didn't go see about the canal," she said, looking away.

He froze. He didn't know what she was talking about.

"I'm not just making words over here."

"You said a canal?"

"The *dig*, Izzy."

Right. Several days ago she'd handed him a classified ad, clipped from the Tiltons' copy of the *Times-Picayune*. Men were wanted for a major industrial project at the eastern edge of the city. They were digging a river. It would connect the Mississippi to the lake, crossing the city at its narrowest point, in the Ninth Ward. It promised to be filthy, grueling work. He was too defeated to lie anymore.

"I haven't asked about the dig. I will. I promise."

Orly walked past him to the door. She placed her hand on the knob—and hesitated. With a surprising nimbleness, a bird hopping from one branch to the next, she pulled back the doily that covered the small blue transom window and just as quickly released it. She covered her mouth to stop herself from screaming.

Isadore approached and slowly lifted the doily. There, on the other side of the door, not four feet away, stood the fat man. One of his eyes was closed and puffed over. He cocked his head, listening.

"I'll kill him," said Isadore beneath his breath.

She put her hand over his mouth.

They stood in the dark, staring through the threadbare doily at the silhouette of the man's derby, a hillock of darkness darker than the night. Had Boyle heard them? Inside Isadore the fear spread like mildew.

"The kids don't wake until seven at the earliest," Orly whispered. "The Rizzo's Grocery truck comes at six. I know the driver, Reginald."

"How?"

"*Shhh.*"

"*How you know driver Reginald?*"

"He delivers the groceries every morning at six o'clock." She sucked her teeth. "He'll take you in the back of the truck, hide you under some rice sacks or something. Rizzo's is at Danneel and Terpsichore. You can walk safely from there."

She tiptoed away from the window. He heard the springs of the bed creak beneath her weight. He counted to fifteen and looked outside again. Boyle was gone. The Paddy's derby was bobbing down the alley toward Carondelet Street.

Orly turned to face the wall and Isadore pulled the revolver from his waistband, balling it in his jacket. It wasn't exactly a goose-down pillow but it would serve and he needed easy access in case Boyle returned. The floor was hard but it beat to hell the crumbling cot in the room he shared with Orly and her mother on Liberty Street.

"Orly," he said, "I'm going to do it."

"He didn't hear us."

"I'm not talking about the watchman. I'm talking about the Slim Izzy Quartet."

"I know, honey," she said, after a pause. "I know you will."

"We're just about there. Lot of people come in Savocca's. Kid Ory last week. George Baquet comes between gigs at the Funky Butt. Then there's the bookers—from the Country Club, Jackson Hall. Even the advance man from the Butt, looking for new acts.

They just have to hear me." He was surprised at the urgency in his voice. Orly, judging by her silence, was surprised too. But he felt it powerfully, the desire to prove his greatness. He wasn't convinced, despite Orly's praise, that he had even proved it to her, not yet. He carried the secret of his genius like a bellyache. He felt relief when he played but it was never enough relief, and too many things kept trying to pull him away from the music: money trouble, the tone of his flesh, the human hostility to original sound.

"Why are you on the ground?" said Orly.

"Figure if I lie across the doorway, Mr. Boyle won't be able to force it in."

She sucked her teeth. The bedsprings creaked. Isadore could see, through the darkness, that Orly was rubbing her stomach.

"I'm sorry," he said. "Orly, I'm sorry." In his mind he heard an echo of Boyle's eye socket popping.

"Don't say sorry," said Orly quietly, "when you know how much I love you."

"I'm going to work the dig. And I'm going to get some big shows."

"Hm."

"I'm lying here on the floor begging you, woman."

"You're lying all right."

"*Begging* your mercy."

She gave a low laugh. "All right, rough boy." Her voice was so quiet he had to strain to hear it. "Come get onto this bed."

MAY 26, 1918—HEINEMANN PARK

Pels salivaballer Dick Robertson, unbeaten in his first six starts, will put his perfect record to the test against the Little Rock Travelers in today's tilt between the Southern League's two top squads. How to win a ball game off the Pelicans with "Robby" on the hill: this is the conundrum that none of the Pels' rivals have mastered. "A lucky victory," said the Mobile Bears, on April 21, after being held to five hits and zero runs; "fortune flew with him," said the Birmingham Barons, whose nine hits came to naught on April 27, and who did no better five days later ("luck was a rueful chippy this afternoon"). From the Memphis Chicks, the Chattanooga Lookouts, and the Nashville Vols, the same response, the sentiment more pathetic with each iteration. Robby is now the leading pitcher in the Southern League and undoubtedly at the top of his form, the slender spitballist flinging better than at any point in his career—and at a discount no less, as Prexy Heinemann purchased him off the Barons for a piddling five hundred dollars in advance of the 1917 season. But today Robby draws his toughest challenge yet in Kid Elberfeld's Travelers, who will send out Ham Hyatt, Bob Fisher, and Dutch Distel: batters that will not be easily intimidated by the saliva-ball expert.

And what a glorious day for a ball game—pale blue heavens, high sun, a casual breeze off the Mississippi—so glorious that even Detective Bill Bastrop, emerging from beneath the grandstand, was momentarily distracted from his inner seethings. The sight of Heinemann Park's vast grassy atrium restored in him the old boyish excitement. The Pelicans arrayed across the outfield, lazily warming up in their cream uniforms, their left breasts stamped with a baseball framed by the Star of David. Dick Robertson, cap doffed, flannel jacket loose on his shoulders, chatted to a small crowd of women along the third-base grandstand. The colors were sharp, the air bright, having been scrubbed by the storm. Rising heat, full sky—nowhere to hide.

This was reassuring as Bill had begun to suspect that things were hiding from him. Strange things, hiding in plain sight, glimpsed in his peripheral vision. When he squinted at St. Louis Cathedral, it transfigured itself into the Ypres belfry tower; the ghost of Leonard Perl of the 69th Regiment stared with his one eye from a passing streetcar; a black cur in Lafayette Square, at least until Bill turned to look at it directly, had walked upright on its hind legs like a man, as if only to mock him. He had seen an identical dog, with the same white snub nose, striding briskly through the Forest of Purroy at the end of his tour, but he had assumed then it was a product of his wartime delirium. Now he wasn't certain.

Surely there could be no tricks of sight in Heinemann Park on such a clear bright day. Bill was relieved to spot Maisie immediately, or at least her wide yellow straw hat, a purple iris fastened to the brim. She sat in the box behind the Pelicans' dugout, alone in the last seat of the row, which had been reserved for the soldiers and their guests. It might have been the fatigue—it was probably the fatigue—but the sight of that great big hat on her small delicate head made him want to weep. An innocent woman, bursting with so many contradictions and obscurities it was a wonder she could get out of bed. When he came up behind her he lifted the hat straight off her head, causing her to whirl around in shock. He laughed and handed it back to her.

"*Billy.*" She frowned. "You pulled out my hairs." With a dainty, almost comically refined gesture, she smoothed her thin brown hair over her white ears, gleaming like cockleshells, and rebalanced the hat on her head. "I got enough problems."

When she'd first showed him, not long after his return, the clumps that collected like miniature hassocks of dead grass on her pillow, he'd tried to reassure her. Hair came out; it was a natural process. But the tangles that appeared on her pillow grew denser. She'd tried every scalp bath ballyhooed in the newspaper columns: Knowlton's Danderine, Honic's Baldpate Tonic, Frenchy's Follicle Cure. Her hats, meanwhile, grew larger and wider, until he couldn't sit beside her unless he arranged himself at a cockeyed angle. She attributed the hair loss to anxiety—first the anxiety of failing to find a job, later the anxiety of being yelled at, by her boss at the law office of Dufour and Janvier, for misfiling meal receipts. Bill didn't argue but he didn't think she had it right, exactly. Anxiety may have plucked out her hairs—and inscribed inky lines beneath her eyes and flattened her belly until the ribs started to show—but it wasn't *her* anxiety. It was his.

Bill once read a story about a man whose outward appearance never changed even as he defiled his body with liquor, drugs, and criminal sex. But a painting of the man, hidden in his attic, revealed the toll of his behavior, becoming bloated, liver-spotted, diseased. Bill wondered whether a similar transference was taking place in his marriage. His appearance had barely changed since he'd left for basic training. He returned from Europe the "same old Billy Bastrop"—that's what everyone said. But Maze had altered significantly and their reunion seemed only to accelerate the transformation. She wasn't going to pieces or anything, but she had suffered a more gradual, elusive transformation. It was as if she were being poisoned by his nightmares. He hadn't told her what had happened in the Forest of Purroy in any detail—she couldn't possibly comprehend—but a wife could intuit evil. Once she learned what had occurred that morning at the Louisiana Demolishing Company, whatever was changing inside her would only change faster.

"It's glorious," she said.

"It is a strange green, the field."

"You can scream as loud as you want and nobody looks at you funny."

"You can be as silent as you want and nobody looks at you funny."

"You didn't sleep," she said, noting his rumpled uniform, the dried mud on his pant cuffs. His bloodshot eyes. "Again."

"How can you tell?"

"You're the same color as the sand."

He followed her eyes to the manicured diamond, with its smoothly raked base paths. They were also a peculiar hue, a grayish white. It wasn't sand, exactly, but silt dredged from the Mississippi at Point Manchac, about a hundred miles upriver, by Jahncke Service, Inc., a sponsor of Heinemann Park. JAHNCKE proclaimed a banner on the left-field fence, the letters bright red against a black background. WE GETS OUR HANDS DIRTY, SO YOU DON'T GOTS TO.

"I intended to come home before the game. But it didn't fall out that way."

"I guess I'll never understand why you have to work nights."

"Have you seen the papers?"

"I saw the *States*. 'U-boat Sunk by the British.' 'Wilson Marches for Red Cross.' 'Digging of the Industrial Canal, Triumph of the South, Set to Commence.' "

A young girl squealed as a ball bounced into the stands several rows ahead. Two boys raced down the aisle, competing with the girl's father for the ball.

"A navy got killed," said Bill.

"What?" Maze's eyes widened. They were still magnificent: hazel, lucid, shielded by long, fluttering lashes.

"Teddy Obitz."

One of the boys, having crawled beneath a seat to grab the ball, emerged triumphantly, dancing in the aisle.

"The man who trained you? The handsome blond man?"

"They called him Big Blond."

Maze visibly shuddered.

"He has a wife and two daughters," Bill heard himself say. The boy threw the ball on a line to the Pelican fielder and whooped with joy. "It was the Negro highwayman who did it."

Maze had stopped listening. The shudder had intensified into a convulsion of rage. "Just quit, won't you?"

"You're right. We don't need to talk about it."

"No—quit the Department."

"Maze."

"It's too horrible. I never thought I'd survive the war, but this—it's an endless war, war forever."

"I guess I won the war."

"What is that supposed to mean?"

"I killed the highwayman." Bill chuckled in a way that he hoped she might interpret as blithely heroic.

He looked out over the field, surveying the players. They tossed baseballs, they joked, they lay on the grass, stretching hamstrings. Yes, thanks to him—and the other navies—these men could play a child's game under the sun and thousands of complacent citizens could assemble in peace on a Sunday afternoon, worrying about nothing more than the viscosity of Dick Robertson's saliva. Bill glanced at Maze to gauge the effect of his bravura. Her mouth was twisted all the way to one side.

"What?"

"You *killed* a man?"

"Not a man. A murderer."

"Murderers are men too." She shook her head. "My God. You must be upset."

"Can't say I am."

She paused, studying him. "Why not?"

Someone leaned over and tapped the rim of Bill's cap. He turned and stared into the damp, grinning face of Captain Thomas Capo.

"Billy Bastrop." Capo was cleanly shaven and when he removed his cap his black hair was bright with brilliantine. Apparently he had found time to go home this morning, likely while Bill was still in the interrogation room. After an excruciating visit to Obitz's widow, Eloise, Bill had helped to interview nearly two dozen potential witnesses—anyone they could find outdoors in the Irish Channel between 3:00 and 6:00 a.m. Only two were willing to identify the corpse as the man who had shot Obitz and fled to the Louisiana Demolishing Company. The first was a petty foon with several outstanding warrants. The other was a Spaniard without papers. Bill cleared the warrants and sent a note to a friend in Immigration. But the witnesses' statements were merely corroborative and would have had no value were it not for the testimony of Obitz's partner.

A navy of fourteen years experience, Harry Dodson understood that he needed to give a clean account, and quickly. Not only for Bill—he didn't owe Bill a thing—but for the Department, for the easily panicked public, for Captain Capo and Superintendent Mooney, and, most of all, for Obitz's widow and little girls. At the Obitzes', after Dodson and Bill had delivered the news, Teddy's eight-year-old, Carrie, insisted on giving them a tour of her father's war garden, proudly listing the names of the exotic vegetables they were cultivating for Uncle Sam: chard, salsify, kohlrabi. The whole business was unsettling, frightening. After a painful half hour in which Carrie explained fertilization strategies and canning processes, Dodson mentioned delicately that he had to return to the station. Carrie burst into tears. It was a grim tableau: Dodson standing in the doorway of his fallen partner's house; Carrie, sobbing, tugging on his legs; Mrs. Obitz, sobbing, tugging on Carrie's legs.

If Dodson said that the man Bill had shot was the highwayman, and Captain Capo was satisfied, then Bill figured he ought to be satisfied too. He rose to greet his boss.

"Captain Cap." Bill smiled tightly. "Have you met my wife, Maisie Bastrop?"

Bill was relieved to see that Maze had recomposed her face into a pantomime of polite expectation.

"You war heroes." Capo shook his head. "You always attract the most fetching female company."

Bastrop noted that he hadn't used the word *beautiful*. It was a precipitous fall from beautiful to fetching and Maze had tumbled the full distance in less than seven months. Not that fetching was unlovable, or undesirable. Fetching was wonderful. But there was a distinction.

Capo—stout, firm, with professional creases around his mouth and a purple liver spot beneath his left eye, the same size as the eye—touched Bastrop's shoulder.

"Give us a sec, would you?" said Bill.

Maze seemed relieved to turn back to the field. She appeared to give her attention to it fully, as if instead of pepper and lazy games of catch it were the ninth inning of a tie game, runner in scoring position, two outs, full count.

"The teenagers," Capo was saying, as he steered Bastrop up the aisle, "they were giddy. Never been inside a morgue before."

"You're saying that they took suggestions well."

"Didn't have to suggest anything. Not in words, that is. The Hun—Bodemuller? He said he was 'almost positive' that the Negro on the table was the same who held him up on Friday. And little Richard Bray says, 'Yah, he looks like the same Negro, but they all look the same if you want my professional opinion.' "

Capo gave a vacant laugh. The stress of the last days showed on the captain's face—his jowls, already pendulous, had begun to melt.

"How long is this going to go?" said Bill. "Not to be ungrateful."

"You trot out to the mound, throw the pitch, shake some hands. Then you can go home." Capo again touched Bill's shoulder. "Superintendent Mooney wanted me to thank you. These are on the house."

Capo waved two nickels in the air, rubbing them between

thumb and forefinger. A Dixie boy promptly appeared by his side and traded him two mugs for the coins.

"I'm happy to represent the company," said Bill.

"I meant last night."

"Mooney was pleased?" It was difficult to tell what the boss thought without reading the newspapers. There were rumors he would run for higher office; Mayor Behrman was in his fourth term and aging in dog years. Beside Capo, who possessed the bearing of a career navy—relaxed in his authority, courtly, generous—Mooney could pass for a desk clerk. He was at heart a politician. Before Behrman named Mooney superintendent he had been a railroad executive. It was difficult to credit a man like that.

"He was elated," said Cap. "Can you imagine if the Negro was loose even a day longer? Mooney asked me to thank you personally." Capo's jowls wobbled. "A hero abroad and now a hero at home. Billy, it's an honor. 'S'really a damn honor."

Bill forced himself to look directly into Capo's liquid eyes as they shook hands.

In their row Maze had been joined by two other police wives. Bill recognized one as John Mestre's wife, a brassy heavyset girl with lips painted bright carmine. She traced Dick Robertson with her eyes. The pitcher removed his jacket and began a light toss with his catcher along the third-base line.

"Wish he wasn't always licking that dirty baseball," said the other woman, whose nose twisted upward at the tip, as if its designer had lingered a beat too long with his pen.

"But he does it so delicately. With such affection."

"Ruth!" The women looked around to see if they had been overheard and turned pink when they saw Capo and Bill at the end of the row, trailed by John Mestre and a man Capo introduced as Okie. Capo raised two more nickels in the air. The wives moved down the aisle to make room and Bill noticed that Maze was being ignored by the other women, who inclined toward each other, laughing conspiratorially.

The Pelicans jogged around the field. Robertson lagged twenty yards behind, escorted by a ball boy. The boy handed him a small jar, from which he took a swig. The jar appeared to contain a white liquid, though Bill knew not to believe his eyes. But Mestre, following Bill's gaze, had reached the same conclusion.

"Milk!" he said, in amazement. "He's going to make himself pump ship." Mestre had been sent back in February after some kind of accident and had yet to recover full use of his hearing. "You cain't drink milk and run at the same time."

"It's probably a chalk potion," said Okie. "With rejuvenating vitamins."

"Spoken like an actual Okie," said Capo. "Milk makes the saliva thick. Old spitballer's trick."

Okie scratched his ear. "Maybe it's both."

"You cain't drink milk and run," said oblivious Mestre. "He's going to make himself chuckle."

"You're not from Oklahoma?" said Bill, turning to Okie.

"I was born the eleven hundred block of Melpomene." He snorted. "Captain Cap thinks just because he served in Manila twenty years ago that he can bully with actual trenchers. You saw the trenches?"

Bill nodded, a vague gesture that communicated either he was in a trench or agreed that Capo was taking too much license with his manner of address.

"I was at Cambrai." *Cam*-bry. "Eleventh Engineers. Got in the way of a tank. It burped boiling metal." He turned to face Bill for the first time and Bill saw the scar, dark purple, branded across his jaw. It looked like a stovepot with a handle. Or the state of Oklahoma. "My name is Guy."

"Bill."

"Bill, I commend you on killing that nigger highwayman."

"I did what any navy would do."

Bill glanced down the row but Maze was blocked by the two other wives, who waved their hands and laughed. A cheer rose in the grandstand. Marching down the aisle was a Prussian brigade commander dressed in a field tunic, with rounded back flaps like a skirt, a high collar embroidered by red piping, and turned-back cuffs. The *Generalmajor* was briefly obscured behind a passing vendor of Broussard's peanuts and when he reappeared he had been transformed, like a magician's assistant, into A. J. Heinemann, the Pelicans' owner, who had begun his pre-game tour of the stadium. A chewed-over stogie protruded from his lip. He twirled a cane and fanned himself with a wad of dollar bills. The fans jeered playfully as he strolled the concourse.

"Cheapskate!"

"Skinflint!"

"Criminal!"

Heinemann grinned and mooned and twirled his cane. Since buying the Pels he'd taken it upon himself to direct the fans' ire away from the woeful product on the field and onto himself. But now that the Pels were decent—second in the Southern League last year—the boos were lighthearted. Heinemann, noticing the cops, pointed his cane at Capo. The navies rose from their seats.

"Gentlemen," said Heinemann broadly, the cigar sticking to his lip. A tangerine bounced off his shoulder and caromed onto the field. Heinemann didn't flinch. "Your sacrifices have conferred honor and dignity upon our great city."

The big man had thick sticky lips, wide ears, and tiny melancholy eyes that withdrew deep into their sockets, like sea creatures shrinking from sunlight, when he smiled. For his act he had applied kohl around his eyes and rouge on his cheeks like a clown, or harlot.

"Great dignity," added Heinemann. A grapefruit landed in the small of his back with a juicy thud. Heinemann turned to Bill. "Detective Bastrop, I presume?"

"Yes, sir," said Capo. "That's the slob hisself."

"So you're the man to stop the highwayman? A heroic act."

"Thank you, sir." *Heroic!* Bill felt a wild laughter chattering inside him.

"These Negroes running wild with guns in our streets," said Heinemann. "It's as terrifying a prospect as the human mind can conjure."

"I did what any New Orleans officer would do, sir." Bill winced internally.

"That detective."

"Theodore Obitz," said Capo. "A damn good man." He seemed instantly on the verge of tears.

"Wasn't he the one working on the ax murder?"

"Maggio." Capo nodded. "The Italian grocer on Magnolia and Upperline. Detective Obitz was overseeing the investigation."

"This city is plum going to shit." Heinemann shook his head. "Thank the Lord for people like you, Detective Bastrop. You're our last line of defense."

The laughter rose again and Bill could not suppress it but managed, at the last moment, to turn it into a cough that he covered with his fist. Heinemann gave him a scrutinizing look but was distracted by the Six and Seven-Eighths String Band, which had taken up position behind home plate, twanging the first bars of "Clarinet Marmalade." Heinemann led the officers down the aisle. They had to go slowly because, as Bill noticed for the first time, Mestre walked with a limp; in place of his right foot was a block of wood, secured by leather stirrups. An initial burst of jeers at the sight of Heinemann taking the field tapered once the crowd noticed the navy jackets beside him. Heinemann raised his hand and addressed his stadium in his loudest baritone:

"Pelicans and Pelicanettes," he began, "I present to you three local heroes worthy of the highest honor. They have sacrificed their lives for our nation, only to return home to sacrifice their lives each day for our city."

Vigorous applause. In the front row Maze had reappeared beside the two other wives. She alone did not clap.

"Officer John Mestre, born in the Seventh Ward, represented us in the Rainbow Division. With gallantry and grit, John marched fifty miles through blinding blizzards, on frozen roads over icy hills, in service of our freedom. He lacked earmuffs or proper boots and suffered a grievous frostbite." Heinemann looked up from the paper that Capo had handed him and grinned at Mestre. "John, I know you must be relieved as we are to have you back under the skee-*orch*-ing Louisiana sun."

Mestre, unable to hear Heinemann's speech, stared down at his good foot.

"Officer Guy Molony fought at the Battle of Cam, of Cam—"

"*Cam*-bry," said Molony, absently rubbing his Oklahoma scar.

"The Battle of *Cam*-bry—and with great distinction. He served alongside a battalion of British fighting tanks, dodging the enemy's machine-gun fire, shells, and horses. Everybody, a Pelican cheer!"

Guy snorted. "If'n I'd dodged them," he said beneath his breath, "I wouldn't be ruined." Bill noticed that Mrs. Molony was sobbing into Ruth Mestre's shoulder.

"Detective William Bastrop, First Ward, was fighting in the trenches at Rouge Bouquet when a shell landed on the roof of his dugout. He and twenty-one other members of the 69th Regiment were buried alive beneath soil and wooden beams."

Men doffed hats and wiped brows with handkerchiefs.

"Exhibiting tremendous fortitude and valor, Detective Bastrop escaped his muddy grave and, in the midst of bombardment, summoned aid for his trapped comrades."

To his surprise the crowd rose—the front sections first, followed by those behind. Soon the entire stadium was cheering, including the Pelicans and the Travelers, who stepped onto the top stair of their dugouts. Even Maze applauded. What did they think they were applauding? They weren't applauding for him, he was certain, at least not for what he had actually done in the Forest of Purroy. But the force of the roaring stadium began to work on him. Maybe he had achieved something great. Wasn't the ardor of the applause all the evidence he needed? He had brought them joy, after all. They were cheering the idea of heroism, or themselves—applauding their own freedom. It was no small thing to make people feel freedom with such force that they rose to their feet and clapped their palms together. Hero or coward, it had led to the same place, hadn't it? Just as reports of the highwayman's death had restored to the city a sense of calm, regardless of whether the dead man was in fact the highwayman. It all came out the same in the end—provided that the truth remained hidden.

Heinemann handed each officer a baseball inscribed in blue ink with the words OFFICIAL SOUTHERN LEAGUE, PAT'D AUG-31-09. Three Pelicans stood in a line behind home plate to receive the pitches. Mestre threw first, an impressive zip. From Molony, a lazy lob. As Bill cocked the ball behind his ear, he spotted behind the visitors' dugout, about eight rows back, sitting beside a trio of starchy sailors in starched white uniforms, a single person who did not applaud. The man stood out because of his attire—a forest-green greatcoat, much too heavy for the season, and a black bowler, which marked him trebly, for he was also the only person in sight who had neglected to remove his hat. As Bill began to wheel his arm he realized that the man wore an eye patch.

Bill's pitch veered violently awry. A ball boy standing in front of the Pelicans' dugout dove theatrically out of the way. The crowd laughed and everyone took their seats. The Pelicans filed out of the dugout, jogging lazily to their positions.

Bill looked wildly for Leonard Perl. His gaze fell on a teenager gurgling a Dixie and children's faces stretching into scream masks and a woman blithely fanning herself with a program before at last he found the white uniforms of the three sailors. He scanned to the end of the aisle, expecting to discover that Perl had reconstituted, transfigured, or transformed into a different person. But it was worse than that. The seat that Perl had occupied was empty. He was gone. Which meant that in the first place he had been there.

MAY 29, 1918—THE BATTLEFIELD

Isadore sat on the floor of the bedroom near the base of an old chifforobe. Termites had devoured two square feet of the floorboard. The termites seemed to have gotten started on the chifforobe too: its legs were maculated with cavities the circumference of No. 2 pencils. A nudge and it would collapse; the whole dresser, for that matter, might fall through the floor. He could see clear to the ground, some four feet below—a patch of black mud clotted with balled-up glassine papers.

"Virginia throws her Creoleans wrappers down there," said Bailey from the bed.

"Pralines?"

"She has a sweet tooth. Seven of them actually. The rest fell out."

Virginia's bedroom smelled like rot and sickness. To avoid prying eyes she hadn't cracked the windows or blinds for more than a week, though this perhaps was better than the alternative since the room faced a back alley where the neighbors left their trash. In May the aroma of decomposition in those close, shaded New Orleans alleys was tyrannical. But inside the darkened room it was suffocating too. The only infusion of air came from the hole in the floor, a damp, fetid whisper. The claustrophobia was heightened by the walls' maroon color, a shade darker than congealed blood. A vanity mirror propped on the chifforobe was overlaid with a coating of green mold. The bed resembled nothing more than a hammock, sinking heavily, as if it were trying to escape through the floor. Isadore empathized with the bed.

"Is Verge supposed to be home soon?" he asked.

"Supposed," said Frank Bailey, "is a funny word. When you come to think of it."

He sat at the head of the bed, his small bare feet dangling off the edge. A single candle weakly illuminated his cheek. The cheek was soft, boyish. His eyes, however, were dull, the eyes of an older man. Isadore sat on the floor below the window, reading the *States* by the sliver of streetlamp light that stole beneath the blind. The rest of the hideout—a shotgun composed of two other rooms, a kitchen and a parlor—was dark. The night outside was dark. But it wasn't a steady darkness. The darkness advanced from all sides.

"She said she'd be home by ten." Bailey's jaw moved mechanically.

Isadore checked his new watch, a black trench with a silver case that said *JW Benson*. He had inherited it from the driver of the Leidenheimer Bakery wagon they'd ripped off on Melpomene. The man's lips had quivered, snot leaked from his nose, he wailed something about his mother. Isadore had wanted to console him—explain that he and Bailey were just jobbing, they wouldn't hurt him. But that wasn't true, it turned out. Bailey was dangerous. He would shoot—a cop, even! Isadore made a mental note to pawn the watch in the morning. "Five before eleven," he said.

Bailey shrugged. "The man shot by the police the other night . . ."

"At the Louisiana Demolishing Company. On Girod. Abraham Price, shot by Detective William Bastrop."

"How they come to know Price ain the highwayman?"

"First because his boss said he was a night watchman," said Isadore. With Bailey it was like talking to a child. A child with the memory of a senior citizen. "Second, because you did five more stickups the very next night."

"You say it like I have a choice." Bailey pulled a small parcel, bound up in a red rag, from the drawer of the bedside table. "You want me to go back to painting houses?"

"That's a choice."

"Between survival and starvation."

"The dead detective's partner even made the identification. He identified the wrong man, which means the case would have been dropped. But you couldn't give it a single *night*. So they had to admit their mistake."

"When you're hot, you're hot." When Bailey smiled the diamonds in his teeth sparkled. "Can't take greens off the stove and expect them to keep warm."

Isadore shook his head and shook the paper. Not for the first time he questioned throwing his lot in with Bailey. He had joined him in a spirit of wildness and rebellion—against settling down, becoming a husband, accepting a slave job. Bailey said things were easy on the other side, after you left behind the stiff dread of indentured manual labor and became a pirate. Isadore figured he would go along once, for kicks. But one night became two, a week, three weeks. His role was minimal, performed at an antiseptic distance from the action; he had only to stand several yards behind Bailey and flash a weapon, or look out for passersby or navies. He told himself he was doing it to supplant the beer-lacquered pennies he scraped out of honky-tonk tip jars, until his music began to pay for itself. And briefly the pirate life had satisfied more than his money troubles. It had quenched a desire for revenge. He did not know exactly what he was avenging, but robbing the wealthy Uptown grandsons of plantation owners seemed to help. The satisfaction did not last. As Bailey broadened his victim pool to include deliverymen, teenagers, even the occasional Negro—anyone who crossed his path—the original thrill was suffocated by a haze of regret and alarm. The more brazen Bailey grew, the more difficult it became for Isadore to extricate himself. Their fates were scrambled. He had to make sure Bailey didn't get caught and give up the whole operation. He had to control Bailey. If only he knew how.

There was yet a final perverse twist. The highway jobs, instead of enabling his musicianship, cannibalized it. The staking out of locations and getaway routes was full-time work, if you did it carefully, which meant that the Slim Izzy Quartet had not held a practice in two weeks. But the holdups fought against the music in a more damaging way. Isadore had always understood music as a conversation with the Dark Unknown—the dimension of the world that was hidden to the world, that bubbled beneath the surface, or above the surface, or in parallel to the surface, what Miss Daisy called the "spirit realm," or what he'd once heard Kid Ory describe, in a set at Economy Hall, as "the dominion of the imperceivable." When you played, the conversation went both ways. The imperceivable spoke back to you. It gave you the feeling that there was more to human existence than hard labor. It consoled you.

The highway jobs, however, were one-directional: take, take, take. It was bad enough to be scared all the time, scared of losing the house on Liberty Street, of failing Orly and Miss Daisy, of starvation. But with Bailey he was terrified all the time. The money diluted the fear, but not enough. It was not nearly enough money for that.

"'One negro,'" he began in his newspaperman voice, a high, over-enunciating voice meant to disguise the dread that surged upward toward his throat. "'One negro was killed outright and another wounded as a result of the activity of police and citizens in the search Monday night for the negro who shot to death Detective Theodore Obitz.'"

"I didn't shoot any detective." Bailey unfolded the red rag, revealing its contents: a wire brush, a bone toothbrush, a bore brush, a single threadbare white sock, a jar of aluminum polish, a green-glass bottle with a beige label (JED'S RED GUN CLEAN), a rusted cigar tin containing a dozen bullets, and the disassembled sections of his revolver: Colt caliber .45, U.S. Army model 1917, finish full blued, the stock smooth walnut, the lacquer lightly chipped, and a pair of spring-steel half-moon clips to hold the cartridges in place. Bailey glanced at himself in the pockmarked reflection of the cigar tin. Did he see what Isadore saw? A young boy with barely any fuzz above his lip, eyes too close together, dimpled cheeks. A boy trying so hard to look like a man that he only made himself more childish.

"That big yellow navy on Baronne?" said Isadore. "That was a detective. A patrolman would've been bad enough. But come about you shot a dick."

"Didn't shoot him."

Bailey's insolence—infantile, silken, irrational—tried his nerves. Did Bailey really think he had to playact when it was just the two of them? He reassumed his newspaperman cadence: "'The dead negro is Louis Johnson. He was killed following a scuffle with two white men at Napoleon Avenue and Magnolia Street who stopped their automobile upon seeing two negroes at one o'clock Tuesday morning and began questioning them. When the slain negro showed fight, Charles E. Jones, cattle dealer, fired the shot that resulted in the negro's death.'"

"That's good—'the shot that resulted in the negro's death.' That means he shot the man's brains out, right?"

"It could have been his heart."

Bailey nodded diplomatically. "Maybe his heart."

"Aren't you worried we'll be caught?"

Bailey looked at him like he was crazy.

Galaxies spun in his stomach. He glanced at the hole in the floor where the bad air seeped in. Or perhaps they secreted it themselves, this miasma of fear and blind ignorance. From Isadore the fear, from Bailey the ignorance. But was it only ignorance, Bailey's lack of concern about the danger he'd brought upon them when he'd shot the yellow-haired detective? Or had he already given up? To Isadore the idea—resignation to death!—was impossible to stomach. Yet since the shooting Bailey had become calmer while Isadore, haunted by the faces of their victims, had traveled in the opposite direction.

"I think I know Louis," said Bailey. "Big country boy?"

"They want to revenge the white detective."

"Don't credit everything you read."

"Look at this Louis Johnson—walking in the street like any evening and *bam*."

"Some men die before their time."

"Forget Louis Johnson. Look at *me*. The other night I was almost shot by a watchman outside the house where Orly works. And that was before you shot the navy."

"They got money lying around up there, the family where Orly works?"

Isadore thought of the lantern in Orly's room casting fluttery shadow wings across the wall, as if a panicked raven had been trapped in the low-ceilinged space. "I won't dignify that," he said, though he suspected Bailey might have been joking about robbing the Tiltons. He next decided Bailey was serious, before concluding that he was no longer able to tell the difference, which was worst of all.

"How's the horn coming?" Bailey dumped the cigar tin upside down, spilling the bullets on the bedspread.

"I've had to put it aside."

"Promise me you'll keep on it." Bailey dipped the bone toothbrush's bristles into the aluminum polish and selected the first bullet. "I may be a pretty good highwayman, but you're the greatest cornet man in this town. I've known it since the Colored Waifs' Band. Everyone has."

"Jass doesn't pay like robbing Paddies."

"It's not all about money, Izzy."

Both men laughed.

"How much it cost to put those diamonds in your teeth?"

"I'm serious about your music."

"I don't know anyone else that is."

"They will be." Bailey licked his teeth. "I haven't done my molars yet. I'm fixing to do my molars."

"Diamond molars," Isadore acknowledged, "would be pretty Spanish."

Bailey resumed polishing the bullets with the bone toothbrush. He admired the smoothness of each bullet like a jewelry appraiser, before dropping it into the tin. When he shifted his weight on the bed the bullets in the tin clinked against each other like marbles.

"Say, Frank. Does Virginia know about my involvement in all this?"

"Verge don't know nothing except that her man brings her poppy-seed loaves whenever she wants them. What time is it?"

Isadore consulted his JW Benson. "Six past eleven."

"She'll be here soon." It was as if Bailey was trying to convince himself.

"It's a manhunt, Frank. Shoot first and investigate after."

"The navies get to figuring there's too many Negroes in the streets so they take some off. It happens now and again. Nothing unusual to it."

"Not taking off. Murdering." Isadore was too agitated to remember to use his newspaperman voice. "'A negro at Clio and Dryades was being questioned when suddenly the negro darted off. He was overtaken by a crowd and was found to be wounded in the neck. It is not known who shot him. The negro, Herbert Foster of 3817 Chartres Street, told the police that he ran because he was afraid of being harmed.'"

"Cain't blame him for running," said Bailey. "Only for not running fast enough."

Bailey dropped the final bullet into the tin. He peered into the business end of the revolver like an astronomer into a telescope. Isadore had an urge to leap onto the bed and smash the barrel into Bailey's eye. That would end this nightmare finally. The police knew the highwayman had partners. What would stop Bailey from fingering Isadore if he could gain an advantage?

"What else does it say?"

"'The better element of the negro race in New Orleans is cooperating with the police. The leading negro preachers and citizens are advising their people not to give the fugitive the slightest encouragement. Fearing a race riot, they are seeking to track the dark griffe down and turn him over to the authorities.'"

"Another lie." Bailey was cleaning the muzzle with the bone toothbrush. "No man in the community going to come turn us in."

"What about a woman?"

Bailey looked up. "You mean Virginia?"

"Listen: 'Laura Smith, negress, living in Julia Street, said she saw a man step from behind a lumber stack at Saratoga and the Basin, a few minutes after the shots that killed the negro workman were fired.'"

Bailey stuck his wire brush in the air like a magic wand. "That's me!"

"'The man, apparently a negro—'"

"What'd I say?"

"'—apparently a negro, was seen by her from her upstairs gallery to cross the basin bridge and meet another man on the other side.'"

"That's you!"

"No shit, Frank."

"You're famous," said Bailey.

Isadore felt hammering inside his temple. An accomplice had been mentioned in some of the pieces, but never so explicitly. They'd be looking for the other man on the other side.

"That's five blocks from here," said Bailey.

To avoid thinking, Isadore continued to read. "'The highwayman is described as a dark griffe negro, five feet seven inches in height, weighs about 140 pounds, and wore a blue shirt, black trousers pulled high over waistline, and white-checked cloth cap.'"

"I'm not that dark. I'm not as light as you, but I'm not that dark. Besides I'm one fifty if I'm anything. Probably more, on account of all those poppy-seed loaves."

Bailey wore a blue work shirt and black trousers. His white-checked cloth cap had flown off his head when they ran away from their last job. On their hunting trips Bailey had stolen three bakery wagons and lost three hats. They only kept the bakery wagons long enough to drive out of sight and they grabbed as many loaves as they could fit under their arms. Virginia favored poppy-seed. Bailey always checked for poppy-seed.

"We can't be found here," said Bailey. With a loud crack he locked the chamber. "Clean." The word seemed absurd when spoken aloud in Virginia's bedroom, with its dust menageries skittering beneath the bed and the hole in the floor making its fetid exhalations. Isadore couldn't take it anymore. Maybe it wasn't such a bad idea to allow Bailey to go on another spree. Every white man in New Orleans was intent on shooting the first Negro to give him cause. If Bailey was stupid enough to try again, he'd get himself killed. Isadore remembered Orly's advice about the job at the Industrial Canal. Perhaps the canal job wouldn't be so grueling after all. Compared to this, the canal would be a parade.

"Where you going?" said Bailey.

"Fresh air."

Isadore began to feel better as soon as he opened the door. He shot through the kitchen to the parlor, sidling between the green couch and the upright stove. He pulled the dead bolt and stepped onto the porch. He breathed deeply, inhaling magnolia and horse manure. Before he could exhale, he spotted a police car at the corner. The automobile was empty but the sound of two men conferring came from the side of the house.

"—facing the alley, but only the single egress."

"Yay."

"What."

"You hear that?"

Isadore dashed back inside and gently closed the door behind him, sliding the dead bolt. He was grateful for the humidity now because the moisture kept the bolt from squeaking. Boots marched up the porch steps. Isadore leaped back across the parlor, through the kitchen—never allowing his heels to touch the floor—and into the bedroom, slipping around the doorframe. In Virginia's house the doors all lined up; he didn't want to stand in the path a bullet might take if fired from the front door by a shotgun. In the moldy mirror he caught a glimpse of his terrified eyes, his cheeks hairless and pale.

Bailey regarded Isadore with mute indifference. He balled his gun-cleaning equipment into the rag and twisted it tight.

"The navies are here," whispered Isadore.

Bailey looked up. "What navies?"

"Turn the light."

Bailey stared at him, uncomprehendingly, for a beat too long.

"*Snuff out the light.*"

It was too late. There came a violent knocking.

"New Orleans Police Department. We know it's you, Frank Bailey. Open up."

Bailey rose and silently walked to the kitchen. Isadore peeked around the doorframe. He watched in horror as Bailey bent to his knees before the front door and brought his eye to the keyhole.

The navy spoke again, in a tone that was almost gentle. "Hello there."

Bailey lurched backward, spun, and returned in a sprint to Virginia's bedroom. He pivoted sharply around the doorframe and leaned against the wall next to Isadore, catching his breath.

"I saw the man's eye," Bailey whispered.

"Whose eye?"

"The navy's eye." Bailey said it like a curse. He trembled, his chest rising in erratic flutters. "Through the keyhole," he gasped, "the man's eyeball stared at my eyeball."

Pounding came from the front door.

"I saw you, Frank." It was a hearty voice, taunting, self-impressed.

"The floor," whispered Bailey. "See if there's men in the back."

Isadore realized that Bailey had visualized this scenario before. The hole in the floor near the foot of the chifforobe was just large enough for Isadore to stick a leg through. He stared at it and wanted to cry. The pounding was getting louder and he couldn't tell if it was coming from the front door or inside his brain.

"Pull the wood," said Bailey, and Isadore was struck anew by his assuredness. Bailey was an idiot in many ways but had a talent for crime: a crime savant. Isadore, on the other hand, was a crime idiot. Criminal activity gave him head pains, like difficult math.

Bailey was right—the floorboards had been bored so thin by termites that when Isadore pulled on a plank, it snapped like a cracker, coughing sawdust. He sat with his feet inside the hole and slid down. With his feet in the muck beneath the elevated cottage, he was chest-level with the floor of Virginia's room. Beneath the bed he could see the dust menagerie herding, the dust bunnies joined by dust tigers and dust elephants and, in the distance, a dust giraffe nuzzling the bottom of the mattress.

From this vantage Bailey appeared very tall and strong. With his gun in hand he leaned into the doorway.

"I will kill the first man that walks through the door," he yelled. "I swear on the soul of Robert Charles." When, glancing behind him, he saw Isadore, protruding like a gopher from the hole in the floor, he made an urgent gesture, as if to say, *You still here?*

Isadore ducked beneath the floor and was enclosed in darkness. By squatting, he could see into the alley that ran behind the house. There, lit by a dim streetlamp, were three pairs of legs, each terminating in hobnailed boots. The only people who wore hobnailed boots were decommissioned soldiers.

When Isadore popped his head back up, Bailey was shouting at the bedroom door: "You're going to have to get reinforcements because I'm going to kill the first white son of a bitch that enters this house."

"Bailey," Isadore whispered. "There are three of them behind the house. We can't escape that way."

Bailey regarded Isadore as he might a scurrying cockroach. "Your head looks stupid." Bailey laughed. "Here." He removed from the bedside table the Webley & Scott revolver Isadore had used during the holdups and kicked it across the floor. Isadore tucked it under his belt.

The police pounded on the door like they intended to break it down.

"Come on in!" shouted Bailey. The veins in his neck articulated themselves. He was able to access a staggering depth of rage almost instantaneously. But it passed like a shiver. When Bailey turned to Isadore, his face was calm and untroubled.

"Hide under the house," said Bailey. "They don't know anything about you."

Isadore tried to think. Beneath the house he would be defenseless, cornered. Even if he could scamper out, there was nowhere to go. The alley continued around the cottage to the street. There were navies in front of the house and navies in the back. Someone would spot him and they would fire their guns. He felt an overwhelming urge to urinate.

There came the sound of splintering wood.

"*Duck*," said Bailey.

Isadore ducked. Bailey shoved the chifforobe until it covered the hole in the floor. The message was clear: Isadore would not be popping up again.

The legs in the alley had doubled. Isadore crawled through the mud until he was under the center of the cottage, beneath the doorway to the bedroom. Creoleans wrappers clung to his elbows and knees. The praline residue smelled atrocious, sickly sweet grotesque.

"We're not going to kill you," shouted the officer from the front door. "We just want to talk." Isadore, without understanding what he was doing, unbuckled his pants.

"You're going to kill me anyway," screamed Bailey, five feet and seven inches above Isadore's head. "You're going to kill me, but not before I kill some of you. I'll shoot the first man in this room."

Isadore wedged the revolver in his armpit and pushed down his pants, not an easy maneuver while kneeling, let alone with one arm. He nudged his trousers down to his knees and, stifling a groan, urinated forcefully in the mud. The stream was checked by an explosion near the front of the house. This was followed, less than a second later, by a thud on the floor above Isadore's head.

"Don't shoot!" screamed Bailey. "I threw down my weapon. Don't shoot!"

"Hold fire!"

"C'mon, Cap. Serious?"

"I command you, hold fire!"

The floorboard above Isadore's head creaked.

"I got his gun!" someone said.

Here was Bailey's chance. He could snitch any moment, beginning now. Isadore pulled up his pants and returned the .38 to his belt. If he was going to be shot, it would be with his pants on.

There were some rough noises, grunts and smacks, and the mattress creaked. More footsteps. The click of a metal clasp.

"Blue jumper, black trousers. Alpine hat."

"Dark griffe."

"Five foot seven. One forty, one forty-five tops."

"It's him."

"Rest your guns," said a tired voice. It was received by restive muttering. "Frank Bailey, my name is Captain Thomas Capo. You are under arrest for the murder of Detective Theodore Obitz."

"I didn't kill the detective."

More rough noises followed.

Isadore crawled toward the back of the house.

". . . out of the front *door* alive," said a cop standing there. "But not farther."

"Nobody wants to miss it," said another. "Least of all me."

If Isadore burst out from beneath the house, would the surprise give him an advantage? He supposed it might, but the men had guns, and he barely knew how to work his. A new pair of legs turned down the alley, barked a command, and all the legs ran off together. Isadore counted to ten, fifteen, thirty. He crawled in a desperate scamper to the back alley. His spine protested when he stood upright and a sudden dizziness forced him to lean against the cottage for support. He picked Creoleans wrappers off his arms and peeked around the corner to make sure the alley was clear.

Isadore crept along the side of the house, prepared to roll beneath it at the first sight of a navy, but he encountered nobody. Perdido Street was thronged with people—navies, of course, armed with high-powered shotguns, repeating rifles, and revolvers, sparking in the moonlight, but they were outnumbered. There was a raging mass of angry white men at front, and behind them more cautious black men and families. Steadily the mob accreted. An inner cordon of police, holding walking sticks chest-high to form a barricade, struggled to prevent the most aggressive of the men from leaping onto the porch. The crowd bulged into the side alley. Isadore pressed behind them and, like that, he was no longer a fleeing accomplice. He was just a face in the crowd.

An older policeman stepped out of the cottage onto the porch. The crowd surged.

"Lynch him!" someone yelled.

"Throw him to us."

"Gentlemen!" The man raised his hands in placation. "My name is Captain Thomas Capo. I implore you."

"We will tear him apart."

Capo repeated himself sternly and the crowd settled. Isadore focused on the captain's purple liver spot, about the size of a silver dollar, directly beneath his eye. It was like the mark of a demon.

"I appeal to your better nature," said Capo.

"Kill the nigger!" a woman shouted. Isadore had an impulse to echo her.

"We have the man under arrest. We took him alive and we're going to escort him to the station—alive. Many of these crimes remain to be solved. This Negro is the only person who can solve them for us."

More booing and grumbling. Isadore booed too.

"The police will not hesitate to loose their guns in the defense of their prisoner," Capo continued. "Any man who is responsible for the Negro's death will be charged with the crime before the law."

When Bailey emerged from the cottage, surrounded by a phalanx of officers, the crowd pushed forward again, but halfheartedly. They were more curious than angry. Who was this monster that had terrorized New Orleans? Isadore saw Frank Bailey as a stranger might and understood the confusion that swept over the shoulders and heads craning for a view. Why, Bailey was just a sliver of a man, shorter and skinnier than the officers who surrounded him. He didn't even look his age: eighteen years old.

A sea of navies carried Bailey into a police wagon. As the automobile advanced toward police headquarters, a crowd trailed like a second line. Isadore split off and wandered down Perdido. When he could be certain that nobody was near enough to see, he transferred the Webley & Scott to his hip pocket, where he felt the crinkle of newsprint. He pulled out the paper, the torn quarter page from the *Times-Picayune*, unfolded it, and reread the job posting:

> WANTED AT ONCE—:
>
> FOR CONSTRUCTION OF INDUSTRIAL CANAL
>
> in Third District, through old Ursulines Tract;
>
> Machinists, Mechanical Engineers, Electricians, Contractors, Foremen, Superintendents, Crane Operators, Dredge Operators, Carpenters, Iron and Brass Melters, Welters, Smelters, Bricklayers, Truck Drivers, Cement Mixers, Fitters, Turners, Shifters, Improvers, experience an asset but not necessary; Boys, eager and willing to learn, not less than 10 years of age;
>
> And 200 Negroes, for Digging.
>
> Days no longer than eleven hours; splendid opportunity; salary secondary to opportunity offered.

Address petitions to Hercules Construction Company, Ltd., 821 Hibernia Bldg., New Orleans.

Isadore had laughed the first time he'd read the ad. Splendid opportunity! He didn't laugh now. It *was* a splendid opportunity.

The mob dissolved, though police continued to traffic through the house, gathering evidence and jotting reports on yellow notepads. On the porch two officers interviewed a black woman. Isadore walked close enough to be certain he had recognized her correctly. He had. It was Virginia, good old Virginia Gabriel, and though he couldn't make out words, he could see that she spoke in a rapid, furtive manner. He noticed another thing that made his flesh creep: Virginia wasn't crying, not even close.

MAY 31, 1918—THE INDUSTRIAL CANAL

Unngh, went the motortruck, tripping over a root. *Uck!*

"I'm terrifically sorry, ma'am!" Hugs shouted to be heard over the enraged engine. His face glazed with perspiration. He did not jerk the wheel quickly enough to avoid rumbling over a loose railroad tie and the truck clattered like a bag of bones. "I'm achingly sorry, ma'am."

"Go faster," said Beatrice. "That way, if we hit something, maybe it'll knock your brains back into place."

"Yes, ma'am." Hugs manipulated the brake. *Ahhh!* went the motor. *Ahhh!*

"Not that slow," growled Beatrice. "We might as well walk."

"Good point, ma'am."

She had to remind herself that she did not dislike Hugs for anything he had done. It wasn't his fault that she could not call him Hugs to his fine-boned face, or even Hugh, but was obliged by the unspoken rules of legitimate business, of which she was making a desperate study, to address him as Mr. Davenport. She did not hate him because of his aquiline nose or girlish figure or even the toadyish, nepotistic pride with which he spoke of his uncle, Hibernia president Rudolph S. Denzler, to whom he owed his position in the bank's bond department. No, she hated him because he was thirty-two years old—the same age as Giorgio. She hated Hugs because Giorgio had not taken advantage of her own nepotistic largesse, because Giorgio was too blockheaded to have any professional ambition, because Giorgio, despite his immense brawn and physical power, was powerless, ineffective, puny—as weak as Hugs, with his concave chest and pipe-stem arms, looked. She reminded herself of all this. But still she hated Hugs.

"Have you ever been on a motortruck before?"

"No," shouted Beatrice. "Have you?"

Hugs chuckled, blushing.

The ground passed in jolts and rushes. She held her hand over her chest to prevent her coat's buttons from bursting off. Silently she chastised herself for wearing the delicate white muslin dress and not a coarser dark garment that would hide the streaks of mud thrown by the motor's tires. She had prepared for a business meeting, not a country jaunt. So that her gold rings, which encircled each of her fingers except the thumbs, would not be tempted to slip off, she clenched her fists.

They sped across the vast, richly green meadow, uninhabited but for the occasional farmer's shack, grazing cow, and a single live-oak tree, like a lone umbrella opened on a beach. The meadow ran along a gentle declivity from the Mississippi River's natural levee to Florida Walk, the country road that traversed the plain like a belt in its midsection, and where Raymond sat inside Beatrice's Peerless Model 56, which never lurched. She cursed herself for not thinking to insist that Raymond, who was after all a professional, pilot the motortruck instead of Hugs. The terrain became even rougher beyond Florida Walk. The meadow attenuated into a muddy alley, a long brown tongue, that terminated in a dense cypress swamp. It was not easy to appreciate, at this vantage point, and so early in the process, that the spongy land beneath them would one day be a grand man-made river, a marvel of engineering that would allow commercial ships to pass between the Mississippi and the ocean, through the heart of New Orleans.

The truck sank into the turf, the wheels spinning before gaining purchase. They bumped over wooden planks, cow patties, a confusion of discarded shovels. The truck doglegged alarmingly close to the live-oak tree, under which two cows and a mule shaded themselves from the hopeless heat.

"Have you noticed the tree?" said Beatrice.

"What?" Hugs turned to face her.

"The tree!" she shouted, over the engine. "The tree!"

Hugs chuckled. The truck skidded through branches and came to rest several feet from the trunk. The cows stared impassively. The only indication of stress came from the mule, which expelled a shower of feces. Hugs chuckled.

"I wanted to show you this tree," he said, "because it is the last tree."

Beatrice anticipated one of Hugs's self-satisfied monologues. She felt in her brain a twitchiness, an electric circuit sparking to life—the telltale sign of a swelling migraine.

"We are sitting in what was, just four weeks ago, an ancient cypress and oak forest," said Hugs. "So ancient, it was described in Bienville's earliest logs. A dense swamp too, five hundred trees to the acre. But in only thirty days, our men—"

"*My* men."

"Of course." Hugs blushed. "The men of Hercules Construction, armed with axes and saws, attacked this swamp and created this right-of-way, extending from Florida Walk to the lake, some four and a half miles. They've cleared three hundred and seventy-five acres of primeval forest. Two hundred thousand trees. Just like that."

"My men are good. They spend so much time building things they've developed a passion for destroying things."

"We are grateful—and I speak for my uncle—we are grateful for the work your men are doing."

She believed him. Already he had shown her the mile of Public Belt Railroad track that had been removed in just eight days (except for the stray ties, which the wheels of the motortruck had a way of seeking out); the small, orange-peel-colored dredge that had eaten a channel from Bayou Bienvenue to the site of the future canal; the cypress stumps that studded the dredge's path, some of them centuries old and buried fourteen feet belowground; and the plots, marked in the meadow by blue stakes, where the Foundation Company and Doullut & Williams would build shipyards. Hercules Construction had won those contracts too. Thanks to Beatrice and her . . . professionalism.

But the radiance of her triumph, her lucrative monopolization of the Industrial Canal project, had been fogged by disappointment. How ardently she had hoped that her little Giorgio—Giorgio the oaf, Giorgio the sloth, Giorgio the dolt—would mature, if not into Giorgio the wise or Giorgio the industrious, then at least into Giorgio the competent guardian of the family business. But though she had tried for years to prepare him, teaching him about the value in taking on great public-land projects and introducing him to her key lieutenants, he had not inherited his father's work ethic. She had not forced the issue after Sal's sudden death, when she might have handed control of Hercules to Giorgio, even though her son was twenty-five, four years older than Sal when he had founded the business. In those rocky months she had needed to fend off Sal's decrepit older brother, Zio Zo, who insisted that, as the eldest male

Vizzini, he should inherit the company, despite the fact that his lung problems had become so tenacious that he barely left the house. She had also to appease Zo's daughters, Efigenia and Elba—nearly as robust as Giorgio, with faces like sledgehammers—by offering them management of the family's smaller collection accounts, the laundry services, millineries, and cobblers. She assumed ownership herself only because she believed that her reign would be temporary, that in time Giorgio would come to cherish the family business and its rewards.

It was in this hope that, upon signing the contract for the canal, she named Giorgio vice president of Hercules—the same title that Rudolph Denzler had given Hugs at Hibernia. It was a hopeful title and Giorgio had made no effort to earn it, using it only to wangle drinks at bars from local grunts looking for work. Not that he needed extra leverage to get free drinks. The shadow business meant he never had to pay for a drink in any bar—or a meal in any restaurant, or food in any grocery—so long as that establishment was owned by one of their clients, most of whom were Sicilian. And what establishment not owned by a Sicilian was worth patronizing?

She tried to explain to him that the creation of the Industrial Canal was more than a construction job. It would be a glorious tribute to the family's work—the work begun by Sal. They were redesigning the very surface of the earth to their own specifications. Hercules would move forest, land, sea. They would create a new river. They would make New Orleans the world's greatest port again. They would etch their presence into the land, like a signature under a painting. The signature would read *Vizzini.*

Giorgio's only concession was to make occasional visits to the Ursulines Tract. He claimed to be supervising the construction, but from what she observed, he did little besides drink bottles of Dixie beer and, when the need overtook him, urinate into the excavation, spraying the heads of the laborers cowering below.

"New Orleans is a delightful city," Hugs was saying, "but a laggard one. We want to change that."

"Be careful who you say that to in this town. Particularly in that Chicago accent."

One of the cows farted loudly. Hugs chuckled. "Do you like steak?"

Beatrice declined to respond. The twitchiness had yielded to a low ringing pain—manageable for the moment but grimly foreboding.

"The cattle we own. They came with the land. The farmer is retiring."

"I hope you did not bring me here to show me cows."

"I wanted to show you that everything is coming together. The bond is authorized. The pile drivers have arrived. Tomorrow the men begin digging. The police have been very helpful with the evacuations of the previous tenants."

"Captain Thomas Capo is an old friend. Something like a nephew. His father I know from Palermo."

"Italy?"

"Sicily," she corrected him. "Thomas provided great comfort after Sal's passing. He made a difficult situation easier."

"His men have been professional and diligent. They have the city's best interests in mind."

"And ours."

The mosquitoes were becoming a problem. They migrated from the cows, at first just one or two, but then they were joined by their friends and relations.

"It's one thing to hear about the progress that has resulted from the partnership between Hibernia and Hercules. My uncle wanted me to show it to you. We'll soon be drinking champagne. Or prosecco." Hugs gestured magnanimously at Beatrice. "And eating fresh *bistecca*."

Beatrice waved at the mosquitoes. "Are there no more problems, Mr. Davenport?"

Hugs wiped his sleeve across his brow. "There's always something, I suppose."

"I want to hear about the problems."

"I knew you would, Mrs. Vizzini. That's why you're a natural businessman—businesswoman, excuse me." He blushed. "Before I explain the situation, I would like you to know that my boss—"

"Your uncle." She smacked dead a bug on her arm. It left a crimson smear on the white muslin sleeve.

"My uncle believes that a peaceful resolution is imminent. In fact we didn't even want to bother you about this. But it seems that both the *Times-Picayune* and the *Item* will run stories tomorrow." He paused, blushing, hesitant to go further. Then he spat it out: "We were concerned how you might respond."

"What do you mean by that?" Beatrice rubbed her temples. It was always there, the shadow business—lurking in the shadows—threatening to undermine all the progress she had made. Sometimes she wondered whether she should relent and sign the whole thing over to Zio Zo and the cousins. But if it weren't for the shadow business, she had to remind herself, Hercules would never have won the contract. The Hercules business piggybacked on the shadow business as a sea anemone hitchhikes on a hermit crab, stealing food from the crab's claws and rebuffing predators with its barbs. Its effectiveness was a product of its secrecy. Most of New Orleans believed that the Black Hand had lost its grip more than a decade ago, after the Walter Lamana murder and the mass hangings of Sicilians. And the Black Hand had disappeared. But into the void created by its absence had emerged a stealthier, warier, more modest business operation, founded by Salvatore Vizzini and professionalized by his widow. One day Hercules would consume the shadow business but many shadow transactions needed to occur before that day could arrive.

"The problem," said Hugs, struggling to keep his tone casual, "is named Fishman. Professor Joshua Fishman of Tulane University."

"I suppose he owns one of the remaining land parcels."

"Not exactly."

"I thought Mr. Blank was the last one."

"We thought so too. But a man came forward this week with the deed to plot 1248. It is the block bounded by Manuel, Convent, Tonti, and Rocheblave." Hugs pointed vaguely upriver. "We can drive there."

"Let's stay in the shade." Beatrice preferred the mosquitoes to the direct sun. "The heat makes me intolerant."

"Yes, ma'am."

"You're saying this Fishman owned this land the whole time and didn't know?"

Hugs took a deep breath. "Fishman doesn't own it. But he represents the man who does. This man, Pitt, lives in Lafayette. He inherited the land last year from his father. He didn't know about the canal until Fishman alerted him. Now Pitt refuses to sell."

"Sounds like Blank." Even in the shade of the oak tree, the heat had found her. The heat did not help her headache. The pain fondled the backs of her eyeballs.

"Blank held up the sale of his property out of greed. He wanted more money."

"Then why is the teacher raising trouble? The land isn't even his."

"It's not about money for Fishman. He fancies himself an advocate for the land."

"The dirt?"

"He says the canal will destroy New Orleans—that by introducing the Mississippi River into the city we are inviting flooding and ruin." Hugs laughed.

"So you want that we should convince him how we convinced Blank."

"No," said Hugs, with as much force as he seemed capable of mustering. "That we cannot do."

Beatrice did not understand. Blank, after all, had been an easy job. Efigenia—or perhaps it was Elba—visited his home one night, hat in hand. She begged Blank to accept the offer from Hibernia Bank, not merely for the good of New Orleans, but for the good of the nation, which required the canal for naval operations. Blank shut the door in her face. The next day, Elba—or perhaps Efigenia—visited with a similar message, and Blank set his dog, a vicious chocolate-brown rottweiler named Giant, after her. On the third day, Blank's young son arrived home from school to find on his bed a dog's skull with daggers stuck through the eye sockets. But the skull did not belong to Giant. The day after that the child came home to a second dog skull with daggers through the eye sockets. This one was Giant. On the fifth day, Blank's wife stayed home from work. She admitted no visitors and frequently checked her son's room, alert for signs of an intruder. In the late afternoon, shortly before her son arrived home from school, she found on his bed another skull with daggers stuck through the eyes. This time it was a small human skull—a child's skull, caked with dirt, that appeared to have been freshly exhumed. By the end of the day Blank had sold his plot to Hibernia Bank.

Hugs perspired heavily, the sweat channeling down his ears. "Fishman is an obsessive," he said. "Facts cannot persuade him."

"*Everyone* can be brought to reason." Beatrice spoke in the reassuring tone one might use with a child freshly awoken from a nightmare. Blank, after all, had been brought to reason. Before him, the Jahncke brothers, who had competed with Hercules for the canal contract, had been brought to reason by a series of late-night meetings with androgynous figures in black masks. Even Whitney-Central Bank, which had competed with Hibernia for the city contract to issue bonds for the canal, had yielded after its office was consumed by an electrical fire. Beatrice had warned the cousins not to take senseless risks but she could not quarrel with the results.

"He's written a letter to the editor," said Hugs, removing a sheaf of paper from his inner pocket. "The *Item* will publish it." He used the paper to swat at several circling mosquitoes before unscrolling it.

> People of New Orleans, we must not allow the enemy to breach the fortification! Have we already forgotten the great storm of 1915, the fallen steeples, the ripped-up roofs, the Lake invading through the gutters? Twenty-one of our citizens lost! The excavation of the drainage canals was the first blow. But imagine the devastation should the River *and* the Lake be invited into our boundaries! Why, having spent two centuries defending ourselves from villainous Water, should we invite Her into the intimacy of our homes as if She were a weary traveler? It is not too late to reverse the course of this hastily-planned Industrial Canal. Stand with me—and stand with the city of New Orleans—in defeating this insensate misuse of land.

Hugs shook his head. "My uncle and I have a plan, Mrs. Vizzini."

"I have heard your plans."

"Ma'am? Do you need water?"

"Just a slight headache." The last thing she needed was for Hugs to tell Mr. Denzler that the old lady was impaired. "It's already passed."

"I'm relieved to hear it."

"You mentioned a plan."

"This professor is antiprogress, anti-enterprise, and antipatriotic. It is men like him who have made New Orleans suffer by comparison with the more virile conurbations of the North and the West. He will fool nobody. We will make those points in our response to the newspapers, and he will be defeated in the palaestra of public opinion."

A yell carried across the plain. Hugs, shielding his eyes, squinted into the sunlight. Beatrice didn't have to look. She'd recognize that voice anywhere.

The man stumbled toward them from the swamp. As he approached, his jerky motion became more frantic, his limbs making movements like the hands of a broken watch. His shirt was soaked through with sweat. By the time he reached the oak's canopy she could smell him—animal and woodsy and sour. She'd recognize that scent anywhere.

"Mamma!" said Giorgio, removing his homburg. "I've been looking all over."

Hugs smiled tightly. With a smattering of moos the cows trotted out of the shade, into the hot meadow. The mule galloped in the opposite direction, toward Florida Walk.

"We're almost done, Giugi," said Beatrice. His appearance was a balm; the headache's cruel grip began to unclench. "We can give you a ride home."

"I was worried, I didn't know where you went." Giorgio regarded Hugs. "Hi, Hugh." *Hug*, he pronounced it.

Hugs nodded absently.

"My," said Giorgio. "It's hot with all the trees gone." He wiped his arm across his forehead and with a flinging motion cast a sleeve of perspiration onto the ground. Beatrice handed him her handkerchief.

"Slow day at the practice?"

"No, Mamma. I cleared the schedule to see you."

It was a joke between them. He had no schedule. He had few osteopathy patients. She suspected that she was the only one.

Giorgio returned her handkerchief, now soaked through. "What are y'all talking about?"

"Just business," said Hugs.

"Oh? I'm vice president of this business."

"Of course," said Hugs. "Right. A Tulane professor is holding up the final phase of the excavation, alas. But we will obtain the land soon, even if we must take him to court . . ." Hugs tailed off, noticing that Giorgio was not paying attention.

Giorgio stared blankly in the direction of the dig, blurry in the dazzling heat. A mosquito landed on his cheek. Its abdomen tumesced. It flew away, dizzy drunk.

"Darling?" said Beatrice. "Hugs was explaining our situation."

Giorgio laughed. "I guess I lost focus." He turned to Hugs. "I just don't have a mind for business. I never could put my mind around it. But I try, don't I, Mamma?"

"Yes, darling." It was excruciating to watch Hugs watch her son.

"I try," Giorgio said, with a smile made of plaster, "but each time I fit my mind around the top of it, the bottom pops out. Or I cram in the top and the bottom but the middle spills out sideways."

"Mr. Vizzini?" said Hugs. "You seem to be bleeding. From your scalp."

"It's an old injury," said Beatrice. "Giorgio, take the handkerchief." She felt for it in her pocket and realized it was already waterlogged. A thin trail of blood, mixed with sweat, descended the rim of Giorgio's ear and fell in thin droplets to the dirt. She looked helplessly at Hugs.

"Here," he said halfheartedly. "Take mine."

"Thanks, Hug." Giorgio snagged the handkerchief, pressed it to the wound.

"Is he all right?"

"He got it in the service," said Beatrice. "Never properly healed. Bad stitching. It comes apart when he is physically active. But it doesn't hurt." She raised her voice. "Does it, Giorgio?"

"No, Mamma. It don't hurt at all." He laughed too loudly. "The only thing that hurts is when people give you a hard time." He stopped smiling. "That hurts."

Giorgio held out the bloodied handkerchief to Hugs. Hugs waved him away.

"Better?" said Beatrice.

"Better," said Giorgio, replacing the homburg on his head. "Mr. Davenport?"

Hugs looked up abruptly. His eyes looked tiny and fearful, the eyes of a young boy. "Yes?"

"Thanks for helping my mother with this job. It sure means a lot."

"No need to thank me. If anything, I should thank her. Your mother is an excellent businesswoman."

Beatrice announced that it was time to go. She could not take it anymore. Besides, she had a business meeting to attend. If they hurried, she could drop Giorgio at home and still have time before supper for an impromptu visit to Tulane.

JUNE 26, 1918—THE INDUSTRIAL CANAL

"I have a large appetite," said Sore Dick.

"No shit." Isadore raised his trench digger. "We've been seven hours without a break."

"I consume eight hundred pounds of vegetation every day."

"Here we go."

"I eat conifers. I eat sagebrush. I eat bodark."

"I'm so hungry I would eat sagebrush. I'd eat conifers. I don't know what it is, but I would eat bodark. I would eat bodark."

"I am the length of a streetcar. I am the height of a high ceiling." Sore Dick gave Isadore a meaningful look. "My tusks extend fifteen feet."

"You are a woolly mammoth."

Sore Dick winced. "I am a Columbian elephant."

Isadore's falling shovel connected with wood. A shiver of pain vibrated from his wrists to his shoulders.

"Duckboard?" muttered Sore Dick.

"Stump," said Isadore. "Definitely stump."

"Stump!" hollered Sore Dick.

"Stump!" yelled the foreman at the rim of the Pit, pointing at Sore Dick until several other diggers hastened to help them unearth the mammoth petrified tree.

Isadore shook his head involuntarily. Another day in the Pit. But it hadn't always been the Pit. In the beginning it was the Plot. The Plot, after being dynamited in a series of explosions that boomed, as the *Item* put it, "like guns along the western front," became the Ditch, and later the Crater. But for the last three days it had been, unmistakably, the Pit. What was next—the Hole? The Hole and then, perhaps, the Abyss. Ultimately it would become the Canal, though that was hard to imagine. It was hard enough to imagine another day grinding at the bottom of the Pit.

Already the Pit was beginning to yawn like the mouth of a drowsy dog. It had a radius of about a city block, sloping to a depth of nearly ten feet at the lowest point, though the slope was hardly uniform. They had hit mud after four feet and now stood in a slurry that was more water than soil. The work became more grueling the deeper they dug. And then there was the smell.

It grew more pungent as they descended, passing imperceptibly from a rich humus to a stench that Isadore could only compare to human feces. Gas bubbles rose through the black lava and burst in the air in sick little gasps. At first when the mosquitoes and chiggers bit his face, he avoided slapping at them, lest he splash himself with mud, but soon he realized that a coating of mud was the best prophylactic against insect bites, and besides, it was only a matter of time before every square centimeter of flesh was mud lacquered. The mud was alive, not only breathing but also wiggling into every bodily crevice, matting his hair, oozing down his spine, and he couldn't pretend anymore that it wasn't getting into his mouth. The previous week Sore Dick had retched and there had been nothing to do but shovel mud on top of it, which was effective, since the reek of the mud was stronger. Soon they didn't notice the stench anymore, but the not noticing was even worse than the smell itself. Orly and her mother noticed when he got home, though—they made him enter through the back, where in the tub he scrubbed his boots, work clothes, and his body twice over with the yellow laundry soap. Still Miss Daisy complained that it was like sleeping beside a decaying corpse. "It's an honest job," Orly would say, but usually while pinching her nose. The pay was eight dollars a week. It almost made him nostalgic for his hunting trips with Bailey. He had to remind himself that he could gig with the Quartet whenever he liked—provided he and Sore Dick could stand upright after a day at the Pit. He had to remind himself how terrified he had been the night of the arrest and in the alley with the watchman and how much more terrified he had been in the days that followed.

Yet a month had passed and Bailey had not given him up. Bailey was not only a better criminal than Isadore. He was a better friend. Still there was plenty of time for him to flip. The trial hadn't even begun. Isadore wondered if anyone in prison read Bailey the headlines, such as the one in that morning's *Item*: "Superintendent Mooney: Frank Bailey, Negro, Will Hang." In equal measures Isadore felt remorse for his deathwishing and continued to wish on Bailey a quick, painless death.

"What are we even doing this for?" Sore Dick spit out a mosquito. "Why do they need to connect the lake to the river?"

"Commercial shipping. War boats." That was the official line, but nobody, including Isadore, believed it. The canal was just another way to make money on the hides of workers. Exactly how they would make the money was obscure, but there was no doubt about it, they were digging a fortune out of the ground for some powerful people. Starting with Hercules Construction and Hibernia Bank.

"Slave work." Dick blew at a cloud of mosquitoes hovering near his head. They shifted away, then shifted back. "Slave rates too."

"The slave rate is zero."

"Close enough."

They had it worse than most—of the two hundred diggers, he and Sore Dick were among those stationed closest to the bottom of the Pit, where the mud was thickest. They had planked it with duckboards but the boards were soon swallowed and the men resigned themselves to sinking. With each swing of the trench digger, Isadore subsided deeper; if he didn't step out of the mud before it grabbed his knees, another man had to pull him out. Sore Dick was usually that man and he was ungentle.

But there was an even greater problem with working near the center of the Pit, one worse than the smell and the slipperiness of the mud: the Mouth.

"Hose!" shouted the foreman.

"Hose!"

"Hose!"

"Fuck my head," said Sore Dick.

The hose man at the lip of the Pit wheeled the cart to the edge. He aimed the nozzle, squared his stance, and dug his boots into the turf, bracing himself. The diggers planted their shovels in the ground and trudged across the Pit toward him. Muddy shoulders pressed flush against muddy shoulders, forming a human wall. The foreman made a gesture to somebody out of view. The hose spurted several times, splashing the men below, and burst into a geyser. The hose man pointed the nozzle toward the sky so that the powerful jet didn't hit the men directly, but fell like an extremely localized rainstorm. The men looked upward with their eyes closed and their mouths open to drink as much as they could swallow. The hose couldn't be run long or the Pit would become even more treacherous, so the foreman gave a signal and, with a final spurt, the flow ceased. Somewhere beneath them, the Mouth slurped.

Isadore reminded himself: the cornet and the Dig went together. The cornet did not go with the highway jobs. Cornet and Dig was the only combination that held open the possibility of a future, escape, glory, eternal life.

"My body is protected by a shell five feet high," said Sore Dick, as they treaded back to their stump. Mud trickled down the sides of his face like tears. "I have a snout. My tail resembles a morning star."

"Damn you," said Isadore. "And damn your snout." Sore Dick's ramblings were another kind of mud laid thickly over the mud they already had to wade through. Their show at the Funky Butt Hall was a week away. Isadore had played Savocca's, he'd played Mussachia's, he'd played Mix's Pelican Club. He had played every whorehouse in the District, but none of the tonks were in the same hemisphere as the Funky Butt. King Oliver and Buddy Bolden played the Butt. Kid Ory, whose band Isadore had first seen as a kid at National Park, playing after a ball game, the closest thing to an immortal walking the streets of New Orleans—Kid Ory's Brown Skin Band played the Butt. The uptown Negroes and the downtown Creoles came to the Butt. Even a few white adventurists came to the Funky Butt, once in a while, after some drinks. Drag "Nasty" Wilson, the Quartet's bassist, had heard the downtown hotels wanted to book jass acts and sent advance men to the Butt to scout. The abracadabra of the hotels' names—the Roosevelt, the Grunewald, and, holiest of holies, the Cosmopolitan—rang of immortality. Isadore wanted that golden ring. But first he'd have to get within grabbing reach.

"We need to talk about the second," said Isadore.

"A morning star is like a mace, with spikes."

"I appreciate your learning, Dick. Don't get me wrong."

"You going to pretend that a tail like a mace, with spikes, is not Spanish?"

Isadore exhaled. "It is pretty Spanish."

"So?"

"I don't know, Dick. A giant turtle?"

Sore Dick shook his head. "Closer kin to an armadillo."

"I haven't even seen Sidney since we booked the show."

"I am a glyptodont," said Sore Dick.

"I don't give a shit what you are," interrupted one of the other men, "so long as you dig your portion."

The trunk began to reveal its shape. It was an oak, about the circumference of a barrel, jagged at the top like the neck of a broken beer bottle.

"Gentlemen," said Isadore, tossing a shovelful of black slop over his head, "I hereby invite you to see New Orleans's greatest piano player, Sore Dick, together with Big Nose Sidney on drums, Nasty Wilson on bass, and yours truly on cornet, when we debut as the Slim Izzy Quartet next Tuesday at the Funky Butt Hall."

"Who's Sore Dick?" said someone. "Never heard of him."

"This man right here's Sore Dick!" said Isadore, rallying to his friend's defense.

"That ain Sore Dick," said another man, without looking up. "That's a glyptodont."

"And who the hell is Slim Izzy?"

But the men had exhausted what energy they had for talking. There was only enough left for grunting, which they did repeatedly as they attacked the stump. Dig the shovel into the mud, pull up a reeking patty, toss it over the shoulder. Dig—pull—*toss*, over and over and over. As they excavated the mud, more oozed up to replace it. They still hadn't reached the root. One of the men leaned into the stump with his shoulder but it refused to budge.

"When this oak stood," said Sore Dick, "a glyptodont might have used it for shade. A Columbian elephant would have used it to scratch his back."

"Stump!" someone yelled, about fifteen yards away.

"Stump!"

"Stump!" yelled the foreman from above. "Zeno and Dick, you stay there. The rest of y'all help out the other'ns."

"Guess they don't like jass," said Isadore, when they were alone again. Dig—pull—*toss*.

"People will come." Dig—pull—*toss*. "The way you play? People will notice."

The deeper they dug, the heavier the mud, the more offensive the odor, the louder the noise of the Mouth. A pneumatic tube connected the Mouth to the Texas, a monster suction dredge that stood at the edge of the Pit. The Texas had dug the Panama Canal four years earlier. It worked loudly but invisibly. It was, Sore Dick explained, like an eating man. At one end the Mouth swallowed the earth and masticated it with metal teeth into a fine slurry. The slurry was sucked down the long esophagus of the pneumatic tube, through the Texas's stomach (the storage tank) and lower intestine (the conveyance pipe) before being sprayed into an ever-growing pile of mud beyond the rim of the Pit. Aboveground laborers armed with trenching shovels flattened the slurry into a levee. Though not as grueling as work in the Pit, the construction of the levee was relentless because the Texas never stopped shitting. And the Mouth never stopped eating.

The Mouth was a picky eater, however. It did not like stumps. The duckboards it could handle—it splintered the cheap flat wood into sawdust, a sound like a man chewing a fistful of almonds. But on the larger stumps the Texas choked and asphyxiated; they had to shut off the engine while doctors—the machinists—were called to resuscitate the beast. To avoid this fate, the dredge had tunneled three feet below the Pit's deepest point. With the soil undermined, the stumps could be more easily excavated by the diggers. This made the Pit resemble the upper half of an hourglass, the mud sloping from the sides down to the middle where the Mouth ate.

The stumps, Dick explained, were the remains of an ancient forest. It had been buried by the Mississippi River, which for thousands of years had flooded the forest with silt, raising the land. Buried below this forest was a second prehistoric forest, thirty feet deeper. And below that forest, a third forest. So as they dug deeper, they were also digging back in time. The thought of all those underground forests gave Isadore a sensation of falling down a bottomless well. It didn't seem right. It was like exhuming corpses that had lain in peace for eternities. That might have explained the smell. They were excavating the land's dead things. Dead trees, but also whatever had died and been buried in the ancient forests. Glyptodonts, say. Or people.

The prehistoric forests had made an impression on Sore Dick. At the Lee Circle library he had found a book titled *The Pleistocene Megafauna of Louisiana*.

"Standing on my hind legs," said Sore Dick, "I could peer into a second-story window."

"We keep working these hours," said Isadore, "we won't have time to practice for the second."

"With my giant tongue, I lick leaves off the highest tree branches. I don't need practice."

"This is no honky-tonk, Dick. We have to be the best. We have to change the way people look at us. Otherwise we're going to play for whores at least another year come we get a second chance."

Sore Dick, leaning on the base of his trench digger, gave Isadore a sorrowful look. "I had no enemies for millions of years, until man hunted me."

"If I don't start pulling more jack, Orleania is going to kick me out. She's *been* fed up."

"Please. She is stupid on you. She'd never kick you out. You're married, ain you?"

"Mm. I need to provide."

"Provide? Really?" Sore Dick paused, turning to face Isadore. "I thought you had other avenues of income."

Isadore felt his back stiffen. "Who said so?"

Sore Dick gave a soft whistle and returned to his labor. After a few hauls he took a deep breath and peered longingly into the sky. "I'm twenty feet tall. I can see over most trees. My eyesight is dull, however, as I have no predators."

Isadore wondered if Dick had seen the papers reporting Bailey's indictment for murder. Detective Bastrop, the cop who shot dead the innocent guard at the Louisiana Demolishing Company, had not been charged. "The suspect showed fight," Bastrop had claimed, so he shot him. That reasoning, unsurprisingly, was enough for the district attorney. Bailey, on the other hand, was sure to hang.

Isadore pressed his shoulder into the stump. No amount of force would budge it.

"I am a megatherium," said Dick.

"If Orly kicks me out, just bury me here. Bury me in the Pit."

"A giant sloth."

"There's the giant sloth." Isadore inclined his head toward the lip of the Pit. The foreman and the hose man had been joined by an unusually large, strong white man in coveralls and a dark homburg: the Vizzini son. He surveyed the action below, making playful asides to the foreman. Beside him a laborer approached, carrying a glistening metal bucket of ice. Vizzini tossed a handful of ice in his mouth, chewing pensively as he watched the laborers toil.

"He's big enough," said Sore Dick, raising his voice above the whirring of the Mouth, "but not too clever. A mammy boy too."

Isadore had seen her, Beatrice Vizzini herself, patrolling the rim like a lioness surveying her pride. She looked as if she were plotting something grand—much grander than a mere canal—and the hundreds of laborers were mindless soldiers in a war with designs beyond their comprehension. He felt the old rage returning. He saw himself climbing the side of the Pit and knocking the old woman into it. He saw her tumble down the side and land, crumpled, in the mud. He saw her swallowed by the dredge and chewed up and digested.

There was a reverberation between the violation of the ancient buried forests and the violation of his nature that came about from working this job. It's true that most bandmen had jobs. Old Bob Lyons shined shoes. Bunk Johnson drove trucks. Even Kid Ory worked at the Poland Avenue shipyard five days a week. All right: and Isadore had highway robbing. But Isadore wasn't like them. Slim Izzy—Isadore Pinkett Peyroux Zeno—was better. He could do things with the cornet that nobody else knew to try. He could make it sing, but he could also make it squawk, caper, weep, chatter, and groan. He could make it speak English. The other jassists just didn't know it. Nobody knew it, not even Orly. He hadn't revealed it yet because no one would understand. He had to prepare the audience. He had to prove that he could play the regular hot music before he broke the rules, or they'd dismiss him as a madman. Once he had built up an audience and primed them to the right point, he'd bring it out, and their exuberance would be a hard panic. The old stuff would go out entirely. Everyone would want only to hear his song. That's what real music did: it made a distinction. It did not improve the old forms. It destroyed them.

"What the hell is going on down there?"

Isadore glanced up and saw the foreman staring back. Beside him the Vizzini oaf made a face like a grizzly bear that had just caught a salmon. No doubt it was Vizzini who'd seen that Isadore had slowed down and alerted the foreman. It was unlike the foreman to call anyone out. He knew how miserable the work was, how putrid.

"Stump's buried deep," Sore Dick called back. "We're going our hardest."

"It's buried deep," said Isadore lamely.

"You better not get us fired," said Dick, under his breath. "You think you're the only one with an old lady? I got *three*."

Vizzini murmured in the foreman's ear. The foreman nodded. "Maybe the mud is too thick," he called out.

"That's not the problem," said Isadore. "If anything—"

"Hose!" said the foreman.

"Hose!"

"Hose!"

The hose man wheeled the cart to the lip of the Pit. The diggers wedged their shovels into the ground.

The foreman waved them off. "Get back to work," he said. "This ain a break."

Sore Dick cursed under his breath.

"What's happening?" said Isadore.

Vizzini relieved the hose man and held the nozzle aloft. A grin crawled across his face. He yelped like a man urging his steed.

There sputtered a spray of water, a clearing of the throat, followed by a torrent, the pressure of Bayou Bienvenue forced through an orifice smaller than a man's clenched fist. But Vizzini did not aim the hose toward the sky. He aimed it like a gun at the men. The jet blasted into Isadore's shoulder, spinning him backward, pummeling him to his knees. Sore Dick yelled and then was on the ground beside him, writhing like an electrocution victim. They had brief reprieves as Vizzini alternated the jet between the two men, but never enough to escape. The ground was the consistency of simmering bean soup. And Isadore was drinking it. He couldn't help it. He was facedown in the filth, drowning, and when he opened his mouth to suck air he took another gulp of black slime. Something gave way beneath him and he began to slide, feetfirst toward the center of the Pit, and though it couldn't have been possible—the jet in his ears was too loud, almost as loud as the whirring Mouth, which grew louder by the second—he was certain he heard fat, babyish Giorgio Vizzini on the rim, giggling.

Isadore reached blindly and latched on to the stump. Vizzini trained the jet on his knuckles and he skidded away, half submerged, his eyes stinging. He felt the Mouth at his feet. Its small rotating knives scraped at his boot. Then he knew the tip of the boot was gone because he could wiggle his toes freely. He screamed, swallowed a fresh gulp of mud, gagged, and plunged his arms elbow deep into the mud, hoping to find something to grab. He crawled and reached but it was like trying to climb a waterfall.

The hose had, however, accomplished what the men and their shovels could not—it exposed the base of the stump and the crown of its root system. Isadore's flailing hands grasped its ancient arthritic fingers. He pulled himself up, coughing and spitting. The hose blasted the mud off his face but he held on. Finally the hose turned off.

Sore Dick was wrapped around the trunk like a pair of pants blown off a laundry line. He was speaking though Isadore couldn't hear the words. The other laborers gathered around Isadore. Their faces looked ashen and dark, but maybe it was just the mud. They grabbed his wrists and pulled, hard. The mud released his legs with a loud smack.

Only then did Isadore get a clear look at Giorgio Vizzini. He stood on the edge of the Pit, the flaccid hose dripping in his hand. His forehead was slick with some other liquid—dark red, like blood, but that made no sense; it must have been mud. He stared down with a ghastly cheerfulness at the black men writhing in the Pit, falling over each other as they tried to scurry away from the feeding Mouth. Isadore had the idea that the Mouth was really Vizzini's mouth, that it was Vizzini who was hungrily trying to chew him, to crunch up his bones. This lummox, this man-child, was the devil behind all his suffering. Vizzini was eating him alive.

In the sudden quiet Isadore could finally hear what Sore Dick was saying. He repeated the same words, a pathetic incantation, a prayer to nobody.

"I'm a mastodon," came Dick's battered voice. "I'm a teratorn," he said. "I'm a mammoth."

JUNE 27, 1918—THE IRISH CHANNEL

It was his favorite time of the day—of all creation, maybe—but he only experienced it as a memory. It occurred in that bluish moment between sleep and consciousness, when he was not quite awake, and Maze was not quite awake, but the brass of the rising sun, parting the dimity curtains, called them home from the distant dimensions in which they had traveled. Maze would push her hips into Bill's lap or absently reach for his arm, placing it around her, his hand cupping her breast. Or his head would find the crook of her neck. They would rest like that for a short time—ten minutes? Ten seconds?—before consciousness broke like a cold ocean wave and they remembered who they were. Then one of them, usually Maze, would recoil, as if having awoken beside a viper.

But this morning, for no reason that he could immediately perceive, the bluish moment dilated into a bubble, which inflated, growing large enough to enclose them both, sealing them from their past and their doubt. They lay very close—a necessity on the narrow straw mattress—but unusually, they faced each other, their noses nearly touching. Bill's leg wedged between Maze's thighs and her arm reached around his back. Her light exhalations tickled his cheek. When Bill opened his eyes, Maze's, large and olive, looked back. To his surprise she did not jerk away or flip over in frustration. She held his stare. And in their bubble they floated away, rising to the moon. He wondered if this was what immortality would feel like, forever floating.

"Hello," he whispered at last, and instantly regretted it because his voice pricked the balloon, which began to deflate.

"Hi," she said softly, and that plugged the hole. Their lips met. Bill pressed his leg more firmly between her thighs. Maze accommodated him. He kissed her neck. She sighed. How many months had it been since he'd heard that particular sigh? It was the sound of an undertow, the gentle recession of the tide.

"Wait." Her voice was high and silky. "Wait."

He grabbed her thigh. He bit her neck.

"*Cher.*" Insistent now. "Tell me how it happened."

He froze.

"In France," she said.

He released her thigh. His jaws went slack.

"Tell me, baby," she said. "Tell about the battle. The bad battle."

There was in his head the sound of sucking air. They began to sink. The moon shrank to a pinpoint and they plunged through the lower atmosphere. She kissed him, kissed his cheeks and his eyes, but it made no difference. No air remained in the bubble, not even enough for a breath.

"Later." It's what he always said.

"Now."

"I've told you." He tried to keep his voice steady.

"Yes, you told me. In different ways and different words. And you paint it every night, in reds and blacks."

He could tell that she'd been saving this up. It was coming out fast, all at once.

"I almost didn't make it," he said, hoping that would end it.

"Men died. You were lucky to make it out. I know that bit."

The bubble collapsed around them and he became conscious of the lumpiness of the pillow, the starch of the pillowcase, the thin brown hairs that gathered on the cushion, and the crease of his neck, grimy with sweat. He felt the heat—the sour, tedious June heat—and smelled the dankness of their linens, which during the summer Maze had to wash every day. And he remembered the shame he felt, the previous evening, when he returned from his beat and saw hanging on the line the sheets with their faded crimson stains, like impressions of wilted roses, made by Maze's spotting. The entire neighborhood was witness to the barrenness of their intimate life.

"It's inverting you." Maze's voice was so quiet that he could barely make it out, though his ear was inches from her mouth. "The secrecy. The furtiveness. It's making you act crazy. Running after murderers—"

"That's my job."

"It's not how you used to do your job."

He flushed.

"I didn't mean it like that," she said. "It's just—it's growing deeper inside of you."

"I should get dressed. Charlie will be here."

"Like a horrible fungus."

"Christ, Maze."

"You don't have to carry it by yourself." Her mouth curled the way it did before she wept. "Talk to me. Just once, really talk to me."

The scratching heat of the bed was overwhelming. He thrust off the sheets and, with them, Maze's arm and leg. She whimpered, her hand flying over her face as if to contain some eruption there. Was she afraid? He couldn't blame her. He was afraid too. He had seen this coming, knew it was only a matter of time before the asking became begging, insisting, demanding. He looked into Maze's face—open, vulnerable, freckles—

"The front was southeast of Nancy," he said tentatively, almost an interrogative. "Between the villages of Lunéville and Baccarat."

She touched his side, gentle but firm. "Where's that again?"

"France."

"C'mon, Billy."

He inhaled. "Imagine France is a fat man standing with his stumpy arms extended, like he's about to hug you. Paris is his mouth. Nancy is on his left hand. Almost touching Germany."

Maze smiled. Creases pleasantly disfigured her face. Freckles hopped and resettled.

"Our regiment was to join the French in the trenches, get some battle experience. But when we got to Lunéville in February, it was too cold. So they sent us to the castle."

"Tell about the castle. Was it like a fairy tale?"

It was more like a drunken orgy. The village's young widows supplemented their pensions by hiring themselves out to American soldiers.

"It was a lot of men drinking," he said. "Their beer tastes like chestnuts. It was nice not to have to drink red wine for once. We were there not five days."

Maze was smiling at him, her ethereal, mildly demented smile.

"We marched into the Forest of Purroy in our hobnailed boots. Our socks froze. It was like walking in cement blocks."

"Good. Details are essential. What was the forest like?"

"There was barely any snow on the ground because the trees were so close together. It was dark. No underbrush. No leaves on the trees. The wood was red, brown. Like rust. Or blood. We got to the camp—"

"This is wonderful."

"What?"

"You've already told me more than ever before. Doesn't it feel nice?"

He wanted to ask her how *she* felt, speaking with such high emotion. It was like being reunited with an old childhood friend.

"Sorry," she said. "Pretend I didn't interrupt."

"The castle."

"No—you were in the camp."

Camp New York. It wasn't much of a camp. It was a man-made forest clearing. So it was muddy. They were covered in mud morning to night. It got in their mouths and under their shirts. They grew bored: they wanted to get into the trenches. That's why they were there, after all. To fight.

She rubbed his arm tenderly. A slight breeze lifted the curtains and cooled his skin. Her touch was soothing. So, incredibly, was the talking.

Each battalion had ten days on the line. They'd take orders from French Command, shoot and be shot at, and acclimate themselves to life as a rodent. If they proved themselves capable, they would be invited to join the French on a raid across no-man's-land. That was the idea, at least.

Bill's battalion, the Second, was second up. When the First Battalion returned to Camp New York from the front, they were hollering, triumphant. They'd seen light fire, no serious casualties. The Second all but skipped to the trenches to replace them. On the way, as they walked through the woods, they passed summer cottages, garden benches, plaster gnomes. In stretches it could have passed for City Park. There was no sign of the enemy. They entered a browned pasture and Bill had an infantile urge to run free, to roll in the matted grass. Only when a French commander started screaming did the men realize they'd stumbled into no-man's-land. But nobody shot at them. If only the Germans had shot at them then.

"Did you think of me?" asked Maze.

"I thought of you constantly." His voice rose sharply, and he could tell from her reaction that she knew he was telling the truth.

She rubbed his chest, her nails drawing patterns. Though not especially long, they were sharpened to points. "The trenches."

"Filthy. Better not to describe the trenches."

"Then what?"

"The dugout." A weight dropped through him. "That's more important."

Her nails traced circles around his navel, in increasing circumferences. "What's the dugout?"

"Where we slept. It was also a bomb shelter. But it was difficult to imagine a bombing then. We hadn't been in one yet."

"There was a single dugout for all the men?"

There were four. Dugout One, the largest, was in the most repulsive condition. It was like an underground cave. A sewer. You descended a rickety stair into a pit forty feet deep in the earth.

Triple-decker bunks and small tables with candles. The candles often flickered out because there was never enough oxygen.

"Why not sleep in the trench?"

"Trenches have no roofs. The bombs can fall on your head."

"How did it smell in the dugout?"

"Like rotting meat."

"You had meat?"

"We were the meat."

"*Billy.*"

"There were other smells. Shit, for instance."

"Where were the . . . latrines?"

"Really, Maze?"

"Don't answer if you're embarrassed."

"You dug a hole and covered it. When I called it a sewer I wasn't being poetic."

Maze nodded sagely.

"When the bombs dropped, some of the men shit their pants. But that was later."

"We can move on."

"I told you we didn't see the enemy. That was the problem. That and the bed sacks."

"Does that feel nice?"

"Sleeping on a bed sack?"

"My nails." They scraped tracks from his stomach to the trim of his drawers. "What's a bed sack?"

"A thin mat, stuffed with straw. Those stunk too." Her nails did feel nice, like little biting insects. But pleasantly biting.

"Sweat," said Maze.

"Old sweat. There's a difference. The smell of sweat sharpens as it ages. Like malt vinegar. When we got there the mats were vinegary with the sweat of the men who had slept there the ten previous nights. We thought we should air them out."

"You were spotted. They were watching you all along."

Her fingers drifted lower, curling like fishhooks, snagging on the hem.

"I don't know if the Germans had seen us before. But when we went outside with the mats—they must have seen us then."

A lieutenant yelled at the men and they crawled back into their hole but it was too late. They just didn't know it yet.

"Who was with you?"

The faces weren't vivid anymore. Time had caricatured them: isolated features were all he could make out.

"William Drain," he said. "One of those bearded guys with more fuzz showing than skin. Alf Helmer, the Norwegian, with white hair like an electrocution victim. Philip Finn. His father was a judge in New York. One eye bigger than the other. Most of the men were from New York. Elwood Rayburn: black teeth. John Legall, Jr.: forehead as broad as a bench. Art Hegney: more than six feet tall." And a vile little pickpocket from Brooklyn named Leonard Perl.

Late on the second afternoon, the French bombarded the Germans, firing across no-man's-land, and the sound of artillery was so loud that the men underground couldn't hear themselves speak. The volume increased threefold when the Germans responded, launching mortars, shrapnel, explosives, and other weapons that Bill couldn't identify. For all the chaos and noise, the whole thing seemed like a performance. At that distance, with the target hidden behind dense forest, the exercise seemed futile. It was as if both sides had too much artillery and had to get rid of some of it.

"I wish I could've seen you with the other men." Maze's fingers played in the hair below his stomach. "I bet they loved you."

The Americans were driven to childlike ecstasies by the sounds and the explosions and finally it was too much: they leaped from their dugout so they could see the bright lights. Elwood surfaced first, then Legall and Finn, and after that anybody who stayed underground would've seemed soft, for no shrapnel had landed anywhere near their dugout. Besides, wasn't this exactly the kind of experience they were meant to accrue?

Maze's hand disappeared under his drawers. Her fingers closed around him, squeezing experimentally.

"Don't stop," she said, her grip going slack. "For heaven's sake."

He wouldn't stop. Not just yet.

They weren't outside long. A French lieutenant, seeing the Americans illuminated by the fire in the sky, began shouting and the Americans slouched back into their cave. They sat in darkness for what seemed like days as the fireworks continued overhead. At first the mood was light, festive even. They were schoolboys stuck inside a classroom on a sunny day. Legall organized a betting pool: Who would be the first to kill a Boche, the first to piss his pants, the first to shoot himself in the foot? Dawkers, a small giddy man with a high-pitched laugh, made a game of hiding below a bunk and tying soldiers' bootlaces together. Elwood insisted on speaking in French even though he did not know a word of French.

With time, however, an eeriness filled the dugout, diffused by the dampness of the earth, the guttering candles that were their only source of light, and the clamor—the pounding that made the dugout's walls and ceiling tremble, so it felt like being inside the chamber of an irregularly beating heart. After one particularly close explosion, sawdust showered from the rotten timbers. It was a kind of insanity not to acknowledge any of this, with the dust and soil falling like snow, but nobody did. Soon a single candle remained, flickering in the center of the room. Drain made a skittish joke about the eternal flame. Then a clod from the ceiling fell on it, splashing wax on Bill's leg, and they were submerged in total darkness.

And Perl was standing beside him. Their skins touched.

"You must have been scared." Maze tugged on his pants.

"Not really." Bill lifted himself from the mattress so that she could pull the drawers free. It had been a long time—but he wasn't going to draw attention to it, lest she stop. "We were anxious," he said. "We wanted to fight. We were sick of hiding."

He had been terrified. Never had he come so close to oblivion. He had imagined facing death on the battlefield, often before going to sleep, except on the nights when he drank himself into a stupor—which he did increasingly after arriving in Europe, the rising anxiety meeting halfway the preponderance of cheap wine. But he was not prepared for the reality of the fear. It was like an old friend surprising you from behind at a party, his hands over your eyes. Guess who? He refused to sit there dumbly like the others. But there was no escape and nowhere to escape to. He slipped beneath a bunk in the corner of the dugout, a child hiding under his bed, afraid of nightmares.

"I thought that if the ceiling fell, that's where I'd be safest," he lied. "I'll tell you the rest later." He bent toward her. She moved her mouth away and his lips landed on the wing of her nose.

"I'll slow down," she said, loosening her grip. "And you can speed up."

He accelerated through the rest:

Some hours later, after a particularly long lull, the ceiling fell. There must have been a loud noise but Bill didn't remember it. Perhaps it was so loud that he went temporarily deaf. He'd heard of such things happening. Or perhaps something hit his head because he had no visual memory of the explosion either.

"It's true," he said, to Maze's curled eyebrow. "I don't."

It was true. He didn't know how long he had been unconscious; it might have been seconds. He was alerted by the sound of a boy weeping. The mattress that had been inches above his face was gone. Turning, he saw that the bunk had tipped sideways and was partially buried by earth and rock. There, pinned like a beetle by the bed's metal bracing, was Drain. He was making the whimpering noises. His leg was bent the wrong way at the knee. It would have to be amputated. That was the optimistic scenario. Drain asked Bill, in a weepy falsetto, to tell his mother something. Bill nodded.

"Did you?" asked Maze, working smoothly now.

"Sure I did."

"Those men must have loved you. And admired you. Like I do."

He forgot the message for Drain's mother almost instantly. He had no room in his brain for messages. Every cell worked to ensure his survival. The dust kicked up by the explosion settled at the bottom of the dugout and he choked. He tested his limbs and found that they functioned. He had only a few scratches and a layer of dirt had crusted over his face like a scab. An adjacent triple-decker bed frame, not five feet away, remained upright. It served as a scaffold, preventing a small rectangular section of the ceiling from collapsing. Between the frame and the ceiling was visible a shard of purple sky. He hoisted himself onto the first bed sack and found it felt good to exert himself, good to be aware of his body, his muscles and his joints. He climbed from one bunk to the next as if scaling a ladder.

Perl was beside him. Climbing as he climbed. Only Perl was not as quick.

"I was able to push up a ceiling board enough to wriggle out," he told Maze. "As soon as I was aboveground, the board slammed shut. The ground caved in. Nobody else got out."

Maze paused. He closed his eyes. He was near. "That's it?" she said. "That's the whole thing?"

Perl's screams, Perl's grasping fingers, Perl disappearing.

"A few other men escaped. From a different section of the

dugout, one blocked to me by the collapsed dirt and rock. Helmer, Yourdon, and Axelrod. That's it."

"Why didn't other men try to climb out like you did?"

"Do you have to stop?"

". . . Is that better?"

"That's better."

"Not too much better?"

"The perfect amount of better."

"Go on."

"Most of the men—ah."

"Sorry."

"Most of them were unconscious or too injured to move. We tried to rescue them. We used our helmets as shovels. But the ground kept giving way."

"Giving way?"

"Dirt filled the hole as soon as we dug it. The shooting began again and we were ordered to return to Camp New York."

"Is that what you're running from?" Her hand relaxed again.

"I'm not running from anything."

"Since you've been home, you've acted like something was chasing you. But you did escape. You're safe now."

He felt himself deflate. "I know I'm safe. I know it in my head at least. I just don't always feel it."

"You're safe with me," she said, squeezing him, but it was too late. He was out of bed, running the sink.

Maze sat up. "Maybe you feel bad about the men who died."

If man could build land by draining swamp, as New Orleans had done for a decade, if he could create a new river and uproot ancient forests, as the city was now doing—if he could rearrange the earth to his own satisfaction, why couldn't Bill reconfigure his inner life? He had tried for months, digging and burying, and still the inner terrain was unchanged. He could not drain the watery marsh of his brain into dry land. It remained soaked, like a bloody uniform, with shame, guilt, horror.

"Where's the strop?" he said.

"It's not your fault. You did your best, just like they did. They would have done the same in your place."

He didn't need to shave, really; he just needed to feel cold water on his face. He hastily applied the cream—a gift from Maze, a concoction derived from Mexican orchids that was supposed to be easier on the skin than Colgate's—and realized that he didn't have his razor either.

"C*her*? You can shave later. Won't you let me finish? I was just getting started."

There came a violent knocking.

"The strop's hanging from the hook in the closet," she called, as Bill flew out of the bedroom. "Next to your razor."

At the door Charlie Breaux, hat in hand, wobbled from one giant foot to the other. "Sorry, partner. Realize it's early. See I caught you eating pie." He stuck a fat finger into the cream on Bill's cheek and put it in his mouth.

"I was shaving." Bill became aware of an aching in his groin.

"Tastes like vanilla custard."

"That why you're here? Because you're hungry?"

"Grocer and his wife got hacked in the head by a madman with an ax. The victims are at Charity. It's an ugly one. They ain dead yet."

"Bill?" called Maze.

He poked his head outside and scanned the block. This had become a compulsion with him, each time he left the house. And what was there today? Not much—Tchoupitoulas Street was suspended in a velveteen silence. A lethargic nag dragged an ice wagon across the intersection at Suzette. Two sleepy-eyed boys in suspenders, boots, and grimy gray caps sauntered toward the river, headed to work at the cotton press. He couldn't see the blackberry woman but her rising song disrupted the silence:

Blackberr-ies, *blackberr*-ies! *Fresh and fine.*
I got blackberr-ies, *lady! Fresh from the vine.*
Blackberries, ma'am. Five cents a can.
Get 'em while you can!
Blackberr-ieeeeeees!

"Give me a minute." Bill tilted his head in the direction of Maze's voice.

Charlie winked. "You don't have to draw a map, boss. Just meet me at Charity."

Bill took a final glimpse of the street and saw, incredibly, that a one-eyed figure in a green greatcoat had appeared at the corner of Benjamin. The man slipped around the corner, but not before Bill glimpsed a flash of silver from beneath the greatcoat.

"They're going to be dead directly, though, so *grouille ton casaquin*." Charlie followed Bill's glance. "Billy? What is it, partner?"

Bill burst by him, breaking into a sprint, his bare feet smacking on the broken cobblestones. "Perl!" he yelled. "Perl!"

As he passed the back door of Di Lello's Grocery a sharp pain seized his foot and he stumbled. He saw blood. A few paces behind him gleamed the metallic edge of an open sardine tin; the delivery boys were always throwing them out the window. He made a mental note to reprimand them, perhaps with his thunderstick, but a sardine tin would not stop him. Maze, unwittingly, was right. There was no use trying to escape. If Perl was alive—which was impossible—and if he had come to New Orleans to find Bill—equally impossible—then Bill wanted to get the reunion over with.

He wheeled around the corner and found the one-eyed figure

sitting there, two stoops down. But the pistol, he could see now, was the handle of a cane. The robe was a moth-eaten blanket. The man was an old woman.

Charlie caught up, huffing loudly, gun raised. When he saw the rag lady, her cane clutched under one arm, he burst into laughter. "A killer's loose," he said, laughing harder when she made the sign of a hex, "but I don't think that's her."

Charlie clapped Bill on the back, too hard. Then he stuck his finger into Bill's face and treated himself to another dollop of cream.

JUNE 28, 1918—THE GARDEN DISTRICT

"Giorgio!" shouted Beatrice. "You're killing me!"

The telephone rang, a hysterical peal like a madman playing a musical triangle, and it was nearly enough to ruin the entire session. Not just because it exploded the silence of the darkened library—a tranquil atmosphere was essential to the success of any osteopathic treatment—but because the sound narcotized Giorgio just as his elbow plunged deeper into her flesh.

Giorgio, mumbling apologetically, eased his weight off her.

"*Per l'amore di Santa Rosalia.*" She reached her hand back to rub the sore spot. The flesh was hot. There would be a bruise. "Unplug that phone."

With a bit more force than necessary, Giorgio yanked the cord out of the wall. His lips formed the kind of interrogative pout an infant makes shortly before exploding into sobs. She tried, as she had hundreds of times before, to locate in his face some trace of his father. Sal's features were there, she decided, only they had been grossly inflated: the ears heavier, the eyelids fuller, the forehead broader. The eyes larger.

"It's my fault," said Beatrice, eager to dispel the momentary thunderclap of shame that rebounded to her whenever she reprimanded him. "I forgot to disconnect the wire. I'm sorry to shout. But sometimes, *caro*, you just don't know your own strength."

"Yes, Mamma."

Beatrice knew her son's strength. It was the kind of strength that qualified as a superpower. It could be used for noble purposes or for ill. Applied in limited doses, it might assist Hercules's daily operations, but Giorgio could not be relied upon even to handle a basic collection route. For the serious delinquencies, Beatrice relied on sulky Elba and vicious Efigenia (or was it sulky Efigenia and vicious Elba?). Sal had hoped his son might develop administrative skills but Beatrice knew Giorgio better. He was adept at lifting heavy objects but showed no interest in managing men. She had long ago concluded that he needed another trade, something that made use of his strength, only in a more honorable application than manual labor. She had bought him osteopathic lessons for his twentieth birthday in the hope that the practice, with its flexible hours, would allow him to transact the family's real business—the shadow business—on his own schedule, while developing in him a sense of professionalism (and in the hope that he might be able to treat her chronic head pains and subluxations). But the most professional thing about his practice was the massage couch that she had bought him, a beautiful object, stuffed with horsehair and upholstered in carmine velvet, that did not look out of place in the vast Vizzini library with its curule chairs, dark bookshelves, and boulle table. She bought the couch after Sal's death, when her pains migrated downward, to the base of her spine. The pains were sharp but Giugi knew how to relieve them.

A faint mechanical ringing came from some other quadrant of the house, barely penetrating the oak door, thickly upholstered in maroon leather and insulated with batting. Giorgio applied his palms to the base of Beatrice's back, his thumbs meeting at her spine. They glided up her back, feeling for warmth—an indication of bone displacement, muscular agony, or deranged blood.

"Gentle, Gio," said Beatrice. "It's sore."

Something was wrong. Giorgio lacked his typical firmness.

"I wondered," said Giorgio, "if you saw yesterday's *Item*."

"Since when do you read the *Item*?" Or any newspaper?

"I saw it in the kitchen."

Beatrice knew he was lying because the pain had woken her at dawn and she had taken her papers into the study, where they remained.

"I must have overlooked it," she said. "Anything interesting?"

"Not really." His touch grew firm again. "Said that sale of liquor would end in the U.S. one year from Sunday."

"That's right, *caro*." She tried to hide her surprise. Was he beginning to take an interest in business? "We're well prepared to take advantage of the opportunities that temperance will offer. But by then, with any luck, the canal project will have led to even more lucrative enterprises for Hercules. Higher."

He adjusted his thumbs.

"Our business will be simpler. We will no longer require supplementary streams of income. We will be free of distraction. It will be safer for us, and more profitable. You can press harder, darling."

"Yes, Mamma."

A freshet of blood spurted into her brain. "Gently. I think you've found an enraged nerve."

But the tranquillity was disrupted for good by a tap on the door.

"I'm in a session, Lizzie!"

From behind the heavy door, the maid's voice was a timid whisper.

"Speak up!"

"I'm sorry, ma'am." Lizzie strained her voice to something just short of a scream. "I know it's your session, but . . ."

"Open the door, *Giugi*."

"Sorry, ma'am," said Lizzie when she entered. She refused to make eye contact. "There's a man *furry* eager to talk with you. He's been ringing the telephone—"

"A man? What man comes here uninvited?"

"Did you say man or men?" asked Giorgio.

"A man, sir." Lizzie kept realigning her head in slight increments, a starling searching the ground for grubs, as she sought in vain a safe place to perch. Finally she settled on the far corner of the blue hearthrug. "Mr. Davenport. He is standing in the parlor, Mrs. Vizzini. Says it's urgent."

"I'll talk to him," said Giorgio.

Beatrice was too surprised to speak. She could not remember an occasion when her son had volunteered to engage in any matter of business.

The maid was nodding, and half-curtsying, as she backed away from the door, when she screamed. She had backed into Hugs Davenport. It was Hugs's turn to scream—or at least let out a muffled yelp—at the sight of his half-naked patroness prone on a massage couch beside the looming presence of her overgrown son. Hugs threw an arm over his eyes and turned away but to his credit he did not withdraw from the doorway.

"Mrs. Vizzini, I beg your apology. But we must speak immediately. Alone."

"I'm in the middle of a medical treatment, Mr. Davenport."

"My uncle sent me."

Now it was Beatrice's turn to feel the heat rising off Giorgio. She didn't have to touch him to feel the radiance. It was like standing beside a stove. A droplet of blood formed on his hairline, at the edge of his scalp.

"Very well, Mr. Davenport. I'll join you shortly." Hugs yielded, his arm still shielding his face. Beatrice turned to her son. "Why don't you visit Lizzie in the kitchen? She's heating a cauldron of Oysters Vizzini. Extra cayenne, the way you like it."

"Mamma," he began, in an uncharacteristically beseeching tone—but he gave up his protest there.

Beatrice slipped on her caftan. Her back ached but the pressure had dissipated and the blood again pumped freely through her brain. That was the crucial thing, the flow of the brain blood. When it circulated without impediment she could think clearly, a prerequisite for conversations with Hugs.

She found him in the parlor, pacing between the hearth and the credenza with its cabinets embossed with carvings of mermaids and wood sprites, imported from Palermo when they had moved into the house on First Street, the year that Sal had initiated the shadow business.

"Did you pay a visit to Professor Joshua Fishman?" asked Hugs. "At Tulane?"

"I did," she said. "But he was not available."

Hugs frowned. "You found his address?"

"It's in the book."

"So you went back."

"I did not." She was irritated by the suggestion that she had disappointed him. She hadn't managed to return to Fishman's house, but she would soon, perhaps the following morning. "Besides," she said, "I thought you didn't want me to speak with him."

"I didn't."

"What is the problem then? Has he published some new screed?"

"No. He has done nothing. That's the problem."

"I do not follow."

"He has disappeared."

She tried to make sense of the information. Had Fishman heard that she had visited and fled? But nobody had even answered the door.

"Two days ago," added Hugs.

"So that's the end of the protest?"

Hugs seemed surprised by the question. He moved his jaw as if chewing a recalcitrant piece of taffy. When he spoke again he sounded exhausted. "It seems so. Pitt—the man who owns the last plot of land in the canal right-of-way, the man whom Fishman had persuaded not to sell? Pitt has dropped his claim. He has agreed to sell at market value."

Beatrice gave Hugs a firm business smile and extended her hand, the gold rings clinking. "Excellent." She tried to ignore the misgivings that swam through her like a school of minnows. "Let's hope that is the expiring wail of our civic dyspepsia."

Hugs regarded her hand as he might a pamphlet that had been forced into his palm. He released it abruptly.

"We have reason to suspect—"

"Yes?" Beatrice smiled more broadly, mimicking polite curiosity. It did the trick. Hugs's jaws resumed chewing something that was not in his mouth.

"We suspect foul play," he said at last.

"I can assure you there was none." She had to suppress a twinge of disappointment. Part of her wanted to take credit for silencing Fishman.

Hugs was sweating. The slightest exertion and the man seemed to bubble perspiration from his orifices, his ears leaking, the swells under his eyes puddling, his mustache damp. "Let me be clear. If Hibernia Bank, or Hercules Construction"—he gave these last two words a meaningful inflection—"or anyone else associated with the Industrial Canal is suspected of, well, *complicity* in the professor's disappearance, the entire project is placed in jeopardy. We have worked very hard, and at great expense, to persuade the public of our virtue, and the virtue of the canal—"

"If you like, I can ask my friend in the Police Department, Captain Capo, whether he has any idea about what happened to the professor."

"I don't think that's a very good plan." There was a barely restrained insolence in his manner. Beatrice had noticed that he suppressed this insolence around his uncle. But she was no less his superior. She would have to make him appreciate this.

She took a moment to straighten, calmly, the sleeves of her caftan, after which she treated Hugs to her most condescending smile. Be a professional, she told herself. "Hibernia," she said, "is only as virtuous at Hercules. Without our help, your costs would have trebled, and the delays would have lasted years. We have not merely provided you with diligent, capable laborers. We gave you efficiency. With efficiency comes peace of mind."

"We are anxious, however, that should any of your, ah, *methods* be detected—"

"As I assured your uncle when we reached our agreement, our methods are irrelevant because they cannot be detected. We are as careful as we are persuasive."

Hugs, cheeks blazing, was preparing a response when, sensing a movement in the doorway, he froze. Beatrice turned and saw her son. He carried in one palm a steaming platter of oysters, bobbing in a swamp of melted butter, oil, garlic, and hot-pepper flakes. A thick glaze of oil coated his chin and his fingers.

"Mamma," he said, though he looked at Hugs, "you were right. Lizzie made the oysters just right."

Hugs showed himself out.

"Would you like me to begin again?" said Giorgio.

"No," she said, but her mind was elsewhere.

"What is it?"

"The strangest thing," said Beatrice. "Do you remember the Tulane professor?"

"The Tulane professor?"

"Hugs mentioned him at the canal? He wrote an editorial against the project. He had convinced the last property owner not to sell."

"I'm sorry"—Giorgio licked his finger—"I don't really remember."

"I had intended to speak with him. But before I could, he went missing."

"He left New Orleans?"

"Nobody knows."

Giorgio looked confused. "That's a good thing, isn't it? The man stopped causing trouble."

Beatrice examined her son: oil-glazed, simple, innocent as a child.

She made her tone as gentle and delicate as she could make it, which was not especially gentle or delicate. "I've noticed," she said, "that you have lately taken a greater interest in our business operations."

Giorgio shrugged. "I like to know what's going on," he said. "It's my business too, after all."

"I am delighted." And she was. Only—she was also uneasy. "I'm delighted because Hercules is stronger than ever before. Soon we will be strong enough to leave the shadow business in the shadows."

"Yes, Mamma."

She removed her handkerchief and dabbed at his temple, where the pinprick of blood had expanded to the circumference of a nickel.

"Ouch."

She balled up the handkerchief and returned it to her pocket.

"The reason we have come this far," she said, "is because we have been exceedingly careful. We are persuasive, not cruel. Tough, but not violent. Never violent if we can help it."

Giorgio set the platter of oysters heavily on the fireplace mantel and embraced her. "I love you, Mamma."

She was enveloped by the warmth of his body, its size, its power. Her boy was a man, all right. "Gentle, *caro*, gentle," said Beatrice. "You don't know your own strength."

But was it possible that he did?

JULY 2, 1918—THE FUNKY BUTT HALL

Now that the fever was on him, it no longer mattered that he had spent nine brain-suffocating hours in the Pit trying to avoid being chewed up by the Mouth, nor that his bassist was outside the club entertaining one of his endless coughing jags, nor that Big Nose Sidney still hadn't poked his big nose inside the hall even though they were to go onstage in fifteen minutes, nor that Orly was nowhere to be seen. Well it was a little distracting, Orly's absence—a scrim drawn over the dazzle of the stage lamps, muting the maniac trill of Achille Baquet's clarinet—but she would come. She had promised. It was an unspoken condition of their pact: he would snap his spine digging the Industrial Canal and she would support his playing. In the last year she hadn't made many gigs, which was only reasonable; between her fourteen-hour days at the Tiltons' and her mother's endless demands, she had little time for amusement. But she got the life-historical importance of this night. She got the Funky Butt.

Now Isadore did too. The Fiss Fass Jass Orchestra crested into a full giddy frenzy, teasing apart the "Tiger Rag" like an old sweater until it unraveled into something unrecognizable and frightening.

Big Head Gaspard's hands chased each other across the length of the piano; Little Head bent halfway over as if to keep his saxophone from blowing off the roof; and Zutty Singleton himself—Zutty, the hardest-hitting drummer in New Orleans—hit the tom with such force that the stand began to hop away from the rest of the set. At least three hundred souls were in the old Baptist church—a clergy of pipe fitters, ditchdiggers, bread deliverymen, clockmakers, longshoremen, nurses, maids, sporting women, and pimps, all of them praising creation with their shoulders and hips. They called this Satan's music, did they? Then praise His Satanic Majesty. Praise the demons of the nether regions.

The Butt. A decade earlier the Reverend Right Duplessis, prophesying in which direction the neighborhood was headed, concluded that a dance hall would deliver far richer earthly treasure than a church could provide. He removed the pews and the cross, converted the choir into a stage and the sacristy into a business office, and changed his name to the Reverend Ya-Ya. He hadn't done much since, apart from offering tithes to the fire chief to avoid capacity fines. The room showed its age. French splayed heels, men's dancing pumps, and cap-toed boots had scored the dance floor. The area in front of the stage had been ground into a pit of sawdust. A few more Alligator Stomps and the revelers would find themselves underground. The walls were maculated with black spots the color and texture of a rotting cauliflower. The ceiling was worse—when it rained, the band played under beach umbrellas that the Reverend kept backstage. During the day you could look up and see patches of sky. But nobody except the Baptists on Sunday morning visited the Butt during the day.

Isadore would've been grateful for rain. The air was choked with cigarillo smoke, squalid perfume, the yeasty aroma of spilled beer. He worried how Orly would react when she saw that the clothes she had so lovingly pressed that afternoon were already damp and smoke stained: his brown box-back suit with thin white stripes, his carmine shirt and pale pink tie, his Edwin Clapp shoes, gingerly polished, even his brown John B. Stetson hat, reclaimed from the pawn with the last of the money from the Bailey jobs. He had told Orly to meet him at the right side of the stage, but maybe she was stuck in the back and unable to squeeze through the turbulent mass of humanity. Or maybe she forgot.

"We better go on quick when these boys leave," Sore Dick shouted in his ear. "If we're to hold this crowd."

"We don't have a drummer."

"Crowd's unruly. We can't lose the reins."

It was just like Big Nose Sidney to be late; why should he make any effort just because it was the Funky Butt? He wasn't a professional—no Zutty Singleton, to be sure—but if he practiced more rigorously, he could get there. Provided that he quit dissipating—he'd have to give up cootch and cootchie both. Yeah right. Isadore solemnly warned himself to stop associating with nonprofessionals.

Zutty tied off his final explosive drum attack, concluding the Fiss Fass Orchestra's set. The burst of applause that followed had the effect of a magician snapping his fingers. Orly appeared beside him in her good blue-and-white-checked broadcloth dress, a freshly plucked magnolia in her lavender bell hat, and her formal shoes, a pair of faded red pumps.

"Hi, beautiful." She really did look beautiful. The beauty was intensified for being mixed with a weariness that was also a kind of wariness. She alternated between them: weary, wary, and wearily wary.

"Harold Jr. has his colic," she said. "And when I finally got home, Mama was having one of her spells."

"Baby, I'm just glad—"

But Sore Dick was back in Isadore's ear with his mosquito buzz.

"Five minutes," he said. "Drag's outside expectorating his lung. Big Nose still ain found."

The Reverend Ya-Ya leaped to the stage. "The Fiss Fass Jass Orchestra," he yelled, in his booming Sunday voice. "Praise the devil!"

The crowd, at least those who weren't busy fanning themselves with their hats or pushing toward the keg or lighting cigarettes or standing mute, paralyzed by mud or muggles, applauded. Scattered through the room, Isadore couldn't help but notice, were several pale-skinned men.

"Ladies and gentlemen, bats and cats, tigers and lions and pumas—"

"And bears!" someone yelled.

"Opossum!"

"Beavers!"

"And alligators and snakes," said the Reverend. "Don't go nowhere because in just a few minutes, your prayers will be answered. The Slim Izzy Quartet is in the hall!"

Drag Nasty joined them, a balled-up handkerchief in his fist. "Hiya, Missus Orleania." He nodded.

She gave him a tight smile, which dissolved into a grimace upon observation of his phlegmy handkerchief.

"Can you stand upright long enough to play?" asked Isadore.

"I'm fine," said Drag, before erupting into another coughing fit. He was pale; his eyes were rheumy and bugged.

"Keep hawking like that," said Sore Dick, still sore, "your eyes gone pop out of your head."

"Izzy," said Orly.

"Yay, look—" He opened his suit jacket to reveal, dangling on a red ribbon from a T-bar he had affixed to his inner pocket, a silver fob watch. The case was engraved with intricate garlands, which surrounded the central shield bearing the maker's name: Omega.

Orly had inherited it from her father and had two months earlier given it to Isadore on his nineteenth birthday. Seeing it against his chest, cleanly polished, she softened. "Good-luck charm," he said, patting his pocket. Finally he had done something right.

Drag fell victim to another jag; he sounded as if he were trying to eject his esophagus.

"Better cancel," said Sore Dick. He always looked on the downside of things—that's why they called him Sore. That and because of his hemophilia. Whenever he got cut, he kept bleeding, sometimes for weeks.

"I'm right," said Drag, bending over.

"Doesn't matter," said Sore Dick. "No Sidney, no drums, no show."

Over Dick's shoulder, Isadore saw two blond men enter the hall. One was very tall, hunched over; the other wore spectacles. They had the cautious, cagey look of interlopers.

"Get onstage," said Isadore. "Set up your instruments."

"Don't see how—"

"*Dick*," said Isadore, and his tone must have been sufficiently menacing, or deranged, because Dick began walking to the stage.

"*Izzy*," said Orly, pleading now.

"One minute, honey."

"Can we at least talk later? After the show?"

Across the stage, Zutty Singleton had finished securing his bass drum in its case and was about to vanish into the smoky fervor. "Give me a second," said Isadore, and he turned his back on Orly.

The crowd was too thick to negotiate, so he hopped onto the stage, hurdled across its length, and reached Zutty just as the drummer was being received in the arms of a pale, dark-haired sporting girl. Isadore recognized her: Sadie Levy from Countess Piazza's Octoroon Club.

Zutty started when Isadore touched his shoulder. "Who're you?"

They'd only met about a dozen times, and Zutty must have seen Isadore perform another dozen times in the streets of Storyville, even if he'd never caught one of Isadore's regular gigs at Mix's or Savocca's. But Isadore knew better than to point this out.

"Slim Izzy Zeno." He brightened his face into what he hoped to be a projection of radiant confidence. "I'm on next." He nodded at Sadie, hoping for some affirmation, but the old sporting girl didn't seem to recognize him either. Had he changed so much in the last year? Or perhaps he cherished the ladies of the Octoroon more than they cherished him. The Countess was his first patron; he had begun gigging in the club's greeting room during the morning shift not long after his fourteenth birthday. When Sadie didn't have customers she got boiled on strawberry wine and requested "Careless Love" or "Melancholy Baby." During breaks she dandled Isadore on her lap like an infant and poured wine from the bottle directly into his mouth. She kept that up even after he was fully grown, to the amusement of the other sporting girls. Isadore never complained. Sadie had a soft lap.

"Our drummer didn't show," said Isadore.

"Sorry for hearing it." Zutty turned back to Sadie.

"I'll pay you."

Zutty pivoted halfway around. "Pay what?" he mumbled over his shoulder, so noncommittal he was barely audible.

Isadore considered the arithmetic. The Reverend would pay a group as popular as Fiss Fass about five dollars a musician, give or take. Isadore couldn't match that, of course—the Slim Izzy Quartet usually received eight dollars for their honky-tonk gigs, or two per person, and tonight they were playing at a discount. The Reverend knew he was giving them a break, putting them on after Fiss Fass, so when he offered three dollars and twenty-five cents Isadore accepted without hesitation. He would have played the Butt for free, just for the chance to perform for Achille, Heads Big and Little, and, yes, Zutty, not to mention any advance men who might attend. The advance men were most important of all. In the last year King Oliver, Jimmie Noone, and Sidney Bechet had all fled to Chicago; Fate Marable, Frankie Dusen, and Johnny Dodds had left for the riverboat circuit; Ferd Morton had gone to California, and Bunk Johnson was wandering the Delta. Their positions were vacant, and the advance men needed new men with new style. It was, when Isadore thought about it, the most important night of his life. That's what he had tried to explain to Orly.

To his bandmates too. But they lacked his vision. They claimed to be offended by the Reverend's offer. Finally Isadore proposed that his three bandmates split the take, a buck each, plus tips, leaving him with the remaining two bits. They went along only because they saw how badly he wanted the gig. Though perhaps Sidney's loyalty was not quite as strong. No doubt someone had offered him better pay that night, which was why he was nowhere to be seen, and why Isadore was in trouble.

The Reverend waved at Isadore from across the stage. *Ready?* He tapped his wrist, though he wore no watch.

"One dollar twenty-five cents," said Isadore. "That's Big Nose's share and mine combined."

Zutty turned the rest of the way around. He seemed conflicted, surprised, and also gently patronizing—as if he were going against his own interest by responding, but had no choice. He had a lesson too important to withhold from a youngster who had yet to figure out how the world worked.

"Boy, I asked you an honest question," said Zutty. "The least you can do is deliver an honest answer." He looked at Sadie, hoping for a partner in incredulity, but her eyes were clouded over in a hop glaze. She was at a different bar, in a different city, on a different planet, in a different galaxy. "Now *please*," Zutty continued, pained by the effort. "Do you fail to observe that I have some sweet stuff here?"

Isadore cursed himself. What was he thinking—$1.25 for Zutty Singleton? Sure the man was insulted. Onstage, Sore Dick sat mute at the piano bench scowling at Isadore. Drag hunched behind him, doubled over coughing. His bass remained in its case. Isadore scanned the room but couldn't see whether the two white men were still in the hall. If so, they wouldn't be for long.

"Fifteen dollars," he shouted, much too loud, and he inflated with terror and glee upon hearing himself pronounce the figure. "And twenty-five cents."

Zutty froze, perhaps uncertain whether Isadore was joking or just being stupid.

"Yay," said Sadie, her eyes traveling all over Isadore without ever alighting on his eyes. "Slim Izzy? That you?"

"What you playing?" said Zutty, skeptical.

"The old pretty stuff at first. 'Sweet Adeline.' 'Cornet Marmalade.'"

"Grown big, huh?" said Sadie.

"I know '*Clarinet* Marmalade,'" said Zutty, prodding Sadie out of the way.

"The drum is the same. Hi, Sadie."

Sore Dick glared imploringly from the stage. Isadore checked his fob. It was half past midnight; the larger part of the crowd starting to bleed toward the door. "We work up to 'Pallet on the Floor,'" continued Isadore, speaking double-time, trying delicately to steer Zutty toward the stage. "'Pallet,' 'Chicken Dog,' then we break into full swing. Later there's some inventions of my own but nothing you can't handle."

Zutty stuck out his palm. Isadore took it for a handshake, but when Zutty's eyes narrowed in displeasure, Isadore withdrew his hand as if from a flame. Of course: Zutty wanted the jack up front. Why should Zutty Singleton trust a no-count such as Isadore to make good on fifteen dollars and twenty-five cents?

He checked his pockets—frantically, to sell it—but he was just buying time. He knew what his pockets contained: four dimes and two pennies, all he had left after reclaiming his John B. Stetson. He could ask Drag or Sore Dick for a loan, but even if they had enough coin in their pockets, which they certainly did not, they wouldn't hand it over to another musician, not even Zutty Singleton. And the crowd was tearing out. The Onward Brass Band was playing a block away at Ferrantelli's, Kid Brown's tonk had a two-for-one on Ojen frappés, and the ladies who used to work Mahogany Hall were offering their services at the Christian Woman's Exchange. The Reverend came stomping toward him. Isadore's hand, palpating his inner pockets, closed around the only thing of value he possessed.

"It's worth at least thirty dollars." He detached the ribbon from its T-bar and held out the watch.

"That's a heirloom," said Sadie, resurfacing briefly into consciousness. "Silver."

"It's real?" asked Zutty, analyzing the gleaming metal.

"Real as rock," said Isadore.

Zutty took the fob from Isadore's hand, bent over, slipped his foot out of his purple suede loafer, placed the fob into the shoe, and slid his foot back over it.

"It ain going to break," he said, seeing Isadore's reaction. "If'n it's silver."

"I'm going to need to buy it back from you at a later date."

"You can have it for fifteen dollars and twenty-five cents," said Zutty, suddenly magnanimous. "Let's git."

The Reverend's eyes got white when he saw Zutty making for the drum set.

"Pelicans and pirates!" he whooped, leaping back onto the stage, arms waving at the backs of his receding patrons. "Squirrels and mongoosers! Zutty Singleton is back! Please welcome Zutty Singleton and the Slim Izzy Quartet!"

At least half of the crowd had filed back into the club by the time they rounded into "Sweet Adeline" and some even began to sing along. A few couples Slow Dragged and Fish Tailed—but still Isadore felt the disappointment rise in him like a black fog. He couldn't account for it. He had every reason to be excited. Onstage at the Funky Butt, playing alongside Zutty Singleton no less, and the band, he had to admit, was parlaying a heavily inflected Spanish: Sore Dick's piano was a babbling stream, Drag Nasty was a locomotive, and Zutty hit harder, more precisely than Big Nose ever had, even in the original numbers. Orly was watching pridefully somewhere—where, exactly, Isadore couldn't tell, he couldn't locate her magnolia in the crowd, but no doubt she was somewhere, beaming. The hall wasn't full anymore, but there had to be at least two hundred people, more than he'd ever seen from a stage. The Reverend had to be satisfied. Still he could see no representatives from the hotels. Face it, there was a better chance of encountering someone who'd recognize him as the highwayman's accomplice. The rumor about the hotel men scouting new acts probably wasn't even true. White New Orleans despised jass music. Check that—white New Orleans didn't even recognize jass as music. The *Times-Picayune*, the voice of the gentry, called jass a vice and an atrocity, like *the grease-dripping doughnut and the dime novel, its musical value nil, its possibilities of harm great.* Still—so what? Why should Isadore care about impressing a bunch of ignorant milksops?

Orly had asked him as much when Isadore promised he would only play before the highest society in town.

"The Roosevelt?" The preposterousness of the idea made her sit up in bed. "You think folks like the Tiltons are going to pay to hear your music?"

"They might learn," he said, unable to fortify his voice with anything resembling conviction. "Jass could go the way of ragtime."

"The Tiltons' idea of music is going to the French Opera House. Jass is workingman's music."

"Things change," he said limply.

"Nothing good ever came from trying to be like white people."

"I'm not trying to be like white people. I'm trying to get *paid* by white people."

But even Orly understood it wasn't only money. It was also fame, which was another word for recognition. If jass caught on in the white wide world—on the order of ragtime—then its masters would be as immortal as James Scott or Scott Joplin or W. C. Handy. As immortal, perhaps, as J. P. Sousa himself.

Isadore pressed the cornet to his lips and the old chemical combustion—oxygen plus metal times flesh—blew everything else out of his head. He'd heard other players describe performing as a jubilant mindlessness, a physical sensation as ecstatic as sexual euphoria, but that wasn't quite right. He used his mind too, running through scales the way Mr. Davis at the Waifs' Home had taught him, calculating fourths and fifths; adding crooks, slurs, and drags; scanning ahead four bars in anticipation; posing and, within milliseconds, resolving questions of harmonic density, chordal patterning, and understructure—all of which was a way of saying he was playing what he thought would sound good. But good was an understatement. It was east and west, top and bottom, in and out, all at the same time. It was chaos and freedom. So even as part of his mind was occupied with time signatures, this other, greater part of him reached beyond time. Wasn't that the very definition of immortality?

What use then did he have for the Roosevelt Hotel when he had everything he desired right here on this old choir, before an audience that was Camel Walking and Kangaroo Dipping and Chicken Scratching like maniacs? The red teakettle overflowed and people began to line their coins in pious rows along the lip of the stage. The other fellows felt it too. From the moment Drag started pulling on the bass he hadn't coughed once and Sore Dick hadn't scowled. You could hear his elation in his attack, the keys babbling like a brook, before cascading in a waterfall of notes, splashing the crowd—yes Dick was downright giddy. Even Zutty grinned like an oyster but maybe that was just the promise of fifteen dollars and twenty-five cents working on him, and all the sweet stuff it could buy. Dick tapered, his cascade dwindling to a ripple, and finally eddied back into the melody. The chorus rose around them and the crowd joined along:

Make me a pallet on the floor
Make me a pallet on the floor
Make me a pallet on the floor
Make it soft, make it low
So your sweet man will never know

Zutty blasted the high hat, the signal for the band to return to the refrain for another eight bars. Then it was Isadore's turn. He pointed his horn to the sky like a telescope, the way Buddy Bolden had done, made his chest as big as a keg, and blew until he felt his eyes pop. The audience was with him now, and his spirit was high, so when the key shift presented an opening, he launched into one of his own tricks. Just a little one—a taste of the new style growing inside him. Braiding appoggiaturas with acciaccaturas, he made his horn cry like an infant—a furious, overtired, hungry infant, wanting his mama's milk. *Waaaaah*, yelped the cornet. *Wa-wa-aaaah*.

The crowd cried back at him, whining and wailing, until the entire Funky Butt was shrieking like a big colicky baby.

Isadore meant to transition to "Chicken Dog" but the fever in the Butt had crested and he couldn't delay the inevitable any longer. The crowd was famished and he had to feed it or they wouldn't come back for seconds. He shouted the name of the number to his bandmates and those standing close enough to the stage to hear it started screaming. The excitement carried the length of the room, the rest of the crowd anticipating what was coming. And to think—somewhere out there, Orly was watching! He couldn't wait to hear what she had to say. She'd finally understand why he loved this indescribable, maddening music. She'd know, after tonight, that he wasn't just good. She'd know he was the best.

"Cats and dogs," he yelled, doing his best imitation of the Reverend. "Lambs and lambskins! This one is called 'The Whore's Gone Crazy'!"

After the third encore, the fourth fainting woman who had to be carried to the street, and the fifth (sixth?) complimentary round of beer for the band, Zutty raised his palms.

"I got blisters," he said, cackling. Isadore couldn't remember feeling so happy. So what if he never made hotel money? Johnny St. Cyr was happy working as a plasterer, and Alphonse Picou was happy to hammer tin. Happy enough, at least. He was starting to understand why. For another night like this, he'd be happy to slave in the Pit until the entire Industrial Canal was dug. Happy enough.

The Reverend wanted to book the Slim Izzy Quartet for another date and about a half dozen fillies wanted to ask questions about his technique but he put them off. He had to find Orly. It was like her to stand back, off to one side; she didn't like to traffic with chaos. But he didn't see her at the bar and she wasn't on the floor.

There was, however, one of the blond strangers standing there. He was dressed much too sharply for the Funky Butt, in a periwinkle sack coat with matching trousers and a white straw boater encircled by a periwinkle ribbon. He fixed Isadore in a dead stare. "You got a second, Mr. Slim Izzy?"

"Sir?" said Isadore reflexively, and chided himself for it.

"You blow a whale of a cornet."

"All right," said Isadore, not knowing what else to say.

"You got a ratty tone too. It's rare you encounter a musician with a tone of his own creation. Never heard anything like it, really."

So this was how it happened. Advance men did come to the Butt after all. Come to think, the man looked familiar—he'd seen him on Iberville, hadn't he?

"I'll be following you. Where do you gig next?"

"We're about to solve that. We'll play again here before long, I suppose."

"I'll be there." The man tipped his hat and made to turn to the door.

"Izzy Zeno." Isadore extended his hand.

The man smiled awkwardly as he shook. He gave a British-sounding name.

"Can I ask with which establishment you are affiliated?"

"Establishment?"

"Sorry. Which hotel?"

A beat passed. The pale man gave a strange smile. "I think you mistake me."

"Ah—you're with a benevolent hall?"

"The only establishment I belong to is the International Longshoremen's Association." The man laughed. "I just like Negro jass. Guess there aren't a great deal of folks like me."

Isadore could see now that the cuffs of the man's trousers were frayed, his shirt collar was slack. He was also younger than Isadore had first thought—twenty-two, twenty-four at the oldest. No doubt he was trying to pass himself off as a big-timer.

"Good luck, Izzy." The man backed away. "I'm off to Spanol's. Mary Mack's Merrymakers are on. Say, you oughta come along."

Isadore couldn't bring himself to reply. Desperate, he threw himself around the hall, looking for Orly. The crowd had thinned but still there was no sign of her magnolia. Nor was she outside, where Drag, hacking his lungs out on the sidewalk, confirmed that he hadn't seen her. Isadore burst back into the club.

"Who you looking for, baby?"

Sadie Levy stood at his shoulder. She'd been patiently waiting for Zutty to finish speaking with a group of chippies. Isadore wondered where Sadie had kept herself since the District closed. Most of the sporting girls had taken up with the wealthiest johns they could find. If they were lucky, they got married. If not, they worked freelance, moving between boardinghouses every couple of weeks, trying to outrun the vice squad and venereal damages. If Sadie was timing with a Negro musician, even one as accomplished as Zutty, she hadn't been one of the lucky ones.

"Orleania," said Isadore, scanning the room.

"What?"

"My lady."

"Girl with the oleander in her hat?"

"Magnolia."

"She left a long time ago."

"What do you mean, left?"

Sadie's eyes crossed slightly as she consulted her memory. "A good thing too. Can't be standing all night in her condition."

"Where'd she go?"

Sadie shook her head. "I'd have thought you'd be more supportive."

It was impossible to talk to hopheads. You couldn't get a straight answer. It wasn't only that they hallucinated; they made you feel as if you were hallucinating too.

"Sadie." He touched her elbow. "Did you see Orleania go somewhere?"

"I hope she went home. She looked exhausted."

Maybe that was it. But it hurt that on this particular night she would go home early. "She had a long day I guess," said Isadore. "Her family works her hard."

Sadie giggled. "Hold on, Izzy. Don't you know?"

"Night, Sadie. I'm sick of your nonsense and side answers."

"She's your own girl and you don't know."

He looked for the Reverend. Had he disappeared too? They had business to discuss.

Sadie was laughing to herself. "Men are blind," she said, and there was a strangely coherent quality to her voice that dragged him back.

"Who's blind?"

"That girl is in the family way. She's got that glow. You don't know?"

Isadore's fob watch jolted into life in his inner jacket pocket, beating hard against his chest. It wasn't the normal rhythm, however. It beat much too fast.

"Baby, you remember our sweet days at the Octoroon?" Sadie drew closer, her voice cloying. "Now that you're a big-timer, maybe you can give Auntie a little candy."

Isadore could only gape at her.

"You got a quarter maybe?" she said. "A dime? A dime for Aunt Sadie?"

It was as if a cog had broken and it kept accelerating, the minute and hour hands spinning out of control, and it wasn't until he patted the empty pocket that he remembered he had given his fob watch to Zutty Singleton. He had given it up and he wasn't ever going to get it back. He felt its absence in his pocket, the lightness against his breast, and he was reminded, for the first time since his father's death, what it felt like to lose something forever.

JULY 3, 1918—THE GARDEN DISTRICT

The eight-foot-tall grandfather clock loomed at the foot of her bed, thonging and clicking, each night winding her thoughts and sending them awhirl, transforming her brain into levers, hammers, rotating gears. This was useful when she wanted to solve a puzzle but oppressive when she wanted to sleep. Tonight she felt particularly defenseless against the clock, which was built into a stout pilaster that wouldn't have been out of place supporting the portico of the Palermo Cathedral. In fact she wouldn't have been surprised if the clock, a gift from one of Sal's uncles—"uncles"—had been pilfered from the cathedral itself, a plaster replica substituted in its place. A week after Sal's death, ragged with sleeplessness, Beatrice had asked Giorgio to haul it out of the bedroom, only to awake in the night to see Sal, having grown eight feet tall and as sturdy as oak, standing in the place of the clock at the foot of their marriage bed, glaring down at her. She made Giorgio return the clock the following morning. It must have weighed four hundred pounds, but he lifted it as if it were hollow.

The clock sent her mind revolving around Giorgio, who was currently in the one place over which she had no supervision: out. Home, she could monitor him. Out, anything went. Where did he go and what did he do? Her mental gears clicked through the possibilities. Tick: *He's with his friends.* Tock: *What friends?* Tick: *He's collecting payments.* Tock: *Past midnight? Giugi knows to make rounds at the bars in the mornings, when there are the fewest patrons, and no grocers are up this late, they have to open their stores in less than five hours.* Tick: *He's seeing a girlfriend.* Tock: *What girlfriend? Besides, he left in a sweat, straight from a day at the dig. If he had a date, wouldn't he have bathed?* Tick: *He's doing something he doesn't want you to know about.* Tock: *He tells me everything.* Tick: *He's doing something he doesn't want anybody to know about. The Tulane professor hasn't been found. What if Giorgio was responsible? What if he did more than scare the professor out of town?*

She reminded herself that this line of thought was ludicrous. Her desperate desire for Giorgio to take an interest in the family business, to one day inherit it, so long thwarted, had mutated into a perverse fantasy: that simple, dull Giorgio had overnight become a calculating lieutenant, willing to commit unspeakable acts of terror to protect the Vizzinis' burgeoning empire. She should be ashamed. The preposterous fantasy only reflected her own longing for him to be someone other than who he was.

The only thing capable of soothing her blood in moments like this, besides an osteopathic adjustment, was a pot of warm milk. But what if, while she was in the kitchen, Giorgio came home? She chided herself—she knew exactly what she'd do. She'd ask him, straight out, where he'd been. He was her son, after all. Imagine that, being afraid of one's own little boy!

But she was afraid. And she was afraid that she was afraid.

Her pulse thumped faster than the second hand and she wondered if the clock was not solely to blame. Perhaps one of the mysterious ingredients in Mother Siegel's Longevity Syrup had contributed. The potion tasted like sarsaparilla and metal, an ominous admixture. But in her siege on mortality she had to explore every possible line of attack. Even when it tasted like sarsaparilla and metal and gave her the collywobbles.

With a groan—the groan of a woman fully fifty-five years of age—she sat up, her wiggling toes reaching for her slippers. A cool whisper of air entangled her ankles; in these high-ceilinged Uptown houses the air was always cooler closer to the floor. The clock chose that moment to chime the half hour—half past midnight—and her heart seized. She bit her cheek; this was unlike her, the anxiety, the vacillating, the tiptoeing. She switched on the bedside lamp, her eyes squinting from the sudden electric glare. After glancing one last time to make sure that the clock was still a clock and not her husband risen from the grave, she wrapped herself in her eiderdown bathrobe. Her mind began to quiet. When she thought about it logically, her fear had nothing to do with Giorgio. Her suspicions were but a new manifestation of the big anxiety, the anxiety that warmed all the others like a stove heating a home through its network of interlocking pipes.

She'd studied the question of mortality as long as she could remember, but Sal's death had led her to reach certain conclusions. Lying in the dark, the clock calibrating her thoughts, she had developed her own unified theory of mortality—or, rather, its opposite. Immortality took four forms, not all of them equal. Most useless was poetic immortality, the immortality of place names, art, and great works. Beatrice knew the name of a French duke because he had bequeathed his name to her adopted city. She knew the name of Dante Alighieri because he had written odes to the woman after whom she herself had been named. And she knew the name of George G. Earl, general superintendent of the Sewerage and Water Board, because it was stamped across every sewer cover in New Orleans. The Industrial Canal, the city's "key to the doors of the world," would bear a similar plaque with her name. The contributions of Hercules Construction Co.—a firm named after another mortal who had been immortalized through his labors—would be recorded in history books. But how long would the world remember a poem, or even a city? What if some plucky New Orleanian, centuries hence, built an even wider canal? Where would that leave Hercules Construction Co., Beatrice Vizzini, Proprietor? Her name would corrode like the bolts in the canal's locks.

She flicked on every light she passed along the way to the kitchen. She stepped lightly so that she wouldn't awake Lizzie. She was grateful for Lizzie's help but the girl didn't know when to stop helping.

Nearly as futile as poetic legacy was biological legacy. Beatrice had Giorgio, but his three older sisters—Rosalia, Beatriceta, and Giulia—had been lost to malaria and croup. Giorgio, already thirty-two, showed no inclination to provide her with a grandchild. All it took was a single barren generation to sever the biological chain. Besides, what good was biological legacy when you were dead?

As for the immortality of the soul, she had her doubts, but just in case she had Lizzie deliver a two-dollar banknote every Sunday to Padre Scramuzza at St. Mary's, served as an honorary *principessa* in the annual Santa Rosalia parade, and invited the entire neighborhood to her St. Joseph's Day party, for which Lizzie prepared an altar decorated with candles, chalices overladen with cherries, and pastries molded into the shapes of doves, hammers, and wreaths. At times, she would grant, she had behaved ungodly. One particular time, really. But she had repented.

She poured the remaining milk in the jug into a copper pot. The pot was on the drying rack, otherwise she wouldn't have known in which cupboard to find it. Lizzie was always hiding things, as if to ensure her own indispensability. If she fired Lizzie, Beatrice would be lost in her own house. She lit a match to the range and watched the flame dance beneath the pot. As a schoolgirl she was made to memorize a line of poetry: *If I thought my answer were to one who would ever return to the world, this flame should stay without another movement; but since none ever returned alive from this depth . . .*

The fourth, and by far most desirable form of immortality was not dying. The most recent number of *Popular Science Monthly*—she had taken a subscription in Sal's name years ago, along with subscriptions to *Science*, *Nature*, and *National Geographic*—reported that the average life expectancy of an American woman had increased from fifty years to fifty-seven. And that was just since the turn of the century. There were various explanations, chief among them advancements in public hygiene and early identification of disease. The anopheles mosquito had nearly been eradicated from American cities, if not from the canal site, by the wide distribution of quinine. Malaria—poor Rosalia!—would vanish from the continent within a decade. Science was gaining rapidly on death. An editorial in *Nature* speculated that increases in life expectancy would soon keep pace with the rate at which one aged, making immortality a mathematical possibility. Was it crazy to believe that by, say, 1940, life expectancy might increase two years for every two years that passed? Beatrice only had to make it to 1940.

To ensure that she would, she took every second night an "immortality bath," a remedy used by every centenarian she had known as a girl in Palermo, a tub of scalding water mixed with essential herbs. As she soaked, she felt her pores open like the tiny mouths of feeding chicks, the quotidian poisons draining from her lymphs. Because one also absorbed toxins from insufficiently masticated food, she was a diligent Fletcherist, chewing every mouthful at least thirty-two times before swallowing. Each morning she squeezed half of a lemon into a glass of milk, waited for it to coagulate, and ate the chunks with a tab of honey, following the example of the Russian longevitist Élie Metchnikoff. Lactic acid increased life span, everyone knew that; even the chief chemist of the U.S. Department of Agriculture had endorsed the life-conserving properties of sour milk in its various forms—yogurt, labneh, and koumiss. This diet, combined with Giorgio's weekly osteopathic treatment, kept her blood fresh and her bones fortified. She had the energy of a thirty-year-old. The figure—not quite. But the energy and the mind. Most important, the mind. Her mind had brought her this far and the Industrial Canal was only the beginning. She was living with the expectation that there would be no end. That was why she wore gold on her fingers. Gold was immortal. They had found gold in Saint Peter's Tomb and in the pyramids where the Egyptian pharaohs were buried. If ever she suffered a crisis of confidence, she could glance at her fingers and be reminded of her golden immortality.

She could feel the pulse in her neck without holding a finger to it. Her heart was leaping over itself.

She hovered her hands over the steam of the warming milk. Without the clock's regimental influence, her mind began to open up, allowing more dimly considered facts to intrude. Besides Hugs's insinuations, there had been other signs, however subtle, that Giorgio's behavior had become erratic. A manager she trusted at Hercules had mentioned that Giorgio had been particularly "vigorous" in his supervision of the dig. She had taken that as a compliment—what a relief to hear that he was engaged in the work!—but she wondered now whether the manager spoke euphemistically.

A nacreous membrane congealed on the surface of the milk. It was a guilty pleasure, but she was alone, so she lifted it with her forefinger out of the pot. The milk wrapped around her finger, a second skin. She put her finger into her mouth and as her teeth scraped off the milkskin, she remembered the newspaper. Giorgio had made an odd reference to reading the *Item* during her last osteopathic treatment—on its face an absurdity as Giorgio was barely literate. And because the paper had been on the divan in her study. But she hadn't given his lie much thought, so happy was she to discover his interest in the coming prohibition of liquor. It was reasonable that he should be concerned, since much of the shadow business's income came from liquor sales at the grocery stores, bars, and honky-tonks that they protected. It was reasonable—just not that reasonable.

She flew to the study. Lizzie was under strict instructions never to throw out a paper until she had finished with it, which she indicated by tossing it onto the floor. The oldest newspaper, at the bottom of the stack, was dated June 29 ("World's Biggest War Budget Passes U.S. Senate"). On Friday, Giorgio had mentioned the previous day's paper, which meant the twenty-seventh. A muddy panic settled around her. When had she read the Thursday paper? Was it possible that it hadn't yet been taken by the trashman? She saw herself outside the back gate on Chestnut Street, rooting through her trash in full view of the neighbors, and the image alone was enough to knock sense into her head.

She returned to the kitchen to find the milk boiling. She picked up the pot with a hand towel but it was too heavy and she overpoured, the milk slapping onto the counter and onto the floor. Cursing the milk, cursing the unwieldy copper pot, and cursing herself for acting like a dippy old lady, driven from her bed in the middle of the night by anxiety about her grown son, she began swinging open cupboards. She finally found the rags below the sink with the rest of the cleaning supplies. The white vinegar, the silver polish, the Old Dutch Cleanser, the scrub brush—and the newspapers. Of course: Lizzie used old newspapers, soaked in vinegar, to clean the windows. The *Item* of the twenty-seventh was the second in the pile.

She scanned it, looking for clues. Beneath the headline "Sale of Beer to Stop in U.S. Sept. 30, 1919" were stories about the emergency appropriation bill that would prohibit liquor manufacture; the death of a New Orleans boy, Sidney Hellman, on a French battlefield; and recent developments, favorable and lamentable, in Berlin, Paris, and the Austrian Alps. In local news the Besemers, a grocer and his wife, were attacked by an ax-wielding maniac as they slept (Beatrice had sent a bouquet of camellias to the convalescing couple, new clients who had bought the business from a retiring grocer from Agrigento); progress had been made on the expansion of New Orleans rail lines; and businesses would close Friday to encourage the raising of War Saving Stamps by all citizens. There was nothing about the canal, nothing about the Tulane professor. So why did her brain feel heavy with blood?

"Hiya, Mamma." Her son stood in the doorway.

"It's late!" Her voice was much too loud. It was nearly a scream.

Giorgio advanced. She thought he would embrace her but he continued past her to the range, where he turned the gas valve shut. The milk in the pot had evaporated, leaving a black resin that had begun to smoke.

"I suppose it's past my bedtime." She couldn't tell if she was more amazed by her forgetfulness or the assuredness with which Giorgio strode across the room and extinguished the flame. When he passed her, she caught an unusual scent—fresh, floral, clean—that she couldn't immediately identify.

"Reading about the Besemers?"

She looked down and remembered the newspaper in her hands. "I had trouble sleeping. Did you have a nice evening?"

"I did, Mamma." He made no attempt to elaborate. He smiled, but it was not his typical befuddled smile. An unsightly flutter played at the corner of his mouth. She had the startling suspicion that there lurked, in this rotten smile, the shadow of condescension. She felt blanketed by a sudden fatigue.

"I'll see you in the morning," she said.

"Mamma." He crossed the distance between them in a single bound and hugged her. "Good night, Mamma." He kissed the crown of her skull.

In bed she returned to the Besemer article. She wanted to stop reading, but couldn't—the ticking of the grandfather clock forced her eyes ahead, one line at a time:

GROCER AND WIFE HACKED NEARLY TO DEATH; WON'T TELL WHO DID IT

Louis Besemer and Spouse Found with Skulls Fractured; Able to Talk, Say Nothing

An intruder attacked Louis Besemer and his wife with the ax that fractured the skulls of both, rifling the cash register of the little grocery at the corner of Laharpe and Dorgenois.

Both Besemer and his wife flatly denied to Superintendent Mooney that either owned the ax, which, stained with blood, was found in the rear of the house on the gallery where the desperate struggle took place.

John Zanca, baker, of 827 Congress street, stood puzzled at 7 a.m., at the corner of Laharpe street. Regularly Zanca had delivered bread to that grocery. Never before had he found it locked. Repeatedly he pounded.

Shuffling foot-steps at last rewarded his hammering.

"Come around to the side door," came the message in a weak voice.

In through the side door Zanca carried the bread.

"My God, what's happened?" he called.

Splashes of blood covered the face into which he stared.

"Aw, nothing's the matter. Don't worry," said the grocer.

Zanca pushed roughly past him, grabbed the telephone receiver from the hook, and shouted into the transmitter for police.

TWO FOUND WITH FRACTURED SKULLS

"There's been a murder or somethin' here," called Zanca—and left hurriedly, before the wrath of the grocer.

A squad from the fifth precinct, a few minutes later, pounded on the door. At last, just as they were preparing to break it down, the key turned in the lock.

In the doorway stood Louis Besemer, 60, the grocer. Blood streaming from his right eye had coagulated on his face. Past him the police pushed. In a bed-room back of the grocery they found Harriet Lowe Besemer, 29, his wife, stretched on her bed, covered with a sheet. Above her ear gaped a deep cut. A heavy blow had laid open the top of her head. One arm was gashed.

"Fractured skulls—both cases," pronounced the Charity hospital staff a few minutes later. Both are conscious, but close to death . . .

Tick: *Why did Giorgio ask if she was reading about Besemer?* Tock: *Because Besemer was a client. Giorgio collected the grocer's tributes on his weekly rounds.* Tick: *Why didn't Besemer want to call the cops or bring his wife to the hospital for treatment, even at the risk of death?*

She placed it now, the scent she had caught off Giorgio when he walked past. Ivory soap. His hair had lain straight on his head and his clothes had been unrumpled, unstained, and undampened by sweat. He had recently bathed. But where? And why? Perhaps he'd been to one of the more expensive whorehouses, which offered bath service. Yes, that's where he had been, at a brothel. Safe at a brothel, no different from any other man.

Tick: *Why did Besemer refuse to call the cops?* Tock: *Why didn't Besemer call the cops?* Tick: *Why was Besemer afraid to call the cops?*

JULY 4, 1918—CITY PARK—THE IRISH CHANNEL—THE WHARF

The barrel of a pistol—a .45 semiautomatic he guessed, army-model issue—pressed into the small of his back, making his shoulder blades pinch. A trickle of urine entered his urethra. So this was how he would wind up: slain in broad daylight, in the middle of a giant carnival, amid thousands of people, in piss-stained trousers. Opposite him Charlie was silently hysterical, his eyes closing up the way they did when he was overmastered by mirth.

"Stick 'em up, mister!"

Bill turned to find a dark-haired girl—fifteen, five foot one, eighty-five pounds—in a cornflower-blue summer frock and a wide-brimmed straw hat. Around her shoulder hung a crimson sash on which gold letters spelled out NEW ORLEANS LODGE OF ELKS. In her free hand she held out two noisemakers.

"Happy Fourth!" she shouted. "Five cents each. Proceeds benefit the naval relief fund."

"You should know better than to sneak up behind an officer of the law," said Bill. He realized that he was holding the paper noisemaker lamely in his hand; he tossed it to the grass. Charlie, trembling with joy, flipped the girl a dime. She pocketed the coin, put her toy gun to her temple and, giving Bill a wink, pulled the trigger.

Charlie's eyes cracked open just enough to allow a fat tear to trickle down his cheek.

"Funny, huh?" said Bill.

"Where's your war spirit?" said Charlie, once he was able to take a breath. "You're the only person here lacking it." He swept his arms over the tens of thousands of revelers swarming across City Park for the annual Biff Bang celebration. The elderly and the children; the young men ashamed not to be in uniform, hiding their faces beneath wide-brimmed Cady hats; the young women hoisting up their dresses to avoid grass stains (and to show off their calves)—they all shuffled from the racetrack, where the Algiers Naval Reserves had bested the Army Reserves in the track-and-field competition, to the inner field, where members of the Forty-Third Infantry positioned themselves for their sham battle. Bill and Charlie followed, having been detailed to the field's southern perimeter. The battlefield was cordoned merely by a red string, tied around stakes spaced ten yards apart, and police were needed to restrain any spectators from joining the battle. The rifles were filled with blanks, but one thousand men stampeding with bayonets posed safety risks. It wasn't the bayonets that worried Bill, however, but the noise. The repeated crack of the starter pistol at the track meet had unsettled him; he didn't think his nerves could withstand an entire sham battle, let alone the fireworks that were to follow. He couldn't withstand a toy gun pointed at him by a teenage girl.

For he had seen, across the track, a man with an eye patch staring back at him. It was true that, ever since the Obitz murder, he had spotted one-eyed men everywhere: at the Pelicans game, in a crowd across Canal Street, on his own street corner. The track was a good hundred yards from where he and Charlie patrolled, and the incident passed in a second: a shot was fired for the hundred-yard dash, the crowd shifted, and the man vanished. Still Bill was certain: Leonard Perl was here. The only possible counterexplanation was even more outlandish: that he had seen Perl's ghost.

"What I don't get," said Charlie, picking up the conversation he'd begun minutes earlier, before the pretty *bandetta* had held them up, "is why he lied about his wife."

Since the outbreak of war, more men had been walking around New Orleans with eye patches—or in wheelchairs, or missing arms. Most of those men were young hearty fellows, just released from service. He felt them staring at him, a herd of maniacal, vengeful Cyclopes. What did they know? More to the point: How *could* they know? The only men who knew the truth about what had happened in the Forest of Purroy were buried beneath a collapsed dugout eight miles southeast of Lunéville.

"So Besemer was stepping out," said Charlie. "But did he really think homicide cops would've cared one way or another about his matrimonial particularities?"

The revelation that the second ax victim, Harriet Lowe, was not, in fact, Louis Besemer's wife was one of several peculiar pieces of information that had emerged during the otherwise profitless investigation into the ax attack on Dorgenois Street. First it was discovered that Besemer, a Jew born in Poland, spoke a number of foreign languages, including Yiddish, Russian, and German. Superintendent Mooney suspected he might be a German propagandist: "Hatchet Mystery May Lead to Spy Nest," ran the *Times-Picayune* headline. Next Besemer claimed that Lowe was not his wife, but a housekeeper. His actual wife, he said, was an invalid, living in Cincinnati.

"Lowe was his mistress," said Bill, with some effort. "Once the ax attack made the front page, Besemer probably figured word would reach Cincinnati. So he got honest in a hurry."

"Married, not married—it's hinky. Then you throw in the German-spy business."

"You think Besemer did it."

"I *did*. I did think so, I'll admit it. Figured he might have given himself a superficial wound to cover up. But then I remembered Maggio."

"Maggio," said Bill vacantly. The name was familiar. He scanned the crowd. All the men had two eyes. The battalions from Jackson Barracks marched into the inner field and took up their positions. One battalion settled into a drainage ditch that was posing as a trench. The men of the other battalion, two hundred yards away and flanked by cannons, gripped bayonets. Medics stood by with stretchers and first-aid boxes. The crowd quieted. The adults in the audience affected a somber mien in deference to the solemnity of warfare—even sham warfare—but every few minutes a schoolboy squealed in anticipation. Bill was grateful he hadn't eaten. He felt that he was going to be sick.

"Maggio, the gibroney who ran the grocery on Magnolia. Killed with his wife."

"That the one from a couple months back?"

"They were killed with an ax, Billy. An ax."

"You sure?"

Charlie nodded heavily. "It's hinky."

Bill remembered. It was the week of the Negro highwayman job: the week he shot the wrong man. Charlie must have recalled the timing and must have decided to avoid mentioning the connection to spare Bill the bad memory. For all his clodding heaviness and patent buffoonery, Charlie could be delicate too.

"Didn't they bust someone on Maggio? A cousin?"

"They arrested Maggio's brother," said Charlie. "A barber. Found him with a bloody shirt."

"That's right."

"They released him. The blood was a wine stain. Never made another suspect."

"You think Maggio's brother tried to kill Besemer and his mistress?"

"Well, you have the ax." Charlie enumerated the coincidences on his fingers. "You have two gibroneys and their wives, or so-called wives."

"I'm with you, Charlie."

"Right. Same weapon, same class of victim." Charlie redid the count. "That's two. Then you have the attack in the middle of the night. You have two grocers." Charlie had one finger left. He paused, trying to find a fifth point of concordance. "You have two unsolved murders," he said at last, triumphant.

An excited susurration swept through the crowd. Soldiers dragged machine guns into position, flanking the cannons. They were old models—Browning M1917s, already displaced in Europe by more modern machines—but still capable of firing ten rounds a second from a barrel the size of a circus giant's thigh. Everything felt too realistic. Bill didn't like to see the guns trained on the callow recruits. Was it still a game to them, a chance to show off their uniforms before their girlfriends and parents? Or had they realized that they would soon find themselves in the same position five thousand miles away, in a French forest instead of City Park, across from war-hardened enemies firing live ammunition. Each of these boys would shortly have to face the prospect of his own annihilation.

But Bill wasn't there to gawk at the exhibition. He was on duty. He resumed scanning the crowd for overzealous spectators who might consider rushing the field. And eye patches.

"Yay, Charlie—you happen to notice any one-eyed men today? In the park?"

"You think the man that killed Besemer had one eye? I know for a fact Maggio's brother has both eyes."

"It's nothing to do with Besemer."

Charlie evaluated his partner as he might a suspect. "You feeling right?"

Bill was not feeling right. He felt like a sewer. He watched a soldier feed a cartridge belt into a machine gun. Did they make blank rounds for machine guns?

"Look, Charlie, if you really think that the Maggio brothers are connected to Besemer, take it up with the lead investigator."

Charlie nodded resignedly, as if he had been dreading this suggestion. "Unfortunately," he said, "that's impossible."

"Why? Who's lead on Maggio?"

"It was Teddy Obitz." Charlie monitored his partner's reaction. "He was working the Maggio case the day he died. Captain Cap said Blond was onto something, but he didn't know what."

The captain of the drainage-ditch battalion blew a whistle three times. The captain of the bayonet battalion blew his whistle three times. The soldiers, in unison, saluted their counterparts. They raised their weapons.

"I did see a man with an eye patch," said Charlie, as he surveyed the crowd. "About an hour ago. Lots of men come back ruined from the war." He paused, glancing quickly at Bill. "Physically, I mean."

"What did he look like?"

"Just a man," said Charlie. "Black hat, green greatcoat. That's all I remember."

Bill stared at Charlie to see whether he was joking. But Charlie was never joking. He didn't know how. "Did you think to ask yourself, Detective, why a man would be wearing a greatcoat in the middle of July in New Orleans?"

A shot fired, loud and close. Bill ducked. Charlie seemed newly concerned about his partner's disposition but said nothing because the sky shook with the clangor of two cannons, four machine guns, and several thousand rifles, a sound that rose from a sputtering carburetor to a thunderstorm before crescendoing into Niagara Falls. The men from the bayonet battalion whooped and set out for the trench. They made rush attacks, scurrying ahead ten yards and falling to the ground, while the next company leapfrogged them. The opposite battalion was invisible behind a curtain of fog. The air thickened with lead, graphite, and the balsam scent of rifle lubricant. Men dropped lit fireworks into the mouths of the cannons, from which they burst in large belches of smoke. Bill's heart skipped when a young soldier leaped into the air, grabbing his chest, and collapsed violently on the field. Bill was ducking under the cordon when Charlie's hand landed on his shoulder. Two men from the Ambulance Corps darted over with a stretcher and began to minister to their fallen comrade by sneaking him a flask, which the dead man accepted with a grin and chugged.

The crowd laughed and applauded. Bill must have been the only person in City Park made ill by the sight of the soldiers clutching histrionically at their chests, writhing in the grass. Charlie, getting in on the fun, spun around, grabbed his shoulder, and fell to his knees.

"C'mon, Charlie." It was too loud for Charlie to hear Bill, so he tapped his partner's arm. It wasn't a good example to set, an officer playing like a child. Bill tapped harder, but Charlie didn't respond, and Bill pushed him. Charlie went over like a felled oak, flat on his face, his head rebounding off the turf.

Bill crouched to inspect his partner. Charlie's arms were twisted beneath him. Pulling with all of his strength—in a flash Bill saw Teddy Obitz, slumped on top of Harry Dodson—Bill lifted Charlie's shoulder and flipped him. His face was purple, his eyes flickering. The hand covering his shoulder was greasy red. A young boy beside them screamed; the sound was drowned out by the detonations but his mouth opened so wide that Bill could see the pink, webbed tonsils.

On the field, not fifteen feet away, the two Ambulance Corps members tended to another playacting soldier. Bill ducked under the red string and raced toward them, barely dodging a soldier running with his bayonet extended, and grabbed a medic's arm.

"Yay! What's this?"

"My partner's been shot," shouted Bill. "Bring your gear."

"The bullets are blanks," said the patient, sitting up.

"This one wasn't."

The two medics exchanged a look. "We haven't passed certification," said one, fondling his crush hat. "The first-aid cases are empty. Except for a bottle of hooch."

"Find help," said Bill. "*Fast.*"

The boys nodded and, dropping their cases, raced along the edge of the field against their rushing comrades. Bill dodged another pair of sprinting bayoneters and ducked back under the red string. A group of men had surrounded Charlie, shielding the children and women from seeing the only fallen man in City Park who was actually wounded. One of Charlie's feet slowly pedaled the air. Pink spittle bubbled from his lips. A man tied his shirt around Charlie's shoulder to stanch the bleeding.

"One of the guns must have been loaded with a real bullet,"

shouted the man, shaking his head. He removed his straw hat to shade Charlie's head from the sun. "What a horrible accident."

"We ought to stop the battle," yelled a boy with a harelip who looked nearly old enough for service. "It's unsafe."

It would be just as easy to call off the fighting in Verdun. "We're going to need to carry him to the perimeter," said Bill. "I called for help but I don't think we can wait." The bubbles on Charlie's lip expanded and popped with each breath. His eyes found Bill. Bill leaned over and pressed his ear to Charlie's mouth.

"Who did this, Billy?" said Charlie. "A soldier?"

The boy interrupted to report that his sister was getting their father, a doctor. He should be there any second. Already the crowd was parting to admit a new entrant. He moved insistently, impatient, pushing his way closer.

"Yay!" someone yelled. "Cool it!"

"Is that him?"

"Let 'im through!"

"*Careful*, fella! It's tight in here."

"Move aside! It's the doctor!"

It wasn't the doctor.

Bill saw the eye patch first. A millisecond later he locked with the man's eye, which, seeing him, darkened like a rotted lemon. Bill turned and ran, pushing out of the circle that surrounded Charlie, back toward the battlefield. He tried to leap over the red string but it caught his foot and he fell headfirst to the grass, where he was stampeded by two soldiers advancing in the bayonet charge. He leaped to his feet and sprinted along the string, staying in the flow of the battle. He glanced back in time to see Perl duck under the string. Perl aimed a pistol down the line at Bill and it erupted in flame. Either Perl's depth perception was shaky or he was too far away, but it was his second miss in as many chances. On the first occasion Perl must have figured that he had a clear shot at Bill but instead Charlie was writhing on the ground and Bill was running free.

Bill ducked under the cordon. Holding his service revolver aloft—screaming, *"Police!"*—he pushed between startled spectators, diagonaling away from the sham battle until he found enough open space to run.

He ran.

Maze was in the kitchen preparing a giant saddle of mutton. Her hands were caked with flour. Her yellow apron was streaked with blood.

"I thought you didn't finish till seven."

"There was a shooting," said Bill. "Charlie caught a bullet."

"What? Where?"

"The Biff Bang carnival."

"Where on his *body*? Is he dead?"

"It just grazed his shoulder. He'll be fine. He's at the hospital."

"Jesus, Billy!"

"One of the soldiers loaded his gun with the wrong kind of bullet. Only explanation."

"It might've been you!" She moved to embrace him, but stopped abruptly, removed her apron, and placed it on the counter. She hugged him with her elbows, holding her hands behind his neck to avoid dirtying his uniform.

"Should we go to the hospital?" she said uncertainly. "I can stop cooking—"

"There's nothing we can do right now."

"If you're certain." She appeared relieved for the permission to return to her apron and the mutton. "As long as Charlie is all right."

Bill began to breathe normally again. It was good to be back in the cool, dark home, the dimity curtains muting the sunlight, his wife's strange miniature porcelain animal figurines parading along the mantelpiece, and his half-completed watercolor on the dining table where he'd left it the night before, when he fell asleep with his face on the old newspapers he used as canvas. It was calming too, Maze at the stove in her canary-yellow apron, preparing a feast. Tomatoes and okra simmered in a Dutch oven, six boiled eggs cooled in a bowl on the counter, and the rich, fatty smell of the mutton thickened the air. Only now could he take the full measure of his exhaustion. The muscles in his legs were sore, his lungs were singed. But he was relieved. The truth had finally articulated itself. For weeks it had been advancing toward him, from some faraway distance, a gloom at the end of a long canal that, emerging from the fog, took the form of a giant steamship, coming to run him over. Perl was alive. He wasn't insane. It was easier to face a man than a ghoul. He only needed rest, some mutton, a few minutes to think. Perl would return. But Bill would be ready.

Still his instinct protested. Something was askew. The dining table, for instance, was covered with a white cloth and the good china—the Bones' wedding gift—was stacked on the counter. Mutton, when he thought about it, seemed far too rich a meal for two people, particularly if one of those people was Maze, who rarely possessed an appetite. Through the bedroom door he noticed her blue toile dress, which she hadn't worn since the going-away party the officers' union threw for the cadets, laid out on the bedspread. Most peculiar, however, was what she had done with his painting—one of the watercolors, a cacophony of orange and red and brown that bore some resemblance to a rotted pineapple, superimposed on a broadsheet from the *New Orleans States*, on which a headline was still visible: MAN SHOOTS SELF AS GIRL LOOKS ON. Maze had pinned the painting to the wall.

"You might profit from a wash." She smiled. "Should I draw the bath?"

"The painting."

"Oh?" she said, as if just noticing it. "It's one of my favorites. I wanted to put it where I can see it more often. It seems silly to hide it away in the closet."

She was lying and she was also guilty of going through his stuff behind his back, but this wasn't the time to take it up. "The tablecloth," he said. "The dress. The mutton."

"It's a holiday," she said brightly. "I thought I'd put the day to use, do something nice." Her smile broadened to unnatural dimensions.

"Maze."

She laughed. "Worst part of being married to a detective—you can't get away with anything."

"You make a terrible criminal." He removed his boots and his socks, careful not to spill too much sod on the mop-streaked floor. "So what am I taking a bath for?"

"You're taking a bath in the interest of public hygiene. And because we're having company." She wrinkled her nose. "It was going to be a surprise."

"Your folks?" He removed his jacket and folded it on top of his shoes. He detached his holster from his belt. "You know how much I love surprises. And your folks."

"But this was going to be such a *nice* surprise."

"I don't think I've ever heard you call your parents *nice*."

"Drat." She sighed. "So much for fun."

"What's that mean?"

"I ran into an old friend of yours."

Bill froze, one pant leg on, one off.

"Don't bother. I've taken care of everything."

"What friend?" asked Bill, through a warped grin. But he knew the answer. He pulled his pants back on.

"Your old friend from the war. Lenny. He's a plum. But I should warn you."

"Lenny."

"He's got a disability. He lost an eye." She paused, spatula in hand. "What are you doing? Take those off, I'll soak them."

"Tell me exactly what happened."

"I thought you'd be happy to see him."

Bill went to the window. The street was clear in both directions. Everyone was at the Biff Bang. There was only the rag lady, making her regular circuit of the neighborhood. "Did he come here?"

She shook her head halfway. "I was making groceries."

Bill saw Perl, the wily former pickpocket, trailing his wife to the market. He'd have waited for the right moment before approaching, hat in hand, with a broad smile. *Ma'am, I don't intend to bother you, but I think I've seen you before—in a sweetheart photograph. Are you by any chance married to my old friend Bill Bastrop?*

He was breathing heavy again, so heavy that he had to sit. Then he stood back up. This was no time for sitting.

"What has gotten into you?"

"Losing an eye's the least of it," he said. "The man has lost his mind."

"Really, Bill."

"He's not a friend of mine."

"He said you saved his life."

"What else did he say?"

She paused. "It was actually a funny coincidence."

Bill paced, trying to put it together. Perl had followed her to the market. Why? What did he want with Maze?

"He just got into town. He was trying to find you."

"He's *been* in town. I've seen him."

"This is getting strange, Bill."

"He's an angry, mixed-up man." Bill's blood was high and it was all he could do to retain consciousness, but he had to avoid setting any snares for himself. "Somehow he got the crazy idea that I'm the person responsible for his misery. I got promoted over him. Never forgave me for it."

"You must be thinking of someone else. This fellow was a gentleman. He owes his life to you. He loves you."

Bill was beginning to understand Perl's game. "Go back to the beginning," he said. "Tell me everything."

There wasn't much to tell. The market was closing at noon for the Fourth, so she got there early to shop for supper. She had purchased the greens, eggs, and tomatoes and was standing at the butcher's stall, sizing up the pork chops, when a man with an eye patch and a warm smell approached the counter.

"A warm smell?"

"Like oak. Like cigars. Or old furniture. But none of those exactly."

The butcher informed the one-eyed man of his specials on beef tail and suet. The customer, smiling, explained that he was not looking for meat, but for a citizen—a friend from the service. I figured I might begin at the market because, well, everyone's got to eat, don't they? He gave Bill's name and Maze's heart jumped.

Why this is his wife! the butcher exclaimed. Imagine that!

"Imagine," said Bill.

"You think he followed me into the store?"

Bill had an image of Charlie moaning on the ground like a hunted bison, the blood staining the grass black.

The war veteran introduced himself as Leonard Perl. He said

he'd served with her husband in France. He pointed to his eye patch. He might have mentioned me, said Perl. He laughed. Bill *better* have mentioned me!

Maze's excitement gave way to embarrassment. She did not recall hearing about a Leonard Perl. She suspected Bill was beloved by his comrades, even if he was too modest to say, but—she apologized—the only man she remembered from her husband's platoon was a tall fellow from Houston who had sat with Bill on the train home. He must forgive her—

That's funny, said Perl. 'Course all I ever do back home is blubber about Billy Bastrop. A good man, your husband. Made of the real stuff.

You were close with Billy?

Ma'am, he saved my life.

A right man, said the butcher, Mr. Bastrop. Once you get to know'm.

Perl noticed that the butcher had given her a stack of old newspapers. She explained it was for Billy, that he painted on the paper. The paintings were his release.

"You told him about my pictures?"

"He was impressed."

I know the feeling, Perl had said. War can tear out a man's nerves. Playing with paint is less harmful than most of the other methods men use. Nobody but a man's wife could understand what he felt and even most wives didn't understand.

It was Maze's idea, the surprise supper party. Bill would be gone all day at the carnival so she'd have time to prepare an elaborate meal. She'd been reserved lately, morose, but here was a chance for a new beginning.

Perl was delighted to be invited, grateful. Maze asked if he had a good appetite.

He did, he said. He had a tremendous appetite.

He volunteered to bring a bottle of wine, the finest he could find—best to splurge on the good stuff before it became contraband. She ordered the saddle of mutton. Perl insisted on treating. She wrote their address on a scrap of newspaper and asked Perl to show up at six thirty.

It was five past six. Perl, clearly, had never expected to show up to supper. Once he'd learned that Bill was working the carnival, he headed to City Park. But having lost Bill at the park, Perl would have built up an appetite all right.

In a blur Bill turned off the stove, reclipped his holster to his waist, and grabbed Maze's wrist. She was too stunned to resist. They paused at the door while Bill clocked the street. Empty. At the corner he realized that she was still wearing her apron. It was tight around her knees, preventing her from running. He tore it off and threw it to the ground. She sobbed. Her sudden transformation, from winsome optimism to pained dread, lodged a splinter of sadness into his heart but there was no time for sadness. Her parents' house on Camp was seven blocks away. They ran most of the way, Maze letting the fringe of her white cotton dress drag in the street, pausing only at Magazine Street to dodge the crowds returning from the fireworks.

"What a joyful surprise!" said Maze's mother. "Why are you sweating?"

"Stove is busted." Maze forced a smile. Her eyes were dry.

"What's that?" came the gruff, baffled voice of Mr. Bone.

"The kids are here," shouted Mrs. Bone, her voice echoing down the side hall.

"Is it Sunday?"

"I can't stay, unfortunately," said Bill. "No holidays for police."

"I am terrifically sorry to hear that," said Mrs. Bone, but her back was already to him. She puttered down the hall to the kitchen, where she began giving commands to their cooking woman.

"I'll be back soon," said Bill.

"Stay." Maze grabbed his hand. "We're safe here."

Bill shook his head. He felt blunted, vague, as if observing the world through a dirty glass. "We won't be safe until I see Perl."

"Is he really that sick?"

"He's deranged and violent."

"He seemed so . . . normal." Her eyes glazed. "How could a man keep secret so much hate?"

"Only a monster could do that." It was the most honest thing Bill had said all day.

"To think—I invited him in our house. Our *home*."

"I'll solve it."

"Can you get him arrested?"

"Yes," said Bill, grateful for the excuse. "I'll arrest him."

She wasn't entirely convinced, he could tell, but she must also have realized that there was nothing else she could say. When they kissed, she pressed her lips into his, hard, as if she wanted to leave an impression. And she did.

Leonard Perl stood on Tchoupitoulas Street in front of Bill's house holding a giant bouquet of red begonias. He peered into the window. Bill slipped back behind the corner, catching his breath, palpating the waffled handle of his service revolver. About forty feet separated them. The revolver was accurate within twice that distance. But it was now evening and civilians were returning from the park in loud, jangly groups, swaying drunkenly and singing "It's a Long, Long Way to Tipperary" and "Over There" (or at least the song's first two words, repeatedly). Di Lello's had reopened for business; it would be busy with neighborhood women buying last-minute items for supper. Across Suzette Street a trio of boys, brandishing the wooden pistols that had been distributed by the Elks at

City Park, played Doughboys versus Huns, arguing over who were the Huns. Bill couldn't just open fire in the middle of a busy neighborhood street. Could he?

A cloud of begonias pressed into his face. He inhaled sharply, his lungs filling with an extravagance of pollen that choked his shout into a jagged cough. The boys on the stoop paused long enough to laugh at the funny sight of a man giving another man a bouquet of flowers, before continuing their game. "Got me a live Hun!" one of them shouted. "Shoot 'em dead! Dig a grave! Harvest his skull!"

"I don't want to kill you yet," said the begonias. The petals stuck in Bill's eyes and their lurid fragrance suffocated him but instinct prevented him from jerking too violently. "You're still alive," said Perl. "Stop and smell the flowers. There. There you are."

Bill's eyes teared and his coughing became rougher, scratching his lungs. Some part of him felt grateful to have forfeited agency. It was easier this way, to give up—to have good reason to give up. Nobody could fault him for giving up.

"Take the flowers, Bill."

He put his arms around the bouquet. Red bouquet, he thought. Rouge Bouquet. He felt a slight depression of his waistband and realized that Perl had removed his .45. He heard the clinking of bullets dropping to the sidewalk. It had happened so fast. Perl wasn't a particularly good marksman—certainly inferior to Bill, who'd had the benefit of training as a cop even before he entered the army. But Perl had his own talents, sharpened by years of experience picking the pockets of stevedores on the Brooklyn waterfront.

"Scream," said Perl, "and you will die slowly through your belly in front of these children. Your wife will find you."

Bill coughed helplessly.

Perl placed his palm in the small of Bill's back and guided him in the direction of the river. They walked nearly a block before Perl spoke.

"Are you satisfied?"

Bill did not want to respond but his voice did not cooperate. "Yes."

"It would've been better if I came as a phantom, returning from the after realm. But this will do."

"Leave my wife alone. She doesn't know anything."

"She knows you're a hero."

Bill heard laughter. Three young women approached, arms interlocked. Perl pressed harder into Bill's back. The men nodded, the women smiled, and the block cleared again.

"I know what you want to know," said Perl.

"Then I won't ask."

"The hole was closing. You were nearest to the top but there were other men close. I was below you."

Bill remembered the men below him, squirming like a tangle of earthworms, struggling to reach the air. He remembered the peristaltic opening in the mud above him, dilating and tightening. Standing on the crossbar of the top bunk, he had extended his fingers through the opening but no farther. A person on the ground might have been able to grab Bill's wrist but there was nobody. With each contraction, the opening narrowed. As the men climbed the bunk beds toward the light, their weight sank them deeper. Bill tentatively explored the wall with one of his boots, seeking out a ledge or branch, but it was all crumbling sand. The walls quaked, the ceiling quaked, and he knew that there could only be so many quakes before total collapse. In camp they had trained for this exact situation. Should a group of men be trapped in a collapsed trench or dugout, the protocol was to help each man out, beginning with the man farthest from the open passage. They were to form a bucket brigade, the men being lifted, one by one, toward the air. But Bill saw the thatch closing and doubted there would be enough time.

His boot, still searching for purchase, alighted on a human head. The man was pulling himself onto the top bunk to join Bill. Without thinking—or acting so quickly that it was impossible to separate thought from action—Bill used the man's head as a footstool. He strained, his boot twisting on the man's scalp, and extended his arm far enough to gain purchase. The fractured ceiling boards buckled but did not collapse and he hauled himself out of the dugout. Later he remembered feeling the soldier's fingertips grasping at his boot, but he convinced himself that he had invented this.

After a few sharp gasps of fresh air he reached his arm into the hole, feeling for another hand. He shouted but could not hear his own voice. In the burning forest there was no hearing and he wondered if he was making any noise or if he was only screaming inside his head. For an eternity—or perhaps a minute—he kept at it, his cheek pressed against the thatch roof of the dugout and his arm reaching down, grasping only air. Finally he ran to the next dugout for help. By the time they returned the thatch roof was no longer visible. There was only a steep pit.

"I tried to rescue the others," Bill said. "When that failed, I sought help. But it was too late."

"You ground the heel of your boot in my eye."

"That isn't true."

Perl jabbed his own gun—a Colt semiautomatic by the feel of it—into Bill's rib. "You ground your boot into my eye." He spat forcefully. He seemed in danger of executing Bill in the middle of Suzette Street.

They walked the final block in silence. The wharf was empty. Even the skeleton staff that manned the warehouses and fuel stations during the holiday had left for supper. The westering sun, sparking the cheap tin roofs, made his eyes water. He considered the mechanics of reaching for Perl's weapon. They'd walked three blocks already; Perl's guard would be down. He could grab Perl's wrist with both hands and twist the gun out. He was stronger and, if not quicker, he would at least have the advantage of surprise. He thought about how easy it would be and thought about it some more but still he kept walking with his arms hugging the begonias.

"You ground your boot into my eye," said Perl with a note of wonder, as if happening upon a startling detail for the first time.

They passed through the waterfront shantytown—the warren of shacks in which the port's business was conducted. The asphalt beneath their feet gave way to gravel. They weaved amid sandbags and shipping pallets. The city was no longer visible behind them.

"Drop the flowers."

The overwhelming fragrance of the begonias was replaced by the overwhelming fragrance of roasted beans. They had entered the coffee wharf, dominated by a warehouse filled with large white sacks of beans like overstuffed couch cushions. It would be so nice, so lung-inflatingly pleasant, to lie on a coffee cushion and take a nap in the falling light. He thought again about making a move for the semiautomatic but the desire had grown even fainter. In the grip of real hazard, mortal danger, the recklessness had evaporated. He had regressed to his old condition, which perhaps was his permanent condition: a cowardice thick as wet cement. Maze came into his head: Maze's hazel eyes as the breeze played with the bedroom curtain; Maze listening faithfully to his account of Rouge Bouquet; Maze's terror and confusion when he left her with her parents. He wondered if she could see through the clothing of his heroic language to the nakedness of his fear. She must have sensed on some lower level that at Rouge Bouquet he had disgraced himself irreparably. If so, did she feel disgust—the same disgust he felt when he thought of the men trapped in the dugout beneath him?

The Mississippi rose before them as they stepped onto the boardwalk. A triple-decked steamboat with white iron railings, a floating wedding cake, was anchored at the nearest pier. At the other slender piers, extending like aristocratic fingers into the water, fishing boats and dinghies docked. Perl had done his research: the port was one of the few places in New Orleans deserted on the evening of July 4. Just as it seemed that he might lead them both off the boardwalk and into the river, he withdrew the semiautomatic from Bill's side.

"You are responsible for the deaths of eighteen men. Good men. Men better, and stronger, than you."

"What could I have done?"

Perl spit into the river. "You knew the protocol. Bucket brigade."

"I went for help."

"Drain had just boosted me when the roof collapsed. I might have saved him if I had help. My eyeball was hanging out of my head."

Bill could make the river in two paces and dive. A lot of good that would gain him. He'd still be an easy target. Besides, every boy who grew up in New Orleans knew that the Mississippi sucked downward. The corpses of suicides, drunks, and thrill seekers washed up at English Turn every weekend.

"When the hole collapsed," said Perl, "I ran into the woods for help. But I became disoriented and passed out. When I came to, it was too late. I made a promise then to the men. I have brought you here to satisfy it."

The falling sun multiplied in the rippling river and the tin roofs. Bill wanted badly to close his eyes.

"It is amazing to me," said Perl, "that you have made no effort to take my weapon. What kind of a cop are you?"

"Do you think that shooting me is going to make any difference to Drain? To Hegney? Finn?"

"I'm disappointed because I had prepared for a fight. I thought there might have been a flash of manhood left in you. But you don't have any fight, and you probably never did." He pointed the gun toward the sky and released the magazine. It was unloaded. "I never intended to use this."

Perl placed the gun on the boardwalk behind him. He placed Bill's empty revolver beside it.

"I was fortunate only to lose an eye. Can you begin to imagine what it is like to be buried alive?" He shook his head. "I have no desire to shoot you. My intention was always to murder you with my hands."

Perl removed his jacket, folded it twice, and placed it on top of the guns. Bill was surprised to see that Perl had sweated through his shirt. Ovals of perspiration descended beneath his arms and a wide butterfly-pattern of sweat broadened across his chest. It reminded him that Perl was a real man. After thinking him dead for so long, it was difficult to believe, even now, that he was not a ghost.

Perl removed his watch and placed it on his jacket. He unbuttoned his sleeves and rolled them above his elbows. Finally he removed his eye patch. The place where his eye had been was a smooth brownish mound of flesh, like the cap of a cremini mushroom. Perl's knuckles whitened.

Something shifted in Bill. Death, even at Rouge Bouquet, had seemed an impossibility, but now it materialized before him. More precisely, the world began to dematerialize. The river began to rise, the clutter of buildings hovered above the wharf, the railroad tracks levitated. His body grew as vaporous as air. Then he was air. The crust of the earth peeled away like a banana. And what lay beneath? A gray haze, a whiteness, a blackness, none of these—a vast expanse without end or beginning. There was no comfort in this roiling insanity, no relief or satisfaction, only void. He floated here unthinkingly, staring into this chaos: a foresight of eternity. Then it was over. He returned to his body, the ground solidified, and the expanse before him was not an abyss but the brown brindled Mississippi.

He deserved to answer for the lives lost at Rouge Bouquet. He would pay whatever cost necessary—short of his life. If death was oblivion, what kind of penance would his death offer? It would only abridge his atonement. These were some of the things that occurred to Bill in the short but infinite stretch of time between the clenching of Perl's fist and the force of the fist against Bill's jaw.

Bill fell to the ground but sprang up as if he had landed on a trampoline. He was stronger than Perl and, as a police officer, better trained for fighting in close quarters. Perl's eye put him at a further disadvantage. Did Perl believe that a righteous sense of vengeance could make up the disparity between them?

Bill swung with his right hand. Perl dodged with a quick step back. Bill followed with a left, which was less forceful but connected.

"There you are," said Perl. "There's Billy."

Perl plunged his forearm into Bill's throat. Perl was stronger than he appeared; he had within him all the strength of insanity. But he had used his left arm and Bill did not fall. Perl's eye was now turned away and Bill did a clever little move. He led with a soft right jab. Because he was off-balance it was weaker than he would have liked but it turned Perl from a three-quarter profile to a full profile. This gave Bill an extra moment to regain his balance. As Perl swung his head around, Bill's right fist flew at full speed to meet Perl's cheek. There was a loud crack and Perl spun sharply, spilling across the boardwalk.

Bill bent over him. Perl was not unconscious but he seemed unwilling to rise. A gurgling noise came from his eye. He tried ineffectively, with the movements of a man twice his age, to wipe away the blood. Bill noticed his own breathing settle. He could kill the man now. That would end it finally. He wouldn't have to worry about being exposed for his act of wartime cowardice or losing his job or being sent before a court-martial. He wouldn't have to fear for Maze's life. He wouldn't have to fear for his own. He wouldn't have to fear.

A kick to the head would do it. Or he could roll Perl into the river and let the current do the rest. That was his choice: head or river. Otherwise Perl would return and the next time he wouldn't hesitate to use a bullet. Bill decided he should do it, one way or the other, but he didn't do it. He didn't do anything.

Perl's movements became more fluid. He spit blood. He raised himself to his hands and knees.

"I don't want to do this," said Bill. "But I don't know what else I can do."

Perl spat again, a blackish red clot. He sat on his heels.

"I wish you hadn't come to New Orleans, Lenny."

Perl tried to speak but it came out in an incoherent demented babble. He shook his head with disgust and tried again. "You're as much of a coward now as you were at Rouge Bouquet." He said *Boo-ket*. His bloody eye regarded Bill. "If you were a man you would kill me."

Bill didn't respond. Perl rose to one knee. After two breaths he stood up.

"You're not just a coward, you're stupid." Perl reached into his back pocket and brought out a small blade. It was not a knife, exactly, as the blade was in a strange crescent shape, like a miniature ax or the chine of a scythe. When Perl transferred it to his right hand Bill saw that its cast-iron handle ended in a loop and he recognized it: a Bully Beef can opener, the model presented to every serviceman upon arrival in Europe. Running along the blade was a bull's head, carved into the iron; the tail curled in on itself to create the loop.

"Yay! Hold it there!"

Three policemen ran forward, pistols aloft. One stopped as he reached the edge of the alley; the others continued briskly toward the tracks. Bill was reminded of the bayonet battalion making their rushes through City Park. Perl rotated his body, blocking the can opener from view. Bill raised his hands in the air. He backed away from Perl. The sky had turned the color of oyster flesh but Bill was able to recognize Guy Molony. Or rather he recognized Molony's scar, the purple stovepot extending across his cheek.

"It's me, Molony. Detective William Bastrop."

"Bill Bastrop?"

"Sir," said the other. "Is this man molesting you?"

"It's nothing, Officer." Bill realized that blood was leaking from a wound above his left eye. "A misunderstanding between old friends."

Perl, incredulous, glanced between Bill and the officers.

"What's in his hand?" asked Molony.

Bill began to respond and Perl interrupted. "William Bastrop is a disgrace to the New Orleans Police Department." His voice rose with each word. "He is a disgrace to America. He is a war criminal."

"Bill?"

"The man is crazy as a betsy bug. War-deranged."

"Bill, is that the man that shot Officer Breaux?"

Molony's men closed the distance. Bill held up his hand, as if to halt them, but it would've been easier to stop time.

Perl's voice became urgent, desperate. "I act in the name of Philip Finn!" He addressed neither the officers nor Bill but the night.

"Put your hands above your head!"

"I act for William Drain. I act for Elwood Rayburn. I act for John Legall, Jr."

The men continued to approach. They avoided sudden movements. More emerged from the lengthening shadows of the waterfront shantytown, their guns aimed at Perl. The sound of boots on gravel was as loud as a landslide. A fuzzy small white form trailed the men.

"Art Hegney," said Perl, addressing the stars. "Daniel Laughlin. Alf Helmer. Roscoe Washington."

"Put down your weapon!" shouted Molony.

"I act in the names of all eighteen men who died because of your cowardice at Rouge Bouquet."

Perl lunged, the crescent dagger of the Bully Beef can opener twisting toward Bill's eye. Bill threw his arm up in defense and the blade sliced his elbow. He felt a tear. He pushed Perl back, not hard, but enough to create separation between them. There was an explosion and Perl staggered to one knee. Bill pulled his arm back and saw that Perl's good eye was missing. A fusillade erupted. Perl tumbled backward. He landed at the edge of the boardwalk. His head, or what was left of it, snapped backward.

The next thing Bill saw was his wife in her white cotton dress running across the tracks. She hugged him and screamed his name and he couldn't tell if his face was wet from her tears or his tears or blood. He put one arm around her but the other was paralyzed with pain. He restrained a sob; he tried to trap it in himself. If it started to come out it would never stop and it would carry everything away with it. Maze buried her face in his neck. She repeated his name until it became part of a question and then the one question became two questions.

"Oh Billy, are you hurt? Is it true what he said? Oh Billy, are you all right? It's not true, is it? Say it's not true. Are you in pain? Billy? Oh God. Are you in pain?"

"It's true," Bill whispered into her neck. "Everything Leonard said is the truth."

Maze recoiled as if she were the one who had been shot.

PART TWO

TOWNS WITHIN TOWNS

New Orleans Times-Picayune, 8/6/18:

POLICE BELIEVE AX-MAN MAY BE ACTIVE IN CITY

Is an ax-man at large in New Orleans?

This belief was expressed by the police Monday night, following an investigation of the assault on Mrs. Edward Schneider, 28 years old, of 1820 Elmira street, early Monday morning.

Detectives found a hatchet in the yard adjoining the Schneider home. An ax, also stolen, cannot be found.

"Where is the ax?" the police are asking.

Considering it probable that Mrs. Schneider was attacked by the hatchetman who murdered Joseph Maggio and his wife and attempted to kill Louis Besemer and Mrs. Harriet Lowe, the police Monday night took every precaution to prevent a repetition of the bloody deeds.

New Orleans States, 8/7/18:

AXMAN THEORY DECLARED ABSURD

Recent Crimes Thought to Be Separate and Distinct

Certain situations affect different persons differently. It all depends on the temperament of a person. For instance, take the sensational stories that have appeared in certain newspapers during the past two days about "the ax man."

A detective, like any other mortal, is human. There are a dozen or more of these engaged in an effort to solve the recent attack made on Mrs. Edward Schneider in her home, 1820 Elmira street. She was struck on the head with a blunt instrument by an early morning intruder Monday. Mrs. Schneider is recovering from a scalp wound and the effects of childbirth in Charity Hospital.

Tuesday in a newspaper appeared a sensational story about the "ax man at large"—one of those thrilling things full of action and color. It stated that citizens were arming themselves and had determined upon all-night vigils, with shotguns, to protect their sleeping families. It stated that the entire community was terror-stricken and living in mortal fear, lest the beast in human form descend upon them.

VETERANS SCOUT THEORY

Older members of the force take no stock in the ax-man theory. They assert there is no such person as "the axman" going about committing these assaults. To liken the ax cases, such as the Maggio case, to the assault upon Mrs. Schneider, they assert, is ridiculous. The Schneider case is not without its peculiarities, however.

REMEMBER NOTHING

Mrs. Schneider recalls absolutely nothing of the assault.

After she emerged from under the influence of anesthetics at the Charity Hospital Tuesday afternoon, Superintendent Mooney questioned her.

"Struck? Oh no, I was not struck. Who said that anyone assaulted me?" Mrs. Schneider believed that the suffering she endured as a result of the attack was attributable to childbirth. Although hardly twelve hours had elapsed since the birth of her baby girl, Mrs. Schneider stated, in answer to a question from the superintendent, that her baby was four days old.

New Orleans States, 8/10/18:

ROBBER'S AX SLAYS MAN AS HE LIES ASLEEP

The fourth ax case within the year and the third person to lose his life as a result, occurred at 3 o'clock Saturday morning at Gravier and Tonti streets.

Joseph Romano, 30, living with his sister and nieces adjoining their little grocery store, was chopped across the left side of the head twice, his skull being fractured. He died in the Charity Hospital two hours later.

The butchery early Saturday morning is similar in many respects to the Maggio case, both as to the method employed by the murderer and the lay of the premises. There is now little doubt left in the minds of the police that the series of recent ax cases have robbery behind them as a motive.

New Orleans Times-Picayune, 9/21/18:

FRUIT STEAMER WITH INFLUENZA ABOARD ARRIVES

A United Fruit Company's steamer arrived at quarantine Thursday from Colón with a passenger list consisting of fifty civilians and fifty-one soldiers and a crew of eighty-six. There were eleven cases of influenza aboard, all soldiers. After a detention of twenty-four hours the steamer was permitted to come up to New Orleans to unload her perishable cargo of bananas, but no one was allowed to leave her, except the soldiers, who were placed in an ambulance. After it left the ship it was in collision in Tchoupitoulas street with a streetcar. One of the soldiers was badly injured, the others slightly.

New Orleans Times-Picayune, 9/29/18:

INFLUENZA GOES IN ORLEANS HOME TO GET VICTIM

The first death of a resident of New Orleans from influenza since the disease began spreading throughout the country was that of Morris William Maurier, age 16 years, of 5918 Coliseum street. There have been recent deaths from Spanish influenza in New Orleans, but they were of sailors from a merchant ship who developed the disease while on the high seas en route here.

New Orleans States, 9/30/18:

INFLUENZA CASES UP IN THOUSANDS

Situation Is Believed by Physicians to Be Under Control

New Orleans Times-Picayune, 10/10/18:

ALL SHOWS, CHURCHES ARE ORDERED CLOSED TO FIGHT EPIDEMIC CASES IN THE STATE TOTAL 100,000

State and City Health Board Heads May Take More Drastic Steps

Spanish influenza continued its alarming spread in New Orleans and throughout Louisiana Wednesday, while state and city health authorities took drastic steps to combat the epidemic. Here is the situation in New Orleans at a glance:

All schools, public, private and parochial, and all colleges closed.

All motion picture and other theaters closed.

All churches closed.

All public meetings, concerts, and sporting events called off.

Public weddings and public funerals ordered discontinued.

Gathering of crowds in the streets, stopped.
Burial of influenza victims, prompt.
Crowding of streetcars ordered stopped.
Closing of saloons, poolrooms, ice cream and soft drink places considered.

New Orleans Times-Picayune, 11/17/18:

SPANISH INFLUENZA TAKES HEAVY TOLL

Louisiana Had Approximately 350,000 Cases, Say Reports

New Orleans Item, 1/21/19:

TRIAL OF KILLER OF OBITZ IS POSTPONED

Luzenberg Asks Case Go Over Because of Flu

When the case of Frank Bailey, 19, negro, charged with the murder of Detective Theodore Obitz was called Tuesday morning in Judge Baker's section of the criminal district court, District Attorney Luzenberg asked the court to postpone the trial for a few weeks because of the influenza situation in the city.

New Orleans Times-Picayune, 2/10/19:

INFLUENZA ABATES SLIGHTLY

Eight New Cases Reported by City in Week

New Orleans Times-Picayune, 2/27/19:

DOCK BOARD SELLS NEW SIX MILLION BOND ISSUE

Expenditure Will Permit New Orleans to Complete the Industrial Canal

A $6,000,000 bond issue to be used in completing the Industrial Canal was authorized Wednesday night by unanimous vote of the members of the Board of Port Commissioners.

The board also voted to sell the bonds immediately by private sale, offered by the Hibernia Bank and Trust Company.

This bond issue of $6,000,000 is in addition to the $6,000,000 of bonds recently issued to finance the Industrial Canal.

"We are constructing a great waterway system which will take the lid off the development of New Orleans," said President Thompson of the Dock Board. "With the canal, New Orleans can become one of the great manufacturing cities of the United States and one of the greatest world ports; without, we must content ourselves with a position of mediocrity and a reputation for incapacity."

Mr. Thompson reviewed the history of the canal project from its inception, characterizing those who had opposed it as "a small minority of moss-backs, doubting Thomases and selfish private interests." He charged that the former bond terms had caused "vicious and spectacular" attacks by hostile private interests. Revised costs estimates convinced the members of the board, said he, that the original $6,000,000 would not be adequate for the work. He stated that material benefits from the canal have already accrued to the city, employing thousands of men at the site. However, said Mr. Thompson, illustrating the need of additional funds, the people of New Orleans cannot expect a "gusher" if they insist upon "boring with a gimlet."

MARCH 1, 1919—THE INDUSTRIAL CANAL—UPTOWN—SEVENTH WARD

They found the body in the canal. It made no sense. The corpse was buried twenty-five feet underground. But it wasn't a skeleton. The man was barely dead.

They were alerted by the choking of the Texas. The body—the pelvic bone, to be precise—caught in the teeth of the dredge. From a forensic perspective, it was a miracle. Though the machine had digested the lower body, everything above the pelvis remained intact. The diggers found this half of the body dangling upside down from the teeth of the dredge like a mouse from a cat's mouth. The coroner sent four men from his body squad to the scene. They pried what they could out of the teeth and covered it to the neck with a blanket. Bill noticed that the man's mouth was stretched open. He had seen that before, in the Forest of Purroy. It meant the man died screaming.

"Don't figure," said Charlie, shaking his head. Since the July 4 shooting he had developed a strange way of shaking his head: using both hands, he rotated the cranium, as if trying gingerly to crack his neck. Bill couldn't tell whether this was an affectation or the result of nerve damage but he didn't want to ask in case Charlie was unaware of it.

They stood on the rim of the canal, which was more like a canyon. The body squad had erected four stakes around the corpse. The laborers, just a few yards away, had resumed their digging. There was no thought of taking a break. The dig had fallen far behind and Hercules couldn't find enough able-bodied men. The conditions were unwholesome, hospitable to the plague, the mud attracting mosquitoes, blackflies, chiggers, opossums, rats—scourges that only multiplied when the project's scope was doubled to accommodate the larger ships built since the war began. The deepening of the canal forced the diggers to go back over their tracks. That's when they found the body.

Bill realized that his partner had been staring at him for a long time. Charlie had been speaking too, but Bill hadn't heard any words.

"You shaking?" asked Charlie.

Bill looked down at his arms, his legs. He was as still as the corpse.

"I'll admit it. I'm shaken myself."

Bill caught the meaning. No, he wasn't shaken. One more corpse meant nothing to him but more footwork, more questioning, more reports. If it turned out to be a homicide, as seemed likely, they would find the murderer or they wouldn't. What difference did it make? Another corpse would appear the next day, or the next week. And so on. After Maze left, days, weeks merged. He wondered whether this was what immortality would feel like. As you rounded your first centenary and approached your second, your loved ones long dead, your interests curdled, novelty impossible, what could happen that had not already happened many times before? Ten, twenty, thirty decades in: at a great enough distance, all terrestrial concerns squiggled over the horizon. All, that is, but loss. Loss couldn't escape beyond the horizon. It was the horizon.

Charlie put a clumsy hand to Bill's forehead. "You don't feel hot."

"Tired." Bill shook him off.

"Ever try sleeping?"

Bill did not know whether the fatigue had begun the day in October when Maze finally quit her job and her parents took her across the lake to their camp in Abita Springs, ostensibly to hide out from the influenza, or on July 4, the night Leonard Perl died. Or perhaps it began when he had seen Perl in the grandstand at the Pelicans game. Or beneath the Forest of Purroy.

"A laborer." Charlie waved at a dive-bombing mosquito. "Guy gets tired—like you—and he falls down during the dig. No one sees. Mud falls on top."

"He don't look like a laborer." The corpse was white. None of the diggers were white.

"He gets preserved in the mud. Like one of those monsters they find buried in ice at the North Pole."

The body squad had borrowed tools from the diggers: pickaxes, a trenching shovel, a bucket of water that they poured over the torn flesh to loosen the soil.

"Why would anyone bury a man so deep?" said Charlie. "People would anyway notice a man digging a twenty-five-foot ditch."

Bill had nothing to add. What detective instincts he once possessed had been siphoned by his investigation into the only mystery that still mattered to him: When had Maze decided to leave? The night of Perl's death? He didn't think so. She stayed another three months. They spoke most of that time—or at least she spoke, asking questions. He wanted to answer. But he couldn't think of an answer that would reveal him as anything but a coward. *I thought there might have been a flash of manhood in you. But you don't have any fight and you probably never did.*

He searched his memory for clues, behavior that might seem suspicious in retrospect. But he found no hard evidence, only circumstantial fact: the evaporation of sexual desire, which began shortly after his return from Europe; an awkward, silent supper on the night of his birthday in April, heavy with unspoken accusation; a subtle but persistent decline in the tidiness of the home. Perl's death marked a turning point, and by October neither of them could take it anymore. They must have been the only two people in New Orleans relieved by the outbreak of the Spanish Death. It gave Maze's parents an excuse to quarantine her across the lake, where they could nourish their vital humors with springwater, fresh air, and ample ventilation. He had not seen her since, apart from a single disastrous visit in January. He had often tried to determine when everything had turned between them but maybe that was the wrong question. A better question: When had everything turned inside him? Turned from strong to weak, brave to craven, alive to . . . whatever this was.

A man on the body squad waved up at them, trying to get their attention.

"I don't see why we bother," said Bill.

"The stink ain going to mellow with time," said Charlie.

A ladder leaned against the lip of the artificial cavern. Bill let Charlie go first. Since the hospital, Charlie moved slower; he had lost some coordination and had gained weight. The buttered beans and fried chicken served in the Charity commissary, combined with a month of bed rest, had contributed about ten pounds, but since his release the weight gain had accelerated. His appetite, always healthy, had become violent, as if he were desperately trying to fill the hole that the bullet had made. Bill didn't want to be beneath him.

But the ladder barely creaked, and Bill followed. He had descended only a few rungs when the smell swaddled him. Sour, ripe, thick, it sought out his eyes and the back of his throat. He paused halfway down, blinking. "Hell."

"That ain the body," said Charlie. "It's the mud."

Bill knew how mud smelled. Every New Orleanian did. After a rain the sewer gates clotted with it and the streets caked like the floor of a dried lake. But this was a different mud. Its stench was like a protest. The mud was outraged, violated by exposure to fresh air after hiding underground for millennia.

One of the coroner's men pulled back the sheet. The corpse wore a torn undershirt through which bloodstains bloomed like roses from the stomach, heart, and shoulder. A whitish organ of some kind, a shrinking sea anemone exposed from beneath an overturned rock, oozed from a laceration in the neck. The pink nub of a cracked rib protruded from the chest. Blackflies danced on the skin, crawled, fed. The eyes were still obscured though Bill could tell from the position of the eyelashes that they were open. The body man tried to shut the jaw but it had hardened stiff.

"I'm not fixing to break it," said the man. He had rubber plugs stuck in his nostrils. Bill asked if he had extras.

The body man nodded toward a sack on the ground. "I'd get 'em for you but—" He held up his hands; they were stained with blood and mud and worse.

"Nah," said Charlie, when Bill offered him a pair. "I'm used to it already."

Bill removed his jacket, rolled up his cuffs. He didn't mind touching corpses but couldn't afford to ruin his shirt. He wasn't much for laundering since Maze left.

"Looks like an Albanian," said Charlie. "Has the nose at least."

"I wouldn't assume the nose always looked like that." Bill felt inside the mouth. The tongue was a dead salamander. The gums were dry, tacky. He found a few loose teeth enclosed in clods of mud.

"Maybe a Arab," offered one of the body men.

"Anyone check the pockets?" asked Bill.

"Eighty-three cents. A pair of spectacles, shattered. A notepad, blank. A timepiece, ticking."

"Cute."

The man spat.

"Cause?"

"Cain say until the autopsy. But looks like death by sharp object."

"You don't need to be a coroner to figure that." Purplish streaks had begun to form on the fleshy mass oozing from the neck.

"You don't think—?"

"Not necessarily," said Bill. "Could be a knife."

"A big damn knife."

"Or the teeth of that thing. The dredge."

"That's what the diggers seem to think."

The machine slumped fifteen yards distant. It was still but its open mouth, crowded with sharp blades, gave it a grinning, predatory aspect, as if it were hungry for its next snack.

"The diggers are superstitious," said the body man.

"They think it's alive?" asked Charlie.

"They don't think it's alive. But they don't think it's dead."

Bill considered this.

"Probably an ax," Charlie concluded.

"Copycat?" said the body man.

Charlie pulled Bill aside.

"Mooney isn't going to want to hear about this," said Bill.

"Maybe not," said Charlie. "But we better start asking questions."

"The diggers won't know a thing."

Charlie looked at Bill blankly. "Why do I hafta keep explaining our job to you?"

Bill wasn't ready to climb out of the canal. He wanted to look again at the corpse. Its eyes, specifically.

"Can you clear the mud off his face?"

The lead body man signaled to one of the others for the bucket. He poured what was left of the water over the head while another man brushed the corpse's cheeks and nose. The mud flowed off. The eyes were open. They stared at Bill.

"He's not Albanian," he said.

"Dago?"

"I'd wager."

"C'mon, Billy. Let's get."

Something itched at him. He thought it was the mud-clotted eyes, but that didn't scratch it. He tried to remember the last time he did any police work beyond the exact minimum. Not since the Besemer attack; maybe as long ago as the highwayman case. "His pockets."

The evidence bag was produced. There were the coins; eyeglasses, which not only had smashed lenses but bent frames, as if stepped upon; gum wrapper; notepad.

"Forgot about the gum wrapper."

"Don't worry about it." They had overlooked something more important. The notepad wasn't blank, not exactly. There was no handwriting but each page was embossed with the words ROSETTA'S GROCERY CO., 3241 COLISEUM ST. in light brown ink. Bill showed it to Charlie.

"Hell."

"Thirty-two forty-one," said Bill. "Where's that?"

"Below Louisiana. Toledano about. You think he lived by there?"

"I don't think he lived near the grocery. I think he lived in it."

Charlie shook his head. "What now?"

"Do I have to explain our job to you?"

"There's Detective Bastrop." Charlie slapped Bill's back. "I thought I'd lost him."

Bill didn't smile but he thought about smiling, which was something. He turned to the body men and pointed at his nostrils. "Mind if I keep these?"

In all but a single aspect did Rosetta's resemble exactly every other Uptown corner grocery. Here was the chamfered corner, the porticoed doorway, the deep basins of olives, swimming in their blackish juices, all but blocking the entrance, and the rectangular side window filled with hanging salami, bronze cans of mustard, stacked anchovy tins. The name of the previous owner was visible under the single layer of paint slathered above the entrance. Inside, preserved vegetables floated like apothecary specimens in glass jars behind the counter and tubs of sweetly fragrant, fresh produce lined the wall. Charlie was immediately distracted by a pallet from a California farm containing white figs, black Mission figs, brown turkeys.

"A new shipment came today," said a salesboy, approaching from the recesses of the stockroom, with its wine-stained kegs of zinfandel, Chablis, and sauterne, on sale for twenty-five cents a fifth.

"Where's the grocer?" said Bill.

The boy puffed up. "I'm the grocer."

Bill looked at Charlie, but he was fixated on the figs. "There an officers' discount?"

Bill interrupted before the boy could respond. He thrust in the boy's face the notepad with the grocery's name. "Where do you keep these?"

"Right here." The boy grinned sheepishly. "Behind the counter."

"Show me," said Bill.

When the boy turned, Charlie crammed a fistful of brown turkeys into his mouth.

Only in one way did Rosetta's Grocery not resemble any other corner grocery: there was no grocer. Sometimes a grocer took on a stock boy, usually a son or a nephew, but no grocer in New Orleans would leave the operation and protection of a store to a child. The boy couldn't have been more than twelve years old.

"Who do you give the notebooks to?"

"Why are you asking me?"

"Good point. Where is Mr. Rosetta?"

The boy's tone turned formal, practiced. "Mr. Rosetta left on a trip, sir. Family emergency. It's not known when he'll be back."

"Not known. And Mrs. Rosetta?"

"She's with him."

"You don't say."

"Trouble back home."

"Where's home?"

"Contessa Entellina."

"What's that?"

"It's in Sicily."

"Since when did they go back there?"

"Since when do I answer your questions? You want to buy something or nay?" The boy glanced at Charlie. "Sir? You owe me for four figs. That's eight cents."

Bill flipped the boy a dime. "Rosetta said he was taking a trip? Or he just left?"

The boy took the dime to the register. He pulled the lever, the change drawer clanged open, and he removed two pennies.

"I got nothing left to tell you, sir." The child smacked the pennies on the counter. "Gentlemen? I have a business to run."

No one in the neighborhood seemed to know the kid's name or how long he had been running the store. Old men feigned senility; old women crossed themselves or claimed incomprehension of English. A young man three doors down just smiled idiotically.

"I have nothing for you."

"You shop at Rosetta's?"

He smiled some more. "What's Rosetta's?"

This behavior was familiar. During the summer a source reported that the grocer Arthur Recknagel had his ax stolen from his yard. When an investigator called, Recknagel claimed he never owned an ax and could not explain why a panel was missing from his back door. Another grocer, Joseph LeBoeuf, called for police when he was awoken at night by a man chiseling a panel in the back door of *his* grocery. He told the beat officer that the suspect was tall, with a heavy build. But the next day, when Superintendent Mooney himself visited, LeBoeuf described the intruder as short, with a medium built. A couple of Negroes were arrested but after enthusiastic interrogations they were released.

It did not take a professional to see the similarities between the Recknagel and LeBoeuf cases and the attack on the Besemer couple. Or the earlier Maggio case, in which a grocer and his wife had their throats opened by an ax. More confusing was the August attack on poor pregnant Mary Schneider. Her sister found her bashed over the head with her own bedside lamp. Four teeth lay on the floor and a laceration traced the length of her scalp. As soon as she regained consciousness, she went into labor. There appeared to be no grocery connection. Schneider's husband, who was not home at the time of the attack, was a downtown businessman. The crime seemed to be a burglary: seven dollars were taken from Mrs. Schneider's wardrobe. But when Mr. Schneider searched his backyard, he discovered that his ax was missing.

The journalists got carried away. The *Times-Picayune* claimed an "ax-man" was on the prowl. The *States* ran an item mocking "sensational stories in other newspapers about the 'ax man at large,'" but it was too late. By linking the crimes, and giving a name to the bogeyman, the *States* had legitimized the story. The "Axman" was born.

Once born, he went to work. Five days after the Schneider attack, as if summoned by public anxiety, he struck again. Two teenage sisters awoke at 3:00 a.m. on a Saturday to the dying groans of their uncle, Joseph Romano. An intruder—"tall, heavy-set"—stood in their doorway, body heaving, watching the children. The girls shrieked and he ran away, but only after dropping an ax on the kitchen floor.

The Romano, Recknagel, and LeBoeuf groceries stood within seven blocks of each other. Two were in Bill's district. But Mooney, citing the public's ungovernable panic, announced that he would investigate the attacks himself. It was typical Mooney. The Axman had, after all, become the biggest story in New Orleans—not even the final throes of the European war or the excavation of the Industrial Canal could compete. Mayor Behrman was in his fourth term and would be vulnerable in 1920. Some of the navies gossiped that Mooney was positioning himself to replace his boss but Bill didn't believe it until he read what Mooney told reporters after the Romano killing.

"I am of the belief," said Mooney, "that the murderer is a depraved criminal, a madman with no regard for human life."

It wasn't how a navy talked. It was how a politician talked.

Bill could only watch Mooney investigate the case from afar, like the rest of New Orleans. It didn't particularly bother Bill. Since Leonard Perl's death he had experienced everything from afar—his job, his marriage, his life. Everything was easier from afar.

Mooney's speech achieved the desired effect: pandemonium. The epicenter of the paranoia was Bill's back-of-town district. A night after the Romano murder, a teenager on White Street claimed she saw the Axman in her backyard as she was going to bed. Navies swarming the neighborhood found no suspect, though an old pensioner, boiled on home brew, and a blind carpenter both claimed that the Axman had escaped through their backyards. Nevertheless Superintendent Mooney declared he was "certain" it was the Axman. "He was probably going back to the stable," he told a reporter, "to find an ax."

As August melted into September there came reports of a female Axman, a cross-dressing Axman, and countless Negro Axmen. The weakness of Mooney's strategy became conspicuous. Every public declaration only reminded terrified citizens that the Axman remained uncaptured. "We are going to get him," Mooney insisted. "If only we could make our plans known, the public would appreciate what we are doing to bring to an end this series of ax cases." He made dozens of arrests, mostly Negroes. None stuck. As the panic rose, shame yielded to ridicule. Advertisements began to appear in the *Item*:

Attention Mr. Mooney, and All Citizens of New Orleans!

THE AXMAN

Will Appear in This City on Saturday, August 24th

AT THE FOLLOWING PLACES:

No. 420 South Rampart Street

No. 4326 Magazine Street

No. 1936 Magazine Street, Cor. St. Andrew

He will ruthlessly use the "Piggly Wiggly" ax in cutting off the heads of all High-Priced Groceries. His weapon is wonderful, and his system is unique.

DON'T MISS SEEING HIM!

There were no attacks for a month, which only heightened the anxiety. Men stood guard with rifles on their doorsteps. Parents forbade children from going outside after dark. Children taunted each other with nursery rhymes:

Cross your hands and tie your shoes
The Axman is coming for you

Say your prayers and cross your chest
The Axman likes young ones the best

Brush your teeth and count your sheep
The Axman knows where you sleep

Cross your hands and tie your shoes
The Axman will chop your head in two

On September 15, a grocer at North Robertson and Marigny Streets named Paul Durel, Jr., awoke to discover that the oblong panel on his back door had been chiseled out. The intruder reached through, trying to turn the key, only to be denied by a pallet of canned tomatoes piled against the door.

"It undoubtedly was the Axman," Superintendent Mooney told the *Times-Picayune*. "His method of work was the same as in the Maggio, the LeBoeuf, and the other cases."

The hysteria might have continued unabated were it not for the arrival of the SS *Harold Walker.* Four crew members were brought off in an ambulance, which collided with a streetcar; the passengers of both vehicles were tossed together on the pavement. The Sick was out. Dozens fell ill the following week and local quarantines failed to arrest the disease's galloping spread. The city was immersed in a panic far more intimate, and deadly, than that caused by the Axman's grocery raids. Maze moved across the lake.

In November, Superintendent Mooney quietly paused the Axman investigation. Mayor Behrman charged him with enforcing quarantines, quelling public protests, and monitoring streetcars to make sure they did not overcrowd. Cops were granted paid furloughs. Bill did not accept one. In his mind the flu took the shape of Leonard Perl's sneering grin. He knew it was only a matter of days, perhaps weeks, before it found him. He welcomed it. Maze would mourn, perhaps, but her grief would give way to relief. And Perl's dying prayer would be answered.

Bill volunteered for extra shifts. He accepted a posting at Charity Hospital, which had dedicated seventeen of its wards to the influenza. But as the months passed and he failed to contract so much as a cough, he realized that the Spanish Death had played on him a trick crueler than death. It spared him. It forced him to live.

If anyone gave a thought to the Axman during the six months that followed the arrival of the Plague Ship, it was only to recall in a spirit of nostalgia that innocent time when a single man, and not a shapeless vast silent plague, could terrorize an entire city. For the Axman had vanished. He had either fled New Orleans or, more likely, been claimed by the Spanish Death. What other explanation could there be?

"If that kid been working two months by himself," said Charlie, after they left the grocery, "why ain he been ripped off yet?"

"Funny, don't you think?" Bill figured that Charlie, even in his compromised state, would be able to put it together.

"I'd speculate someone else is running the business." One of Charlie's hands rested absentmindedly on his stomach.

"I'd speculate you're right."

"We should go to the office and study Mooney's Axman files."

Bill shrugged. He was thinking of Maze in Abita Springs. Was she still hiding inside, avoiding the vapors? Had she grown tired of her parents? Did she speak to strangers? He tried to imagine her life but it came out blurry.

"What don't pay," said Charlie, "is the fact that the body ain barely decomposed."

"It does not pay."

"But the Axman ain even tried to break into a grocery since October—let alone commit a homicide."

"Maybe one of those things isn't true."

Charlie took his head in both hands and rotated it from one side to the other. "I still don't see how a man could find himself buried that deep underground."

The kid dragged the olive basins inside Rosetta's Grocery. He hung a signboard on the doornail: CLOSED.

As they walked back to the station, Bill kept returning to the image of the body in the canal, its mouth filled with mud. What would it feel like to be buried so far underground? What did the men at Rouge Bouquet feel? Would you feel as if you were being crushed? Or would it feel cozy, like being tucked into a well-made bed?

Charlie rotated his head again. "A thing buried that far underground," he said, "don't want to get found."

MARCH 2, 1919—THE BATTLEFIELD—THE GRUNEWALD HOTEL

"Playing for the whores again?"

"I haven't played the cribs for years." Isadore tried to keep his voice level. "I play respected joints."

Miss Daisy snorted. It had never been easy to be alone with his mother-in-law but Orly's advancing condition had made it worse. Every conversation had a way of finding a tributary back to the main conversation.

"I don't know how a man that plays concerts at night can help take care of a newborn child." There it was—even faster than usual. The interval was narrowing. The interval correlated inversely to the size of Orly's stomach. He wanted to say, *Would you prefer I go back to robbing people at gunpoint on the street?* But he could only say what he always said.

"I'll stop once the baby is born." He expected he'd say it about three hundred more times in the next month. "I figure we better save as much money as we can before then."

Daisy snorted.

"In fact," he said, unable to resist, "I'm playing a luxury venue this very evening."

"Luxury? What's that supposed to mean? *White?*" She said it as if she were putting on airs.

"It means the Grunewald Hotel."

Daisy sat in the creaky rocker in which she spent most of her days. It was set by the window so that she could keep an eye on the street. She only rose from the chair to use the privy, to go down the block to St. Augustine, or to refill with holy water the spirit glasses, one on every flat surface in the apartment. For the first time she turned to face him. "They pay more?"

1@
NEWS
1@ 9
LONELY PLA
1@ 2.50 NE
NEWSPAPERS
@ 3.00 NEWS
SPAPERS
S 0.10 B
Bag Fee
GRAND

TENDER:
Cc XXXXXXXXXXX 16
TOTAL TENDER 16.5

CHANGE $0.00

TYPE: Credit
CARD: VISA
ENTRY: MANUAL
TRAN ID: 83055128
APPROVAL CODE: 006835

Shop online at www.booktable.net. Returns within 10 days with a receipt. Gift receipts valid 30 days with a receipt for credit and exchanges only. All sales final on special orders. No returns on opened shrinkwrapped items or clearance items.

Please visit us at www.booktable.net

00604205

CUSTOMER COPY

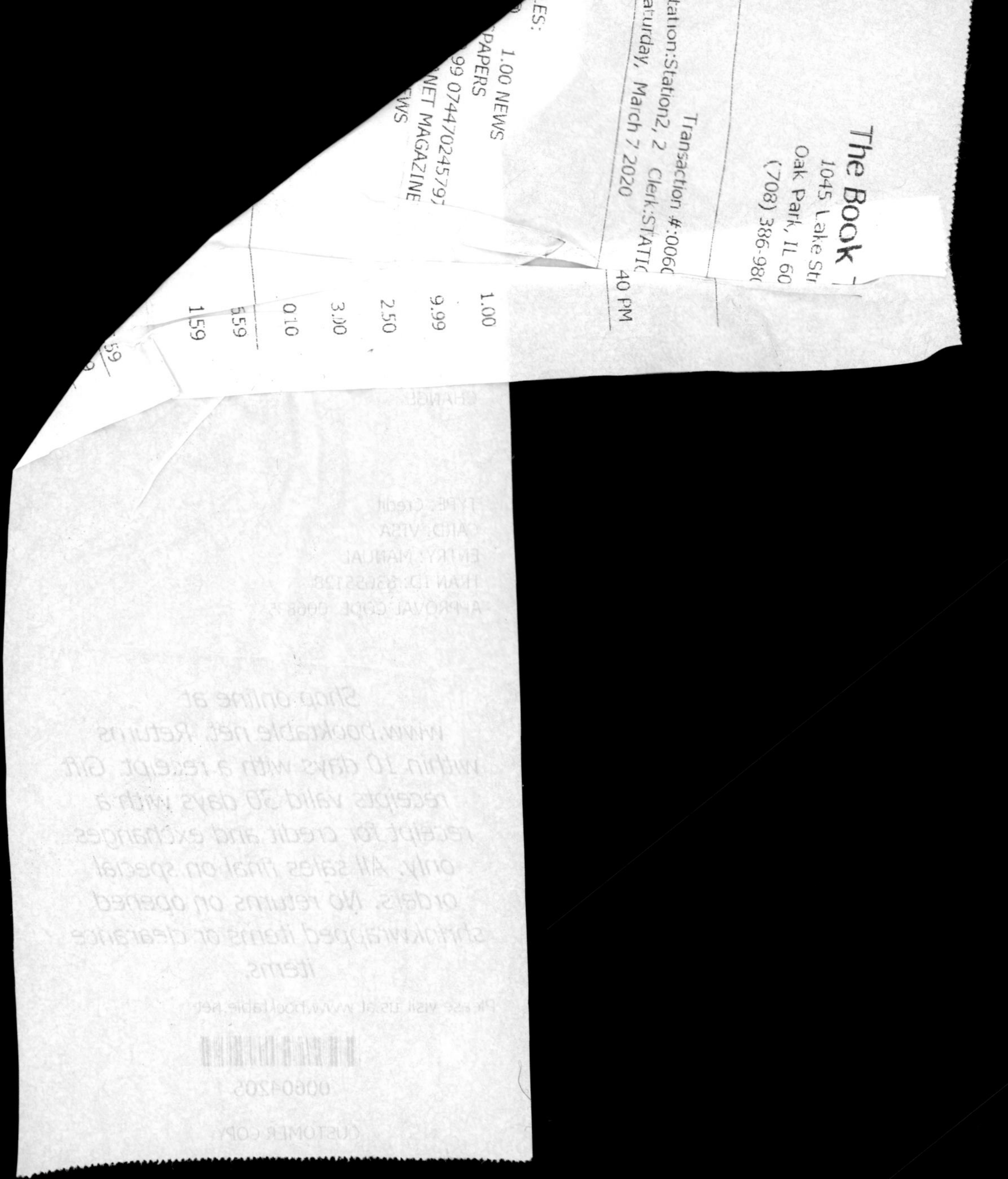
The Book
1045 Lake Str
Oak Park, IL 60
(708) 386-98
Transaction #:006
tation:Station2, 2 Clerk:STATI
aturday, March 7 2020
40 PM
1.00 NEWS
PAPERS
1.00
99 07447024579
NET MAGAZINE
9.99
2.50
3.00
0.10
5.59
1.59

"Yes, ma'am." He broke away from her gaze so she couldn't see that he was lying. Daisy might be half-blind but she knew him as well as anybody, after Orly. She was roommate, mother-in-law, and adopted mother all in one. Between them had grown a casual intimacy made of equal parts comfort, familiarity, love, irritation, and rage. Still she didn't understand his heart—she couldn't. A person who believed so fervently in the hereafter couldn't understand the desire to make something that would live forever.

"You think jassy music is going to impress the toits at Hotel Grunewald?" she said. "I know that's a lie and I haven't left this room since the war."

"The Civil War."

Isadore knew better than to push it further. He knew also that she was right. Nobody cared about jazz, as they were now calling it, outside of a small group of people in the back of town. But if jazz had no future in New Orleans, Isadore had no future in New Orleans. This was a problem because he would not go North or West; he couldn't bring himself to betray Orly and Miss Daisy. Beneath his mother-in-law's irritation was a more profound grievance that, despite her volubility and general lack of inhibition, she had never put into words. Isadore was in danger of defaulting on their unspoken agreement. If it weren't for Orly—if it weren't for Daisy—he would've had to fend for himself after leaving the Waifs' Home. He'd have been no different from Frank Bailey, cast into the streets with only his wits for armor. In exchange for adopting Isadore, and allowing him to marry Orly, Daisy made it understood that Isadore would support the three of them, plus any children that might follow. Apart from signing the marriage license, Isadore had not kept up his end of the bargain. They were already two months behind on rent and could be cast out at any time. It was her greatest terror, the prospect of becoming, as Isadore had once been, a ward of the state.

Isadore shut his cornet case and slipped into his jacket. He was half out the door when he was caught short by Daisy's voice. It was too loud, too urgent, and he felt his stomach turn even before he could understand the meaning of the words.

"Do you believe in the redeeming power of art?"

She stood shakily, leaning on the bedpost for support. Her cataract-clouded eyes searched for his through the gloom. "Do you believe in the redeeming power of art? Do you believe music will bring eternal life?"

Isadore froze. "Times are turning, Mama," he said at last. "You're going to see."

Daisy snorted. "Times change," she said. "People don't."

Isadore had never been inside a cave. He'd never even been underground, unless you counted the Industrial Canal. But beneath the lobby of the Grunewald, he found himself dodging stalagmites and stalactites—he couldn't remember which was which, but both were represented. The walls and ceilings appeared to have been slathered with melting vanilla ice cream. In recesses spaced along the wall stood pools fed by iridescent waterfalls, trickling at the rate of snowmelt. Plaster naiads dipped their toes in the water, gazing pensively into distant eternities. The air was dank, chill, poorly ventilated: ideal conditions for the Spanish Death. In a central pond, ringed with bright green ferns, a reclining nymph, her posterior arching out of the water, cast an inviting look over her shoulder. Isadore looked away out of instinct and told himself it was only a sculpture but still he didn't look back. He could feel the weight of Mr. Stumpf's gaze resting on him.

"I suspect you're the Creole musician." Stumpf had emerged from behind an elf. He was as Zutty had described: short, pink, bow-tied, a voice two octaves too high. "Zutty says you can read music."

"Sir, I can play anything." He was proud of this answer. It was important to display confidence, to prove he belonged.

According to Zutty, Stumpf paid a dollar to fill-ins, less even than what Countess Piazza paid at the Octoroon, but that was beside the point. If he earned Stumpf's respect, he might win a gig for the Slim Izzy Quartet. Stumpf regularly featured Johnny DeDroit's band. They were white and wore tuxedos but they did play something approximating jazz. Stumpf even gave a show to Armand Piron's New Orleans Orchestra, the highest-paid Creole group in town, though they stuck to ragtime when they played the Cave. It was close enough. The Cave was the most advanced of the white venues. Mr. Stumpf didn't look the part—he looked more like the red-haired watchman outside the Tiltons' house—but he had hired Isadore, after all. He was open to change.

"You won't need that," said Stumpf, registering Isadore's cornet case.

Isadore did not understand but he was not going to leave his cornet on the floor. He followed Stumpf, weaving around the nightclub's glass-topped tables, and narrowly avoided tripping on a melting ice castle. Two waiters in the back, folding linen napkins into scallop shells, avoided Isadore's eye. The cornet was a dead animal in his arms. What had Zutty told Stumpf? He could handle trumpet or trombone, but what if he was asked to play clarinet, or standing bass? What if Stumpf sat him at a piano? Did Stumpf not know that he was one of the best cornet players in New Orleans?

They mounted the bandstand, garlanded with ferns and rocky plinths and gnomes, and passed through to the practice room. Three white men with stubble-darkened cheeks sat around a small table, playing cards. A fourth lay facedown on the floor.

"What's with him?" asked Stumpf.

The cardplayers glanced up balefully.

Stumpf's voice became strained. "Does he have a fever?"

"He's all right, boss. Still gassed from last night. He'll be ready."

Stumpf seemed unconvinced. "This here's Izzy. Izzy, this is the Hans Marble Quintet." He read Isadore's confusion. "What, didn't Zutty give you the details?"

"No, sir. He just told me when to show up."

One of the cardplayers stood and extended his hand. "Hans Marble." He had a small tidy mouth and brilliantined dark hair that reflected light. Isadore hesitated, thinking of the waiters setting the tables. But he wasn't a waiter. He was a musician. He was an artist, like them. He shook the man's hand.

"You got an hour before first supper service," said Stumpf. "So start studying."

"It won't take but a minute," said Marble, once Stumpf was gone. He appraised Isadore's cornet case. "You a jasser or something?"

"That's right."

"We don't play anything that complected. Only simple stuff. Tunes so old they got whiskers."

Isadore forced a smile. His stomach went sour.

"Some light rag, some show tunes. 'By the Light of the Silvery Moon.' 'At the Darktown Strutters' Ball.' 'Hello, Frisco!' "

Isadore tried to hide his disappointment. Though *disappointment* was a gentle word for it. *Despair* was more like it.

"It's an easy gig," said Marble. "You can split the tips."

One of the cardplayers glanced up from his hand.

"It's only fair," said Marble.

Frowning, the musician resumed studying his cards.

"Mr. Stumpf said something about not needing my cornet."

"He's right. That's all you'll need." Marble pointed to the card table, which Isadore now realized was a bass drum laid on its side.

"I never really played percussion," he heard himself say.

"Can you keep a tempo?"

Isadore nodded. He felt as if he might be sick.

"That's all we need. A nice, easy tempo."

The man on the floor groaned.

"Don't go too close to him," said Marble. "He's suffering an ague fit. Just look at his tongue. Or don't, actually."

For the next four hours Isadore sat at the back of the bandstand, in the shadow of a plaster grotto, beside a petrified mermaid, tapping a 4/4 beat. Each beat was a tap on his shoulder, telling him that his time as a professional musician was running out. The audience seemed largely oblivious of the Hans Marble Quintet, but there wasn't much audience, mostly drunks mistaking the plaster nymphs for former wives—it was Sunday, after all, and who wanted to be in the dank Cave when the influenza was about? The bassist, the one with the fever, retreated backstage halfway through the set, but nobody, onstage or off, seemed to notice. So much for jazz. So much for impressing Mr. Stumpf. So much for the Cave. So much for New Orleans. For all the bluster about its sophistication and grandeur—"the American Paris," "the Metropolis of the South," and poised, upon completion of the Industrial Canal, to be a "city of the future"—there was no escaping that it was run by water-brained bureaucrats and unreconstructed bigots who couldn't make it in St. Louis or Cincinnati, let alone New York City. What did it say that King Oliver had to supplement his income by working as a butler in the Garden District, before the shame forced him to flee for Chicago? That Buddy Bolden was locked away at the State Insane Asylum? The kings knew New Orleans was dead. To believe otherwise, that it was possible to nurse a fledgling career in this misbegotten music, was delusional coming on insane.

Hans Marble was singing "Something Seems Tingle-Ingling." The sourness in Isadore's stomach had spread into his brain. He couldn't pinpoint exactly when it happened—certainly by the end of the evening, before he received his dollar plus twenty-one cents in tips—but at some point during the concert it hit him as strongly as it ever had, the undeniable knowledge that he was floating through life in steerage.

When he went backstage after the show to retrieve his cornet—maybe the pawn would give him a deal, if it wasn't already flush with abandoned instruments—he found the bassist on hands and knees, vomiting blood.

MARCH 3, 1919—THE GARDEN DISTRICT

During those lost months, as her suspicion hardened into grim knowledge, Beatrice kept returning to the story of Bobby Dunbar.

The four-year-old was last seen on a family fishing trip to Swayze Lake of about fifteen people—Bobby's parents and younger brother, aunts and uncles, cousins and friends. Around noon, the women were busy tidying up the cabin and preparing for dinner; the men had just returned from fishing. When Lessie, Bobby's mother, emerged from the kitchen with a platter of trout, she knew something was wrong.

"Who is left at the shore?" she asked.

"No one," said the men.

The platter fell to the gravel, breaking into shards. Several of the men followed Lessie, screaming Bobby's name, as she ran to the lake. When they returned to the cabin and Bobby was still missing, she collapsed to the ground.

Three men ran to the wagon trail. Bobby's father, Percy, had earlier set off for the family farm in Opelousas, summoned by a messenger to notarize a business deal. Perhaps Bobby had followed his father? The men caught up to Percy. He sat astride his horse: the farm was not a half day's journey but Percy had a cork leg and used the horse when possible. The men explained that Bobby was missing. Percy galloped back to the camp, kicking the horse hard with his cork leg.

Percy jumped from the horse and ran in his troubled fashion past his prostrate wife through the canebrake. At the lake Percy crawled on hands and knees through the brambles, his cork leg dragging a rut through the mud.

A whoop came from the wagon road. The men had discovered small prints in the dirt. Lessie came to her senses long enough to locate a pair of Bobby's sandals and place them beside the footprints. That they matched she was certain. The party followed the footprints down an incline, across a railroad track, and over an embankment, where they vanished. It was as if the boy had jumped into the sky and floated away.

The search lasted days, joined by hundreds of volunteers. The local fire department dynamited the lake but the only body that rose to the surface was the bloated carcass of a drowned deer. They dragged the lake bed and searched the reed-clogged coves. They shot and disembowled alligators. The dragnet widened to a radius of eight miles. They found no trace of Bobby Dunbar.

Percy set out across the South, searching flophouses, dive bars, and drugstores. He stayed a week in New Orleans.

Beatrice had read in the papers about Percy Dunbar's search for his son but forgot the story until the following spring, when a boy matching Bobby's description was located. His guardian was a poor piano tuner named Walters in Poplarville, Mississippi, seventy-five miles northeast of New Orleans. Percy took an overnight train and met the boy at the sheriff's office. The child's cheek was blackened with grime, his hair grease matted, his feet scaled with dirt.

"Bobby!" shouted Percy, unable to control himself.

The boy looked up. He looked down. He had lost weight and was obviously malnourished; his eyes were different, squinty. Percy was positive he had found his son. When the cork-legged man approached, arms stretched wide, the boy shrieked in terror.

A parade greeted the Dunbars when they returned to Opelousas. Bands played, schoolchildren marched. But when Lessie was brought to see the boy, she faltered. She couldn't find the scar above Bobby's right eye, the trace of a collision with her sewing machine when he was an infant. Also vanished was the mole on his left big toe. Bobby did not appear to recognize her either. But Percy reassured her. Of course the boy was her son.

After the news spread through the South, a woman named Julia Anderson came forward. She claimed that the foundling was not Bobby Dunbar but *her* son, one Charles Bruce Anderson. The piano tuner Walters had taken Charles for a short trip a year earlier and never returned. Walters himself corroborated the story, at least the identity of the boy—he claimed that Julia Anderson had given away her son willingly. Anderson visited Opelousas, where the reluctant sheriff allowed her one chance to identify the boy in a lineup. She picked wrong and was sent home sobbing.

Walters was convicted of kidnapping Bobby Dunbar in 1914. His lawyers appealed successfully. The first trial had been so expensive, and the evidence so weak, that the prosecutors declined to seek a retrial. Walters had wandered the land ever since, a free but forsaken man.

Two days after the article about poor Louis Besemer and his mistress, Harriet Lowe, the *States* carried an item about the piano tuner Walters. He had arrived in New Orleans to perform a one-man show he had written about the plight of Charles Bruce Anderson, now Bobby Dunbar. Walters sang and played a harp he had constructed himself, with 287 strings—piano strings, ordered by pitch into discrete sections that, when strummed together, made a chord. It was the largest harp ever built. Walters performed mournful songs about mistaken identity, parental love, and carniverous swamp creatures over baroque chords strummed on his maniac harp.

The grainy newspaper photograph showed, beneath the cheap bowler, a face reticulated by suffering and poverty. But Walters's eyes were filled with light. They were tricky, mocking. They saw through her.

How was it to live as mother of a stranger? Lessie Dunbar must have known the boy was not her child. It did not come down to a question of scars or eye shapes. A thousand more intimate signs connect mother and son. Lessie had passed the eight months after Bobby's disappearance in bed. Undoubtedly she craved release from her nightmare. Her husband certainly did. In a moment of weakness, she capitulated to him. She changed her mind, she later told reporters, after she gave the boy a bath. The insinuation was that, seeing him naked and clean, she could more easily identify her son. But Beatrice suspected that something different occurred: Lessie had exchanged a moment of tenderness with the child and it was the tenderness that brought her back to herself. It was the tenderness—not the boy. But then she was stuck with the boy.

Beatrice could empathize. The man who went by the name of Giorgio Vizzini these last eight months resembled her Giugi all right, down to the scar below his chin and the mysteriously bloody forehead and the strange flap of skin on the helix of his left ear, but the psychic cord between them had stretched and finally snapped. She did not know him anymore. It was a subtle thing. A third party would not tell the difference. Outward appearances remained the same; he hugged her just as forcefully when they saw each other, he smiled his big ursine grin, he called her "Mamma" with the old simpering sweetness. He never missed a Sunday-night supper of Oysters Vizzini and he said that he loved her. But she knew that this Giorgio was an impostor.

Fortunately she had figured out how to stop him.

MARCH 4, 1919—THE IRISH CHANNEL

If he failed immediately to recognize his wife it was because his mind was crowded with Italian grocers—hairy, overweight, sebaceous—and Italian groceries—mold-dusted barrels of pickled pork, greasy tins of anchovies, giant steel *fusti* oozing olive oil, pallets of prunes, and purple heads of garlic. Bill had never before given thought to how all Italian groceries in New Orleans were nearly identical. It wasn't just the architecture and layout but the prices. Had the strategy of underselling occurred to no grocer? Variety? Competition? Each grocery was named after its proprietor, that was the main distinction. But it seemed as if they were all run by the same person.

He had had Italian grocers and groceries on his brain since his visit to Rosetta's. After they reported the body, Captain Capo sent them to canvass the groceries victimized by the Axman. They found Arthur Recknagel behind the counter, scooping salt into a small brown paper bag.

"Officers," he said, as if overjoyed to see them. "I told your pals everything they wanted to know."

Bill nodded. "Recknagel's not an Italian name."

"German." The grocer raised his hand in supplication. "But American for three generations."

"So why do you run a grocery?"

Recknagel gave him a broad smile. "It was an Italian grocery when I bought it in 1916. The business works, so why monkey with it? Only I added sausages."

They dangled from hooks behind the counter like disembodied limbs. Charlie gravitated toward them.

"Don't you know the Axman died in the Sick?" said Recknagel.

Bill bit the inside of his cheek. He knew there was a question that would elicit a revealing response from the German; he only had to summon it out of the ether. But he couldn't. Yet another navy instinct he didn't have. Charlie was closing in on the sausages, however, so he had better ask something.

"You have any trouble since your door got broken down? Burglaries?"

Judging by the relief in Recknagel's face, it was the wrong question. "Nope." He weighed the package on his scale. "Guess it was a fluke."

LeBoeuf was no more helpful and his mood less receptive.

"They arrested some Negroes," he said. "Had nothing to do with no Axman, no bogeyman, no Needle Man, no Gown Man."

Bill remembered the Needle Man: a creep who lurked at night in vacant lots, jumping out of the weeds to stab women with trephine needles. He was never caught.

"The Gown Man?"

LeBoeuf laughed. "They say he's tall and slender and wears a long black cape. Some men say he's a ghost. Not women—they know he's real."

Bill removed his notebook, wrote down *Gown Man*, and returned it to his back pocket. In recent weeks his notebook had become a surreal farrago of disconnected words and phrases: *false river, blues for dancing, inner harbor, underwater forest*. He didn't know what they meant or why he wrote them down.

"Your grocery is a block from Joseph Romano's. The stores sell the same stuff at the same prices. How does the block support two groceries?"

LeBoeuf's eyes deadened at the mention of Romano. "Joseph was my friend. Nobody mourns him more than me."

Romano's had been bought by a man who spoke just enough English to inform Bill that the surviving members of the Romano family had left town.

"I don't get it," said Charlie, when they were through. "What can they tell us that they didn't already tell Mooney?"

"They're saying something. We just have to listen."

"What beats me is why the man didn't use a gun. I mean, sure, Gunman doesn't have the ring of Axman. But the gun is the more effective instrument."

"You might have something there," said Bill, but he was thinking about Maze, about the way she laughed when they first met, showing her pink gums and covering her mouth out of embarrassment, before deciding she didn't care and laughing even harder.

"It ain so hard to come across a pistol. That beats me right up."

"I see what you mean."

"The gun," said Charlie meaningfully, "is the more effective instrument."

Charlie wouldn't let it rest until he got a response so Bill forced himself to go through the old catechism. There had to be a connection between the corpse in the Industrial Canal, most likely the grocer Rosetta, and the other grocery murders—but what? Was the so-called Axman still alive and active? If so, what explained his long dormancy? The questions weaved together into a woolen sweater that abraded his neck. But at the end of the day he could take off the sweater. That was the difference since he lost Maze. Six months ago the confluence of clues would have driven him into a frenzy, the old navy instincts crackling and sparking. But Maze's departure drained him of the old energies. He saw the facts and the connections between them but he couldn't quite bring himself to study the problem. Then he saw Maze.

He saw her exiting a grocery: Gino's on Magazine Street, in their neighborhood. He was on his way home when she emerged, hugging a brown satchel. Her face in the moment before she saw him was bright, amused, free. But when she recognized him she stiffened. A wordless conversation passed between them: Bill asking questions, Maze declining to answer. She looked different but he couldn't tell how. Maybe her skin was darker; maybe her hair was thicker; maybe her lips were fuller; maybe she was more beautiful than ever. Or maybe nothing had changed and only he was changed, his own internal filters knocked off-kilter, making everything he had known seem strange.

"Can I take that for you?"

She handed over the parcel. It was bulky. He smelled rosewater on her neck.

"I didn't tell you because I can't stay."

"When did you get back?"

She hesitated. "My parents were concerned about the house. Pipes. Mold."

"You could have asked me to check it."

"Bill."

"Paper says the Spanish flu is on the way out. Fewer cases this month than last. Much fewer than January."

For a moment she resembled the old Maze, the Maze who encouraged him to fight, who said she'd wait for him forever. But only for a moment.

"They said the same thing in November, December. Then it started again."

"When are you coming back?"

"You lied to me." She spoke with an odd, mirthless smile. "I thought you were lying about only one thing but then I realized that the one thing was everything."

"Maze—"

"You lied about that soldier, you lied about what happened in the war. But none of that would have mattered if you hadn't lied about you."

Something about her tone brought water to his eyes and he heard himself say, "I don't know what to say. I don't know what to do."

"I loved you. I understand how it was in the war. I'm not a child. Of course I wanted you to live, desperately, no matter what the cost. *No matter what*. But you lied about you."

The past tense of *love* entered him like a grappling hook.

"That's what it means to be married to someone. You're on the same side."

"We're still married." He instantly regretted this; perhaps, being reminded of the fact, she might begin taking steps to negate it.

"I realized the person sleeping beside me was a plaster cast. Meanwhile you, whoever you are—"

"Whoever am I?"

"You were somewhere else, wandering. You still are, as far as I can tell. Wandering." When she said the word she made a flighty gesture with her arm that seemed to indicate the entire universe. He saw an asteroid boomeranging around a star and careening out of orbit.

He wanted to tell her that she was talking crazy but he reflected that it was the cold sanity of her words that disturbed him. "How long have you been in New Orleans?" he said finally, to say anything, to break the tears.

"Four days."

He tried to remember what he had done the last four days. He couldn't remember anything except for Arthur Recknagel's gray sausages, dangling from their hooks.

"I'm leaving tonight. On the nine o'clock."

"I worried you might have caught sick," he said. "I worried you might have died."

She was about to reply when some internal tremor distorted her features and she pressed her hand to her mouth to restrain it. It made her face look really beautiful. Four days, seven blocks from their home, and she had made no effort to contact him.

"Stay another night. You're not acting like yourself."

"I'm not acting."

As she took the package from his arms, he inhaled deeply: rose-water, yes, but also salt water and another aroma that he could only describe as the scent of her skin when she slept. He tried to picture what he must have looked like, sleeping in bed on the morning when Maze glanced over and decided that he was a plaster mannequin.

That night in bed he rode the boomeranging asteroid into outer space. It sped beyond the galaxies, escaping the stellar universe, entering an oceanic abyss as dark as it was infinite. Against this blackness his thoughts assumed clarity, like shadows projected on a screen.

You lied to me. She meant something different, he decided. She meant *You're a coward.* She was right. He had been a coward. He had been a coward in war and a coward at home. And where had that taken him? His cowardice had rescued him from death, at least once if not twice. But his big sin—his fear of death—had also cost him. It had taken from him the very thing he had tried so hard to preserve: his life. What was the point of living if he was entombed inside the skin of a mannequin? The line of logic continued straight from there. If cowardice was the way in, courage would be the way out. But what kind of courage? What feat would do it? He could appear on the Bones' doorstep on the North Shore and demand for a second time that Maze return with him to New Orleans, but that hardly seemed bold. When he had tried it before he earned nothing more than a sharp rebuke from Maze's father on the Bones' front porch. He returned to the train station without seeing his wife.

The war was over and there was no glory in reenlisting to do aid work. He had already volunteered at influenza wards, but that was hardly extraordinary: thousands of New Orleanians were doing the same. No, he had to find something grander. He had to pursue a great work. He had to defeat a problem that no other man had been able to solve.

He laughed because it was right in front of him. How could he have missed it? He laughed and the asteroid reached its apogee and began to fall back to Earth. It had never left its orbit after all, it was just a big orbit, and now it was falling at the speed of light through the galaxies, reentering the solar system. He laughed because he couldn't believe he had not seen the thing that had been hovering in front of his face the whole time like a bright glowing star. He laughed all the way back to Earth.

MARCH 5, 1919—ESPLANADE RIDGE

The whorehouse was a traditional shotgun with a side porch that faced an inattentively tended garden of orange snapdragons, lavender swamp irises, and cream calendulas. It stood at the edge of Esplanade Ridge, a site chosen for strategic reasons. It was convenient to wealthy married men who might not want to traffic the city's more louche precincts, and inconspicuous among the surrounding cottages and manors in the leafy residential neighborhood. It was about halfway between the grimy cribs of the Tenderloin and the sumptuous vulgarities of the Ritz Palace, Rosalba Bucca's old Storyville bordello, with its three terraced stories and red awning embossed in gold lettering, designed to resemble the Ritz Hotel, or at least a chintzy fairy-tale approximation. Upon entering the Ritz Palace, a maid checked men's shoes to make sure they were well-heeled; a waiter served tumblers of Raleigh rye; a ragtime band played in a drawing room decorated with robust leather chairs, oil paintings of the Normandy coast, and wine-colored damask drapes dense enough to block daylight. Every hour Rosie's women, the Palacettes, presented themselves like debutantes in ball gowns along the staircase. They coated their faces with powder, rouge, eyeliner, and Rosie's tawdry pink lipstick. They looked expensive, like jewelry or rare coins. This was not the Ritz Palace.

"Ma'am," said Raymond, as he helped Beatrice to the curb, "you want I should escort you?"

"Don't be foolish."

"No, ma'am. I sure won't."

A woman dressed in a man's grimy overcoat opened the door. Her hair drooped in greasy clusters and her mouth was dismal with sagging gums, though, in a nostalgic touch, the lips were painted Rosie Bucca pink.

"Rosie!" the woman shouted over her shoulder. Her coat flapped open, exposing a tattered turquoise chippie that hung above the knobs of her blackened knees.

If Beatrice had been able to come up with a better plan, she would have tried it. But she had to protect her son and protect herself, and there was no time. For she had become certain that Giorgio, poor dundering Giugi, was the one they called the Axman. After reading about the Besemer attack in July she checked her files and was unsurprised to discover that Besemer's grocery was on the yellow list—the list of addresses, written on foolscap and running a dozen pages, that she kept locked in her library bureau. The yellow list included not only the groceries but bars, laundry services, millinery shops, tailors, cobblers, newsstands, and pharmacies—every business engaged by Hercules's shadow wing. Many were owned by Sicilian families, but not all—in recent years they had expanded to Negro bars in the Battlefield, ignored by the police, whose owners were grateful for the protection. Each time an ax attack was reported, she consulted the list. She had an ember of hope when she could not find Arthur Recknagel's name. Then she located his grocery's address; the previous owner had died and his sons sold the business to Recknagel, who changed its name. Joseph LeBoeuf was on the list, as was Joseph Romano. The pregnant woman, Mrs. Schneider, was not—she had no connection to a grocery or any other shadow business that Beatrice could determine—but when Beatrice read in September about the break-in attempt at the grocery run by Paul Durel, Jr. (son of Paolo Durello, native of Taormina), she could delude herself no longer.

Her first thought was to have Giorgio arrested, but it took no time to realize that an investigation would expose the entire shadow business to the corrosive air of public inquiry, destroying not only Giorgio but also Hercules and herself. Nor, heaven forbid, could she have harm done to him—the thought alone was unconscionable (though late at night, tormented by Sal's grandfather clock, she had occasionally been consoled by an image of Giorgio smiling moronically from the safety of a wheelchair). She might discuss the matter openly with Giorgio, urging him to stop committing violence, but she had already done so in subtle ways, giving him every opportunity to absolve himself, without success. Giorgio had noble intentions, she was certain of it. In his own way, he must have felt that he was helping Hercules, or at least the shadow business, eliminating risks, enforcing rules, putting the fear of death in anyone who considered cheating the family. His sudden assertiveness in the business, after such a long dormancy, might have charmed her if it hadn't taken such gruesome form. It almost did charm her, she admitted to herself, but more than that it scared her. He had come under the sway of primitive urges for which filial devotion was no match. She had long ago accepted that she could not control him with commands or reprimands. It was like training a bear for the circus: the act might go off without trouble for months or years but inevitably the day would come when the bear leaped into the audience and mauled a child.

Her solution derived from a principle that had never, in her experience, been disproved. A man could be deterred from the path of violence by a steady application of venery. The method was as old as civilization. Every Italian child learned in primary school that the Romans would still rule the world were it not for the rampant dissipation of the rulers, first in Rome, later in the court of Ravenna. The converse was equally true. During the war the Italian generals ordered soldiers to avoid female contact for one week before battle, lest they lose their nerve. Gavrilo Princip was a nineteen-year-old virgin who abstained from liquor, raised by Christian peasants who were strict even by the standards of their superstitious village; was it a surprise that such a man would be driven to murder a prince famous for his lust marriage to a lowly countess? The principle had held for Giorgio's father too. Sal lost his mastery of the family business once he began debauching. His own venery had achieved what his rivals never could.

There was only Giorgio's relationship with women to consider. They seemed suspicious of him. He had never figured out how to be gentle. He would not caress but paw. Did he know, when he kissed, not to bare his teeth? It was probably Beatrice's fault: she had never figured out how to be gentle either. It was not a quality that interested her, gentleness, but desperation had driven her to it. She saw now that gentleness, when deployed ruthlessly, could be effective. Gentleness could save lives.

A whorehouse offered a relatively safe, controlled environment, enabling easy supervision. It was just a question of selecting the *right* whorehouse. Sal had always supervised the crib collections, and after his death she had handed them to the cousins, so she wasn't familiar with, so to speak, the lay of the land. With prostitution outlawed, protection services were in higher demand. But Beatrice couldn't consult the cousins and she didn't know any sporting girls directly, save one: Rosalba Bucca, native of Linguaglossa, known in the Tenderloin as Rosie the Mouth.

Beatrice could only guess how Rosalba acquired the nickname, but it suited her. It was, after all, Rosie who, despite never having met Salvatore Vizzini's wife, had alerted Beatrice to the unscrupulous activities in which he engaged during the final year of his life. A summary of Sal's transgressions had arrived in a pale blue sealed envelope dropped off not at the Vizzinis' home but at Canal Street Chapeaux, a millinery shop of which Rosie was a silent owner. When Beatrice made her weekly visit to the store, the salesclerk handed her two envelopes, the regular collection envelope and a second, unmarked. A request for a meeting was written in a simple, uneducated hand.

Beatrice was not prepared to take seriously the slander of a prostitute but she had begun to nurse suspicions. Rosie's information confirmed them. Beatrice met with Rosie twice to confirm certain details but never bothered to thank her afterward. What would she say: *Thank you for ruining my life*? Since Sal's death, she had seen Rosie twice in public, but did not acknowledge her: in Jackson Square, walking alone, and at Antoine's on a date with an out-of-town businessman, her amaranth lipstick smudged thickly over her enormous mouth, giving her the appearance of having been caught devouring a fresh carcass.

When Beatrice returned to Canal Street Chapeaux last September, shortly after the Durel grocery break-in, the salesclerk took one glimpse of the gold rings on her fingers and went pale. The girl reversed the CLOSED sign on the door, pulled the dead bolt, and, after an inaudible mumble, ran out the back. She reappeared with the owner, both of them panting. Beatrice left soon after, carrying a black box tied with velvet string. It contained a slip on which was written Rosalba Bucca's new address: 2631 DeSoto Street.

"You can wait in the parlor," said Rosie's pink-lipped employee. She sank heavily into the nearest chair.

Beatrice followed her inside. Before her eyes could adjust to the gloom—the windows were covered by louvered shutters—she became aware of a repeated percussion: the sound of a rusty bed traveling, a centimeter at a time, across the floor. The rate of locomotion seemed gradually to be increasing. But she was spared from further sordid contemplation by the appearance of Rosie the Mouth.

"Go to the back," said Rosie.

The pink-lipped woman delivered a profound sigh and, with heroic effort, pulled herself to standing. She dragged herself out of the room.

"I'm all fixed with protection, ma'am," said Rosie. "I squared with your agent the day before yesterday." Her accent—flat, nasal, squeaky like a sharpening knife, several octaves removed from the rich Sicilian dialect of her birth—made Beatrice grind her teeth. It drove her crazy, the immigrant instinct for assimilation, the panicked desire to out-American the Americans. "I think it was Efigenia?" said Rosie. "Maybe Elba. I get them confused."

"I'm here to talk about my son. Maybe you've met him." Rosie began to respond but Beatrice interrupted with a wave of her hand. She didn't want to know. "I am promoting him from his supervisory job at the canal. He is available to assume new responsibilities."

"Mr. Vizzini will be the new collector?"

The hammering grew louder.

"We are countrywomen. You did a great service for me. I haven't forgotten."

"Yes, ma'am."

"This operation isn't much to admire." The commotion in the bedroom was becoming intolerable. A thin film of sweat coated the back of Beatrice's neck. She removed her scarf. The whole scenario was highly distasteful but there was no better solution. She had thought about it plenty and there was no better solution.

"No, ma'am." Rosie's accent was broadening, losing the crass Americanismo. "I concede this."

The unseen woman shrieked. She screamed obscenities. And begged. Begging and screaming, in alternation. Beatrice and Rosie stared at each other.

"What is the hourly rate?" said Beatrice finally.

"Eight dollars."

Beatrice removed one of her gloves, opened her purse, and found a ten. "I cannot take it anymore."

Rosie stuffed the bill into her dress and walked through the bedroom where the pink-lipped woman lay sprawled on a mold-spotted mattress, oblivious. Rosie knocked sharply on the door of a second bedroom. The noises abruptly ceased. The door opened a crack. A terse communication concluded with the emergence of a portly, red-faced man, in an undershirt and white drawers, cradling the rest of his clothes in his arms. He was made to dress on the porch.

The two women resumed their conversation. It wasn't much of a conversation: Beatrice spoke, Rosie nodded. The deal was simple. Rosie's Ritz Palace would be allowed to continue operations. Rosie would receive from Beatrice a weekly installment of three hundred and fifty dollars. In exchange, Rosie would hire Giorgio Vizzini as manager. He would be responsible for developing a more profitable business model. This, at least, was what he'd be told. What he would not know and would not be explained to him under any circumstance was that Rosie would be the one providing the protection. She would be protecting Beatrice. She was to keep careful record of Giorgio's behavior and activities, noting his movements in a letter that she would deliver to Beatrice at the end of each business day. Her sporting house would by this means become a shadow business to the shadow business.

"The more time he spends here, the more you will be able to observe him, and the more value you will have to me."

"What if he doesn't want to be here?"

"Then you are to make him want to be here." Beatrice did not feel it necessary to elaborate. From Rosie's response, or rather her silence, it was clear Beatrice didn't have to. She produced an envelope containing the first payment. "Use that to get some cleaner girls." She glanced meaningfully at the pink-lipped woman passed out in the next room. The last thing Beatrice needed was for Giorgio to acquire some awful infection.

"*Vi ringrazio, signora,*" said Rosie, and her accent was perfect, as syrupy and sun kissed as the island of Sicily itself.

Operation Ritz Palace, Beatrice called it, when she presented Giorgio with her plan for an important new endeavor at supper the following Sunday. She chose her words carefully. The closure of Storyville, she explained, presented a major business opportunity. The grand sex alcazars were demolished and the madams had gone underground. But that did not mean that they had to go sleazy. The men who patronized Arlington Annex or Mahogany Hall did not feel comfortable stalking like criminals to hovels in the Tango Belt. Why not offer clean, discreet houses in affluent residential neighborhoods, businesses so respectable that they could be operated in plain sight without raising suspicion? The sporting girls would no longer dress in diamonds and ostrich plumes but—at least when entering and exiting the premises—in attire that made them resemble the daughters of an Uptown family. Yes, she assured him, she was as determined as ever to retire the shadow business. The Industrial Canal remained more than a year from completion, however. There was still time to entertain, in a cautious way, other opportunities. But she needed someone in charge whom she could trust.

Giorgio, to her surprise, accepted immediately. He said he was tired. He would be happy to take a break from the canal. It might even allow him more time to work on his osteopathy business. In fact, he announced, he would move into the apartment in Jackson Square he kept for his practice and leave the house on First Street for good.

To think—he had needed just the slightest push. She only regretted she hadn't thought of it sooner. On the night that Giorgio accepted his new assignment, for the first time since Sal's death, Beatrice went to bed without a headache. The ticking of the grandfather clock was a lullaby in her ears.

MARCH 6, 1919—THE BATTLEFIELD

As he fumbled with the key, the door opened. Orly wore her blue terry-cloth bathrobe, the only thing she owned that still fit.

"Hush," she said, before he could speak.

"What is it? Your mother?"

She closed the door behind her and cinched her belt. "Let's go for a walk."

Some part of him wondered whether she was about to give birth. He knew it made no sense, but where was the sense in taking a walk at one thirty in the morning?

"I was hoping to get off my feet," he said. "I've been upright twenty hours."

"We'll go to Sis Pinky's."

Now he knew there was trouble. Orly didn't like going to bars even when she was in a good mood, and particularly not Sis Pinky's, which she called Piss Stinky's. She must have appreciated how tired he was, his first day of working a second job, an apprenticeship for Drag's deaf old uncle at the Pelican Cooperage. But she appeared not to care.

"Why aren't you asleep?"

"I was thinking about you."

"I don't believe it."

"And I can't find a comfortable position." She patted her stomach. "She's up, so I'm up."

It was the first time Orly had said *she*. He didn't understand how she could know but he didn't doubt her. He rested his palm on her stomach. The movement inside was no less bizarre than it had been the first time he felt it. It was irresistibly, exhilaratingly bizarre, an alien life frantic to escape.

"When did we even see each other last?" Orly wore a jacket over her robe but the terry-cloth hem glided just inches above the sidewalk.

"Monday?" said Isadore.

"You were asleep when I got back from the Tiltons. Sunday."

"It's not enough."

Orly had worked longer hours, knowing she would have to miss at least a couple of days of work when the baby came; she worried Mrs. Tilton would replace her. Increasingly she slept Uptown, in the maid's room. And now Isadore was working nights.

"It's too long," she said, "when you can't remember the day."

Sis Pinky's wasn't such a bad place to talk—it wasn't exceedingly dirty, the drinks were strong, and ever since Pinky had negotiated a protection arrangement with some Uptown Italians, the rougher Battlefield characters tended to keep away. Tonight it was nearly empty: an old drunk slumped at the last stool and a youngish couple chatted conspiratorially at one of the tables. Neither looked up when the Zenos arrived but old Pinky herself was tending bar and she missed nothing.

"Boy, you smell like a barnyard."

Isadore tried to formulate a retort about how her bar reeked of piss, but his exhaustion rendered him mute.

"Look at *this*!" Pinky exclaimed, noticing Orly's stomach. "You're fixing to burst! Just hold till I get the mop."

Orly gave a weak smile. "Two whiskeys straight."

"Yours is a double."

"Single will do."

"It's on Sissy. You're drinking for two, ain you?"

"Thanks, ma'am. She could use a nap, to tell the truth."

"So could her mam."

Isadore held the stool beneath Orly as she settled herself. Pinky poured the drinks and splashed two extra drops into a small glass, which she swirled and held to her nose, inhaling histrionically to cleanse her nostrils of Isadore's odor.

"Tell me," said Orly, once Pinky had drifted to the other end of the bar, "about the new job."

The new job: a cathedral of a warehouse with vaulted ceilings two stories high, lit carelessly by occasional candles, populated by the skeletons of wooden barrels, metal staves with bladed edges, and pyres of stripped cypress trees. Drag's uncle himself resembled a stave, slender, taut, with a spine bent by a life spent hunched over barrels. Isadore supposed he would look that way soon enough. Better to be stooped over from hard labor than bending over a horn for audiences who couldn't recognize real music when they heard it.

"Drag's uncle said I'll be a proper cooper in no time."

"You hated it."

Making barrels was a pain in the ass. The lining had to be pulled tight, and when it slipped, the metallic edge sliced his hand. The pay for night-shift assistants, working from eight to one, was only four dollars a week—what you could make in about two hours at Savocca's. But he hadn't played Savocca's since before the outbreak, nor any other tonk, and just about nobody else had either. "It beats digging in a swamp," he said.

"But you're still digging in the swamp."

Outside the wide glass windows the streetlamp atomized the mist. Liberty Street shivered as if underwater. This time of year you expected alligators to climb out of the gutters, fish to swim through the air. Then came the spring floods and the streets really did go underwater.

"I appreciate that you stayed with the canal job." It was as if the mist had seeped inside the bar and coated her face. "And now a second job, just like you promised. Baby, I'm proud of you." She let out a sob.

"Or."

She laughed through her tears. "You know how the baby swings my mood. I don't know why I'm crying." She cried.

"I think we should get you to bed." He found two quarters in his pocket and put them on the counter, thinking, Four dollars a week minus fifty cents makes three dollars and fifty cents—in two minutes they had drunk nearly his night's work.

"I'm not ready." She wiped her face with the sleeve of her robe.

"You still haven't told me what this is about."

"You're going to hate it, huh?" she said. "The cooper job."

"Not like I hate the dig. Compared to the dig, it's the Taj Mahal."

"How much does it pay?"

He told her and watched her do the mental calculations. He knew what she was thinking: it wasn't enough. Between them they could barely cover basic expenses. Soon they'd be four. Miss Daisy couldn't care for an infant, and the Tiltons would never allow Orly's child to play with their own children. She would have to quit, and they would have even less. The last six months had been devoted to raising a cushion but they had failed. The money from the Bailey jobs was long gone—all that was left in the Egyptienne Luxury cigar tin was the Webley & Scott revolver, which wouldn't fetch much at the pawn now that the city had been glutted with unwanted service guns. They would soon have to leave Liberty Street, and that didn't take into account if the baby got sick or, God forbid, the influenza found them. Would they starve? Would Miss Daisy die?

"Why's it so hard? Just to slip by?"

"It's a hard time, Or."

"It has always been hard."

"It has been," he conceded. "It always has been."

"You look different."

"Dignified. Serious. A real workingman."

She smiled, but it was a rueful and unpleasant smile. "You look like a workingman all right. Beaten down."

"I work all day for us and you start complaining about how I look?"

"Iz! I don't mean that. Nothing wrong with how you look. You have muscles in places you never did before. I like that."

"There you go."

"I mean in your eyes. You're tired."

"That's all right. Daisy is the only person I know that isn't tired."

"You've *been* tired. I haven't said anything because I know you're trying, but I've been watching. I don't like what I see."

Isadore had to laugh. First he wasn't working enough and now he was working too much.

"I know I'm not making sense," said Orly.

The old drunk stumbled past them, into the night. At the end of the bar Sis Pinky poured the watery remains of his whiskey through a funnel back into the bottle.

"I've been unfair," said Orly. "That's all I'm saying."

"Life is unfair. Work is unfair. But you're not unfair."

"I keep thinking about the night at the Funky Butt."

"That was an age ago."

"Remember how downcast I was?"

"You had other things on your mind."

"I'd known about her for weeks." She patted her stomach. "No, I was downcast because I saw how excited you were in the club. And on the stage! You were possessed by spirits. It gave me a memory of when we met."

"Please. I was still in short pants."

"Hustling in the street with Dick, playing outside the clubs, blowing so hard it looked like you were carrying lemons in your cheeks."

"That's another life." He shook his head. "That boy is gone."

He thought of the nightmare at the Cave. Being forced to play "At the Darktown Strutters' Ball" for a few chattering white drunks should have been enough to crush finally his dream of musical glory, of creating a new sound that would live forever, flowing from one generation to the next down the river of time into the sea of immortality. But two days later he got a call to audition with Kid Ory himself. With King Oliver having fled to Chicago, Ory's band needed a new cornet player. In the audition Isadore had played it straight, not wanting to alarm Ory, but apparently it wasn't straight enough. Ory had hired Dipper Armstrong, an old classmate of Isadore and Bailey's from the Waifs' Home—a fine technical player, nothing special. At the end of their appointment Ory had playfully called Isadore "King Zeno" and said he'd be keeping watch on him. But there was no job for him—not with Ory's Brown Skin Band or anyone else. Music had not respected him, so he could not respect music. He would learn to respect barrels. He would learn to respect mud.

"Isn't there some way you can still play?" said Orly.

"You're really saying this."

"What about weekends? How you used to do in the second lines."

"That was kid stuff. I don't traffic with rag anymore."

"Maybe you could play with Dick, or Drag. I used to think it exhausted you but I've come to see it gave you life."

"This kind of talk isn't going to do anyone any good."

She seemed on the verge of weeping again so he pushed her glass closer to her. She took a tentative sip. "I don't like the taste anymore."

He finished it for her and finished his own. His vision sharpened. He noticed that the fringe of Orly's blue bathrobe was caked with sawdust.

"I love you," she said after a little while. "That's all I'm trying to say."

"I'll get a hang of coopering." He tried to be gentle. He didn't want her getting the idea that he was miserable, that each day he went without playing his music felt like another window closing, the air getting smokier, the escape routes being sealed off, in a house on fire. "Before too long," he said, "they'll increase my pay."

Orly wiped her eyes.

"I can play with the boys on the weekend. Maybe even a Saturday show, make a few extra dollars. Or if a band needs a sideman, like the other night at the Cave."

"It was a dumb idea."

"It was a good idea. But I'm not even worried about music anymore."

"Don't talk like that."

"I'm not just talking. Yes, I have been tired. But once the baby is born, that'll be my music."

"*She*."

"How do you know?

"I just do."

"All right, *she*. I won't need to gig. I'll have her."

She winced. "You believe that?"

"I know it." The whiskey bubbled in the caldera of his stomach. His future was becoming as clear as the polished mirror behind the bar, where he spied Orly's face, wise and trusting and open, and his own, pinched and dry, mud streaked across the forehead, the mustache a little wild, two days' growth of stubble tracing the jaw. He looked older than usual, but with enough soap and shaving cream, he might still pass for a ward of the Waifs' Home. His Parisian grandfather, a cabinetmaker named Louis Bouillet, who never learned English though he arrived in New Orleans as a young man, whose framed portrait was one of the few possessions that Isadore had brought with him from the orphanage, survived in Isadore's hazel eyes and delicate ears; his mother was visible in his full, expressive mouth. This was a mixed-up fellow, brazen and fearful both, divided between continents, families, races, lives. Nobody could trust such a man. Not even Isadore could trust this man.

"We will have money," he told Orly. "And we will have joy."

She leaned into him, resting her head on his shoulder. "I hope so."

"Don't have to hope. That's what a husband is for."

Orly took his face between her large hands. In her eyes he could see that he had reached the place she had wanted him to reach. "I'm ready," she said, "to sleep."

She winced with pain when he helped her off the stool. After she went outside, her bathrobe dragging sawdust and who knew what else with her, he took a final glance at the bar mirror. He had been mistaken, he realized. He could not be confused for a child. That fellow in the mirror was a grown man, with grown responsibilities. He was a grown man who was going to do what any grown man in his position must do.

MARCH 7, 1919—GENTILLY

The old clarity began to return. The problem, he realized, was that they had been talking to exactly the wrong people. They had interviewed the owners of grocery stores. Of course the grocers wouldn't talk. They were vulnerable, they had businesses to run. He needed witnesses with nothing to lose. Or who had already lost everything.

Eloise Obitz opened the door on Havana Street on the second knock.

"Billy Bastrop," she said, a strange grin playing across her face.

He was disarmed by the speed with which she had answered the door. It was as if she had been standing on the other side, waiting.

"Orchids are my favorite." She took them out of his hands and carried them into the kitchen. He heard running water. He didn't know whether to follow her, so he remained in the doorway, hat in hand. He had not visited since the sleepless morning after her husband's murder, when Bill and Harry Dodson had undertaken the grim errand of informing the victim's family. After a tour of the Obitzes' victory garden with the older daughter and a long, incoherent monologue by Eloise, they had made every plausible excuse to leave, but neither mother nor daughters would permit it. The encounter only ended when Bill pried the older daughter off Dodson's leg and the female Obitzes melted together onto the living-room floor in a puddle of tears. If he had to revisit this scene, it would be better to go without Charlie, alone. Besides, this was no longer police work, at least not *only* police work. By solving this unsolvable case, he would solve Maze. He would prove his courage, regain his confidence. He would win her back. He would not have been able to explain all this to Charlie, which was another reason he left his partner behind. But he felt it was true. Instinct told him so.

He had expected to find the Obitz house messy and dark—like his home in Maze's absence—but the living room was immaculate. The sofa cushions were puffed, the chairs aligned exactly with the edge of the coffee table, the floors cleanly swept. He felt as if he should remove his hobnailed boots.

Eloise poked her head out of the kitchen. It was a fine head, a doll's head—a standard deviation too large for her torso, suggesting a measure of jocularity ill suited to a woman recently widowed.

"You'll stay for a moment, won't you?"

"Yes, ma'am."

"Eloise to you, Officer." She winked. "Sit on the couch. The chairs are hard."

The house was silent, childless. Eloise returned with two wineglasses and a bottle. As she poured, Bill was struck by how *normal* she seemed. Her skin was soft and uncreased; her color high; her hair, nearly as blond as her late husband's, coiled into a neat bun. She was pretty, if slightly drawn around the lips, roughly Maze's build but narrower in her hips and shoulders. The only concession to mourning was the long black skirt, though it was dappled with white checks. Her blouse was white. She sat beside him on the couch, tucking her knees beneath her so that she could face him.

She held up her glass. "To surprise visits."

She winked again. It was not voluntary, he decided, but a kind of twitch. They touched glasses and their eyes met.

"Your daughters."

She laughed. "You'd have heard them. They're with my sister."

"I know it's been a hard time."

"It's a small town." Her smile dampened only slightly. "He's everywhere."

"I understand how that can be."

"But lives go on." Again the wink—yes, it was definitely inadvertent.

"Yes, ma'am. That is, Eloise."

She beamed again.

It *was* a small town. In a small town people spoke the same way. He recalled something Andrew Maggio had said that morning. They stood on Tonti Street, around the corner from his barbershop. He had been giving a shave, but when he saw Bill's uniform in the doorway he handed his blade to his partner and walked silently into the street. They did the regular duet—"I already told them everything," etc.—but when Bill bluffed that he had a new lead, Maggio tightened.

I've been cleared, he said. There's nothing attaching me to the crime.

I know it wasn't you, said Bill. But I think the killer is still alive.

I hope you're wrong.

I went to your brother's grocery yesterday. It's closed.

I sold it.

Why?

After what happened, you think I'd want to go into groceries?

Who bought it?

I sold my note to the bank. That ended my involvement.

With the grocery?

With your investigation.

Bill tried to summon the right question but as always it evaded him.

Someone in New Orleans knows what's going on, he said at last, if only to extend the conversation. I won't stop until I find that person.

You'll have to look hard.

I am. I'm searching the whole town.

Ah, said Maggio. But there are towns within towns.

"I have a strange question," said Bill, in the Obitz living room. "'There are towns within towns.' Have you ever heard someone say that?"

"'There are towns within towns'?" Eloise tilted her head, as if listening for an echo. When none came, she provided one. "There are towns," she said, "within towns."

"It's nonsense, probably."

She shook her head. He noticed that her wineglass was empty. He did not remember seeing her take a sip.

"Maybe it's like this," she said. "Within the city there are lots of different communities. And each community exists apart from the others."

"What kind of communities?"

"The community of officers and their families, for instance.

I take it that's why you visited this evening—to honor our little community?"

He hesitated. "I did want to pay respects. I looked up to Teddy. He was the best detective I've known." It was the truth. He'd shadowed Obitz when he'd joined the Department. Nobody had better navy instincts than Obitz, which was why the entire Department was especially spooked by his death. A navy with excellent instincts shouldn't die in action. At least that's what they were told in training.

Eloise nodded blankly. She'd heard it before. Bill found it awkward to be on the couch beside her; he had to rotate unnaturally to face her. His neck was sore. It'd be easier to sit in one of the chairs opposite but he worried that she would be offended if he moved, so he remained beside her, craning his neck.

"I'm afraid I also have some professional questions. But first I want to know about you and your family. Is the Department doing enough to help?"

"We've been lonely. To tell the truth."

"They haven't been around, to help? We've made collections—"

She waved him off. "Business first. Then we'll get to the other things." She folded her hands on her lap. Her bright smile returned. Perhaps she was sick of talking about her husband. Bill couldn't blame her. He didn't like talking to other people about Maze and she was alive.

"It's grisly business."

"I was married to a policeman."

"Do you remember the Maggio murders? The Italian grocer and his wife?"

"The Axman." She filled their glasses.

"Teddy was working the case."

She seemed to be turning over an idea in her mind. Maybe something had occurred to her. Detective work was like that: a lot of fruitful research and hard work with no result, and then a single question to the right person turns the lock.

"Is this the reason you came here, Detective? To discuss the Axman?"

"Anything you remember—"

"I heard your wife left."

It stopped him.

"Small town," Eloise said.

"She went with her parents across the lake. To avoid the influenza."

"Has she?"

"Has she left?"

"Has she avoided the influenza?"

"So far," he said. "So far as I know."

"It's very terrible," she said. "The influenza."

It was not quite a question but not quite a statement either. He recognized the tactic. It was the interrogator's noncommittal inquiry, used to elicit information without seeming particularly eager to have it. She assumed a concerned expression though he sensed a playful fluttering behind her pursed mouth. She did not wear lipstick but her lips were moist. Her slender little fingers played lightly with the top button of her blouse. Well, he was an actual detective. He could wait too. Time elapsed. Her mouth opened. Her mouth closed. It was a soft mouth, filled with bright white teeth. In fact, he thought, my wife is the reason I'm here today. But he did not say this.

"Teddy might have mentioned Maggio," said Eloise. "Teddy mentioned all kinds of things." She leaned very slightly forward, an inch or perhaps less, but it was enough to alter the atmosphere. "He kept everything in his files."

"Are they here?"

"They're in the kids' room."

"I would like to see the files," said Bill, but he was no longer thinking about the files. He was thinking of the blond strands that had come loose from her bun and fell over her forehead. Her hand slipped from her blouse. The top button slipped out of the buttonhole. He waited for a wink but it was not forthcoming. She stood abruptly.

"Should I follow you?"

She disappeared down the hall. He waited for an invitation. It did not come. He followed.

The children's bedroom had no windows, only two single beds lying against perpendicular walls. Eloise Obitz's back was to him; she faced the bed along the far wall. When she turned, her blouse was fully unbuttoned. The fabric parted to reveal a cream-colored corset with its own row of buttons set between folds of ruffled fabric. Towns within towns. Buttons beneath buttons.

"There aren't any files," he heard himself say.

She closed the distance between them. Advancing, she was all sharp cutting shoulders and quick little hands. Her face, clear and blank, stared up at him, and he felt her hands find his belt. It was not an easy belt to remove, the service belt. It had two rows of holes and two separate loops. But she had experience with the model. With a click the belt was loose. He felt stomach-sick and frenzied with desire. A hit of some narcotic burst in the brain stem and flushed downward in rolling waves. He had not felt it for months, maybe longer, not with such intensity—there had been a hit when he saw Maze outside Gino's, but it was swiftly overcome by stronger emotion. Eloise looked down and her yellow hair was in his nose, giving off a strong scent of powder. He grabbed her shoulders. They were like the wings of a small bird.

"The files are under the bed." Her tiny fingers worked into the coils of hair beneath the band of his drawers. "You can have all the files you want."

He forgot why he had cared about the files in the first place. Maze was gone, perhaps forever. Even if he did solve the case, what good would it do? Would she care? Would she take him back just because he solved a big case? What kind of logic was that?

A door slammed open and shut. It took a second for them both to realize that it was not Eloise's front door, but the neighbors'. Even so, the clatter and the prospect of being interrupted by her daughters made Eloise stiffen and in the caesura a sliver of mental clarity entered Bill's lust-addled brain. He reminded himself that he wasn't only chasing the Axman for Maze. He was doing it for himself. If he had learned anything this year, it was that cowardice led only to ruin. And what was more cowardly than taking advantage of the lonely widow of his former mentor?

But now Eloise Obitz's lips were pressing wetly against his own and her busy little fingers were closing around his cock.

MARCH 8, 1919—THE GARDEN DISTRICT

It was a good thing that Operation Ritz Palace was a success because the Industrial Canal—the great dream that the shadow business and Hercules Construction served, the seed of her immortality—was a fiasco. Giorgio's transfer to the DeSoto house coincided with the beginning of a precipitous decline at the work site. It wasn't his absence that caused it, she didn't think. She couldn't put her finger on any single decisive problem, which was itself the problem. The Texas dredge was slowed by its delicate gastrointestinal system, and as the men dug deeper, quicksand conditions took hold. Marsh gas burst from the ground in explosive belches. When laborers weren't threatened with being sucked under to a sandy grave or poisoned by gas, they risked drowning as groundwater seeped into the canal more quickly than it could be pumped out. The Spanish Death, on top of everything else, seemed to breed in the damp recesses of the canal. At the height of the first outbreak, Beatrice consented to a weeklong cessation of activities. The second outbreak in January led to another furlough. The budget doubled. This was not so bad in itself—much of the money would end up going to Hercules, after all, and much of that to Beatrice Vizzini—but it required a second municipal bond. The public indignation drew scrutiny to the exclusive nature of Hercules's unusual contract. Hercules Construction, unlike the shadow business, was meant to operate in the light of day, but Beatrice was unaccustomed to the brightness of the glare. Hugs became impatient, even wondering aloud, during one particularly high-strung meeting at Hibernia's downtown office, whether they should reconsider hiring additional construction firms. None of these troubles pained her acutely, however, for Giorgio, miraculously, had been cured.

She did not think it was a coincidence that there had been no attacks in the eight months since he began working with Rosie. Every man had a rowdy age, but she had helped him through his. It was even perhaps not too late for Giorgio to become the family leader she had hoped for, the man Sal never was. Her intercession had diverted Giorgio's violent energies to productive use. He had, to her delight and amazement, transformed Ritz Palace into a highly profitable concern. Giorgio had become a businessman.

He ran the Ritz Palace like a doctor's office: no drinks or cigars sold, no music played, no card tables. Less romance, more lust. It turned out most clients did not mind as long as the main service was delivered. The girls were booked a full week in advance, the house was clean, and there were no complaints from neighbors or police. The work calmed him. Or perhaps it was all the sex. Though Beatrice did not like to dwell on it, she had concluded that he was engaging several if not all of the women under his employ. He might have even engaged Rosie despite the age difference—she was at least ten years older than him. Who was Beatrice kidding? He was engaging Rosie.

In February, with Beatrice's blessing, Giorgio opened two additional cribs, installing three women in each. They were situated in former grocery apartments that had been sitting vacant in good neighborhoods—one in the Garden District, the other in Faubourg Bouligny. Giorgio spent his days moving among the houses. Every evening Rosie left her sealed report beneath a pot of pink azaleas on Beatrice's front porch. Her letters varied little but were highly detailed. They were more glowing than any assessments Giorgio had received in elementary school. Reading the letters at night in the library, she dared to imagine a new future unfolding before her. Gradually she would hand over to Giorgio greater responsibility. She would begin to include him in meetings with Hibernia, tutor him in the intricate financial structure that linked the shadow business and Hercules, and deputize him to oversee Zo and the cousins. Within a couple of years, once Hercules had terminated the shadow business for good, she might even retire. She could join the boards of cultural institutions: the French Opera House, say, or the Delgado Museum of Art. The Vizzini name would come to be associated with charity, fine taste, discretion. She would embark on this new stage of life secure in the knowledge that her son would lead Hercules to ever-greater business success, expanding from construction to, perhaps, shipbuilding, engineering, real estate speculation. One day, perhaps, in the not too distant future, Giorgio would find a respectable woman with whom he would produce a new generation of Vizzinis, and so on, through time immemorial.

Still a line in one of Rosie's recent letters struck her as odd. *Giorgio has shown an unnatural talent for this work,* Rosie wrote. It was an anodyne statement, written without emphasis, but it lingered in Beatrice's mind. The more she thought about it, the more it bothered her. It was *unnatural* that did it. The word reminded her of something Sal had said, toward the end, after she confronted him with evidence of sloppiness in his business affairs. Sal had first laughed, as if charmed by the idea of her investigation, before growing angry. In their final argument he had used that exact word, *unnatural*. He had called Beatrice's determination to reform Hercules "unnatural." He didn't understand why it wasn't enough to make money and live comfortably. He didn't understand her yearning for higher things. He found it unnatural that she should favor the phantom of future glory over present happiness. He found unnatural the ends to which she would go to achieve this glory. Beatrice had tried to explain that nothing was unnatural about her views—or her methods. What Sal called "unnatural," she called strategic. She called it wise, bold, visionary.

She called it cunning.

MARCH 9, 1919—CARONDELET WALK

The first candidate was short, slight, bundled tightly in a dark hooded coat. He walked with the swaying, horizontal motion that came on after a fourth drink. It was unlikely he would put up a fight. He couldn't do Isadore much damage anyway, and if he made a big noise, nobody would hear. At this hour Carondelet Walk, a narrow, rutted horse path that separated the Old Basin Canal from a grim procession of shuttered warehouses, was empty and silent. There was no escape. A crabbing boat was tied to the nearest mooring but the deck was too far away to be reached in a leap. Isadore had a decent disguise—he had cut a patch of netting from the boat's hawser and secured it beneath his black alpine hat, wearing it like a mask. He was proud of the disguise. It was also a dark night, a platinum cloud obscuring the moon. It added up to ideal ambush conditions, better than any Bailey had obtained. But with Bailey, Isadore had only to stay in the shadows, serve as a lookout. This was a different business altogether. As the figure approached, Isadore tightened the crab netting over his face and gripped his Webley & Scott revolver, but he couldn't bring himself to move. A picture of Orleania rubbing her stomach, her eyes moist with fear of the future, entered his mind, and the next thing he knew, he had leaped from behind the loading dock.

"Hold it," he said, rough.

The candidate, after a brief hesitation, walked faster.

"I am pointing a gun at your head," he shouted.

"I have the crabs," came a female voice. She turned slowly, her hands rising over her head. "If you rape me, you will also have the crabs."

"Good heavens. I—"

"Take pity."

"I did not see you were a woman," he said stiffly. What would he do if Orly were held up by a low-down tough? He would murder the man. That was one scenario in which he could see committing murder. Imagine: holding up a woman!

"The crabs are only the smallest portion of my misery. My husband has gone, and he was the source of the crabs."

Isadore resumed his position behind the dock in a precarious moral state. He had no time to reconsider his plan, however, for another candidate approached. The man—Isadore could see his Stetson from half a block away—was white, tall, striding with a quick, assured pace. This hour, 3:00 a.m., was the height of the so-called Tango Slobber, the steady dribble of men oozing home from the nightclubs, gambling parlors, and sporting houses in the Tango Belt. The clubs around Iberville and Rampart stayed open all night on Saturdays but around three o'clock the conscience of any man intending to go to church with his family began to churn. If a man was in a rush, or not thinking clearly, he might find himself walking along the fetid canal that divided the former Storyville district from Black Storyville. It was the shortest route to the back of town, a straight line, and it avoided the enticements and dangers of both nightlife districts. No enticements lay along the Old Basin Canal, only a procession of slumbering shrimp boats, shell barges, garbage scows, charcoal schooners, oyster luggers. And Isadore Zeno, lurking.

This man appeared not to be egregiously boiled, was several inches taller than Isadore, and had strong shoulders. Best to let him pass. Isadore held his breath. When the man came flush with the dock, he turned and stared at Isadore.

"Yay!" The man's voice was deep. "Who goes there?"

Isadore could not speak. In his pocket he fondled the Webley & Scott. Should he shoot? What if he missed? What if he hit? He did not want to fight and he did not want to kill because he did not want to be fought or be killed. So he remained squatting. He forced himself again to think of Orly and their unborn child but it no longer had an effect.

"Why is there fishnet over your face?"

After a pause, Isadore said, "Do you have a nickel for a poor fisherman?"

"It is a poor fisherman indeed who must resort to begging." The man removed a coin from his pocket and placed it in Isadore's trembling palm.

"Appreciate it, sir."

The man shook his head in sorrow. "It used to be enough to teach a man to fish."

Bailey had taught Isadore how to fish. A victim should be preoccupied, incautious, physically compromised: fat, short legged, disabled. He should offer the promise of a good payday, meaning he should either dress well or in a uniform that suggested he carried cash—knife sharpener, say, or bakery deliveryman. The greatest danger was a man who sought eye contact, a surefire sign of aggression. Should a confrontation occur, it was essential to attack with overwhelming ferocity. Bailey had no fear: he would have slugged the gentleman in the face, no matter how tall or white he was, and kicked him into the canal. That's why he was a successful highwayman. It was also why he was in jail, facing death.

It had become difficult to imagine any other outcome. The newspapers reported that Capo, the sweaty swinish police captain, assured Bailey that he would be rewarded for cooperation, and in September he confessed to six of the holdups—without mentioning an accomplice. He also pled guilty to murdering Detective Theodore Obitz. But the judge refused to accept the plea. He wanted Bailey hanged. Obitz's widow wanted him hanged. The Police Department wanted him hanged. Bailey was not so brave anymore. He told the judge he had made a mistake—could he change his plea to manslaughter? The judge laughed. Bailey tried again: Was there anything he could do to avoid a murder charge? You could kill yourself, replied the judge.

There was death on one side and death on the other. Then came the Spanish Death and the trial was delayed three months, depriving Bailey of a short confinement before his inevitable end. "I'm looking straight into the darkness now," he told a reporter. "I'm looking straight into it and I can't see no reflection." Isadore had wanted to visit him, he felt guilty for not yet having done it, but the risk was too great. His presence might cause Bailey, desperate and panicked, to report Isadore's role in the crimes to the police. No, it was better not to visit at all, better not to agitate him. A real friend would be careful not to cause any unnecessary harm.

Perhaps a new series of holdups would help Bailey's case. The police had believed the grocer Besemer to be the Axman until another attack occurred while he was in jail. Might another series of highwayman attacks cause Bailey's case to be reevaluated? But Isadore could not hold that idea in his head. He wasn't doing this for Bailey. He was doing it for Orly and the child inside her, which was another way of saying that he was doing it for himself. Enough—another candidate approached.

He was small, pale, skinny. His jerky walk meant he was either drunk or infirm. He carried a long suitcase in one hand and hummed a tune beneath his breath. Think: You're Bailey. You're fearless. You've done this thirty times. Maybe the suitcase carried winnings from one of the casinos. Wait too long and you'll risk being surprised in your own hiding spot. So jump. *Jump.*

"Hands over your head!"

The man froze but made no movement with his arms. Close up, Isadore could see that he was not white but was even lighter than himself. Very well—an Uptown Creole would still be liable to have money on him and would not file a police report. But Isadore did not look long because the holes in the crab netting were wide and head-on he might be more easily identified. He held the gun directly in front of his face.

"Would you mind, young man, if I first put down this case? It is heavy."

"Go on."

"There. Now I am raising my hands. There is no need to shoot."

The Creole's movements had a sinuous fluidity that unnerved Isadore. But why should he be more anxious than his victim? He circled quickly and, pressing the revolver between the man's shoulder blades, passed his free hand into the jacket pockets. He watched alertly for any sudden movement, but the Creole was still, his breathing even. Close like this, he could smell the man's odor—oaky, touched with gin. It was an intimate thing, going through another man's clothes, and it did not sit well with him. He had never been physically close to a victim on a Bailey job and was unprepared for the man's damp skin, the gravel of his breath, the pulse of his jugular. Isadore found a folded handkerchief in one of the pockets. From the other he removed a set of keys, a pocket watch, and a plug of tobacco. He dropped everything but the timepiece, which he slipped into his own jacket.

"What you're looking for is in the right pocket of my trousers."

Isadore swiped the man's waist to make sure there was no weapon. From the right trouser pocket he extracted a wallet and some coins. The left pocket was empty but in the back pocket he felt a thin metal rod that terminated in a bell. He held it up to his face to get a better look. It was gold plated—a mouthpiece for a trombone. Dread rose in him: Was this someone he knew? Had played with? The crab netting had come untucked from his shirt collar and he paused to replace it. He placed the wallet and the mouthpiece into his jacket and withdrew his weapon.

"What's in the case?" he asked. But he was stalling. He already knew.

"Nothing that would interest you." The man laughed. "I guess that's the last thing I should say to a thief."

"I'm not a thief." Isadore had to stop himself from adding, *I'm a musician.*

"Of course not. You're a professional purloiner. A career nightbird. A maestro of the pinching art—"

"Remove your shoes."

The Creole bent slowly and untied his shoes with dainty precision. They were Chicago Flats with cork soles and treble clefs embossed on the toes. Isadore didn't like the treble clefs. No ordinary jobbing trombonist could afford a gold mouthpiece and cork-soled loafers specially embossed. A voice inside him whispered a name.

"Hands back up," he ordered, affecting gruffness.

"Please leave my instrument." The man's calm was eroding. "It's my living. Take my jack, but leave me my living."

Isadore popped the case. The brass found the moonlight and the reflection shot into his eye. When the glare dissipated, there appeared in its place, as he had feared, a slide trombone. Not just any slide trombone: the bell was unusually small, the slide was wrapped in a green plastic band, and engraved on the lip of the bell was its owner's name. It confirmed what Isadore already knew and would have known sooner if he had gotten a clear look.

Isadore was jarred from his reverie by the crash of his revolver against the warehouse's corrugated iron siding. He became conscious a moment later of a burning sensation in his wrist. Dutt Ory kicked him again, sending Isadore to his stomach. Ory throttled him, pushed his cheek into the gravel. Isadore tasted metal and dust and hair.

"I draw the line," said Ory, "at taking away my livelihood."

"I don't want your horn."

"You were just appreciating it. Admiring how it glows."

Ory weighed a lot less than Orleania; if Isadore stood up, Ory would slide off. Hard from eight months toiling in the Pit, Isadore could easily toss the older man into the canal or retrieve the gun and do worse. But he had no desire to hurt Ory, or to risk further indignation. So he did not resist while Ory went through his pockets, reclaiming the wallet, watch, and mouthpiece.

"Skulking like a rat along the wharf," said Ory. "Striking from the shadows. What kind of a man does that?"

"Just get your stuff and leave."

"I could kill you. I could grab that gun and finish you for good."

"You could." Isadore knew he could beat the older man to the revolver. "I don't doubt it."

"But I am a merciful man. I know how hard the rough life can be."

The condescension chafed him. Ory might have known once, yes, but what did he know anymore? He was the embodiment of professional music success, and not just in New Orleans—in clubs from California to Chicago, Ory's acolytes played his music and sang his legend, building him, note by note, a monument to eternity. It was enough indignity to toil in obscurity and poverty and mud, smothered by the weight of Ory's shadow, driven even to criminality, but to be thwarted in his desperate effort to support his wife and child by that same man—it was too much to bear.

The weight abruptly lifted and Ory backed away, case in hand.

Here was an opportunity. With a single motion Isadore could snatch the revolver and fire. Just like that, he would be forevermore the man who killed Kid Ory. Or more than that—if Ory was the man responsible for popularizing jazz, then might killing him destroy the music at its root? Isadore Zeno, the man who killed jazz. Yet he didn't move.

"I'm going to leave you there because I trust you," said Ory, as he faded into the night. "You will find your way. King Zeno, I place my faith in you!"

Before he could respond, Ory was gone. Isadore rose creakily to his feet and threw off the crab netting. He considered the handgun. Compared to the slide trombone—hell, compared to his own pockmarked cornet—it was a poor instrument. It shot only one kind of bullet.

The cornet was the one instrument he knew how to play and he could make it sing better than anyone else could. How had he doubted it? He was better than Dipper, better than Buddie Petit, and better than Ory. That was why Ory didn't want Isadore in the Brown Skin Band—he understood that now. Ory was afraid of Isadore's sound, so new and so big. No, his problem was not the playing.

The problem was getting people to listen—enough people, the right people. As soon as the world heard him, it would not be able to hear any other music. The music would come first. Everything else—joy, security, life eternal—would follow.

Isadore tossed the revolver into the canal. He saw a splash but the sound was drowned out by the singing in his brain.

MARCH 10, 1919—THE GARDEN DISTRICT

She could be cunning too.

At eight thirty she blew out the candles and sank into the leather chair in the bay window that gave a clear view of the front gate. She retrieved Rosie's pale blue envelope every evening at ten o'clock, not wanting to wait until morning, when someone might notice it sticking out beneath the pot of pink azaleas. It wasn't there yet so Beatrice waited.

Two nights earlier, while reading the evening papers in the library, she had noticed Rosie's fluttery shape drifting past the gate. Beatrice tapped the window, indicating that she wanted to speak, but by the time she was outside, Rosie had vanished. Beatrice might have concluded that Rosie had not understood the gesture, were it not for the rapid pattering of Rosie's heels as she turned the corner and raced down First Street.

Nothing in Rosie's letter that night gave any indication of a problem. The letter she left the next evening was also mundane, but mundane to the point of absurdity. It wasn't the blandness itself—the reports were often unembroidered lists of events and appointments. Bland was normal. What was abnormal was the absence of detail. The report—when she thought about it, most of the reports of the last several weeks—had been poorly reported. In the first letters, back in September, Rosie had splurged on detail, as Beatrice had requested. A letter might note, for instance, that Giorgio settled a dispute with a john who demanded two girls in a single appointment, though he had only reserved one. Or that Giorgio, between 12:45 and 1:10 in the afternoon, consumed an oyster loaf in the second bedroom; between 1:35 and 1:50 speculated with one of the girls about the origins of the Spanish Death; between 2:10 and 2:45 repaired a hinge on the side gate; and between 2:35 and 3:00, due to the aforementioned exertion, bled from his head. Bleeding stanched at 3:01.

The details had dried up. Perhaps, after a listless six months, Rosie had grown as confident as Beatrice had of her son's transformation. That was the most charitable explanation. But Beatrice did not pay Rosie to be a judge of character. She paid for details. One entry stated simply: *noon–5pm, supervising at Washington Street crib.* The next day: *10am–2pm, errands.* What errands? And if Rosie was at the DeSoto house, how could she be certain that Giorgio was at the Bouligny crib? Rosie knew Beatrice would not tolerate such carelessness. Had she taken sick? Unlikely—she was healthy enough to hand-deliver the letters, after all. If you had Spanish flu, you didn't leave your bed unless you thought you could get to the bathroom without spilling fluids on the way.

The clock on the library's mantelpiece read nine o'clock. It was a cool vaporous evening, breezeless and dark—precisely the kind of evening that unsettled her. Too quiet, too still, a dress rehearsal for oblivion. Better the wind should blow, the cold should ache the bones. Somatic discomforts had their uses; they reminded you that you possessed a body, perceived, were alive. Beatrice lifted the window a few inches so that she could hear footsteps approaching and was rewarded with the distant sound of piano keys. A child played a clumsy ostinato. Her thoughts followed the line, meandering and disjointed, curling into half-completed thoughts that never resolved but returned to the beginning of the phrase and repeated. Rosie's omissions could not be credited to cockiness, laziness, illness, or carelessness. Was it fear? If Rosie neglected her duties, she might be afraid to fill the gaps with lies. If caught, the sin of a lie would be greater than the sin of neglect. But that excuse didn't ring either. The reports only drew attention to Rosie's inattentiveness. They were *conspicuously* blank. An entry such as *2pm–6pm: DeSoto Street* was a frank admission of incompetence. So why the provocation of a blank report?

Beatrice must have allowed her vigilance to lapse, for Rosalba Bucca was standing before the front gate. Beatrice had not heard the clicking of her heels, but soon had the explanation: Rosie held her shoes in one hand. In the other she held a blue envelope. Beatrice was at the front door in a heartbeat—a sharp, ragged heartbeat that tinged her vision red. Rosie was resettling the flowerpot when she saw Beatrice on the porch. Rosie looked as if she might speak, but a competing impulse overtook her and she pivoted in her stockinged feet, clutching her coat around her, and began to run.

"Wait!" Beatrice descended the porch steps in two bounds, crossed the garden path, and cleared the front gate. Rosie seemed determined to perpetuate the illusion that she had somehow failed to notice Beatrice. But despite being about fifteen years Rosie's senior, and perhaps twice her weight, Beatrice was, thanks to Messrs. Fletcher and Metchnikoff, as fit as a Carpathian maiden. She caught Rosie at the corner, beneath the dim yellow streetlamp. Rosie's eyes looked everywhere but at Beatrice, as if trying to follow simultaneously the paths of a dozen fireflies.

"If you want to quit," said Beatrice, "I'll find someone else."

Rosie shook her head in a kind of silent pleading.

"Do you think your services are no longer needed? Or do you want more money?"

Rosie shook her head more sharply and Beatrice realized her mistake. In Rosie's evasiveness there was not deceit or cunning. There was only fear.

"Why are you scared of me? Is that why you skulk like a thief—so I wouldn't hear your approach?"

Even in the dark Beatrice could see how pale Rosie had become.

"You're afraid of Giorgio." The fact had a finality to it, once spoken aloud. Beatrice intimidated, she bullied, she caused trepidation. But Giorgio inspired terror. If she were envious of her son, it was for his easy way with fear. He was a clambering bear whose mere presence made the smaller forest animals scurry underfoot.

Lessie Dunbar, after eight months apart, had been able to convince herself that a stranger was her son. Beatrice recalled that the foundling Charles Bruce Anderson, preferring the wealth and love of the Dunbars to the indifference and poverty of the piano tuner Walters, began to answer to the name Bobby Dunbar. Had Giorgio simply become a more persuasive impostor?

A sudden exhaustion consumed her. Denial had been exhausting, all-consuming. She had felt it in her joints, guts, brain. "You've been trying to tell me something with your letters," she said. "Here I am. Tell it to my face."

"Non lo posso . . . non adesso." I can't—not now. It was as if Rosie couldn't bring herself to speak in English. Or, in her panic, had forgotten English. She stared past Beatrice, into the dark.

"Rosie, please. Nobody is here but you and me and the night."

The night interrupted.

"Mamma."

She turned but didn't see him. Then she realized that she didn't see her son because he was so close that his bulk blotted out everything else.

"Rosie here giving you a hard time?"

Beatrice found that she too had lost her breath.

"I was coming to visit." His voice wasn't cheerful. It was grim. He sounded as exhausted as Beatrice felt. "What are you doing here, Miss Rosie?"

Rosie put her hand to her mouth as if to stifle a scream.

"You're bleeding," said Beatrice finally. She touched her son's forehead with her forefinger, her gold rings clinking like small cymbals. When she withdrew her hand, one of the rings was smeared.

There followed a moment's silence. Giorgio was considering something. A thin file of blood, merging with sweat, flowed down his jaw.

"My head," he said at last. "It's acting up."

"Here." Rosie produced a folded handkerchief. She seemed to surprise herself with the gesture.

"Thank you, Miss Rosie." Giorgio removed his homburg. The satin lining was stained pink.

"You can go, Rosie," said Beatrice.

"I'll be seeing you, Miss Rosie," said Giorgio.

Rosie turned the corner and, heels in hand, raced into the night.

"She's in a hurry," said Giorgio.

"Let's go inside." Beatrice told herself to take a reasonable tone. She worked hard at it but could no longer tell whether she was controlling her voice. For all she knew she might have been shrieking. "Then you can tell me why you're here."

She had no desire to bring Giorgio into the house with her. But she wanted to give Rosie a head start. Giorgio didn't protest. He loped to the front gate.

Beatrice tarried, letting him walk ahead of her. She lifted the azalea pot gently and plucked the blue envelope without taking her eyes off her son's broad, powerful back. Inside, once Giorgio went to the bathroom to clean his head, she tore open the letter.

It contained a single page, on which were printed only thirteen words:

All day long: Giorgio behaved very well. I have nothing more to report.

She forgave Rosie. There really was nothing more to report. Beatrice knew everything she needed to know. Bad Giorgio—plotting Giorgio, violent Giorgio, murderous Giorgio—had returned. For all she knew, he had never left.

She shoved the letter into her pocket and waited for her gigantic son to come out of the bathroom.

MARCH 11, 1919—CENTRAL BUSINESS DISTRICT

Capo claimed he was too busy to meet but Bill found him alone in his office, a rosary dangling from his hand, staring into nothingness. He reclined in his black wicker desk chair, which seemed insufficiently fortified to support the weight of his torso. His mouth worked soundlessly.

"Captain?"

Capo looked up, his fist clenching the rosary. "I said tomorrow at four."

"I found Obitz's files. There's new information."

Capo pursed his lips. They were gray and wet, oversize oysters. "We've seen those files. Mooney pulled them last summer."

"No—his personal files. He didn't take them into the Department."

Capo opened a drawer of his immense desk, placed the rosary inside it, and closed it. Before him stood eight neat stacks of documents, most of them in manila folders, each a different open investigation. On top of each stack lay a slip of orange paper on which his secretary had written a single word in neat cursive: HUN, PIETY, ROOSTER. The slip on the tallest stack read AX. Capo patted each pile, enacting some private compulsive ritual, before gesturing to Bill to sit in the oaken armchair opposite.

"Joseph Maggio was paying maintenance fees." Bill had to sit very erect to see Capo over the papers. "Obitz wrote it in his notes: 'maintenance fees.' "

"Protection?"

"Exactly. Black Hand. Obitz even drew a little black hand."

"What's that mean?"

"A doodle, like. A hand colored in with black ink." Bill had a momentary image of Eloise Obitz, her black underwear clinging to one ankle, her hands clenching. This was followed by an image of Maze in front of Gino's, saying, *You lied about you*. She was right, of course. She didn't know how right.

"There isn't any Black Hand." Capo said this as he might have said, *Stop wasting my time*. It was common wisdom among navies that the "Black Hand" was not an actual Italian Mafia crime syndicate but a catchall term for any criminal acts committed by New Orleans's Italian population. But a Black Hand crime hadn't made headlines for a dozen years, not since the kidnapping of Walter Lamana, the eight-year-old son of an Italian undertaker. When his father refused to pay a ransom, the child was decapitated and buried in a swamp; the kidnappers were found and convicted, their ringleader executed. It was understandable that superstitious beliefs should persist in the port city where the American Mafia originated, but if racketeering did persist, Captain Capo would know about it. Besides being second-in-command at the NOPD, Capo was also the Department's liaison to the city's Italian community. His father was born in Palermo; Capo spoke Sicilian at home.

"I know there's no Black Hand," said Bill, backtracking. "But it seems that Obitz found evidence of Black Hand–like activity."

"You interrupted me for this?" Behind Capo, a window looked out to Saratoga Street. A preacher stood on the tailgate of a church wagon parked in front of the station, declaiming loudly to passing officers. A sign on his wagon said MR. JOHN BARLEYCORN BROUGHT US THE PLAGUE.

"I also spoke with Andrew Maggio. Brother of the deceased."

"Christ, Billy. You haven't been this excited since—I don't know. Before the war certainly."

Excited—a delicate way of saying crazed or obsessed. Bill had a vision of Leonard Perl pressed beside him, saying, *What kind of cop are you?*

"I'm close," said Bill.

"No need to yell."

Bill lowered his voice. "Maggio told me there were 'towns within towns.'"

"I'll be honest, Bill. I'm running out of tolerance."

"Towns without towns: he's talking about a protection racket. That's why Maggio didn't talk. He was afraid of a reprisal."

Capo gave him a lidded look.

"Then I spoke with Louis Besemer," said Bill.

"I suppose he claimed he was innocent."

"He said that, yes."

"He's being charged for murdering his mistress. What do you expect?"

"I don't think he did it. Unless the ax attacks, despite being nearly identical in method, are totally unrelated. But that's not the point."

"I'm waiting for the point."

"Besemer said something funny. He said that if he did know something, and the Axman were alive, then he—Besemer—wouldn't be safe even in prison."

"So you think the syndicates are coming back."

"Seems that way."

Capo shifted laboriously in his seat. "Slow down, Billy. Think about it. What do you really have? Mooney has been over this business for months with nothing to show."

On Saratoga Street the preacher replaced the sign on his wagon. The new sign read JAZZ KILLS.

"There's more," said Bill.

Capo's face remained impassive, heavy, molded of damp clay.

"Andrew Maggio said he'd sold the family business to a bank. I looked in the city records. The bank was *Hibernia*."

"You're going to have to back up."

"Right. Hibernia. There's one ax crime that doesn't match the others."

"Mrs. Schneider. She's not Italian. Not a grocer. Lives at home with her kids."

"But her husband works as an auditor at a bank."

"Let me guess."

"I know—it's rickety."

"Hibernia is what, the second-largest bank in New Orleans?"

"It's enough to get you thinking."

Capo smiled. With visible effort, he pressed down on the desk and hoisted himself out of the wicker chair. The chair and the desk groaned in mutual sympathy. Capo walked past Bill, toward the doorway. Bill took this to mean that the conversation was over.

But Capo closed the door and flipped the lock. "There is a problem with your story."

"Mrs. Schneider?"

Capo shook his head—slowly. Everything he did was slow. He moved through honey instead of air. "You said the attacks were 'nearly identical in method.'"

Bill was surprised by Capo's recall. He had appeared to be half-asleep during that part of the conversation. But Capo was not half-asleep anymore. He eyes bored out of his head.

"So how do you explain the body in the canal?"

"I was working up to that. Charlie and I have a theory."

"An Italian?"

Bill nodded. "A Sicilian grocer. Ernesto Rosetta."

Capo returned to his chair and collapsed into it. The chair groaned. The floorboards groaned. Capo groaned.

"Why haven't I heard about this?"

"Nobody reported him missing."

"Is he married?"

"She's missing too."

Capo reached for the stack labeled AX, then withdrew his hand. "Explain."

"There's a boy running Rosetta's Grocery—a child. He said Rosetta told him to look after the shop while they went to Sicily."

"Let me make sure I get this: Rosetta put a kid in charge of his store and he went on a vacation."

"Some vacation."

"Nobody claimed the body."

"The corpse had a note from the grocery in his pocket."

Capo leaned back. There came the sound of splintering wicker. "Anything else?"

Bill wondered about Maze. Was she back across the lake, preparing supper for her parents? Did she think of him?

"Captain, with respect—I thought you'd have a little more enthusiasm. The case has been dead six months. And now these new incidents. Some journalist will make the connection."

"The journalists in this town . . ."

"The point is that the killer is back. The panic is back too." The line surprised Bill and he decided he liked it. *The panic is back*. If

Capo didn't understand the urgency of the situation, Bill would keep reminding him.

"You're rather energized."

"It's right in front of us."

Capo pulled open a desk drawer and removed two log-size cigars. He produced a matchbook from his breast pocket.

"Smoke?"

"I wouldn't want you to waste one on me."

Capo shrugged and returned one of the cigars to the box. The other he inserted into a silver cutter mounted to his desk. He lit a match. Bill tried to tell whether the cigar lighting was an act of celebration or deferral.

"Don't get me wrong," Capo said at last, exhaling. "I'm glad to see you excited. But I've been working this job a little longer than you."

"Yes, sir." The smoke smelled delicious: sweet, with a shadow of cinnamon. It had been a mistake not to accept. His demurral had given Capo an advantage.

"I don't mean to patronize. It's just that I don't get excited until I hear something that sounds like evidence. That at least rhymes with evidence."

"Here's another thing."

Capo sighed smoke.

"The construction company running the dig? Hercules? The owner is Beatrice Vizzini. Widow of one Sal Vizzini."

"Vizzini was a nothing," said Capo through smoke. Out the window two officers brought the preacher a mug of coffee. The preacher blessed the officers, who laughed.

"I checked his file," said Bill. "He protected grocery stores. Ten, fifteen years ago. There were a few charges but nothing stuck."

"You don't have to tell me about the old reports. I wrote those reports. Vizzini has been dead nearly a decade."

Capo sucked his cigar thoughtfully. Bill wanted to grab him. It was true Bill's instincts were imperfect. But he wasn't one easily carried away in speculation. Just that morning he had imagined telling Maze all about it. She would be awed, proud. Her eyes would get big as he told her about the child running Rosetta's Grocery, Andrew Maggio's strange declaration—but then came Eloise Obitz and the image shattered.

"Let's review." Capo held up one of his meaty hands, as if to forestall any interruptions. "The brother of one victim says something cryptic and probably nonsensical. He sells his brother's grocery to the bank. The same bank, one of the city's largest, employs a man who is the husband of victim two. We have no evidence linking the two attacks. A third victim, Besemer, on trial for murder, claims innocence. A fourth victim is found in the canal. Again, no evidence linking that crime to the others. You believe that John Doe is in fact a grocer who, according to his closest associates, has traveled to Italy. For all we know the grocer did travel to Italy. What was the last one?"

"The canal," Bill heard himself say. Capo appeared to gain energy with each recited doubt. And each dealt Bill a wound. None was mortal in itself, but his theory was dying from blood loss.

"Right," said Capo. "John Doe's burial site. The construction company is owned by the wife of a man who once ran a small protection business for grocers. Which makes him one of about a dozen Italians who did the same. And he's been dead for years!"

Bill knew not to take it personally. But the case had become personal. It was personal because his interest had nothing to do with the Axman. It had to do with Maze, and with himself. Solving the case and winning back Maze were entangled in his mind. It made no sense. It was irrational. Even so, hearing Capo ridicule his theory, he began to suspect that he had lost Maze forever.

"Besides," Capo was saying, "why would the killer dump the body of a grocer in the canal? The other bodies were found in the groceries. What would make the killer drag the body across the city and bury it twenty-five feet underground?"

Bill shook his head. "I guess I hadn't considered that, boss."

"Look, Bill. You've had a lot to absorb this year."

Bill began to see what this was all about.

"It's no easy thing coming home from war and going straight back to work. I know that. Then the scene with your old comrade—"

"The man was deranged."

"Furthermore," said Capo, addressing the glowing tip of his cigar, "though I don't like to mention it, I understand that things aren't going well at home. It's a lot of burden for one man to carry."

So he had become himself an unreliable witness. He didn't realize his behavior had been that transparent.

"Hand over your files." Capo crushed his cigar against the desk. "Maybe I'll come to see it your way."

"Thanks, Cap," Bill said woodenly.

Capo sprang from his seat, suddenly as light as a pillow, and rested his arm on Bill's shoulder. "That's what I'm here for. To consider it all. We'll solve this. Don't crack up."

Capo's voice had taken on an avuncular tone, the kind you might use with an impaired relative who was not strong enough to face the truth. "Take this for gospel: We're going to get him. I'm going to do everything in human power to run down this maniac." Capo opened the door. "Oh, and Bill?"

"Yes?"

"Don't forget to bring me your reports. Especially the Obitz file. I need it all."

Capo's words were still ringing in Bill's head when he arrived home to discover a note wedged under his door. He recognized immediately the handwriting. Under his name, she had written the words *Urgent: Deliver By Hand*. His heart leaped, before plunging a much greater distance, as he flipped the envelope and read the words printed on the back:

CHARITY HOSPITAL

NEW ORLEANS

And stamped over that, in red ink:

DISINFECTED

MARCH 12, 1919—CENTRAL BUSINESS DISTRICT—ESPLANADE RIDGE

"'I am convinced,'" read Hugs Davenport, "'that the murders are the work of an ax-wielding degenerate who has no robbery motive, but who has taken small sums to throw the police off the track.'" He glanced up from the paper, peering narrowly over his spectacles—a new addition to his toilet, the spectacles, like his wispy blond mustache, could only be explained as a strategy to make himself look older. When he read the newspaper he looked below the lenses at the text, so that he was always looking above or under the lenses, never through them. "Mooney continues, 'I am likewise convinced that he is a sadist, a man whose obsession is to hack people with an ax.'"

"That is quite enough." Beatrice reminded herself to sit still, to avoid playing with her rings, to take normal, shallow breaths—to eliminate any manifestation of the alarm that caused her vision to turn purple at the edges. "That is beyond enough."

Hugs ruffled the paper at her in a way that she considered profoundly unprofessional. "You hadn't heard about this?"

"I have been too busy this week to keep up on the local press." It was a lie, but no version of the truth was remotely possible.

"The Axman has returned."

"You asked me here to discuss business."

Hugs glared over his spectacles. He had perfected his uncle's demeanor: skeptical, exacting, supercilious. She doubted that he dared to assume this attitude with his colleagues, but now he flung at her the full weight of his disdain. "Exactly. Business."

He slid the *States* across the table. It contained nothing that surprised her. She had read it, as well as similar accounts in the *Item* and the *Times-Picayune.* But dutifully, gamely, trying to preserve the last particle of her sanity, she forced her eyes to advance through the text. It was like trudging through a pit of mud:

GRETNA ITALIANS LATEST VICTIMS OF AX MURDERER

Keeper of Grocery, His Wife and Child Attacked as They Slept

LITTLE GIRL KILLED, MAN FATALLY HURT

An axman murderer, who laid his plans with fiendish cunning and executed them with revolting brutality, chose Charles Cortimiglia, his wife, and their 2-year-old daughter, Mary, Second and Jefferson streets, Gretna, for his victims early Sunday morning.

The child was killed outright, the father was in a

dying condition Sunday night in the Charity Hospital, and the mother unconscious and piteously crying, "Mary, Mary," the name of her murdered child, was fighting for her life with five wounds in her head and a depressed fracture of the skull just over the left ear. She may recover.

Meantime the police of New Orleans and Gretna were without a clue to the identity of the murderer.

FIFTH AXMAN MURDER

This Gretna murder is the fifth perpetrated in New Orleans and vicinity by an axman murderer since last May. In every case except one the victims have lived back of corner groceries, their homes have been entered in early morning hours, entrances have been effected by removing a panel from rear doors and an ax has been the weapon.

While the police have put forth every effort to bring the murderer to justice, they admit themselves baffled and without any satisfactory clue.

The murderer who attacked the Cortimiglia family while they slept in the early hours of Sunday worked with all the cunning of a degenerate maniac. The child, sleeping in her mother's arms, apparently was killed first, the mother next was attacked, and the condition of the room indicated that the father, roused from sleep, had battled the fiend until he fell unconscious beneath blows from the ax which crushed his skull. The murder was done in a tiny room, where pictures of the Crucifixion, the Virgin and her Child and a Sister of Mercy at prayers looked down upon the scene.

"A two-year-old child!" exclaimed Hugs, as if just absorbing the fact.

Giorgio at two: fat, languorous, refusing to be weaned, a bear cub who did not know his own strength. At two he told his first lie: that he hadn't eaten an Elmer's Mint Bublet from the candy jar. He said so through lips flaked with chocolate. She had indulged him, laughing.

"My uncle—" Hugs could not bear to complete the sentence. "We have endured tremendous scrutiny since the bond issue."

"It's a sad story. But I don't see the connection."

"Don't you really?"

"I do not. Now. You were going to provide an update on the progression of the Texas dredge."

Hugs was examining his nails very closely.

She tried again: "How many yards did it advance last week?"

Hugs peered over his spectacles at Beatrice. "I had hoped you would not compel me to spell it out."

"I am afraid," she said, as calmly as she could manage, aware of a slight tremor of her lower lip, "that you will have to."

"We had a major delay one week ago. Perhaps you recall? The Texas dredge was not designed to digest human skeletons."

"I remember."

"If it weren't for my uncle's intercession with his friends at the *States*, *Item*, and the *Times-Picayune*, the story would be everywhere."

"A dead laborer. A shame. Likely he did not take the proper precautions. Is there any problem with insurance?"

"The papers reported it was a dead laborer. But he was not a laborer."

"A machinist? A truck driver?"

"A grocer."

She did not know whether she responded. Her mind was elsewhere.

"An Italian grocer."

Beatrice thought about this for a while. "What was he doing at the canal?"

"His murderer buried him there."

"A murderer? Why a murderer?" She felt herself on the verge of falling to pieces. She must avoid that. She must keep all the pieces attached as long as possible. Once unstuck, she would not be able to put herself back together.

"The autopsy found that his wounds were not inflicted by the Texas. The wounds, I quote, were 'consistent with the profile of a large chopping implement, such as a hatchet, or ax.'"

Beatrice redoubled her barricade of placid indifference. It was a last-ditch defense, but as in the case of all last-ditch defenses, it was the only one available to her.

"That I suspect your son may be responsible is irrelevant. The problem for you is that my uncle thinks so too."

"My *son*?" The outrage in her voice startled her. But it was real, the outrage. That much was not an act. She *was* outraged.

"If we know, how long before the police discover the truth?"

"I must speak with Mr. Denzler immediately."

"We have no interest in your family's business—at least the aspects that do not relate to the canal. But the police are asking questions."

"What police?"

"The New Orleans Police Department."

The police, she thought inanely. The police.

"My uncle is scheduling meetings with other contracting companies."

Denzler was not an idiot; he understood, perhaps better than

Hugs, that the fates of Hercules and Hibernia were entwined; no investigation would fail to uncover that awkward fact. Still Hibernia could try to dilute their union, hiring rival competitors to assume much of the work. She rose abruptly, knocking her knee against the table. She tried not to show pain.

"Where is he, your uncle? I demand to see him."

"He is not working in the bank today. I do not know his whereabouts."

"Has Hercules let you down in any way? Professionally?"

"A corpse in the work site? I'd judge that a letdown."

"Hercules, despite your lurid fantasies, has nothing to do with that. The police will reach the same conclusion."

"I hope so." Hugs's voice was impassive, polite, dull.

"I was speaking about the dig. Have we not been as efficient as possible, given the circumstances?"

"Efficiency is not our concern. Our concern is that the carelessness of your methods may undo the great work we've begun."

It was a reasonable concern. It was her concern too, after all. "Please advise Mr. Denzler," she said with what remaining authority she was able to muster, "to cancel any meetings he's made with our competitors."

Hugs laughed. "I can convey the message."

"Convey this: Hercules will finish the canal. That is written in our contract. And it is binding."

"I don't know that it is binding."

"I am telling you. It is binding."

The police.

No one answered the door at DeSoto Street, but when she tried the knob, it was unlocked. A muted arpeggio of laughter came from one of the rooms. She called out Rosie's name—once, twice, a third time.

"Rosie ain here!" A bedroom door opened. A plump woman in a semitranslucent white slip appeared, red faced, breathless, a thick curl of greasy black hair dangling over one of her eyes. Her areolas—brown, diffuse—were visible through the sheer fabric. "Rosie ain here."

"Where is she?"

From inside the room, a male voice: "Mamma?"

The prostitute turned in wonder.

"Mamma, is that you?"

"Giorgio?"

"One minute, Mamma."

The prostitute, shaking her head in disgust, retreated from sight.

There came a creak of mattress springs, followed by a creak of floorboards. Giorgio appeared in the door: vast, muscular, grinning. His neck was slick with perspiration. He wore his navy trench coat. She could not tell whether anything was underneath it.

"Let's parley in the parlor." He giggled slightly and indicated the way with a gallant sweep of his hand.

"I don't want to sit. Where's Rosie?"

"I haven't seen her since, well, since the other night. At your house."

"What did you do to her, Giorgio?"

Giorgio gave her a look that she had never before seen. It so surprised her that she required a moment to decode its emotional valence. Then it hit her: condescension. Giorgio was regarding his mother with a look of pure, unabashed condescension. It was as if he were trying to imitate Hugs Davenport.

"I'm running the sporting business now," he said. "Soon I will relieve Zio Zo and the cousins of their duties. And one day, when the time comes, I'll relieve you." He laughed, as if it were all just a joke.

"Is that so?"

"I know that I wasn't always a good business partner to you. Sometimes I think that's because of how things ended with Papa. But it don't matter anymore. I'm older. I understand how business works. I'm good at it too. If it weren't for me, who knows which company would be in charge of the canal project."

"*I* am in charge of the canal project. I've seen it through. It's not easy, to see something like that through."

The condescending smile returned. "Mr. Blank, who wouldn't sell his land. The Tulane professor, Fishman. The laborers who slacked off."

"*Murder*," she said, "is not a solution." She was coming unstuck. Or had she already come unstuck? Talking with her son openly about murder! It would be better to come unstuck once and for all. Have it done finally. So much easier than trying to summon the energy required to hold all the pieces together all the time.

"Murder," she said, "only causes more problems. The police are investigating. They have been to the canal."

"Yes, Mamma."

"Don't 'Yes, Mamma' me."

"Yes, Mam—ma'am."

"Do you know anything about this Cortimiglia couple in Gretna? With the small child!"

"Don't believe everything you read."

"Or the grocer buried in the canal?"

"The only detective who knew anything was killed by the Negro highwayman last year."

"I did not raise you to be a monster!"

"*Calmatevi.* You are agitated unnecessarily. Let me examine your back."

"I will not sit down." She rapped the frame of the chair with her palm.

"I am not a monster. I am your son, your Giugi. That hasn't changed."

"I can't take this anymore."

"Your blood is deranged." He raised his hands. "May I?"

"You may not!"

He lowered his hands. When he spoke again his voice was cool, distant. "You did not raise me to be a monster. But you did raise me."

"What does that mean?"

"I am talking about Papa."

"What does he have to do with this?" But she was beginning to understand. The shape of it dawned as big as the moon.

"You taught me that when you want something, you got to grab it. If a person blocks you, you knock him down. No matter who he is."

She had never heard him speak this way. Perhaps running the business did it. Professional success conferred a dignity that was not otherwise available. But it was more than that. Giorgio had traveled beyond confidence and into the next territory, arrogance. He had, perhaps, gone even further: into monomania, the darkest, swampiest country of them all.

"You hated your father."

Giorgio nodded gamely. "Papa was cruel. Worse than that: incompetent. I don't blame you."

They had never come so close to addressing it. She knew that Giorgio understood the general ingredients of Sal's death: Lizzie sent home early; Beatrice seated beside Zio Zo all evening in the loge of the French Opera House for all of New Orleans to see, though she detested opera; Sal collapsed over his nightly glass of marsala superiore. The coroner asked to test the bottle but Beatrice could not find it—Lizzie must have thrown it out, she told the investigating officer, Captain Thomas Capo. But she had never explicitly discussed the incident with her son. She had not mentioned the letter from Rosalba Bucca, the final bitter argument, the blue vial of mercury bichloride.

"If Sal lived any longer," said Beatrice, "we would not have secured the contract for the Industrial Canal."

"I know that."

"While he dissipated the last of the family fortune in Storyville, our competitors would have run us over."

"Don't you understand, Mamma? I'm grateful for what you did."

"And what do you think I did?"

He laughed. "You gave me another chance at life."

She leaned on the chair for support. Giorgio, observing her shakiness, guided her into it. It was a relief to unburden herself, to let the heavy cushion absorb her weight.

"I'm only saying, Mamma, that you taught me well."

When Giorgio was a little boy, she thought he looked exactly like Sal. Not anymore. It's true he had his father's imposing size, his flat, squashed turnip nose, and his dark, wide-spaced eyes. But look into those eyes, and there was Beatrice—deep inside of him, staring back at herself.

MARCH 13, 1919—CRIMINAL COURT BUILDING

The clock on the red stone tower of the Criminal Court Building was broken: it read five minutes before ten. A trail of men in business suits weaved through the neutral ground of Elks Place, returning unsteadily from luncheon at the downtown hotels. One pretended to mount the bronze elk that stood at the end of the park; another wobbled into traffic, causing a hansom horse to rear up. None of this elicited any response from the pair of navies stationed in front of the court. They were fixed on Isadore. They had monitored him since he'd turned the corner. It made sense, the clock on the court building being stopped. Justice had stopped. Bailey would soon be forced to stand trial, despite not having any chance of victory; he had even been forbidden from pleading guilty. The state sought his life, all for the crime of being poor, black, and desperate. And, to be fair, for killing a police detective.

"Why you smiling?" The cop's hand rested casually, but firmly, on his gun.

Isadore was certain that he was not smiling. If his mouth was doing something funny, it was not inspired by cheer but terror. He had deferred the visit for nine months, fearful that his old friend might have let slip the name of his accomplice, fearful that the police might be waiting for him, using Bailey as bait. But Bailey had remained loyal. Isadore owed him, though that wasn't all. He had become convinced that Bailey, the smartest and stupidest man he had ever met, who knew him as nobody, not even Orly, could—that Bailey was the only person he could trust. Still Isadore couldn't help but wonder if he was volunteering himself to the gallows. Four police eyes devoured him with gratuitous disdain.

"I'm here to visit an inmate, sir."

They gave nothing.

"Do I enter through this building, sir? Or better I should go around back?"

"Depends," said the navy. "You guilty of something?"

The other cop laughed.

Isadore went around back. He entered an antechamber in which an enormous man sat at a broad desk, his bulk framed by a grilled iron door. The jail had the violent smell of raw chicken left out in the sun. Suppressing a gag, Isadore searched the face of the guard to see whether he was aware of the offense, but he was as impassive as a mountain. As Isadore began to wonder whether the officer was sleeping with his eyes open, he slid a visitor's form across the desk. Isadore selected a dull pencil from a hollow coffee tin. He wrote his name, Bailey's name, and the time. The clock in the waiting room was not broken: it read ten past three. In jail, the clocks never stopped. Jail was a dress rehearsal for oblivion. Time kept marching while you sat still, doing nothing, thinking nothing.

Isadore did not notice the officer glance at the form, but he must have because suddenly he came to life. He was a volcano trembling before an eruption.

"You're here to see Detective Obitz's killer?"

Isadore saw himself being hauled behind the door and thrown onto the floor of a cell. He saw himself kicked and beaten. He saw himself getting used to the stench of rotting meat until he didn't notice it anymore.

"A miracle he's still alive," the officer snarled. His glare invited a response.

"Sir?"

"The boys were fixing to tear him apart. But the chief forbade it."

"Yes, sir."

"I figured he wouldn't last a month. But he's still here."

". . . Yessir."

"Not for long."

"Nosir."

"He won't outlast Judge Baker. It'll be a glorious day for this city when he hangs. I hope they do it in Jackson Square so folks can bring their families. Make a picnic of it."

Isadore glanced at the iron door. He had the impression that prisons were loud places, that some kind of camaraderie set in among the inmates, as at the Waifs' Home—that you would hear people razzing each other and laughing and flapping cards. But it was silent.

The officer squinted. "What are you, one of his partners?"

"No, sir. Just a friend."

"You're the only one."

Isadore waited, hat in hand. He concentrated on a section of the wall where the paint bulged and bubbled, unable to suppress some liquid force trying to burst through.

The jailer rose, unbolted the door, and disappeared behind it. An interval of silence was followed by another series of clanks, metal grinding metal, and beneath those a rushed conversation in a tone of low menace. The iron door opened.

"Enter," said the jailer.

The door led into a second room even smaller than the first. Bailey sat shackled by his wrists and ankles to a rusting metal chair bolted to the floor. The restraints hardly seemed necessary. Bailey had changed. Always he had been hyperactive, carbonated, unwilling to turn off his voice, but now he sat still. He was leaner, almost gaunt. They had clipped his hair too short. His flesh was puckered with insect bites. His features had been adjusted somehow, shifted slightly, the way the furniture looks after a party. Isadore figured it out: Bailey was nearly a year older. The last time Isadore had seen Bailey, he was eighteen. He was nineteen now.

"Izzy?"

"Here I am."

"I didn't suspect you'd ever come."

"I'm sorry, Frank." Isadore glanced at the officer, who stood with his back to the door, cracking his knuckles. "I've been wanting to."

"Don't say anything. I'm pleased to see you."

With nowhere to sit Isadore leaned against the damp cement

wall. A small, high window, heavily smeared with grime, permitted a shaft of gray light.

"You look different," said Isadore.

"I've spent nine months and twelve days facing death."

"C'mon. It's not going to come to that."

Bailey gave Isadore a look that mingled sarcasm and pity. "The first thing that goes is all the stories you tell yourself to quiet your fears. I had a great deal of those stories. Like: All I needed was one more holdup and I'd be set for jack. I would never get caught. I had no choice but to run holdups. I would look Spanish if I wore diamonds in my teeth."

Isadore laughed. "No one says *Spanish* anymore. It makes people think about the sickness. *Tough* is more up-to-the-minute. Or *clever. Clever like a professor.*"

"I didn't look clever with diamonds in my teeth."

"I heard your lawyer has a good defense."

"I bought that lawyer with the diamonds." Bailey sighed. "It would've been better if I hadn't already pled."

"It's not too late."

Bailey snorted. "When I got taken in—when Verge sold me out—they used the third-degree method."

"I read that."

"You know what it means?" Bailey's jaw moved in a wounded way.

"They did you physical damage."

"One navy struck me with a stick. Another twisted my arm. They shouted in my face. Spit on me. They punched me in the stomach, where it doesn't leave a mark. They're animals."

Isadore looked at the jailer, expecting him to stride over with heavy fists, but he stared emptily into the middle distance.

"That's the first defense: illegally obtained confession. They dictated the whole rap to me."

"I'm not a lawyer," said Isadore. "I'm just a ditchdigger and barrel maker."

"You're a musician."

"What's the second?"

"Second?"

"The other defense."

"Detective Obitz's partner, Dodson. He identified a different man as the murderer. That's number two. The old nightman at the Demolishing Company. Abraham Price."

"I remember."

"Big country darky."

"It stands to reason. The judge is supposed to believe that the officer, when he fingered Mr. Price, was lying?"

"It won't amount to nothing. I haven't got a Chinaman's chance."

"It's not for you to say."

A series of inscriptions and drawings was scratched into the green walls. A frowning stick-figure man hung from the bough of a live oak. Next to it was written MY FAMILY TREE.

"Many folks heard me cry out in pain while I was in custody but nobody will admit it." Bailey caught himself returning to his old excitability and resumed his matter-of-fact tone: "They want my life and they'll have it. To the gallows I'll walk without a whimper and not one word will I say after leaving my cell. They won't hear nothing so I won't say nothing."

"It won't hurt none, having your lawyer make those arguments. I can't say if it will help. But it won't hurt none."

"People in this town think a Negro is nothing. If there is such a thing as a spirit returning to earth, I don't want to come back. The people want to send nothing from this world and that nothing will stay away forever."

"Is there mercy for the fact of your youth?" Isadore snuck a glance at the guard, standing behind Bailey, on the opposite wall. The guard appeared comatose.

"They like to get us as soon as they can."

It made Isadore uneasy, hearing Bailey speak this way. But wouldn't he feel the same in Bailey's place? On the wall a prisoner had made a tracing of his hand. Beneath he'd written MY GIRLFRIEND FOR THE NEXT 9 YRS.

"You just got on the left side of bad luck," said Isadore. "Many get away with much worse."

"When nothing leaves this earth," said Bailey, "nothing can be returned."

"You got your people behind you. You got me."

"You and my mother. No one else."

Isadore knew better than to ask about Virginia. He heard she had taken up with a hard man, a grifter type who worked on the wharf. "A lot of people are behind you," he said. "They just aren't fixing to come to jail."

Bailey made to swat his hand, as if to change the subject, but the chains yanked back his wrist, making him wince. "Here's my question. Who's going to answer for the deaths of Abraham Price and Louis Johnson, innocent men, who were shot down for the crime that I am to hang for?"

Isadore glanced at the mountain man. He remained as nonreactive as limestone. On the wall behind him was written IF JESUS WAS A NEGRO WHY HE HATE NEGROES.

"I'll tell you," said Bailey. "Nobody will answer for the deaths of those innocent men. Because the killers are white. Whiter than white: one's an Uptown businessman, the other's a cop." He shook his head. "The crazy thing," he said, more stunned than angry, "is that I didn't kill the detective. I didn't do it."

Isadore didn't know how to respond. It hurt, Bailey's not being honest even with him. But the jailer was not ten feet away, listening, even if he pretended not to.

"I just wanted to say, I appreciate what you've done." Isadore nodded toward the navy and hoped that made his meaning clear. He couldn't out and say, *Thanks for not turning over on me*. "It means a lot. Means everything."

"Yah? Then you can do me a favor. We don't have mosquito bars in there, and the mattresses are crawling with chinches. I got a terrible itch here above my eye."

"What about—"

"He don't care. Please. I'm dying."

Isadore rose slowly. The guard did not budge. Isadore walked slowly toward Bailey. Above one of his eyes a bite had burst and scabbed over. After another glance at the guard, Isadore scratched carefully around the bite's circumference. Bailey's skin was raw, moist. It was like touching a fresh corpse.

"A little harder." Bailey gritted his teeth. "There it is. Thanks. Thank you."

Isadore returned to the wall. His hand shook. His back was sore. His head was fuzzy.

"And what, can I ask, have you been doing with your freedom?"

He thought of Dutt Ory twisting his cheek into the gravel on Carondelet Walk. "I've been struggling, to be honest."

Bailey's eyes went somewhere far away. "Sometimes I remember the Waifs' Home Brass Band."

"It was Mr. Davis got me started on the cornet."

"Seefus on trombone. Gateface on drum. Me on bass. Dippermouth on second cornet. Who was the foundling with the fucked-up hair who played clarinet?"

"Family Haircut. Don't recall his Christian name."

"That boy could play, Family Haircut. Him and Dipper too. But you were best."

"I appreciate it, Frank. Not enough people see it your way."

"You could make sounds on that horn that nobody heard before. Made it cry like a baby, growl like a tiger. You still making it growl like a tiger?"

"I've all but given it up, to tell the truth."

Bailey scowled. "Why? You have a real touch for jass."

"They call it jazz now."

Bailey scowled again.

"There's no audience for jazz in this city," said Isadore. "Not the real hot kind."

"For your playing, there's an audience."

"We played the Butt. It's not a living, though."

"Five minutes," said the jailer, without looking at them or, as far as Isadore could tell, moving his lips.

Bailey gave Isadore a curious look. "You were at the Butt?"

"You should've seen us. Zutty Singleton played with us."

"Hey! That's all right."

"But we didn't get any other chances out of it. I got an audition with Ory but . . . it didn't come to pass."

"No hotel gigs?"

"I did a show at the Cave, but it was a fill-in. It wasn't even jazz."

Bailey thought about that. "What did you play at the Funky Butt? What's your routine?"

"You got to play the old milky stuff, so they get accustomed to you. 'Clarinet Marmalade,' 'Tiger Rag,' 'Livery Stable Blues.' That's the way to get gigs. Then, after you get to the top, you deliver the piping-hot stuff."

"But you never got to the top."

Isadore shook his head. "It's hopeless."

"Don't tell me about hopeless."

"Sorry, Frank, that's not—"

Isadore was interrupted by Bailey's laughter. "You're doing it *all* wrong." Here was the old Bailey: quick to give counsel on things he knew nothing about. "Nobody cares about another young Negro playing the same old music. You need to start *off* with something new. Look, every man who's made it has some trick that gives him glow, right?"

"You mean like Bolden playing three times louder than everyone else?"

"That's right—the people at the front would clear right out. Or King Oliver wearing the bright red fireman's underwear beneath his shirt. The ladies see the flash of red and they're like bulls seeing the flag. And Ory—what'd Ory do? He must have done something."

"He was the first to play trombone in the tailgate fashion. Playing smears and slides in conversation with the trumpet line. Before him trombonists played straight rhythm."

"The point is he did something new. I did something similar myself."

"What, when we were in Mr. Davis's band?"

"No—the holdups. Nobody ever heard of a Negro highwayman making white businessmen before me. Why do you think I got so much play from the newspapers?"

"It doesn't matter what I do if there's only a few people to see it. Since the Spanish flu, the city has gone silent. I'm working two jobs just to survive."

Bailey shook his head. "You're thinking too trifling. You can play, but you're not thinking strategically."

Isadore laughed. Look at Bailey, advising him on strategy. "Is there anything I can do for you from the outside?"

But Bailey was off in his own land. "It's a double trouble." He nodded. "Nobody's going to appreciate your music if they don't see you play it. But nobody is going to come see you if they don't already appreciate the music. You're double-troubled."

"Add the fact that nobody in this town seems to care about jazz music, or want to pay to see it, and you got troubles treble and quadruple."

Bailey thought for some time. The light coming through the window had dimmed. The walls grew dark, olive-hued. The room shrank.

"You have to get their attention," Bailey said at last.

"That's all for palavering," said the jailer, stirring to life. He began separating himself from the wall. "Back to murderers' row."

"I'll come back soon." Isadore tried to sound cheerful.

Bailey ignored him. "What motivates people to do something? How do you get into them and make them go out of their normal ways?"

The jailer lowered himself to one knee to unlock Bailey's ankle shackles.

"I think back on my situation. Why did the whole city turn against me? Why did Superintendent Mooney send the entire police force into the streets to find a Negro highwayman who hadn't stolen more than two dollars from a single person?"

The jailer, having chained the two anklets to each other, rose to unlock Bailey's wrists. Bailey pressed his palms together to make it easier for the officer. It saddened Isadore to see how deeply the routine had become ingrained in Bailey, how easily he participated in his own imprisonment. But perhaps we all do this.

"Because you went after a U.S. district attorney?" asked Isadore.

"Fear," said Bailey. "That's why. Look at this Axman situation. It's got folks hiding in their houses, seeing ghosts, setting up all night with shotguns on their laps."

The jailer pinned Bailey's wrists behind his back and pulled the slack in the chain.

"I guess I'll be seeing you, Frank," said Isadore.

"How do you bring a city to its knees?"

The jailer dragged Bailey to his feet by yanking on his shackled wrists. The metal cuffs pressed into Bailey's wrists, slicing into the flaky skin, but Bailey seemed used to that too. He was in the other place.

"Fear!" Bailey's eyes were getting large. "Fear is how you do it!"

The jailer pulled him toward the door.

"*Fear* them into seeing you play."

"All right, Frank. May it go well with you."

"I don't fear no more because I have seen the darkness. I live in the darkness. But outside these walls?"

Isadore backed away. He would not return to this horrible place. Bailey was not himself. The Bailey he knew was gone. And yet—

"Fear!" Bailey yelled, as he disappeared behind the cellblock door. "That's the answer, Izzy. Fear is the only truth."

The door rattled shut. But still his shout came through.

"*Fear!*"

PART THREE

THE UNDERGROUND FOREST

New Orleans Times-Picayune, 3/16/19:

MYSTERIOUS PERSON'S NOTE DATED 'HELL,' SIGNED 'AXMAN'

Immunity Promised All Families Who Have Jazz Band Playing in Their Homes When 'Fell Demon from Hottest Hell' Flies over City

The Times-Picayune has received a letter from a mysterious person who declares he is the Axman wanted for five murders in New Orleans and vicinity. In it he characterizes himself as "a fell demon from hottest hell." He also admits that he is fond of jazz music and makes the interesting announcement that next Tuesday night at 12:15 he will fly over New Orleans, but promises immunity to all families who have a jazz band playing in their homes.

The letter received by The Times-Picayune came in Friday's mail:

"Editor of The Times-Picayune, New Orleans:

"Esteemed Mortal: They have never caught me and they never will. They have never seen me, for I am invisible, even as the ether which surrounds your earth. I am not a human being, but a spirit and a fell demon from hottest hell. I am what you Orleanians and your foolish police call the Axman."

CALLS POLICE STUPID

"I shall come again and claim other victims. I shall leave no clue, except perhaps my bloody ax, besmeared with the blood and brains of he whom I have sent below to keep me company.

"If you wish you may tell the police to be careful not to rile me. Of course, I am a reasonable spirit. I take no offense at the way in which they have conducted their investigations in the past. In fact, they have been so utterly stupid so as to amuse not only me, but His Satanic Majesty, Francis Josef, etc. But tell them to beware. Let them not try to discover what I am, for it were better that they never were born than for them to incur the wrath of the Axman. I don't think that there is any need of such a warning, for I feel sure that your police will always dodge me, as they have in the past. They are wise and know how to keep away from all harm.

"Undoubtedly you Orleanians think of me as a most horrible murderer, which I am, but I could be much worse if I wanted to. If I wished to I could pay a visit to your city every night. At will I could slay thousands of your best citizens, for I am in close relationship with the Angel of Death.

"Now, to be exact, at 12:15 o'clock (earthly time) on next Tuesday night, I am going to pass over New Orleans. In my infinite mercy, I am going to make a little proposition to the people. Here it is:

"I am very fond of jazz music and I swear by all the devils in the nether regions, that every person shall be spared in whose house a jazz band is in full swing at the time I have just mentioned. If everyone has a jazz band going, well, then, so much the better for the people. One thing is certain and that is some of those persons who do not jazz it on Tuesday night (if there be any) will get the ax.

"Well as I am cold and crave the warmth of my native Tartarus, and as it is about time that I have left your homely earth, I will cease my discourses. Hoping that thou wilt publish this, that it may go well with thee, I have been, am and will be the worst spirit that ever existed either in fact or the realm of fancy,

"THE AXMAN."

The letter is dated "Hell, March 13, 1919." Its authorship will be subjected to the investigation it seems to warrant in view of the recent ax murders.

MARCH 18, 1919—THE INDUSTRIAL CANAL—CHARITY HOSPITAL

They found the body in the canal. It made no sense. The corpse was buried twenty-five feet underground. But it wasn't a skeleton. It wasn't a skeleton. It wasn't a skeleton.

"Don't figure," said Charlie, shaking his head. He had been at the scene for thirty minutes. Bill, arriving from the hospital, had left too quickly to remember his scarf. "Cold? I'd say it's making at least seventy degrees."

Bill pulled his collar as high as it would go. It did not feel like any seventy degrees. It felt like twenty.

They stared into the chasm. The body squad below erected stakes around the corpse. Several hundred feet away the men continued digging. The Texas dredge had made its final pass across Florida Walk and seemed destined to reach the lake by the end of the month. They would next shore the levees and seal the walls with slate panels, before finally opening the gates at either end of the canal. On that day the brackish water of Lake Pontchartrain would rush to meet the freshwater of the Mississippi River and submerge everything between them, but for now there were still underground forests, and the occasional corpse, to exhume.

The foreman from Hercules came rushing in a hansom along

Florida Walk. He gestured out the window and screamed, but the words escaped in the wind. They ignored him.

"What do they have?" said Bill.

"Not much yet. Don't even know the sex."

"How's that possible?"

"They've only found legs and arms."

Bill shook his head. "They blaming the dredge again?"

"The dredge is way yonder." Charlie gestured in the direction of Florida Walk.

"Then how'd they find the body?"

"They didn't." Charlie clapped his hands, obliterating two mosquitoes at once. "Coroner got an anonymous call."

"That so?"

"Said there was something the police would want to see at yard marker ninety-five. Came here and found an arm sticking straight out of the ground."

"Hand-side up?"

"As if the victim was trying to pull himself out a grave."

"I will never understand human nature."

One of the body men ascended the ladder to the brim of the canal. He held under his armpit a heavy parcel wrapped in a yellowed edition of the *New Orleans Item*.

"We don't know who called it in?"

Charlie shook his head. "A male. He hung up."

"That's a new one."

"They dug down, came to see the arm wasn't attached to nothing."

The foreman's hansom came to a stop and he jumped out. "Yay!" he shouted. "You cain't be here! How many times I have to explain this?"

"See this?" Bill indicated his badge. "It says we can go anywhere there's a dead body."

"The dead body was two weeks ago, pal. And it was half a mile that way. Didn't your captain tell you to stop harassing my men? Oh. Oh my."

The body man dropped his parcel at their feet. It landed with a thud, releasing an angry handful of blackflies. The man sliced it open with a knife, and the old newsprint peeled back like a blooming flower, revealing a dismembered leg. It was heavily flaked with mud but they could see patches of red and brown and wrinkled white flesh.

"Look," said the officer. "It still bends at the knee."

The foreman vomited.

"Here's the amazing thing." The officer pointed at the uppermost part of the leg. "Cut clean."

"What's that mean?" asked Charlie.

"Means the killer is strong," said Bill. He thought of Perl on the wharf, removing his jacket, folding it twice, placing it neatly on top of their guns. *My intention all along was to murder you with my hands.*

"Extremely strong," said the body man. "Strong enough to cut straight through the femur. It'd require a sharp tool, but mainly extraordinary physical strength."

"It means another thing too," said Bill. "The victim didn't resist." He felt another shiver coming along. But it wouldn't come. It was like not being able to sneeze, a lingering pressure behind his sinuses.

"More likely the victim was already dead," said the coroner's man. "It's a butcher job. Look at the composition of the corpse."

It wasn't just flies, Bill saw. The decomposing leg seethed with euphoric carrion beetles, their yellow pronota like wriggling jaundiced eyes.

"Who told you about this?" The foreman wiped his mouth. He looked away when he spoke, addressing the distant Mississippi. "Does anyone else know?"

"Just us. And whoever did it."

The foreman nodded and headed back toward the hansom. After several feet he broke into a sprint.

A shout came from the bottom of the canal. They walked to the edge and looked down.

One of the body men had planted his shovel into the ground and was gesturing. "We got a head!" he yelled. "It's a beauty."

"It's my head," she kept saying. Or: "It's inside my head." Or: "Get it out of my head!"

After sprinting to the hospital, Bill had wasted twenty panicked minutes with the receptionist, who could find no record of Maisie Bastrop in the rolls. Was Mr. Bastrop certain that his wife was not at Presbyterian or the Hotel Dieu? He showed her the Charity Hospital envelope addressed in Maze's hand, the terse letter, written with an odd formality: *I caught it, Bill. I'm at Charity. I'm sorry.* The receptionist could only shrug and review the list of two hundred influenza patients admitted to the hospital. After interrupting her search to admit two new cases—a German husband and wife, leaning into each other, the wife's nostrils bleeding profusely—the receptionist consulted patient lists from the other departments. Perhaps Mrs. Bastrop had entered surgery? Some of the most critically ill influenza patients had been sent to the operating room. But she could not locate a Maisie Bastrop. There is another list, she said, in a chilly, remote tone that Bill immediately recognized, having used it himself with wives of murder victims. It could mean only one thing: the list of patients sent to the morgue.

But Mrs. Bastrop's name wasn't there either. In his desperation Bill burst past the receptionist, ignoring her shouts, and ran beneath the archway bearing the inscription WHERE THE UNUSUAL OCCURS AND MIRACLES HAPPEN. He flashed his badge at the security guard at the foot of the stone stairwell and sprinted to the second-floor landing, where he was staggered by the odors of camphor, stale urine, carbolic acid, and the sugary tang of blood. The ward extended before him in a grid of iron bedsteads, each occupied by a miserable. The nurses wore gauze masks and the goggles that motorists used to shield their eyes from dust. They glided among the beds, taking temperatures, handing out ice bags and, in one case, administering an enema with a rubber catheter.

"Officer?" said a goggled nurse, her eyes magnified to the size of golf balls. "It is necessary to don protection." She pointed to a pair of tin boxes set on a table near the doorway. No goggles remained, but he removed his cap and placed a gauze mask over his mouth.

"Have you treated a woman named Maisie Bastrop?"

"The eyes," said the nurse, "are an atrium for disease. Goggles are required."

He continued past her, bile rising in his throat. He stepped over a young woman who had fallen out of her bed and convulsed on the floor. He negotiated bedpans and Murphy drips. It was difficult to make out the patients' faces; he peeled back the sheet of one woman whose thin brownish hair resembled Maze's. When a person died, how much time elapsed before her name was entered on the morgue list?

He climbed to the third floor. A nurse told him it was restricted to male patients.

"Are there influenza patients on any other floors?"

"Negro male patients are on the fifth floor. Additional female patients are in the women's department next door. White women on the second floor, Negroes on the third."

Down the stairs, across the courtyard, into the women's health building, past the guard with another wave of his badge, up a flight of stairs. He shoved through a pair of French doors into yet another, smaller ward, and spotted Maze immediately. She sat up in bed, propped on a pillow. Her hospital gown was open; a breast was visible, the nipple erect. A nurse applied a poultice to Maze's chest. He called her name.

She looked confusedly in his direction. He pulled down his mask. She didn't seem to recognize him. Blinking, she pulled the edges of the gown together.

Should he feel offended that his own wife felt modest before him? Or ashamed that, despite her sickness and the semipublic setting, surrounded by patients and the reek of death—should he be ashamed that he was aroused by the cold nipple, the underswell of her breast?

"Ms. Bone? Do you know this man?"

"Bone?" said Bill.

Maze's eyes came into focus. "He is my husband."

"Officer Bone, I ask that you wear goggles. And please reapply your mask. The influenza is highly contagious."

"It's Detective Bastrop. And she's *Mrs.* Bastrop."

"Nurse," said Maze. "Will you grant us a moment?"

"I'll return with a new poultice in forty minutes." The nurse made a note on Maze's medical chart, wiped her goggles with a sanitary tissue, and delivered Bill a final skeptical glance.

"I was very worried," said Bill. "I thought . . . I didn't know what to think."

"I'm sorry I wrote. It was rash."

"Of course you should've written." The emotion pressed behind his eyes. He took her hand and squeezed. The skin was clammy, the fingers smaller than he remembered. Fatigue gathered around her pinkish eyes and in tense folds beneath her chin. Her greasy hair was tied in a ponytail. It looked fuller than before; perhaps she had stopped losing it once she left him. She did not squeeze his hand back.

"I'm very tired."

"You smell like mustard." He felt like a moron as soon as he said it.

"It's the poultice. Mustard seed."

"How do you feel?"

"I've tried to feel well. I've tried hard. The nurse gave me something."

Her hand absently made flexing movements, as if squeezing a sponge. He took up the chart, which hung by a tether from the bedpost. It was three pages long. The entries, which began more than two days earlier, listed medicines beside their dosages: *ice five mins for fever—cool enemata, sod. bicarbonate for hyperpyrexia—chloral hydrate for delirium—paregoric, codein and whisky for cough—jalap. powder, castor oil w/ turpentine for bowels*. In a parallel column the nurses charted fluctuations in Maze's temperature. She had entered the hospital with a 104 fever; the second day it had increased to 105.5. The most recent reading was 103.

"Doctor said it's going to get worse before it gets better."

"When did you return from Abita?"

She paused. "I don't remember. I developed a fever and found the next train. I wore a cape over my head."

She wiped a strand of sweaty hair from her forehead and he noticed her fingernails for the first time. They were long and blackened down to the quick.

"I'm on the edge of catching the Axman. There are some problems with the investigation—office politics—but I'm close."

She regarded him blankly.

"The Axman—the guy going around hacking grocers to death. There was just another attack a couple days ago. A couple and their child in Gretna."

"Why are you telling me this?"

Before he could respond, she recoiled into a violent cough. She pressed a hand towel over her mouth. When she removed the towel, he saw that it was lightly sprayed with blood. He touched the back of her head, but the gesture felt unnatural and she appeared irritated by the contact. He withdrew his hand.

"Funny," he said. "I guess I never told you about the investigation."

"I'm grateful that you came, Billy. But I need to rest." She shut her eyes. Or eye—one eye was buried in her pillow.

No, he had not told her about the investigation. But he had never thought about the investigation without thinking about her. She had called him a liar but he would be honest now. Honest about all that mattered, at least. Eloise Obitz did not matter. She was a means to obtain evidence. Which was a means to solve the case. Which was a way to win back Maze.

"I want to tell you everything," he said. "I've changed entirely."

She coughed lightly.

"I'm about to solve the biggest murder case in the city. I took it up after everyone else gave up."

"Is it dangerous?" She didn't open her eyes.

"I don't know."

She patted his hand. Her breathing had become heavy, unnatural, as if she were the one struggling to breath through a gauze mask. He yanked off his own mask.

"Why are you telling me this?" She spoke slowly, as if within a dream. "You come here. You see how sick I am."

"You're right."

"You tell me about police business."

"I'm sorry."

"I don't understand."

"It's just that—I'm scared."

"Scared about me? Or scared about your work?"

"I am scared about you. Us. Everything. I guess I'm afraid of everything at once."

She breathed deeply and the pressure of the breath made her wince.

"I was scared about your work," she said. "I was scared the way you threw yourself into it, after the war. It was like you were chasing disaster, violence."

"There's a difference between the way I am now," said Bill, "and the way I was. I'm not letting the fear stop me anymore."

"Did it stop you?"

"It stopped me. Then it started me up again. It made me reckless."

"Scared about everything, you said. What's everything?"

"Everything. Failure. Chaos. Weakness. Confusion. Death."

She opened her eyes. "Are you really afraid of death?"

"Of course. Yes."

"Why 'of course'?"

"Isn't everyone?"

"Death isn't so bad, Bill. The fear is the bad part."

He took in her frail body, her trembling fingers, her flickering eyes. "Death is exactly the worst part."

"What do you think about, when you think about it?"

"Oblivion."

"What's the alternative? Immortal life?"

"Yes."

"I'm glad not to live forever. I'm having trouble keeping my hair as it is. I'd be a bald old lady."

"If we lived longer, we'd get better at doing it."

"The knowledge of death makes life worth something."

"Wouldn't we enjoy life more if we didn't have to worry about dying? Think how free that would make us."

"Why did you pull off your sanitary mask?"

"I guess it's pretty dumb: a navy who's afraid of guns. Whose fear makes him run at guns."

"There's nothing dumb about being afraid. Ouch."

"What—your head?"

"It's just a whisker." She winced. "It passed."

"A whisker?"

"It's like a brief shiver of pain that whisks you away from yourself."

"Should I call the nurse?"

She shook her head to one side. "I don't understand why you never told me about it before—the fear."

"I never told myself."

"I love you. You should tell me everything."

"I love you."

"It's not fear I mind. It's dishonesty." She turned her head and coughed again, into her pillow. "I saw the fear in your paintings."

"What I fear most about death is losing you."

She gazed at him with her one eye—wet, pinkish, piteous. *The eye is an atrium for disease.*

"The pain is getting worse in my head," said Maze. "It gets to where it feels like it *is* my head."

"What do you mean?"

"First it's inside my head. Then it radiates outward until it fills my head and the head is inside the pain. The pain is a bubble that contains my head."

Bill called to the nurse but she was on the other side of the ward, preparing a syringe.

"I wish someone could come and get it out of my head." Maze winced, her mouth straining.

"Nurse!" shouted Bill. "Nurse!"

"It's going to get worse before it gets better."

"I'm not leaving until this is over."

Maze's face fixed in an agonized rictus.

"I'm not afraid." Bill hoped that he sounded confident, strong. He hoped he sounded like a different man. He hoped he was becoming that man. But merely picking up the Axman investigation would not do it. He saw that now. His cowardice had led to too much death already. He had to stop the killer dead.

Maze broke into a sob. Her hand drifted up from the mattress. "I'm glad you're here. Billy? Are you still here?"

"I'm here, Maisie."

"Oh, Billy," she said. "I'm afraid."

Charlie shook his head with both hands in consternation. "Uh-uh. That don't pay."

"It's an arm. What don't you understand? Most bodies come with two."

"That's just it. We found two arms already. This here is three."

A motorcar rumbled toward them across the denuded plain.

"What's this?"

"Foreman come back?"

"Foremen," said Bill, "don't drive automobiles like that."

A man dressed in a shepherd's plaid suit unfolded himself from the passenger seat. His formidable executive neck was secured with a pumpkin-hued cravat, and a gray felt hat rested low over his sharp executive eyes. He stepped gingerly onto the turf, careful not to muddy his loafers.

"Where is Mr. Davenport?" he asked, addressing none of the assembled officers in particular.

"He mean the foreman?" said Charlie.

"I do not mean the foreman." The man spoke with an accent that reminded Bill of the British commanders he'd met abroad. The voice was soft, lilting, indifferent to being heard. "I am speaking of Hugh Davenport, my nephew, vice president of Hibernia Bank. He is the liaison between the foreman and myself."

"I know your nephew."

The man's skeptical glare struck Bill like a stiff breeze.

"I met him a couple of weeks ago," Bill continued. "The last time we visited the canal. I haven't seen him today."

"Very well. My name is Rudolph Denzler. I am bank president. The foreman called my secretary in a frantic state. I gather there has been another accident."

"I wouldn't call it an accident, sir," said Charlie, waving at a mosquito. "We've found three arms so far."

"Excuse me?"

Bill put his hand on Charlie's shoulder, a sign for him to stop speaking. Charlie sighed. He knew better than to blubber to civilians.

"This is a crime scene, Mr. Denzler," said Bill. "We have initiated an investigation. I will be happy to notify you, or Mr. Davenport, of any conclusions we reach."

"After the last incident, Captain Capo assured me that no police would visit the canal site without his accompaniment."

Bill pressed his palm to his temple. The pressure behind his sinuses had diffused into a tickling, undulating vibration; it was almost pleasant, like an alcoholic buzz. "Sir, we have jurisdiction wherever a dead body is found in this city."

A voice shouted from the canal floor, "Another head!"

Bill walked to the edge of the canal. He was followed by Charlie and, belatedly, bank president Denzler. When they came into view, the men at the bottom of the pit backed away to reveal what they had unearthed.

Though some of the mud remained, it was obvious enough: a naked female torso, missing her arms and most of her legs. A large tangled mass of muddy-brown hair sprouted between her thighs and it took Bill a moment to realize that it was not her pubic hair but the back of a decapitated head that had been set there.

"Sir," said Charlie, "you need to move back."

It was too late. Denzler had seen it. He removed his hat. "Who is that?"

"Sir—"

"The head. Show me."

Everyone looked at Bill. He nodded.

One of the men knelt and lifted the head from the corpse's crotch. He held it up so that the men on the lip of the canal could see its face. The eyes were open, the mouth closed and twisted to one side. The bluish neck had been cleanly severed. Bill looked into the open eye and saw Leonard Perl.

The river flows both ways, said the head soundlessly. *It goes out but it comes back too.*

You're dead and I have never regretted it, said Bill, unspeaking.

There are forests buried under forests. There are towns within towns. There are rivers that run down and run back up too.

Go back to hell.

I have seen Maisie in the river.

Perl's face underwent a sudden contortion. It realigned itself into the features of the young man from Hibernia Bank. Of course the head could not have belonged to Perl. Perl's head fell into the Mississippi. This head belonged to the young banker, Hugh Davenport. It wasn't Perl. That would have made no sense. Perl was dead and gone.

Still Bill wasn't certain until he heard the bank president scream.

MARCH 19, 1919—UPTOWN—THE BATTLEFIELD

The first indication that something extraordinary was happening came shortly past one in the morning, after Isadore and Sore Dick left the Van Benthuysen Mansion. Aside from the occasional streetcar, St. Charles Avenue tended to be silent because nearly nobody lived on it. With two or three colossi to each city block, it was not part of any neighborhood but a nostalgic promenade, a refuge of Confederate majesty. As Isadore had learned from his hosts that evening, the Van Benthuysens were relations of Jefferson Davis; Watson Van Benthuysen II, for whom the mansion was built, was a quartermaster for the Grays. Watson's grandchildren, who had hired the Slim Izzy Quartet for that evening's entertainment, supposed that Isadore's band would be excited to learn of their brush with Confederate aristocracy.

The grandchildren, two graying unwed sisters, looked as if they had spent the better part of their energies to ensure that the family fortune did not survive their generation. Their faces were too pink, their hair too thin; they smeared far too much lipstick on their heavy mouths. The dissipation of the family mansion had followed the same careless course: the portraits of Watson Van Benthuysen II and III were jaundiced, and dust coated the ancient oak chest, the pedestal desk, the recamier sofa. Even the porcelain monkey band figurines—miniature monkeys attired in Elizabethan wigs and ruffs, each playing a miniature chamber instrument—were cracked and faded. The sisters seemed to have expected the Negro performers to take delight in the monkey musicians but only Isadore was game enough to feign interest. He felt obliged; the Van Benthuysen wastrels had, after all, paid him fifty dollars. They had wanted the best Axman jazz show on St. Charles Avenue, and by God, the Slim Izzy Quartet had given it.

Lord was it a relief to play. Even for a bunch of drunk fools who thought dancing meant walking in place. Nobody Slow Dragged or Turkey Trotted or did the Grizzly Bear, nor did they even recognize any of the songs. But they were as engaged as the parishioners at the Funky Butt and appeared to love it as much too, in their own ridiculous way. He had done a crazy, harebrained thing and if this evening was the only reward, it was worth it, just to touch the music again. He could admit to himself finally that he wasn't made to be a highwayman or a ditchdigger or a cooper. He was meant to do this thing—this thing that didn't pay, that broke your spirit, that caused trouble and pain and ephemeral joy. Through the horn he shouted, *Love me!* He shouted, *Hear me!* He shouted, *Love me! Hear me! Love me! Hear me!* It was a strange sensation, performing again, like reentering a dream. Or rather it was as if the rest of his life were the dream, vaguely recalled, and this was reality—playing onstage with Sore Dick and Drag Nasty and Zutty. But he knew it wasn't a dream because the fingers that pumped the valves were stained with mud. His fingernails were jammed with the stuff.

At a quarter past midnight, the hour of reckoning, one of the party guests stood atop the stair and raised a champagne bottle to the Axman, thanking him for "a night of merriment and jazz, and on a Tuesday no less!" The reveler smashed the bottle on the banister. The bottle didn't break but slipped from his hand and, barely missing Drag Nasty's head, fell to the marble parlor floor, where it shattered, spraying the players with white froth and slivers of glass. The Van Benthuysens considered this the apex of hilarity and begged the band to play beyond the allotted time—for a tip, of course. Jazz music was a scream: they couldn't get enough. The band played another forty-five minutes before departing to quaking applause.

Drag Nasty and Zutty hopped the streetcar but Isadore and Dick were too exhilarated to go directly home. They walked down St. Charles. The avenue was lit like a carnival, electricity spilling from the windows of the mansions. Even the serpentine branches of the live oaks lacked their usual nefarious quality; they were like elderly arms beckoning the musicians onward.

"The Lord works mysteries," said Dick. "All the Uptown millionaires wanting to hear jazz?"

"Not just any jazz. Our jazz."

"*Your* jazz. Then again, at night all cats are gray."

"Yah, they wouldn't know the difference between the one and the other, let alone between ragtime and Dixie and jazz."

"Don't get me wrong. They fell for the hot stuff."

"Like a baby falls for milk."

"Like a pig falls for slop."

"It wasn't just the gin either."

Sore Dick shook his head. "I never had gin like that. Tasted like daffodils."

"We should've asked for more."

"More than fifty dollars plus fifteen in tips? You're getting greedy. I'm amazed this family found you to begin with."

"Credit the Reverend."

"That's what I don't get. Why didn't he recommend, I don't know, Freddie Keppard?"

"Keppard's in Chicago."

"You know what I mean. Frankie Duson. Lawrence Duhé. Sidney Bechet?"

"Chicago, Chicago, Chicago."

Dick shook his head. "What about Dutt Ory? He still here?"

I draw the line at taking away my livelihood, Isadore thought. *King Zeno, I place my faith in you!* "Maybe he got the first call."

"I guess we're the last men standing. Funny how that comes out."

There was a loud concussion, followed by a horn blast. Streetcars didn't make that kind of noise, and there was no rail track closer than the wharf. The sound grew louder.

"Damn," said Dick. "Some other millionaires had the same idea."

The music rumbled out of Christ Church Cathedral, a block away.

"They're playing the devil's music in the house of the Lord."

"Praise Mr. Axman," said Sore Dick. "These folks are either petrified of the Axman or they just needed a respectable excuse to listen to hot music."

The band at the church was blazing like hellfire.

"Impossible."

"Fuck my head."

The cathedral was overflowing with St. Charles millionaires, spilling onto the avenue. Sore Dick climbed onto a sidewalk bench so that he could see into the nave. Isadore climbed up beside him.

"Shut my mouth," said Dick. "Shut it to the ground."

Hundreds of souls were inside—men, women, child gentlemen and child ladies—dancing and hollering, or at least doing their best guess at how dancing and hollering should look.

"They don't seem scared of any Axman to me," said Isadore.

He couldn't see the musicians' faces clearly across the cathedral but he did notice that the cornet player had a white bath towel hanging around his neck, in the King Oliver style. Only one player in town dared to imitate Oliver so blatantly.

"Can you make out who's playing?" asked Dick.

"I'll be damned."

"Don't tell me. Dippermouth's crew?"

"I won't tell you."

"Shit. How much you think they got?"

"Seventy? Maybe eighty."

"Praise the Axman!"

Isadore cussed. The band swung into "High Society."

The fire spread down the avenue. On nearly every block music poured from the windows of the millionaire palaces, music that the residents of those palaces until that night would have called degenerate, a manifestation of what the *Times-Picayune* called "a low streak in man's tastes that has not yet come out in civilization's wash." Bailey was right. Fear had broken the levee.

They cut into the Garden District at Second Street and it was the same. In the picture window of a mansion on Prytania he spotted Buddie Petit's band. Through an open door he spied a trio of white musicians in blackface. In a backyard garden a sextet was made up of kids Isadore had seen busking outside the Funky Butt, the youngest still in short pants, while the partygoers had colored their faces with charcoal. They drunkenly yelled nonsense such as "Jazz it up!" and "I'll be jinks swing!" and "You're telling I!" It was grotesque, wrong, disgusting. Still the music was playing everywhere.

"We must've been the first band to stop playing tonight," said Sore Dick. "We should've hung on for another session."

A man in blackface shouted from the terrace of a mansion on Coliseum. "Y'all musicians?"

They froze.

"You there!"

"Yes, sir," said Isadore. "We're musicians."

"You play the hot stuff?"

"Yes, sir."

"How about you boys jazz it with us then? A couple of dollars in it for you."

"Yes, sir!" said Sore Dick, but he held up short when he saw Isadore's face.

"Go ahead. But I'm not playing for a bunch of foons at this hour."

"I have no place to be."

"Suit yourself."

"It's not bad, Izzy, all these folks loving hot music. No matter how it came about."

Isadore continued downtown past an endless procession of jazz parties—the music bursting drunkenly out of mansions and town houses and later, as he passed Jackson Street, cottages and run-down shacks. It was a cool night, but the windows were left open to the street so as not to leave any doubt about what music was being played, even though the Axman's witching hour had passed. Where there wasn't a band, a man was playing a horn or a guitar, a record was rotating on a Victor, or a family was singing a cappella. Dick was right. Isn't this what Isadore wanted? It didn't matter that the people discovered the music because of a letter from the Axman. Especially since he was the Axman.

Still, he couldn't enjoy it. Not because Dippermouth Armstrong and apparently every other halfway competent musician in New Orleans had reaped high-paying gigs from his gambit—many probably paying higher than his. Nor because he was sick of having to appeal to bigots who didn't know the difference between rag and swing, treasure and trash. He didn't mind not getting credit either. All these things bit at him, sure, but they just nibbled around the main problem. Yes, he wanted people to learn the music and embrace it, but he had come about it the wrong way. He had taken a shortcut. It was as if he had altered the flow of history, diverting the river, forcing what should have been a slow serpentine meander into a rigid shortcut: a canal. The water had flowed too fast, down an unnatural channel, over dark territories. It was bad water now.

When he drank it in, the music that cascaded from every home he passed, it gave him a stomachache. It made him sick.

Canal Street was a pandemonium. He felt the gravitational pull as he crossed the old district, pedestrians streaming toward the electric marquees of the movie houses and honky-tonks, but he wasn't prepared for what opened in front of him. A dense confusion of brass and percussion and tinkling piano keys clouded the air and crowds spilled from every bar and tonk. A barker sold sandwiches off the back of a wagon, others sold beer and slugs of whiskey, and freelance musicians weaved through the boulevard, blowing horns and banging drums, a dozen spontaneous second lines marching and dividing and merging. A streetcar, engulfed by the crowd, stalled, and its passengers sang and jumped. And Isadore let his mind jump and sing. What if this was not a passing delirium, the convulsions of a city panicked by a masked maniac—and a great plague, the impending prohibition of liquor, the trauma of a global war—what if this was a revelation?

The old hot players had left town because conditions were better in the North: better wages, easier living, black and tan clubs. But it was also true that the music was beloved in those places. White people and Negroes both packed any show that billed New Orleans jazz. It stood to reason the same would ultimately happen in New Orleans. The only thing holding back the new music was old attitudes. Perhaps the Axman's letter really had broken those attitudes. It wasn't the story Isadore had always told himself, about his music showing a new way forward, converting the heathens with his gospel. But if enough people decided they wanted this music, here was a real opportunity. A city hungry for the new music would require a roster of regular players to fill not only every tonk but every hotel lounge, nightclub, and society hall down the line. It would require specialists. It would require maestros. It would require innovators to keep the music expanding and surprising.

The field was open. King Bolden abdicated when he went mad. His successor, King Watzke, was dead, a victim of the Spanish sick. Watzke's heir, King Keppard, was deposed by King Oliver, and both had escaped North. The kingdom was vulnerable for the taking: the ramparts undefended, the moat dried up. If the mania lasted beyond one night, Isadore would have as good a chance as anyone to inherit the throne. He had his army now, didn't he? His hungry listeners? A whole city was prepared to hear his cornet wail, growl, and yell. He could almost hear it, his cornet ringing through the streets, shouting, *Zeno is king, Zeno is king, ZENO IS KING.*

He was feeling pretty good by the time he turned onto Liberty. Even here the music was playing, calling him home. But Miss Daisy's house was quiet. Though it seemed unnecessary, the streets as loud as they were, Isadore made certain, as he entered, not to let the door slam behind him. The room smelled of sleep and baby powder. Daisy was snoring. Gently Isadore slid his cornet case beneath the bed, careful not to let it knock against the frame. He eased off his pants, pulled up the blanket, and sidled beside Orly. It took about one second to know that she was awake: he couldn't hear the regular, heavy inhalations that marked her sleep. Nerves: she had been glad for his gig, particularly when she heard how much the Van Benthuysens were offering, but worried about the circumstances. He had done everything to dispel her anxiety short of saying that he had written the damn letter himself; as an extra precaution, he had not even brought the envelope to the post office himself but had left it with Sis Pinky to send with her mail.

"The baby keeping you up?" he whispered. The darkness was thinning but he couldn't quite make out her features.

She placed her arm around his waist. He inched closer to her, until her full stomach pressed against his. "I was afraid."

He rubbed her head. "That Axman thing was a joke. Probably a prank."

"You got home all right?"

"You wouldn't believe it. The whole city's gone insane. Just about every mansion on St. Charles had a band. The Garden District, downtown, even the big hotels—a circus."

She didn't respond. The darkness cleared some more. He saw that she was crying.

"Baby, what is it? All this worry about the Axman?"

Her voice hitched. "A man came tonight."

"What man?"

"A white man."

"*Here?*"

"Shh. You'll wake Mama."

"What'd he want?"

She shook her head. "He was talking wild. Talking about you played a dirty trick."

"A white man came here to say that to you?"

"Did you play a trick on somebody?"

He forced himself to breathe. "How did he look?"

"Like a giant. Bigger than big. Squashed nose. He had *angry* eyes."

"What do you mean angry?"

"Small. Spread apart. Always focusing in on you. Narrowing you down." She flinched at the memory. "How'd you come to know a man like that, Izzy?"

"I don't know any man fits that description. He probably was just a crazy person. He didn't try anything with you?"

"No."

"You sure?"

She shook her head. "He knew your name."

"The man said my name?" The fear declared itself. It started in his chest but he knew it wouldn't stop there.

"Said he wanted Isadore Zeno."

"What else did he say?"

"Oh, Izzy, what's happening?"

At Orly's raised voice, Miss Daisy's snore rumbled louder; they paused, and it hitched back into its rhythm.

"He said he came from Tartarus." She looked a bit confused. "Where's that—on the north bank? Out by Abita Springs?"

The fear dropped into his bowels. It radiated down his leg. It wrapped cold, tapering fingers around his heart. It whispered from inside his brain.

"It's south of here."

"What, like Gretna?"

He had a manic urge to laugh. But if he started, he knew the laughter would turn into a different animal altogether, and he didn't know what it might devour.

"Uh-huh, baby," he said. "It's a bit past Gretna."

MARCH 20, 1919—CENTRAL BUSINESS DISTRICT—THE GARDEN DISTRICT

She ordered Raymond to take her to Hibernia Bank. She couldn't help herself. Denzler's secretary explained that he was in a meeting of the board. Over the secretary's protests she burst into the conference room. A dozen men sat around an oval table, their hats in their laps. They wore black mourning suits. Denzler sat at the head, facing the double doors.

He glanced up sharply. "That's fine, Miss Kernaghan. I'm glad you can join us, Mrs. Vizzini." As if he had invited her. His poise unnerved her.

"Mr. Denzler." It came out like a shriek. She took a breath and tried again. "Gentlemen, please forgive me. Mr. Denzler, may I speak with you alone?"

"Absolutely not. I want my colleagues to hear everything you have to say."

"Please let me begin," she said, "by conveying what deep sorrow I feel for the loss of your nephew. Mr. Davenport was a brilliant, compassionate man with a promising career before him."

Denzler bared his teeth.

"I cannot imagine how horrible it must be to lose a young family member, a person on whom you rely. A man you hoped to inherit the family's legacy. I think, for instance, of my own son, Giorgio."

Denzler slammed his fist on the table. One of the vice presidents' water glasses overturned, but the man made no effort to dam the rivulet flowing onto his leg.

"I'm sorry," she said, to buy time. The matter was becoming exceedingly delicate. No false moves now. "I did not mean—"

"Giorgio." Denzler's jaw stiffened. "We suspect that your son is the problem."

"The problem," she echoed. "The problem with the work delays?"

"We will be conducting our own investigation."

"Giorgio hasn't worked at the site since last summer."

"We are investigating everything. Privately."

"I don't like your insinuation."

The heads of the bankers turned between the antagonists as if watching a tennis rally from the grandstand. Beatrice glanced down at her fingers, at the gold rings that encircled them, and recomposed herself.

"You can no sooner fire us than we can fire you," she said. "You may recall that Hibernia Bank and Hercules Construction entered jointly into a contract with the city."

"Murder wasn't part of the contract."

It was as bad as she had feared. The ground beneath her turned to mud, sucking her down, and she could hear the sound of mechanical teeth biting, chomping, grinding. "I won't stand for this kind of talk."

"Then leave at once."

What else could she do? She left.

Lizzie had left in the bathroom the bronze tray containing the ingredients for the immortality bath. Beatrice drew the water from the tap and emptied into the tub the finger bowls of pressed garlic, saffron, zedoary, cardamom, anise. The spiced steam began to rise, carrying her anxieties with it. Once Denzler reflected on the situation, he would come to his senses. He could not possibly raise suspicions about Giorgio to one of his police or journalist friends, could not risk revealing that Hibernia Bank had entered into a criminal conspiracy with Hercules Construction. Still it had been his insistence on a single contractor—an insistence inspired by his private agreement with Beatrice—that secured Hercules's exclusive control of the project. He could undo everything, especially if financial profitability was no longer his highest priority.

She sprinkled several drops of grain alcohol into the bath and submerged the cup of olive oil. She had entered into a tacit contract with Giorgio: she would protect him and pardon his sins of overaggression while he mastered the family business in preparation for assuming leadership of it. But Giorgio had signed the contract in invisible ink. His solicitousness—the fawning-son business—was an act. Perhaps he had been acting for years. For all of Hugs Davenport's meddling and condescension, his death was the worst thing that could have befallen Hercules. She wondered if that was Giorgio's strategy after all: to destroy what she had built. *If someone stood in your way, you had the right to remove that person.* Did he believe his own mother stood in his way?

Some men purchased their own deaths with cruelty, meanness, or profligate carelessness—men like Salvatore. But what had those grocers done to offend Giorgio? Were they merely late on payments? Strategic violence, she could understand. But she could not forgive intemperance. She could not forgive him for killing Hugs and she could not forgive him for killing poor Rosalba Bucca. It was as if he had become drunk on the blood of his victims. What explained the manner of assault if not a profound thirst for gore? Even a bear killed for sustenance, only when necessary. Giorgio had plenty of access to pistols. Yet there persisted this grim reliance on the ax.

The bath was drawn but something was missing. Everything was missing. She could try to persuade Denzler against hiring new contractors; she could hope for his temper to subside. But she knew she was powerless to change his mind. If he couldn't have Giorgio arrested without risking his own interests, he would do the next best thing. He would destroy Beatrice Vizzini.

She eased herself into the hot water and, closing her eyes, tried to organize her thoughts. It had been a long time since she had been able to think with clarity or precision—not since September, when she had thought to place Giorgio in Rosie Bucca's care. Perhaps, given Rosie's fate, she had not been thinking clearly then either. No, she'd have to go back further, to the evening last July when she deduced that Giorgio might know something about the Besemer ax attack.

No one could escape detection forever. Certainly not a man who killed so *unnecessarily.* Even if self-interest silenced Denzler, someone would put it together—a journalist, a detective, a city bureaucrat. Beatrice would be dragged into the public glare. It would be worse for her now: after her delusional Operation Ritz Palace experiment, she was not merely the mother of the killer. She was his accomplice. The vultures would peck through the canal project and the family's ancillary businesses, legal and shadow alike.

They would review, with greater scrutiny, the sudden, mysterious death of Sal Vizzini. They would talk about Giorgio, the mad Axman, a cartoonish ghoul and maniac, as they still spoke about Jack the Ripper nearly three decades after his brief, violent career. Giorgio would seize the immortality that Beatrice had cultivated for herself—a sick, shameful immortality it would be, but an immortality nonetheless. The Vizzini name, if not forgotten, would become a blasphemy.

The bath was not working. Her blood was not circulating properly, her pores remained clogged, and her muscles, untreated by osteopathy for so many months, refused to expel their accumulated poisons. The water didn't feel right. It did not soothe. It burned. She was bathing in a pool of fire.

She stood but that was even more disagreeable, her brown, puckered skin smarting in the cold air. Lunging for the bathrobe, she nearly tripped over the lip of the bathtub. She saw her skull colliding with the ceramic sink counter, making her go limp, her body collapsing on the floor, the water and blood gathering into pink pools around the tub's claw feet. With cautious, birdlike movements she wrapped herself in the robe. The bath tray presented itself for scrutiny. Though there were normally six finger bowls, she counted five. From residual flakes and motes she could pick out the zedoary, anise, cardamom, saffron. The last she smelled—garlic. That left what? She went over the recipe in her head.

Blue gentian! Lizzie had forgotten it. Or omitted it purposefully. No wonder the bath had been such a disappointment. Gentian root was a tonic, anthelmintic, and stomachic, promoting digestion, purifying the spleen, dispelling dyspepsia, and counterbalancing the inner poisons. No wonder she felt the way she did. No wonder she felt as if worms were burrowing through her brain, eating her thoughts, squirming deep into the flesh of her heart. No wonder she felt as if her heart were tearing apart.

MARCH 21, 1919—THE IRISH CHANNEL—PRESS ROW

Capo ordered them to clean up an armed robbery in the Irish Channel, ten blocks out of their district. It turned out to be nothing, a few neighborhood kids holding up a tailor with a butter knife. Next he sent them to a murder in Gentilly, nowhere near their district. They arrived to discover it was an accidental suicide, a man cleaning a gun that he didn't realize was loaded. In both cases, after the call had been neatly resolved and they returned to the station to draft their report, Bill could sense a slight irritation when Capo greeted them. "Back so soon?" he said after the Gentilly call, as if they'd traveled to Manchuria. Maybe it was all in his head—Bill's head had been muddy lately—but it didn't require professional detective instincts to figure out what was going on. Capo was treating him like an unreliable witness. An untrustable.

Capo immediately sent them out again, to an amateur laboratory in an attic on South Salcedo and Baudin. They encountered a clutter of hypodermic syringes, lancets, and vials blackened by human blood.

"You're making a catastrophic error," said the suspect. He called himself Dr. Rene Albert but could provide no evidence of a medical degree. He was doughy, middle-aged. Dark rings cradled his eyes, his hair stood stiff with grease, and the teeth were bad, streaked yellow. There were reports that Albert had injected influenza patients with blood from other sick patients. Exactly how many people he had killed in this fashion was a mystery.

"This is low business," said Charlie. A few test tubes had cracked in their initial tussle with Albert and a pool of blood gathered along the edge of the specimen table. "Low-down evil business."

"What you don't realize," said Albert, "is that I've discovered the cure."

"How many people you shoot up?" said Charlie.

"As many as I could."

Charlie shook his head. "This is exactly why we need to be on the street," he said to Bill. "Not digging up the canal or canvassing grocery stores. The Axman has nothing on this monster."

"I save lives." Albert rubbed his jaw against his shoulder, testing the bruise, and grimaced.

The dizzy feeling had returned. It wasn't the exposure to the infected blood, Bill didn't think, the close air of the makeshift laboratory, the grating sound of Albert's handcuffs scraping against the metal ventilation pipe, as unpleasant as all of that was. It must have been the odor. He had encountered it, coppery and acidic, on visits to the women's ward at Charity. There were other similarities: blood and sputum were splattered on surfaces throughout the hospital ward too, as five months of influenza had made the staff exhausted and inattentive to all but the most pressing procedures. When Bill had visited Maze that morning before work, his relief at her stable condition—her fever had weakened, her color was higher—deflated at the sight of a stout brown rat capering brazenly between a dish of butter beans abandoned on the floor and an asterisk-shaped hole in the masonry. He tried to alert the nurse but she was busy suctioning pink foam from the mouth of a convulsing patient.

"Thirty of thirty-two patients have made a full recovery," said Albert. "America must learn about my inoculation cure. Doctors are prescribing aspirin, salt of quinine, and Vicks VapoRub—useless, useless, useless!"

"You admit to shooting up thirty-two people." Charlie wrote the figure on his notepad.

"I do not count those currently with symptoms. There might be another forty."

Frowning, Charlie struck the figure and wrote a new one.

"My patients know the cure works. It's the doctors and pharmacists who don't. But they have an interest in not knowing. They want to keep their hospital beds full, the prescription notices coming."

"Seventy-five people." Charlie glanced at Bill. "You believe this?"

Bill shrugged.

"You appear beige," said Charlie. "You need air?"

Bill shook his head. He intended to shake it only once but it continued to shake, back and forth, a windup toy wound too many times.

"Watch the foon. I'll make the notes." Charlie began to circulate around the room, writing observations in his pad.

"It's amazing how many cures are out there," Albert continued. "But the men in power don't want us to know about them."

"I bet they don't." Charlie sidled up to a table filled with medical journals and textbooks. He copied the titles.

"They got the cure for cancer in the rain forest," said Albert. "They just haven't hooked all the flowers up yet."

"What," said Charlie, "is 'sub . . . cut . . . anywho'?"

Albert turned into Perl and said, *You're still alive, Bill. Stop and smell the flowers.*

"Who's 'Sara Brell'?" said Charlie.

"They got the cure for syphilis in mushrooms. Syphilis is a moneymaker for Fowler's and Donovan's, however, and those men control the politicians, who control the medical boards."

"I could use some air, to be honest," said Bill.

"Arsenic isn't an effective cure," said Albert. "It's expensive too. But mushrooms are free."

"You don't say," said Charlie.

"*Subcutaneous* means 'under the skin,'" said Albert. "*Cerebral* means 'in the brain.'"

Charlie glowered at Albert. "Get some air, Billy. I'll finish with this lunatic all by myself."

"Mushrooms are free." Albert spoke as if having to explain to a small child, for the hundredth time, how to tie his shoes. "Flowers are free. So is blood."

"Keep talking," said Charlie.

A glass syringe exploded beneath Bill's boot as he stumbled to the door.

"The blood of a patient who has recovered from influenza will renew the blood of a sick man," said Albert. "Rehabilitated blood is the most potent medicine we have. Our only medicine!"

From the street Bill heard the sound of Dr. Albert's skull clanging off the ventilation pipe.

Once Bill took his first full draw of fresh air he decided he would not go home. He flagged a streetcar on Tulane Avenue and rode to Camp, where he walked the remaining two blocks to Press Row and the *Times-Picayune* building. The newsroom, on the second floor, resembled a hoarder's attic: stacks of yellow copy paper sloping like snowdrifts, ashtrays invisible beneath smoldering butts, black candlestick telephones gesturing interrogatively. Across the room it was just possible, through the cigarette haze, to make out the sign: POSITIVELY NO SMOKING. A copyboy stationed at a toy desk rose to intercept him.

"Closed to officers, sir." The copyboy had a faint mustache; he couldn't have been more than sixteen.

"I have an active investigation."

"Sir? It's the rules."

"The rules." Bill pushed through the gate, pinning the boy behind it. "The rules say that no property in the city of New Orleans is closed to a police investigation."

Behind the copyboy several newspapermen wearing green eyeshades clustered around a set of proofs; another, listening on a telephone, watched Bill with silvery suspicion. The boy rushed over to this man. He hung up and regarded the boy with heavy-lidded eyes. Bill waited patiently, cap in hands. *The rules.*

"What's the matter, Officer?"

With each step the man kicked up shreds of the torn copy that papered the floor. There were wastebaskets but they were already stuffed to overflowing. On the scraps of newsprint bolded words stood out, disembodied from their headlines:

COTTON

DRYS

GERMANS

DREADNOUGHT

PANIC

"I'd like to speak to the editor."

"I'm afraid this is a closed newsroom."

"I'm here on city business."

"Moore's not in. I'm Croak—the daytime city editor. What do you need?"

"Moore. That's who I need."

The phone rang.

"Come back at four." Croak turned away from Bill and picked up the phone. "Yes," Croak said into the phone. "No," he said. "Yes," he said.

"I'd like to see the Axman letter," said Bill.

The man replaced the receiver. "I thought it was a hoax."

That smarted. There had been no mention of a hoax at the station. Did Capo sincerely believe the letter was a hoax, or had he told this to the *Times-Picayune* to tamp public anxiety? Bill had last heard that Capo was conducting interviews with postal workers, but had no strong evidence of the author.

POTATOES
CANAL
VICTIMS
BOND
ATROCITY

Croak gave Bill a cold, glazed-over look: the professional-journalist glare.

"Sure it's a hoax," said Bill. "Still, we have to figure out what kind of degenerate would make up a hoax like that."

"You should see the letters we get every day. You'd need another police force to investigate them all."

"Yah. I don't doubt it."

"It's a sick city." Croak shook his head.

"That's one word for it."

"It's the swamp gas, if you ask me."

"I take it you're not from here."

"Philadelphia. Followed a girl."

"She a degenerate too?" An old navy instinct: loosen up the witness with bawdry.

"I wish." Croak chuckled. "Look, what'd you say your name was, Officer?"

Vicks came to mind. *Donovan's*. "Fowlers."

"I'd like to help, Officer Fowlers. But Moore is, shall we say, on assignment."

"Don't worry, I won't investigate. You mind if I leave a note?"

Croak sighed. "Across the floor, take a right. Last office at the end of the hall. If it's locked, you can slip a note beneath the door."

Bill nodded. "Swamp gas."

"Tell me about it."

Bill started across the room, keeping his eyes down, the copy shuffling around his feet like sawdust.

DEATH
WETS
HORROR
U-BOATS
ENEMY

He felt the eyes of the copyboy on his nape until he cleared the corner. He passed two occupied offices. Neither man looked up. At the end of the hall, the editor's door was locked. It was a simple lever-tumbler. Bill withdrew his pick—a four-and-a-half-inch piece of steel wire bent at one end into two right angles—and rotated the knob.

The editor's desk was empty but for a mug, lamp, and a snow globe with two birch trees and a snowman. The drawers contained nothing but dead copy. Four filing cabinets, about eye-level high, lined the wall, on top of which were scattered loose papers, yellow, navy, and white. Bill pulled the top drawer on the nearest cabinet and was instantly overwhelmed. The files were not organized in any discernible way; many were unlabeled and most were overstuffed. He found handwritten notes, edited proofs, editorial correspondence, assessor's files. The next drawer was more chaotic. It would take weeks to go through the cabinets. Bill opened another drawer at random, in a different cabinet, and found another farrago of paper. He tried to think. He squinted his mind. Where would an editor keep the Axman's letter? Would he really file it away with all the other letters that came over the transom? But there was no time to puzzle over it—the copyboy or Croak or one of the other newsmen would soon come snooping.

At the doorway he took a final scan of the office. He closed the door. He opened the door. The navy-blue triangle of paper lying on top of the last cabinet—he recognized that particular shade of blue. He tugged and found it was the edge of a folder, the letters NOPD embossed on the cover. Inside, a short scrawled note from Capo (*D.D.—Back to you—we've determined no threat.—Cap. Cap*); behind that, the letter. It was written in florid script, the kind of writing you might see in an official government proclamation. *Hell, March 13, 1919* . . . The torn envelope lay beneath it, postmarked March 13, New Orleans. He read, *I am not a human being, but a spirit and a fell demon from hottest hell.* He saw Perl, pressing red begonias into his face. *It would've been better if I came as a phantom, returning from the after realm.*

"Mr. Officer?" The lightly mustachioed copyboy stood in the doorway. "Did Mr. Moore permit you—"

"I don't need permission." Bill lifted the folder in the air. "Police property."

The boy seemed at pains to muster the skepticism of the profession he sought to join. "What did you say your name was, Officer?"

He thought *Donovan's*. He thought *Fowler's*. "Vicks," said Bill, brushing past the boy, barely able to suppress his laughter. "Officer Donovan F. Vicks."

MARCH 22, 1919—THE BATTLEFIELD

"*Shh*. Don't answer."

"You think it's him?"

The curtains were drawn. A single candle guttered on the far side of the room, faint enough that its glow might not suffuse the fabric. Isadore debated whether to blow it out. He'd have to get off the mattress, which would cause the pallets to creak, and walk across the room, which would cause the floorboards to creak.

"Stay put," he whispered.

Orly nodded, her hand clutching her stomach. Her eyes were as big as tea saucers. "I think it's happening."

"Nothing's happening. We're fine."

"I mean the baby."

The knocking came more urgently.

Isadore glanced at the tin of Egyptienne Luxury cigars on the high shelf above the stove. Could he make it across the room and remove the tin from the shelf without causing too much noise? Then he remembered that the Webley & Scott revolver was no longer inside the tin. It was at the bottom of the Old Basin Canal, thanks to Dutt Ory.

"He'll leave," whispered Isadore. "We just have to wait."

The door rattled in its frame.

"Ain anybody going to answer the damn door?" shouted Daisy from her bed.

"*Shh.*" Isadore raised himself, his finger to his lips.

"If y'all are too lazy—" She shook her head, muttering. "Make an old lady hit the cold floor in the middle of the night."

"Mama!" said Orly. "Quiet!"

Isadore laughed with terror.

"I hear y'all in there," came a familiar voice from outside. "Don't foon me, Izzy!"

Isadore leaped to his feet. When he parted the curtain, every nerve in his body relaxed. He swung the door open so fast he didn't realize he was wearing only his underwear.

"Damn, Izzy," said Sore Dick. "I didn't intend to interrupt."

Izzy scanned Liberty Street. A phantom echo of the fear remained, but nothing was alive out there except for one of the roosters that lived with the Zurkes two doors down, moronically bobbing its head. In the damp night the moon turned the mist silver.

"Miss Orly." Dick removed his hat. "Miss Daisy."

"Who's that?" Daisy sat up in bed.

"It's all right, Mama. It's just my friend Richard."

Orly lifted the blanket up to her chin. "Why don't you two parley in the kitchen?"

"What about the baby? Is it coming?"

"Baby's coming?" said Daisy.

"Baby's coming?" said Dick.

"I think we might have some time," said Orly.

"Ma'am," said Dick, "I'm sorry for jumping in like this—"

"C'mon," said Isadore too loudly. The relief was high in him and he couldn't modulate his voice. No news could be bigger than the news that it was not a white maniac hoisting an ax at the door but only Sore Dick. Isadore led him into the cubby that the house's original owner might have used as a closet but they called a kitchen. Dick's breath smothered him with gin.

"The Reverend Right Duplessis invited us for a gig."

"All right."

"You heard me?"

How could he not? Dick was speaking directly into Isadore's mouth.

"I don't know when I'm going to be able to play again. Baby's about to arrive."

"You ain even heard the details."

"Dick, you came here after dark and terrified my wife, who is about to give birth—"

"Congratulations for that, by the way—"

"—just to tell me about a gig at the Funky Butt? A gig I won't even be able to play?"

"Gig ain at the Butt. It's at the Cosmo." Sore Dick gave a meaningful look but the name meant nothing to Isadore. *"The Cosmopolitan Hotel."* Dick pronounced each syllable as if Isadore were half-deaf.

"They don't put on jazz."

"Their advance man asked the Reverend for a recommendation. He said the Slim Izzy Quartet." Dick slapped Isadore on the chest.

"You're boiled. That doesn't make sense in at least four different ways."

"They said they want the real thing. This coming Friday."

"You spoke to the Reverend?"

"Heard from the holy man directly. Now, they ain paying much."

"I guess that's to be expected."

"Only eighty-five dollars."

"Hell!" Isadore felt light-headed. Was it possible to get drunk off another man's gin breath?

"They're going to hold a showcase. Dipper, Buddie Petit, a few other guys."

"Ah."

"But we get top billing."

"Eighty-five dollars? Hell!"

"Hell is right. Old Axman is taking care of us."

"It's not about him," said Isadore, with a ferocity that surprised them both. "It's about us."

Dick winked. "It's about eighty-five dollars that are going to line our pockets for a single evening of work."

It was as if the kitchen had been slowly filling with water and now it reached their necks. Isadore floated. The water kept rising and he couldn't breathe. But it was a pleasant breathlessness because the water was really gin. He could tell that Dick felt it too and they were swimming together like a pair of tadpoles.

"I feel like a damn tadpole," said Isadore, shaking his head.

Dick cackled. "I feel like a megatherium. Or a mastodon. No—like a Smilodon!"

"*Smilodon?*"

They burst into insane laughter, laughter so loud that Isadore didn't hear Orly when she screamed.

He hadn't run this fast since the night Bailey killed the blond detective. He made St. Claude within the span of a heartbeat. Amazingly a motor was approaching in the uptown lane, one block away. The driver was a white man in a suit and bow tie, with a stern mustache and disinterested eyes. He took one glance at the gesturing Negro and motored on. No sooner had he passed than Isadore spotted in the downtown lane another automobile. He sprinted across the neutral ground and into the road, waving his hands over his head. The motorist honked his horn but Isadore refused to budge. The car sputtered to a stop, the engine belching. Isadore, shielding his eyes from the headlamps, ran to the driver's side, where he was greeted by a young man in a bowler thrusting a pistol out of the window. Beside him a young woman cowered.

"Don't try it, boy!" yelled the man. "You let us go in peace."

Isadore raised his hands. "Sir, my wife is having a child. We need a ride to Charity. Please, take pity—"

The car accelerated, clouding Isadore in exhaust and dirt. He was unable to make out the man's parting obscenity but got the general picture.

Not another automobile or carriage was in sight apart from a

Leidenheimer wagon too far in the distance, headed uptown. He could run into the Marigny and see whether a motor or carriage was parked in front of a house and try to rouse its owners. But he was less likely to get a ride than to get shot. No streetcar route was within walking distance and the St. Claude jitneys stopped running at nine. Their plan had been to use the carriage belonging to their neighbor Harold James, a driver who hired himself freelance to Uptown clients, but he worked on weekend evenings. Harold had jokingly warned Orly that she should make sure not to let her water break between the hours of 7:00 p.m. and 2:00 a.m. on a Friday or Saturday. The joke wasn't funny then and it wasn't one bit funny now.

A wagon appeared at the corner, pulled by a half-asleep mule. Isadore set off in a flat sprint. He would jump on the mule's back if necessary. He would throttle the driver if necessary. If necessary he would kill him.

"Get in, boy!" shouted Sore Dick, pulling the reins.

Isadore leaped onto the footboard.

"Sis Pinky said we could use her delivery dray," said Dick. "She saw that Miss Daisy would've kilt her if not."

"Go. Fast."

"Mule isn't for fast. But it beats walking."

Isadore flipped the door handle and climbed into the carriage. Orly was alone, her head in her arms.

"Tell me," he said.

"The pains are coming regular. I can't really figure the time. Maybe four minutes apart."

"Is that bad?"

"It's not good. It's not bad. But it's not good."

"It's happening, though?"

"She's coming. And none too soon."

"Heavens."

"Don't be nervous."

"I'm not, baby. We'll be at Charity in no time." But he knew that between now and then, and between then and forever, an infinity of bad things could happen. What made it especially bad was that he had no idea what most of the bad things were.

Reading his mind, she said, "If anything happens—"

He didn't let her finish. "Only thing that's going to happen is we're going to have a beautiful baby. But not until we get to the hospital."

The mule's hoofbeats were painfully slow, methodic, indifferent.

"If anything *happens*," said Orly, "I want you to know I'm proud of you."

"I couldn't even find you an automobile."

"You made big sacrifices for me. For our family. It's tried on you."

"You made all the sacrifices. Between the Tiltons and my music nonsense—"

"Don't call it nonsense."

She squeezed his hand hard. He thought it was a gesture of endearment, but she kept squeezing until it felt his hand would break.

"What? What's doing?"

"It's happening." She arched her body back in the seat, gritting her teeth.

"What do I do?"

She shook her head. He reached to wipe sweat from her brow. She pushed his hand away.

"Y'all good back there?" called Dick.

"I have no idea," said Isadore.

"You a real tough baby now, Miss Orly! We're about there."

She grimaced, shaking her head.

"It's bad," said Isadore.

She nodded.

"Can you credit it—the Cosmo?" called Dick.

"What?"

"The Cosmopolitan Hotel!"

"Tell that fool," said Orly, through her teeth, "to shut up and drive."

Isadore sat beside her, as helpless as the sky. He promised himself that he would throw his cornet into the Mississippi if only Orly would stop hurting.

"There," she said. "It passed."

"You sure?"

"Don't worry. I'll tell you when it gets bad."

It got bad seven more times before they reached Charity Hospital. Dick ran inside to get nurses, a wheelchair. The streetlamp illuminated a vein throbbing thickly in Orly's forehead.

"I need something strong," said Orly.

"Squeeze my hand if that helps."

"Oh, baby. That doesn't come close to helping."

Sore Dick was back, his chest heaving. "They ain got any more wheelchairs. And they ain got any nurse or doctor available. Everyone's busy with the flu patients. Asking if we got anyplace else we can go."

Orly growled. Isadore had never heard her growl.

"This is our stop," said Isadore. "Help me, Dick."

It was oddly quiet in the lobby atrium. The desk attendant shook her head as soon as she saw them, Orly in the middle, her arms around the men's shoulders.

"How long between contractions?" asked the attendant.

"I don't know—four minutes?" said Orly. "It's been coming faster, though."

"You have time. I'd go to Presbyterian if I were you. We're chockablock in here."

"We're not going anywhere," said Isadore. Orly squeezed his arm. "We're going to the birthing ward and I'm going to deliver this child myself if I must."

"Tell 'em, Iz," said Dick.

"Suit yourselves," said the attendant. "The Negro women's department is next door. Third floor."

"What are you fools waiting for?" said Orly.

After another set of contractions in the stairwell they reached the ward. They emerged into a miasma of coughing and expectoration and rotting food. In the yellowish electric light they could only make out writhing limbs. Bodies lurched out of the shadows, lying in the cots and on the floor between the cots, in every configuration of agony and derangement. While Orly leaned on Dick for support, Isadore gathered discarded blankets that feverish patients had thrust to the floor and made a nest of them against the wall. Orly declined to sit on the blankets. She was no longer there, not really. Her voice was unfamiliar and it took Isadore a moment to realize that she was not groaning or asking for anything but singing, slightly out of tune, an old folk song:

Sauté crapeau, to chieu va brûler
Prend courage, li va repousser.
Dansé Calinda,
Bou-doum! Bou-doum!

"What's that mean?" said Sore Dick.

Orly, ignoring Dick and everything else, kept singing.

Mo té ain négresse,
Pli belle que Métresse.
Mo té vole belle-belle
Dans l'armoire Mamzelle.

Dansé Calinda,
Bou-doum! Bou-doum!

"Something about a bullfrog," said Isadore, thinking, praying, begging: if the pain ended soon and the baby survived, he would work two jobs the rest of his life. He would never raise his hand in violence against another man. He would never again see the inside of a tonk or hotel cabaret.

Orly paused, pressing her head against the wall, before resuming her song. She urged Calinda to dance even as Isadore went screaming for a doctor and Sore Dick ran downstairs to check on Sis Pinky's dray, even after a physician finally arrived, trailed by a nurse carrying a tray with forceps, tenaculum, hemostat, perforator, syringes, and a vial of cocaine solution.

Dansé Calinda,
Bou-doum! Bou-doum!

Her voice grew louder, the words becoming inarticulate. It could not be called singing anymore but had become a kind of sacramental chanting, which she kept up even as she arched her back and her hips began convulsing, even as the physician injected cocaine into her perineum, even as the doctor made a slight incision and, with a final spasm, the tiny eyes emerged, followed by the nose and the grimacing mouth. The mouth was the last thing Isadore saw before turning away and Orly was still singing, her voice louder even than the baby's wailing:

Bou-doum! Bou-doum! Bou-DOUM!

MARCH 23, 1919—THE GARDEN DISTRICT—THE INDUSTRIAL CANAL

Boys were playing baseball in Laurel Street, but none looked anything like Giugi. The street game had evolved since he was an urchin, when they had used a decapitated broomstick and wrapped their black stockings around the hard rubber balls that sold for a penny at Mackey's General. Giugi returned home with dirty feet and remorse in his face, understanding that it would have been cheaper to buy a new ball than ruin yet another good pair of stockings. He possessed a sense of guilt then. Today on Laurel Street the boys used actual baseballs and a real wooden bat; many wore gloves. Some weren't even Sicilian. In the last decade the neighborhood had diluted. Here was a redheaded Irish boy, a Chinese, an Arab. The boys once spoke in an English-Sicilian pidgin but today even the Italians spoke straight American. No, Giugi wasn't here at all.

"How is your head?" asked Raymond. "Isn't giving you any pain?"

"Go to the next site."

"Yes, ma'am."

"It is the same as driving to the Industrial Canal, only you continue on St. Claude over the bridge. Then left on Flood."

"Yes, ma'am. I recall from taking Mr. Vizzini and your son upon a time."

Good, reliable Raymond, driver and gardener, who compensated for his general dimness with his mastery of geography and geraniums, streets and strelitzia. He was working hard to project an attitude of carefree enthusiasm. He did not understand what she was after. Perhaps in the hope of eliciting information from her, he had begun to speak cavalierly. The comment about Sal and Giorgio, for instance. Raymond had figured out that their excursions had something to do with her family, but he did not understand what. She didn't mind Raymond's confusion. He was smart enough, and loyal enough, not to pry. Lizzie must have warned him against asking stupid questions: Mrs. Vizzini was not quite herself these days.

No, she thought, chuckling to herself. She was not.

"Ma'am?" Raymond glanced in the rearview mirror.

"Oh, nothing. I'm just admiring the beauty of this spring day."

"Yes, ma'am," he replied, in cheerful bafflement. "It's the kind of beautiful makes you laugh just to be alive."

She hoped it augured well, for yesterday's rounds had been a failure. Giorgio, she concluded, was hiding. She had not found him in the Upper Pontalba Building, where he kept his apartment and osteopathy office; Rosie's old sporting house on DeSoto Street; or the dozen or so bars and grocery stores on his old collection route. The men and women they did encounter in those places avoided speaking with Beatrice or feigned ignorance. Overnight, however, the ticking of Sal's grandfather clock had wound her sleepless thoughts into a tight geometry, and the logic came to her. Of course Giorgio would not turn up in those places. He might as well turn himself in to the police or present himself at her front door. But it was just as unlikely that he would have fled New Orleans. Even at the height of the Axman scare, when the entire city was on alert and cops pulled men off the street at the slightest suspicion, he had remained in town. The most logical explanation, the grandfather clock told her, or perhaps Sal himself communicated through the clock's machinery—the most logical explanation was that Giorgio had sought out a place he knew intimately, but where he would not expect to be seen. He would have gone, in other words, to one of the places he loved as a child. No member of the New Orleans Police Department knew those places. Only his mother did.

Raymond piloted them out of the old neighborhood. They passed the one-bedroom house on Josephine Street that Zio Zo, who had preceded them to New Orleans, had rented for Sal, Beatrice, and

Giugi upon their arrival on the SS *Montebello*. Sal had marveled at the central stove, the galvanized tub left behind by the previous tenants and, in the dirt backyard, the cypress cistern that collected rainwater running off the roof. But Beatrice now saw that it was smaller than the guest cottage on First Street where she lodged Lizzie and Raymond. The house itself, if not quite dilapidated, was nevertheless faded—the paint cracked, the window clouded with dirt. Perhaps it was only memory that made the house vivid. Everything seemed more vivid then: the scent of magnolia, the camphor pouches you wore around your neck like a vampire hunter during the yellow-fever scare, the twigs Giorgio bought at Chink's Oriental that, when lit, gave off fumes of cassia and jasmine. The milkman delivered his brimming pail at six in the morning; the baker, his face spectral with flour, at seven; the grocery boy dropped off the tomatoes and peppers at four in the afternoon. At six the coal train gusted smoke into the living room if you forgot to close the windows in time. When Giorgio came home with a sooty face, she removed with the pointed edge of a dampened handkerchief the cinders from his eyes—his large eyes that, if not entirely innocent, were at least trusting.

Sal took him on Saturdays to Bayou Bienvenue. It was not unusual for them to come home with a wagon full of king mackerel, bull croaker, and black jewfish the size of Giorgio himself. Sometimes they stayed the night at a camp belonging to one of Sal's fishing friends. It was swampy country, dense with shadows and blackness. What better place to hide from civilization? What better place to hide from one's mother?

At Sisters Street a security guard stood before a wooden barricade blocking the steel bascule bridge that passed over the Industrial Canal lock. He waved his arms. "The bridge ain open for automobile traffic." He leaned into the driver's-side window. "If you want to go to St. Bernard, you'll have to take Burgundy."

"Hello there, Arnold."

"Mrs. Vizzini! I didn't see you."

"I wondered, Arnold—have you seen my son? Giorgio?"

"Ma'am, I have not."

Two other men approached—the bridge engineer, a short man with nasty, bent features and a rabbity gait, trailed by his assistant, a cherubic young man whom Beatrice had never heard speak.

"Not today?" asked Beatrice. "Or not recently?"

The guard looked uncertain. "Not for some months, I'd hazard. Not since he was overseeing the dig, ma'am."

The engineer poked his face through the window. Raymond decorously withdrew.

"Sightseeing expedition, Mrs. Vizzini?"

"What are you boys doing out here on a Sunday?"

"Final-checking the bridge, ma'am," said the engineer. "It's about set."

From their ingratiating attitude she concluded that news of her dismissal from the Canal Board had not filtered down to the rank and file. "Have you got the drawbridge working correctly?"

"Me and Ernest here are just running some final tests on the counterweights, ma'am. But it's just about ready to go."

"You haven't seen Giorgio, have you?"

"Mr. Vizzini? Can't say I have. Ernest? You seen Mr. Vizzini?"

The assistant shook his head.

"I reassigned him to another project," said Beatrice. "But I wondered if he ever passed through. To admire the work, perhaps."

The engineer and the guard exchanged a look that Beatrice could not interpret.

"Plenty of folks come to marvel at the canal," said the engineer. "It's a treasure you've given New Orleans, Mrs. Vizzini."

"I'm glad that the deserving people of this great city are able to enjoy it." She savored the flavor of the old magnanimity. To shield her pride she glanced down at her hands. The gold rings sparkled so brightly they nearly brought tears to her eyes.

"Say, would you like to try it out? The bridge?"

"If it's safe," said Beatrice. "Raymond, do you think you can make it?"

"Yes, ma'am. If it's safe."

The engineer clapped the door and the men followed him to the barricade. The guard and the assistant lifted either end of the barricade and carried it off the road.

Raymond mashed the starter and they rolled over the steel. Beatrice glanced back once; the men waved. She thought she could see the guard muttering behind his hand to the engineer but they were soon obscured by the rising dust. On one side of the bridge she could see down into the lock, which linked the canal and the river; on the other the canal widened to the point at which it would meet the Mississippi. When the final plugs of land at either end of the canal were dynamited, the project would be complete. Lake would meet river. The great dream would be realized. But it wasn't really her dream anymore, was it? It was Rudolph Denzler's dream. It was her nightmare.

Raymond turned left and they drove along the canal. The bright meadow that Hugs—poor Hugs—had shown her that spring day in his motor truck was a moonscape of sand, mud, cement blocks, twisted fencing, and rusting machine parts scattered like limbs on a battlefield. The cows had long ago been converted to steak and leather. The pelicans, wild turkeys, and snipe had vanished. Beyond Florida Walk, where another bascule steel bridge was under construction, they drove through a barren expanse that a year earlier had been an ancient cypress swamp. The air was noticeably cooler here, and the soil richer, the color of dark chocolate. The bayou materialized in the distance. Its few remaining stands of cypress were the only vegetation visible in any direction. Raymond turned right at the outlet and stopped beside the excavator that had been used to cut a passage into the canal's turning basin. The roughed-up country felt familiar. An excavator had devoured her too, leaving wreck and ruin, or at least a void.

"Are you quite sure that this is it?"

"I'm sorry," said Raymond. "I thought you wanted to see Bayou Bienvenue."

"I did."

Raymond nodded. They sat in silence for a minute, looking at the marsh. "I suspect it don't look the way you recall," he said finally.

She should have anticipated this—the bayou, after all, belonged to the parcel purchased by the city for the canal. The fishing camps that lined the bank would have been seized in advance of the job. Most were demolished, leaving a few splintered stakes behind, sticking out of the ground like the skeletal ribs of an unburied beast. About a hundred yards offshore there floated a rowboat holding two people. One was an adult, the other, unmistakably, was a child. A fishing rod was propped over the stern.

"No," she told Raymond. "This is exactly how I remember it. Let me out."

She leaned on his arm for support. Her shoes, sinking into the mud, were instantly ruined. She didn't care. She only wanted to know who was in the boat.

"It's been a moment since the last pill," said Raymond. "Would you like one?"

"No time."

Raymond followed behind her solicitously. The mud was cake batter. Reeds tugged on her skirt like the fingers of beggar children.

"Careful, ma'am. Ain no place for a lady just here."

"Can you get their attention?" she said, as they approached the bank.

"Ma'am?"

"The two in the boat. Can you call them over?"

Raymond looked between his boss and the rowboat.

"Before they get too far," she said.

Raymond yelled so loudly he seemed to surprise himself. The oars lowered and remained submerged for a moment. Then they rose. The boat pivoted in a wide arc toward shore. Because the man faced backward, and the boy sat on the bench behind him, it was impossible to see their faces. She could hear their voices—the father's low bass hum and the son's persistent chirping. She could not make out the words. But it sounded as if the father spoke in a Sicilian accent. It seemed possible that he was teaching his son to fish, that no time had passed and nothing had changed.

"Ma'am, if I may?"

"Hush now. Can you hear what they're saying?"

"What is it you're thinking they might be saying?"

"*Hush.*"

Gradually their speech clarified.

"But why?" said the boy.

"Because," said the man.

They glided into view.

"Ma'am?" called the boater. "Sir? Y'all lost?"

She was, in fact, lost. The man was slender, with a welcoming, kindly face; he wore a crushed green flat hat and had a poorly trimmed beard. The hair on his face was red. He did not look in the slightest Sicilian, let alone anything like Sal. A moment later she saw the boy's face. But it was not a boy. It was a girl.

"Y'all must be lost if you're all the way out here without a boat."

"Tell them to leave us," she said, under her breath, to Raymond.

"What's the matter?" the girl asked her father.

"I'm sorry, mister," said Raymond. "We mistook you for a friend. Awful sorry to interrupt your fishing."

The man smiled. "Ain't nothing biting anyway. Happy for the exercise."

"What's wrong with that woman?" said the girl.

"We're on our way, darling."

"Why is she staring like that?"

Raymond took Beatrice's elbow and guided her back to the car, the spindles of weeds scraping her arms like knives. He handed her an aspirin. When he turned away, she let the pill fall from her hand. Aspirin was a joke before the force of her headaches; the only relief was total osteopathic reconfiguration. Aspirin could not right displaced bones, loosen contracted muscles, or purify the blood. Raymond would not know anything about that, however, so she did not mention it.

Raymond drove at a much faster speed than before. It felt less like a Sunday tour in the country than an ambulance racing to the hospital.

"I'll ask Miss Lizzie to boil that tea you like," Raymond was saying. "You just go straight upstairs. Miss Lizzie will fetch the tea to your bed."

They sped over the St. Claude bascule bridge, the men rising to salute her. *People of New Orleans, we must not allow the enemy to breach the fortification! Have we already forgotten the great storm of 1915, the fallen steeples of our churches, the ripped-up roofs, the Lake invading through the drainage canals?* In 1915 the collapsed steeples and exploded roofs had been the least of it. Coffins from Lafayette Cemetery burst from the ground and floated down Washington Avenue like canoes; the row houses were laid bare to the world, the exterior walls falling away like drapes; the dray mules, trapped in the district stable on Tchoupitoulas, floated in their flooded pens. Professor Fishman was the only person without a financial stake in the matter to protest the canal. Nobody else had worried how the canal might respond to future inundations. It had seemed intuitive: in high water the canal should flow into the lake or the river. But the natural scientist likely had a different analysis. If he had not disappeared, he might have described more precisely the nature of his fear.

"Folks have their likes and their dislikes," said Raymond, glancing nervously into the mirror. "Childhood rudeness is my dislike. I abominate rudeness in a child. In anyone, mind you, but most especially in a child."

It was true, as Fishman said, that the canal would invite water into the fortified city. It was true that the canal flew against two centuries of municipal strategy, which called for keeping water out of the city at all cost, first with a parapet of earthen levees and later the modern drainage system. But what would happen if the rain kept coming? If all the springs of the great deep burst forth and the floodgates of the heavens opened, overwhelming Mr. Wood's screw pumps? The lake swelling, the river rising. The water finding the weak spots in the canal walls and bursting through crevasses into the defenseless city. The Industrial Canal would no longer be "the realization of a splendid vision" but a ravenous wolf exacting vengeance. Beatrice's river had divided the city; with reinforcements it would conquer. The drowning citizens would curse her name as they fled by rowboat and pirogue, the hospitals overwhelmed, iceboxes left to rot, the houses sinking, the infirm, the cocky, and the weak marooned—

"These touring trips get tiresome, don't they?" said Raymond. "Almost home now, though. Almost to bed."

"Wait. Turn here."

"We're just about home, ma'am. We'll come back another day."

"Turn left. Take me to St. Mary's."

"Service is probably out already," said Raymond, but in a diminuendo that reduced the end of the sentence to a mumble. He turned left.

Mass had ended and a cluster of families lingered by the entrance, waiting for an audience with Father Scramuzza. Beatrice gave Lizzie a two-dollar bill each Sunday to hand to Scramuzza but had not herself attended mass since Sal's funeral. Still she had fond memories from the days when Scramuzza delivered the homily in Sicilian. She had taken pleasure in dressing Giugi for church in his little jacket and tie, combing his blond hair with a dab of pomade, shining his tiny shoes—

She saw her son.

"Stop here!"

Raymond smashed the brake with both feet. "I'm sorry, ma'am. Are you hurt?"

She was already out of the car. Giorgio was tussling with another boy at the end of the block.

"Giugi!"

Giugi wrapped his arms around the boy's shoulders. Laughing, the boy flung him off and began playfully to jab Giugi in the back. Giugi escaped, running in the direction of St. Mary's, toward Beatrice's outstretched arms.

"Giugi!" she yelled. "*Amore mio!*"

The child, suddenly aware of her presence, dodged, but not fast enough. She enveloped him in a giant hug.

"*Darling,*" she said in Sicilian. "*I have been looking for you everywhere.*"

The boy pulled back in shock.

"*I miss you horribly.*"

"Get offa me, lady!"

"*You can still change. I can change too. Let's not hide from each other.*"

The boy tore away and ran to the church. "Help!" he shouted. "This woman is nuts!"

"*Come home, Giugi,*" she yelled. "*It's not too late. Come home.*"

"*Please*, Mrs. Vizzini." Raymond had caught up to her. He stood before her, blocking her from chasing after the child.

"That's him!" she shouted.

"Let's get back into the motor, Mrs. Vizzini."

"*Giugi!*" she yelled, but there was no use. A young couple herded the child around the corner. "*Goodbye, my love,*" she called after him, with all the volume she could muster. But her throat, filled with fluid, would not cooperate. It became difficult even to see; her eyes were hot with tears. Still she tried once more, with the final measure of her energy.

"*Goodbye, Giugi!*" she screamed. "*Goodbye, goodbye, goodbye!*"

MARCH 24, 1919—UPTOWN—CRIMINAL COURT BUILDING

Giving your wife an enema: there was marital intimacy for you.

It had been a blurry weekend of cold sweat, ice bags, temperature taking, vaccine dosing, sodium bicarbonate suppositories. A weekend also of softness, pity, and understanding, which is to say, love. It was not their old love, the teenage fervor and mystery—that was a faded memory—but a new love, mundane and heavy and inevitable. Enema love. He did not want to call her friends and did not want to see the Bones, so he served as nurse himself. His duties included preparation and administration of the enemas: one dram of sodium bicarbonate in a pint of water, inserted every three hours through a soft rubber catheter. It did not bother him, once he got used to it: he was happy to do something. The hours bled. Maze's fever dreams mixed with his own until he couldn't tell whose dream he was dreaming. He felt a faint desire to return to his investigation but he couldn't risk leaving Maze for more than a couple of hours at a time. At night he felt he couldn't risk leaving her long enough to use the bathroom. On Monday morning her fever began to fall. When the doctor appeared shortly after dawn to examine her lungs, kidneys, and heart, he ordered Bill to leave the house. Bill was excessively piqued, the doctor concluded, and his presence could only make matters worse. She would need him to be strong and clear minded for the next stage of her recovery. Better Bill should return to normal life. He laughed at that: "normal life." On his way out, Maze told him not to worry. She told him that she loved him. It restored his strength. It made him want to do good work. Big work. Not to prove anything to her, or even to himself, but because it was right. It was human.

On the street the fresh air was like a foreign climate. It abraded his skin. He began to order his thoughts again. They all led to the same place: the Axman's letter.

It might not be likely to lead to the killer, but it was all he had. Theodore Obitz used to say that clues were like witnesses: each told a different story and even the lies provided information. Even a forged letter might lead to the truth. He was certain at least that Capo had not pursued it sufficiently. He may have shown it to the Department's forensics chief, but Bill didn't trust the old man, whose specialty was ballistics, after all. He only knew to study documents for fingerprints, stains, watermarks. He didn't understand how graphological science had matured. The new theory was that handwriting was itself a kind of fingerprint, capable of revealing aspects of character and habit. Handwriting told its own story. That, at least, was what Mary Eager had taught him.

He had been waiting for nearly an hour outside her office at Sophie Newcomb College when she arrived. She wore a lilac jacket and carried an oversize handbag swinging from her shoulder; her manner was brisk, assured, impatient.

"William Bastrop." He extended his hand.

"The Gallier suicide."

He had consulted with her on a murder case; she testified that a suicide letter was in fact written by the victim's husband. Though a psychologist by training, Eager was an expert in the burgeoning field of handwriting analysis, having published papers with titles such as "Garlands or Arcades: A Crisis in Graphology" and "Bar Sinistrality."

"I telephoned the department on Friday," said Bill. "The secretary said you'd left for the weekend. So I tried your residence."

"I was at my mother's in Slidell." Her eyes paused on his face. She did not appear to be reassured by what she saw. "I have class in an hour. Can you return this afternoon?"

Bill produced the Axman letter.

"I saw that in the paper."

"This is the original."

"Hasn't it been solved?"

"He's still out there."

"If I don't help, I suppose another grocer and his wife will be murdered. Their blood will be on my hands."

"You're already making my job easier."

There were footsteps behind him. Bill's hand went to his hip. He turned to find a boy holding three books under one arm. At the sight of the cop, the student dropped his books.

"Don't be concerned, Henry," said Eager, as she moved behind her desk. "Unless you plan on giving me an excuse for missing today's class."

"I wouldn't miss class for the world, ma'am," said the student, hastily gathering the books. He ran down the stairwell, taking two steps at a time.

Eager gave Bill a professional smile. "I'm sorry to disappoint you. And I'm sorry to doom yet another grocer to a gruesome execution. But there's no way for me to conduct a proper analysis in the next hour."

"Can you cancel class?"

"Absolutely not." She withdrew a file and a pencil from her handbag.

The dizzy feeling was returning, gathering about him like a cloud of bees.

"Don't get torn up about it," she said. "I'll telephone the station with the results this evening."

"Forget the proper analysis. Can you simply take a look?"

"I already did."

"Did you reach any conclusions?"

"None you couldn't have reached yourself."

"You might overestimate me."

"Well, it is obvious that the writer is not the Axman."

"How do you know?"

"You mean apart from the demand that everyone in New Orleans play jazz music?"

"Other than that." He placed the letter on the desk.

She sighed. "The diacritics—the dots of the *i*'s and the crosses of the *t*'s—are consistently sharp. Look at *spirit*. *Invisible*. *Victims*. That tends to indicate wit, originality, imagination."

"The Axman is nothing if not original."

"The clean penmanship indicates that the letter was written with great deliberation. The writing gets slower as it goes. You see the roundness of the vowels toward the end? *Devils*. *Nether regions*. *Tartarus*. The writer is trying to hide something. Or he is anxious to get it right."

"Trying to hide something."

"These are hardly conclusive observations. It would be like a doctor saying that a patient with a sore tooth must have scurvy. In a proper analysis one considers more than three dozen criteria. One looks for commonalities, patterns. One creates a profile."

"Nothing you've said proves the writer isn't the killer."

"You're right. I suppose that's my conclusion as a psychologist, not as a graphologist."

Bill returned the letter to its folder.

"I expect that you've already tried to determine whether any local schools still teach Spencerian?"

"Excuse me?"

"You can see that the letter is written in Spencerian script."

"I don't know what that is."

She put down her pencil. When, after a pause, she resumed, her voice took on a distinctly pedagogical tone. "Spencerian script was taught to American schoolchildren in the second half of the last century. It was designed by the abolitionist Platt Rogers Spencer. He believed that a formal system of penmanship, taught to schoolchildren of every race and creed, was an essential foundation of a democracy."

"You mean how the writing looks like a government document?"

"Or your parents' correspondence."

His parents didn't have "correspondence" but he did not interrupt.

"Schools adopted the Palmer Method by the turn of the century, or the Zaner-Bloser script. Most likely you use Palmer."

"Why would somebody write in Spencerian?"

"Maybe because they're older," said Ms. Eager. "You're the detective."

The old obnoxious New Orleans heat. The sunlight on St. Charles was a thousand needles poking under his collar, beneath the band of his belt where his shirt bunched, in the soles of his feet, along the rim of his hairline. Applied suddenly, in extreme quantities, the heat stirred visions. It made the streetcar driver exactly resemble Leonard Perl. It made Maze materialize in the shade of a palm tree, only to melt into the ringed patterns on the bark. It sent a young man angling toward him down the avenue brandishing an ax. The ax was a baseball bat, he realized, the man heading to Audubon Park, but the shock quickened his pulse. Navy instincts—ha!

Still the fuzziness had its benefits. It shuttled his thoughts out of their regular circuits, creating new transferences and patterns. Was it possible that the Axman was an older man? Perhaps. But what older man would demand jazz music? What older man had heard of jazz music? And if the letter was a hoax, what end did it serve? What kind of lunatic would go through the trouble?

Two police skills Bill did have: observation and memory. They had not abandoned him entirely. He knew because he could feel the weight of a memory pressing into his consciousness, making him uneven, like a hand pushing down on one shoulder. He had seen the Axman's florid script somewhere before, and not in old letters from his parents. He remembered thinking it was silly, particularly given the context, but it was not until he searched through case files at the department that he found it. Frank Bailey, the Negro highwayman—the man who shot Teddy Obitz—wrote his confession in Spencerian script. The lavish loops, the fussy flourishes: it was as if he had written it with a quill. The other navies had laughed at the idea of a griffe Negro writing like a member of King Arthur's court.

Twenty minutes later he was through the Criminal Court Building and into the jail. The mountainous officer at the door led him through an interrogation room to the cellblock. The center tier was murderers' row.

When they appeared at his cell, Bailey leaped from his cot. "Officer—the judge really going to hear my case tomorrow?"

He was smaller than Bill remembered. Perhaps captivity had done that to him: shrunk him. Bill had seen it before. Prison shrank one's world, the action of one's mind, even one's physiognomy. Or perhaps he was confusing Bailey with Abraham Price, the man Bill had shot dead on the night of the murder. He tried to forget about Abraham Price.

"That's a detective," said the prison guard.

"Mr. Detective. Is the judge going to hear my case tomorrow?"

"Tell me first—what school did you attend?"

"You seen my lawyer? Mr. Doyle?"

"Answer his question," said the prison guard.

"Maybe we can have a conversation," said Bailey. "A conversation means two people talking to each other."

"Boy, you will die a convicted cop murderer," said the guard. "And it will not be a pleasant die."

"That's fine, Officer," said Bill. He waited until Bailey resumed eye contact. "You answer my question, Mr. Frank. Then I'll answer yours."

"What *school* did I attend?"

"Yes, sir."

"McDonough 6. Left when I made twelve. They taught me nothing. But teach me this: Do you know Detective Harry Dodson? Theodore Obitz's partner."

"Of course I know him."

"Did you know that he was the man who killed Obitz?"

"Shut your face," said the prison guard, advancing heavily toward the cell.

"That's fine," said Bill. All he needed was the answer to a single question. He could play along. "Let him tell his story."

"I fired three shots as I ran, but none of them took effect. I fired as I ran and could not take aim. It must have been Obitz's partner, Dodson, who did it. One of Dodson's bullets, intended for me."

"That's an interesting theory."

"My question is who is going to pay for the death of Abraham Price and Louis Johnson, the two innocent Negroes who were shot down when they were hunting me?"

"I ask about your schooling because I noticed the quality of your penmanship in your confession note."

"Are they going to hear my case tomorrow?"

"I don't know. I can ask."

"The confession note was coerced. I was given the third degree."

"They taught you to write at McDonough 6? They taught you to make those loops and flourishes?"

"What did you say your name was?"

"I didn't. Detective William Bastrop."

"Bastrop . . . ain you the one who shot Abraham Price?"

Bill realized his mistake. It was too late to lie now.

"Why am I to pay for the death of Detective Obitz," said Bailey, "and you won't pay for the death of Abraham Price?"

Bill silently offered three answers, none of which he could utter without enraging Bailey further.

"There are two innocent Negroes dead on account of Detective Obitz," said Bailey. "I'm going to make three. Where is the justice in that?"

Bill raised his hand to still the guard. "Do you remember," he asked Bailey, "the name of the teacher at McDonough 6 who taught you how to write so fancy?"

"It wasn't anybody at McDonough 6 that taught me script."

"You said that was the only school you attended."

"I learned it out in the country. From Mr. Peter Davis at the Waifs' Home."

Bill wrote the names on his pad. He liked how they looked

there—solid enough to dress up in clothes. They went next to *Gown Man—forests under forests—river flows both ways—jalapeno for bowels—cancer in the rain forest—Spencerian.*

"Have you heard anything about Miss Virginia Gabriel?"

"Is that the woman who turned you in?"

"Wondered if she come ask about me."

"I'll find out. Just a few more questions."

"Ask about Verge and ask about the trial tomorrow."

"I will."

"Is this conversation going into the court proceedings against me?"

"Answering the questions will only help your position. I promise you that."

"Promises from a navy." Bailey shook his head.

Bill touched his temple. Something was active there, a seismic activity beneath his skin, swelling and contracting, fixing to explode. "When were you at the Colored Waifs' Home?"

"From 1913 to 1915. I was charged with stealing thirteen chickens. I trace my misfortune back to the chickens."

"Stealing chickens is a hundred miles away from holding up men. Let alone murdering a detective."

"It wasn't the chickens. It was their number: thirteen. I knew when I counted them that I was cursed." Bailey closed his eyes and opened them. "I didn't kill that policeman."

"Who was there with you at the home? Other students, teachers?"

Bailey's eyes narrowed. "I don't recall. It was a long while ago."

"Four years?"

"Time and me aren't friends anymore."

"You know anything about the Axman murders?"

Bailey looked confused. "Only what I've read," he said. "Hasn't he heard of a gun?"

Bill had had enough. Bailey wasn't nearly as dyspeptic as the others said he was. Or the dyspepsia had been beaten out of him. "I'll mention you to Judge Baker." Bill almost meant it. "I'll say you were helpful."

"If you see Virginia Gabriel, please tell her that I request a word."

As Bill walked past the cells and the shrunken men inside, he felt a strange envy rise through him. These men had been condemned to a life so restricted that there was never any need to ask questions. How different that was from a life of questioning, and of questioning his own questioning!

When he returned to the open air he marveled at his foolishness. The time to think was exactly the problem. What finer torture than being left alone with your thoughts, free to explore the shape of eternity and your position in it? The questioning habit was a kind of game, when you came down to it. The thousands of little questions that arose during an investigation, or during a marriage, were little puzzles that distracted from the big, central puzzle. Without all of life's little questions you would be left alone, in silence, to study the central puzzle. And that puzzle's pieces never fit, no matter how roughly you tried to force the edges together.

Even this brief glimpse of the big question complicated his breathing. Better to think about the Colored Waifs' Home. He could get out there in fifteen minutes if he borrowed one of the Department's automobiles. That would give him just enough time to come up with questions for Peter Davis, a series of little questions that might just lead him to resolve the big question. Now those questions—what were they?

MARCH 25, 1919—CENTRAL CRIMINAL COURT

"If they walk the dog," said Bailey, "you may as well sign my death warrant."

"They're not going to bring in any dog." Isadore hunched forward so he could whisper over the bar into Bailey's ear. "Even the DA has more self-respect than that."

Bailey turned and looked at Isadore as if he were crazy. Isadore frequently received that look from Bailey. He had learned not to be offended by it. Bailey, he could tell, was comforted by Isadore's presence, elated to have someone to listen to his complaints. Isadore was happy to be here. He did not say as much to Bailey, but he saw his presence at the murder trial as a way of thanking Bailey for not revealing his role in the holdups. Bailey had proven his loyalty. Besides, there was little chance that he would even be tried for the highway jobs. They had him dead to rights for murdering a detective.

"It's not about self-respect," Bailey whispered loudly, spraying saliva into Isadore's inner ear. "It's about theater. That's the secret to good prosecution: theater. Don't you know anything?"

Bailey's attorney made a subtle lowering gesture with his palm. It meant *Quiet down, the jury is watching.* The attorney, E. Warren Doyle, was gourd shaped with a bushy yellow mustache and a spray of irregular small reddish moles like fire ants across the left side of his face. When he addressed the jury, he positioned his body in an unnatural profile to avoid showing his moles, which only made the jurors more determined to see them. Isadore could see their distraction whenever Doyle spoke. It wasn't a good sign for Bailey, Isadore didn't suppose.

The prosecutor had proposed the dog experiment during one of the early motions hearings. No mark or ash had been found on Detective Obitz's clothing. A small ring of charred flesh encircled the wound. Both findings, the coroner argued, suggested that the gun was fired from close range, with minimal distance between muzzle and flesh. This was a good break because Obitz's partner, Dodson, had testified that the shooter fired from approximately a dozen yards away. Bailey had known better than to let himself become excited but it was the best news he'd had since the arrest.

That's when the district attorney, Luzenberg, came up with the dog idea. He would wrap an actual police uniform around a dog, press a revolver against the animal's chest, and pull the trigger. The experiment, Luzenberg argued, would show that a revolver so fired would not only singe the flesh but leave distinctive burn marks on the clothing, disproving the coroner's finding.

Doyle had ordered Bailey a close shave for the trial and provided him with a weathered suit and black spats. In this costume Bailey looked older, dignified even, despite his ankles and hands being shackled. His face was darkened by anguish but his eyes did not participate in it. The old irascible spirit flickered within them.

"A daddy, huh?"

"This is the first I left Orly since she was born."

"What's the child's name?"

"Isadora."

"Orly let you leave?"

"The nurses said I was getting in the way."

"They say girls are easier to raise but I wouldn't be so positive about that."

"I'm not positive about anything in this world right now."

Doyle glanced over sharply and Bailey was quiet another minute. Luzenberg was explaining the properties of flesh char.

"I'm glad you came," Bailey whispered. "I need to tell you a few things."

"Like what?"

Bailey nodded in the direction of Doyle. Presently he stood to rebut the district attorney's argument. As he approached the bench in his sideways, crablike manner, Bailey started again.

"A detective came to see me in jail. Man who shot Abraham Price on the night of the Obitz murder."

"You think he's involved?"

Bailey shook his head. "Asking about the Waifs' Home. Questions about penmanship."

Isadore didn't know what to say.

"Handwriting, like."

"Sure—but why?"

"Something to do with the Axman."

Isadore shot a glance at the judge. Had he heard anything? Isadore had the idea that if Judge Baker heard the word *Axman* and looked in Isadore's direction, the judge might just interrupt Bailey's trial to haul Isadore to jail.

As if on cue, Baker interrupted Doyle in the middle of a frantic plea. "Denied. Mr. Luzenberg, call your witness."

Doyle threw up his arms in exasperation. His moles flushed a richer pink.

"I call Barko, Your Honor."

"Barko?" whispered Bailey.

The door to the courtroom swung open. Isadore turned at the sound but saw no witness, only two navies striding in. One of the officers held a leash.

"Bring me the death warrant to sign," said Bailey, a little too loudly. One of the jurors, an older agrarian type, glanced over. Doyle gave Bailey a warning hiss. It made no difference.

"Bring the death warrant!"

The judge pounded the gavel. "Defendant, you are warned!"

The dog, a wolfish mongrel that appeared to have been injected with a sedative, was brought—dragged—through the gate into the middle of the floor.

"I call Mrs. Eloise Obitz," said Luzenberg.

A slim woman in a black drawcoat and long black skirt entered the gallery. Against the blackness of her mourning clothes her yellow hair glowed. She carried a folded garment. Her eyes twitched but the set of her head and the movement of her legs were determined, vengeful. Isadore could not concentrate on the widow, however, or Barko. He could only think about his handwriting. It was a funny handwriting, fancier than what was normally practiced, but that was how Mr. Davis had taught them. If the script was good enough for Platt Rogers Spencer, Mr. Davis said, it was good enough for the children of the Colored Waifs' Home. A man who could not write in a dignified manner should not expect other men to treat him with dignity. It hadn't occurred to Isadore to write the letter in any other script. It would have looked childish if he had tried.

"Why was the officer asking about the Axman?" asked Isadore, leaning forward. "What does that have to do with penmanship?"

"I'm hearing the Axman didn't write the letter to the newspaper."

"Who said that?"

"Guys in the block." Bailey did not elaborate because the widow took the stand.

"Objection," said Bailey under his breath. Doyle nodded but did not say anything.

"Mommy!" shouted a young girl in the gallery, waving. The widow Obitz, sitting in the witness stand, waved at her daughter.

"Mrs. Obitz," said the district attorney, "can you please tell the court what you hold in your arms?"

"This is my late husband's police coat."

"How does it resemble the coat that Detective Obitz was wearing at the time he was attacked by the murderous Negro sitting right there?"

"Objection!" shouted Doyle.

"I sustain," said the judge.

"How does this resemble the jacket worn by Detective Obitz at the time of his death?"

"It is identical. Or, rather, as close to identical as possible without being the same jacket. He had two pairs. They are issued by the New Orleans Police Department."

"Theater," said Bailey. "Help me Christ."

"Please show the coat to the jurors, Mrs. Obitz, so they can see it has not been tampered with."

"Who said the thing about the Axman?" said Isadore.

"I don't know. A few of the dagos. They say the Axman isn't one for writing letters to the editor."

"They know who it is?"

"Sure they do. Ah, Hell."

One officer held down Barko's haunches; the other guided his front paw through a sleeve of the police coat.

"You know that isn't his real coat," said Bailey, appealing to his lawyer. Doyle ignored his client. He looked defeated. He had forgotten to shield his strange moles from the jury. But they didn't appear to notice. They were staring at the cur, which, having been dressed in Obitz's coat, laid its head on its paws. Barko on some primitive level seemed to know what was going on. So did Bailey. He also laid his head in his hands.

"Aren't you going to object?" said Bailey.

Doyle shook his head. "Already objected all I could do."

The clerk handed one of the officers a revolver that had previously been entered into evidence. With a ceremonial air—thumb and forefinger pinching, pinkie extended—the officer extracted a single bullet from a leather pouch on his belt.

A sob erupted in the gallery. Bailey, astonished to find an unexpected ally in the courthouse, looked for the source of the outburst. When he saw it was the widow's daughter—a slim reed of eight or nine with bright blond hair—his eyes widened.

"Don't shoot!" she shouted. "Don't shoot the doggy!"

"Yes, girl," said Bailey. "Tell 'em!"

The officer with the revolver froze, uncertain. Barko froze too. He appeared to have fallen asleep. The adults seated near the child tried to calm her but it was useless.

"Child," said the judge, placating, but that only made her sobs stiffen into a breathless shriek. The judge stood. "Mrs. Obitz, will you please remove your daughter from the courtroom?"

The girl resisted and her mother was powerless to move her. There was agitation in the gallery, murmurs of distress. The officer with the revolver swiveled between the judge and the sobbing girl.

"Your Honor," said Doyle, "I move to suspend the execution of the dog."

"That dog," said the judge, "will be executed."

The girl's shriek could not possibly increase in volume but it increased in pitch.

The judge pounded the gavel. "We'll take a five minute recess," he said. "Somebody tend to that child."

The jurors were led out of the chamber. "Maybe," said Bailey, turning to face Isadore, "this is my lucky day."

The bailiff approached the widow and her daughter. Most of

the audience in the gallery rose to stretch their legs or to leave the courtroom.

"Listen," said Isadore, putting his hand on Bailey's shoulder, "what did you hear about the Axman?"

Bailey gave him a look. "Don't tell me you're involved in that business."

"Why do you say that?"

"Frank," said Doyle. "We need to go over a couple things."

"One second, lawyer Doyle."

Doyle, shaking his head, went to chat with Luzenberg. Obitz's daughter, having been told that the dog would be spared, was led gently up the aisle.

"I'll explain," said Isadore. "But you first."

"Lot of Italians in the block. Southern Italians, you know?"

"They talk to you?"

"They talk to each other. But I hear. There aren't proper walls, you know."

"I thought Italians—southern Italians—talk in . . . Southern Italian."

"They go back and forth. They said the Axman doesn't write letters—that he probably doesn't even know how to write his own name. But he didn't like that someone was writing letters for him."

"How do they know who the Axman is?"

"The Italians like to blabber. All day it's *me parley* this and *tea-parley* that." He paused. "Is this personal with you?"

Isadore didn't know what to say.

"What's going on, Iz?"

"You're going to win this thing, Frank."

"You leaving? Izzy?"

But Isadore was already in the aisle. He passed the trembling Obitz daughter and her overwhelmed mother, burst through the swinging courtroom doors, down the stairs, and out into Elks Place.

He had to get to Orly. When she and the baby were released from Charity, they could not return to the Liberty Street apartment. But where could they go? And what about Miss Daisy? While Isadore had slept on the floor of the women's ward beside Orly's cot the last three nights, Daisy had slept at home. She hadn't said anything about strange visitors but she had only been there to sleep. There was also the matter of the Friday-night gig at the Cosmopolitan Club. That was out of the question. He would tell Sore Dick to cancel it or to find another cornet player.

Outside, as he passed the courtroom window, Isadore realized it wasn't enough to move his family away from Liberty Street and cancel the gig. If the maniac knew Isadore's address, wouldn't he also know that Isadore worked days at the Industrial Canal and nights at Pelican Cooperage? Isadore thought of Barko, tightly collared and wrapped in the clothing of a dead man, resigned to its pitiful fate, a gun pressed into its flank.

But his thoughts were interrupted by the blast of a revolver.

MARCH 28, 1919—THE GARDEN DISTRICT

A normal woman with a normal son living a normal existence would have thought it a lovely spring evening in New Orleans. The sky was pink blending to gold. A few clouds in the west, grimy with a moldlike pattern that might have been detached from the side of a dilapidated white house, sent a breeze to dispel the heat. Had Beatrice been nearly anybody else, it would have been a pleasant day too. In the morning she walked through the Garden District to St. Mary's. At home for dinner she ate like a laborer—a new habit, of which she was not particularly proud. Lizzie prepared a pan of Oysters Vizzini; a third of a pound of spaghetti in garlic, hot-pepper flakes, and olive oil; spinach, stewed in lemon juice and oil; and a loaf of crispy Leidenheimer rolls to sop up the oil from the oysters, spaghetti sauce, and spinach. There followed three *cartocci,* which Lizzie had not quite mastered, but were sweet and filling. Beatrice also drank an entire bottle of Frascati. She did not try to get drunk but she did not try to not get drunk.

After a fitful nap on the library couch—in open revolt against the regimentation of Sal's grandfather clock she had begun sleeping in the library, not only at night but in the afternoon—Raymond drove her back to the Industrial Canal. She avoided Bayou Bienvenue, where the diggers were finishing the excavation. Hibernia had so far hired two additional contracting firms but the Hercules men remained and she did not want to risk having to explain that she no longer had a voice in administrative decisions, would be unavailable for newspaper interviews, and would not appear in the formal ribbon-cutting ceremonies. Her name would be connected to the canal no more closely than the names of Hercules's anonymous Negro laborers. After an hour or so of standing on the lock, at the point where the canal would join the Mississippi, she returned in a blue reverie to the house on First Street.

Had Giugi been a normal son, Beatrice would have been overjoyed when Lizzie announced, at the end of supper, that he had appeared on the porch. But he was not a normal son and she was not a normal mother. She choked on her ice cream.

"Shall I tell him that you are occupied?"

She was occupied, of course—in thoughts about Giorgio. Thoughts, calculations, schemes. Had her brain summoned him into existence, drawn him to her front porch? But she did not have the opportunity to respond.

"Hi, Mamma." He was larger than a dream.

"Your head is bleeding."

He touched his hairline. "Gee. I guess it is."

"Lizzie, please bring a handkerchief for Giorgio. Also a setting."

"It's nice to see you, Mamma."

"Would you like some supper?" She tried to make her voice sound as normal as possible but forgot what her normal voice sounded like. She tried to pretend as if he had never stopped coming over for their weekly supper, as if they had seen each other since Hugs's disappearance. "I believe we still have some veal and creamed onions."

"Chantilly ice cream would be nice. I'm not very hungry but I am hot."

They sat in silence while Lizzie went to fetch the handkerchief and the ice cream. This gave her a chance to think. But she couldn't. She was too distracted by the physical presence of her son. In the days she had spent searching the city in vain, trying to imagine where he might be, what he might be doing, what demon had possessed him and how she might exorcise it, Giorgio had become in her mind more than human. He had become a universal force, like inertia or friction. She had forgotten the scale of his face, the ears like potatoes, the eyes like onions, the turnip nose, the hairs on his forearm like rubber coils. The torso like an icebox. The arms like ham bones. The predatory, ursine grin. The hands like celery roots, heavy, ugly, warped. The hands like mallets. The hands like murder weapons.

"You have been looking for me."

"It's been weeks," she said calmly. "I'm not used to going so long without seeing my son."

"I've been busy."

Fate, or some higher power, had granted her a second chance. Though she was unprepared, she could not waste it. It might be her final chance. She needed time to strategize.

"Busy? How?"

Giorgio grimaced in the shape of a smile. "You know how."

Lizzie returned holding a tray with place mat, the good purple-filigree-on-cream cloth napkins that Beatrice reserved for important guests, a glass of cold water, and a bowl of chocolate Chantilly ice.

"Angelo Brocato's," said Lizzie, proud of herself. "Your favorite, Mr. Giorgio."

"It's good to see you, Miss Lizzie."

"You sure I can't bring you something else? There is a healthy cut of veal piccata, some beans . . . might even be some Oysters Vizzini—"

"Lizzie?" said Beatrice. "Why don't you leave us?"

"Ma'am?"

"Save the dishes for tomorrow."

"Yes, ma'am."

Giorgio became lost in the ice cream. He forgot about the blood on his brow. It descended his forehead at the pace of dripping honey. "It's so cold," he said.

"Darling. Your head."

He glanced up in confusion, spoon in mouth, chocolate smeared on his upper lip.

She gestured to his forehead.

"Ah."

She winced as he pressed the good white napkin to the blood. He pressed another corner of the napkin to his chocolaty lip.

"I came here tonight," he said, "to thank you. In person."

"I can't imagine for what."

"For helping me."

"Setting you up at Rosie's? I went on Saturday. They said they hadn't seen you for weeks." Beatrice tried to keep her tone neutral, even. To her ears it sounded convincing but Giorgio was inscrutable. In the past year he had passed from guileless to cunning to what seemed a calculated guilelessness, which was most cunning of all. Maybe even the Chantilly ice was a cover. Maybe Giorgio, like her, was buying time. Plotting.

"*Mamma*. We're alone now. Lizzie's gone."

She did not like where this was going, did not like her son's cockiness nor the antigravitational feeling that accompanied her realization that her son was controlling the conversation. Still she caught herself admiring Giorgio's newfound confidence, how he sat erect and strong and proud, like a man.

"I thought we had an agreement," she said.

"We did. You protect me. I protect the shadow business."

"That wasn't our agreement."

"It's a funny name, isn't it? The *shadow business*. Me, I don't see shadows. I just see business."

"The deal was that I protect you. And you stop *murdering* people."

"Mamma. Your voice."

"We're alone."

"I guess I'm confused. The business can't work unless people fear us."

"It's not about fear. It's about persuasion."

"Is there more Chantilly?"

"I can bring you the carton."

"*Persuasion* is a big word. I don't really understand it. But I understand fear. I think most people understand fear."

"We didn't need to persuade anymore. We're getting out of the business."

"There's getting out." Giorgio raised his flattened hand to mark an invisible boundary. Then he extended the hand as far from his body as he could. "And there's out."

"The canal was a legitimate job. It was our escape."

"How do you think Hercules got the contract? Why do you think the Jahncke brothers and Hampton Reynolds withdrew their bids?"

"The cousins were helpful during that process. I admit it. But after we won the contract—"

"The cousins were not very helpful."

"They were with Mr. Blank." She saw in her mind a dog's skull with daggers stuck through the eye sockets.

"The cousins paid the first visit to Mr. Blank. They did not persuade him."

"But they told me—"

"They told you what I told them to tell you."

Beatrice sat with this for a minute. The questions sprouted like toadstools but she had no time to ask them all.

"There was also the Tulane professor," said Giorgio. "Fishman."

"He wasn't going to hold anything up." She thought, *People of New Orleans, we must not allow the enemy to breach the fortification!* She thought, *Why, having spent two centuries defending ourselves from villainous Water, should we invite Her into the intimacy of our homes as if She were a weary traveler?*

"Fishman had a meeting with three members of the city council," said Giorgio. "He collected data that showed the canal walls would burst during extreme inundation. The data was convincing."

Those were not sentences Beatrice had ever expected to hear from Giorgio. *The data was convincing.* She needed a moment to recover.

"I never heard about that."

"I didn't think you needed to." Giorgio said it flat, without affect. As if it were just a statement of fact.

"How did *you* know?" She tried to control her voice. "About the data?"

"I found the studies in Fishman's credenza."

She suspected that if she asked where he buried Fishman's body, Giorgio would not hesitate to answer. *In his credenza,* he might say.

"There was also the situation with Hibernia."

"Which situation?"

"Their internal auditor conducted an investigation. He found some odd numbers. He came to Hugh with a whole mess of discrepancies."

"I didn't hear about that either."

"The auditor, Schneider, was threatening to make the numbers public."

"I don't believe you. Hugh mentioned no such thing."

"Hugh didn't think we should tell you about it. I agreed."

"Hugh Davenport—*he* asked you to settle it?"

Giorgio nodded. "I'll take the rest of that Chantilly now."

The information was coming too quickly. Not just the information about Giorgio's mercenary dealings but the information present in Giorgio's face: sobriety, calculation, shrewdness. Intellect. She had not met this Giorgio before.

"Hugh," she said. "What happened to him?"

"His uncle, Denzler, was leaning on him. He was prepared to tell Denzler everything: about the audit and about my work for the canal. The newspapers had started again with the ridiculous Axman stories. He was nervous."

"About what?

"He thought he would be discovered too."

"Hugh threatened you?"

"I could see what was going to happen. I distrust weakness."

Beatrice shivered. She couldn't help it.

"What?"

"An ax . . . it's grotesque."

"Don't believe everything you read in the newspapers. It's not always an ax. Only when the situation calls. A bullet leaves one message. An ax leaves a different message."

Her temples throbbed. Her throat was dry. "All those innocent grocers."

"What innocent? They owed us. They didn't pay."

"How careless could you be?"

Giorgio's eyes became very large. A hot, sudden fear rose in her and she was certain she would scream.

Giorgio smiled. He scratched his elbow. He inhaled. "I was careful," he said. "When it became dangerous to leave the bodies in the groceries, because of all the attention, I found another place."

"There are methods available to us in those situations. When someone is late on a payment. When there is a dispute."

"I am the method of last resort."

I could see what was going to happen, she thought. *I don't trust weakness.* She flashed her son the biggest smile she dared. "I want to apologize. I am the one who should be thanking you."

"Please be serious with me, Mamma."

"I am. I see it now, what you've done. You've held this whole thing together."

Giorgio stared at his empty bowl. She couldn't tell if he was bashful or considering his mother's sincerity or plotting some fresh horror. When he glanced up his face was serene, or more than serene: affectless.

"The ice. I'm sorry. I'll bring the carton."

"On second thought, I am hungry. I think I am very hungry."

"Would you like the oysters?"

"I haven't been eating too well. I've been moving around a lot."

"Home-cooked meals are the best cure for indigestion."

"I think I am very hungry now."

Beatrice rose. "I'll find you something."

"Mamma?"

"Yes, darling?"

"I'm glad there are no secrets anymore between us."

"I am too." She forced herself to place her hand gently on his shoulder. It was like caressing an anvil.

"I was starting to think you were against me."

"No! How could you?"

"We're the same, aren't we? You made the family strong. I'm trying to make us even stronger."

"Of course. We're family. We're mother and son. We're Mamma and Giugi."

"I see it like this: you did things that Papa couldn't bring himself to do. And I can do things that you can't bring yourself to do."

She wondered what he thought she was capable of doing or not doing. But she knew better than to say another word. She gave his shoulder another squeeze.

Giorgio covered her hand with his paw. Its weight was appalling.

On the tray she had arranged a slice of veal piccata, a small bowl of creamed onions, two rolls beside a mound of currant jelly, and a bowl of Oysters Vizzini, with extra oil. Giorgio loved the oil. He had a habit of tilting each oyster into his mouth until the oily juice drained down his throat. He had always been a compulsive, a systematic eater. She also brought a set of silverware. No steak knife, however. Butter.

"Wine?"

"No thank you, Mamma. The water will do."

"Good. Eat, my darling."

He had already begun. He dragged the dull knife through the

veal. He gripped the knife incorrectly, not between thumb and forefinger but in his palm, as one might the handle of a saw. Just as it was becoming more than she could stand he released the knife and tore apart a roll. He used it as a plow to herd the veal and onions on his fork, to sponge the oyster oil.

"I've missed our suppers," she said.

"Delicious," he mumbled through a mouthful. His mind seemed to have gone slack. Food alone disabled him—just not enough. She watched him closely, she couldn't help it, ready to glance away should he notice. But he did not look up until all the oil was gone. With the remaining crust he wiped the residue from his lips and popped it in.

"I have an appointment downtown," he said, after a swig of water.

"Don't you want to let your meal digest?"

"It's a big jazz show. Got to be there on time."

"I didn't know you liked jazz."

"I've become very interested in it lately."

"Yes. I suppose I can see why."

He smiled. "I'm glad we talked."

At the door he gave her a powerful hug and she felt as if she might choke. Then he was off, bounding down the steps and turning toward St. Charles Avenue. Nothing about his gait was abnormal, so far as she could tell. He was a big man, but she had made allowances for his size. She had calculated him to be at least twice the mass of his father, then rounded up. It made sense that the effects would not be felt immediately. Still she watched him closely until he disappeared around the corner.

MARCH 28, 1919—THE FRENCH QUARTER

The Axman was clever, but Bill was clever too. He left his uniform at home and dressed in his nattiest—his only—suit, the black Styleplus he had bought for his wedding. Since France he had lost weight and the suit hung loosely, particularly around his midsection, which was convenient because it meant the pistol would not make an impression. It was not exactly the height of fashion but with a black knit tie, his John Stetson, and a clean shave, he could pass for the kind of Uptown swell that might attend an evening show at the Cosmopolitan Club. When Maze saw him in the suit she thought her hallucinations had returned and let out a surprised laugh-shriek. But the humor caught and withdrew into her, where it twisted into something darker and cutting that brought her hand to her mouth and tears to her eyes.

The crowded club had a murky reddish tint, like a subterranean cave lit by boiling lava. It was an effect of the plush maroon wallpaper, the cirrus clouds of cigarette and cigar smoke, the golden light of the ornate crystal chandeliers. Spaced between the chandeliers, ceiling fans rotated lazily, powerless to dissipate the heat of the bodies pressed against the bar and tightly gathered around the circular tables. The bodies close together in the murky room brought back sensory memories of the dugout in the Forest of Purroy, the stench of the men, the warm clamminess of the air, the cheerful anxiety of imminent death. Sweat dampened his collar, which responded by tightening its grip. Just as he thought to ask the maître d' to lower the lights, the chandeliers did begin to dim and he felt some relief. But when he blinked the lights brightened again and he couldn't tell whether something was wrong with the lights or with him.

If only he had solved it sooner; if only Maze hadn't fallen ill. If Peter Davis's mother hadn't died of the flu in Atlanta over the weekend, Davis would not have left on Monday morning for the funeral, at about the same time Bill was visiting Mary Eager at Sophie Newcomb. When Davis returned on Thursday, Bill was there to greet him at Union Station. Davis, exhausted, did not put up a fight when Bill suggested a visit to the orphanage. The files at the Colored Waifs' Home were poorly organized and a comprehensive list of former students was impossible to find. Davis went patiently through the rolls. On a notepad he copied the names of the students that he had taught and the names of other boys he recalled teaching who did not appear on the lists. He crossed off the names of two boys who had died and another three who he was certain had left the state. Bill counted the remaining names. He got to fifty-six.

"You taught all of these boys how to write?"

"I taught them the Spencerian method, yes."

"Does anyone else teach penmanship at the home?"

"Just me."

"I'll need addresses. Occupations."

"We are not a correctional facility. Most of our boys are guilty of nothing more than losing their parents."

Fifty-six suspects . . . it was possible Bill would get lucky but more likely that a search would drag for weeks.

"Even the boys we accept from the juvenile court we do not believe are capable of sin. A boy under the majority is too young to know his own soul. We help him to find it."

"I see," said Bill, but he did not see anything. Fifty-six suspects, most without permanent addresses. One author of the Axman letter.

"We give a boy direction and teach him to become a leader of men. We educate him in a trade: woodworking, industrial labor, automobile driving, musicianship, tailoring—"

"The only trade Frank Bailey knows is highway robbery."

"That's not true, sir. He also played the bass guitar."

"He's a musician?"

"He played in our jazz band. He wasn't so bad."

"He wasn't so bad at sticking up people either. But not good enough."

"I thought he would continue to pursue music. But that's what I'm trying to explain—he is an exception to the rule. We turn wayward boys into upstanding men. Bailey was a disappointment. But I would be quite surprised if one of our students descended to the level of serial homicide."

"Frank Bailey was a jazzist?"

"He was. Many of our boys are."

"Are there boys on this list—boys you taught to write—who were in the band with Bailey?"

Davis nodded. He went down the list, underlining names. Beside each of the underlined names he wrote additional words in the margin.

"'Family Haircut'—what's that supposed to mean?"

"These are the names they go by in the street. Musician names."

In the margin Davis wrote:

SIDE PORCH

FAMILY HAIRCUT

SEEFUS

GATEFACE

DIPPERMOUTH

TWO ROOMS AND A KITCHEN

GRAND JURY

SLIM IZZY
NICODEMUS
REDHEAD HAPPY
FAT SLOP

The winnowed list was eleven names long. Back at the station, scanning prison and morgue records, Bill narrowed it further. Three of the men besides Bailey were locked away. Another had been in custody during the Besemer and Schneider attacks. A fifth, unbeknownst to Davis, had died. That left six.

Bill took the list to Perdido Street that night and canvassed the honky-tonks. What had seemed like a long shot began to assume the substance of a real theory. He could not believe that the letter's author was motivated only to sell jazz tickets. Miss Eager had said that the writer was imaginative but also deliberate—as a killer such as the Axman would have to be. The further Bill went down this path, the stronger his instinct pulled him. It told him that the letter writer was a murderer and that Bill was getting close.

A few bartenders recognized the names. "Grand Jury" Sam Lamothe had moved a year earlier to Los Angeles to play with his cousin Ferd Morton. "Family Haircut" Henry Rene was a drunk who stood outside clubs hoping for a handout from his old musician friends. Louis "Dippermouth" Armstrong was playing on Fate Marable's steamer and rarely passed through. "Nicodemus" Hubbard unloaded bananas at the Pauline Street Wharf. Isaac "Redhead Happy" Ingram had given up his horn a few years ago and worked as a plumber on the West Bank. That left a single musician. And he was playing a big show the next night.

The Axman might have been clever but Bill was clever too. He knew that it would be foolish to ask blindly around the club for Izzy Zeno, lest someone pass word to the murderer that a wild-eyed man was looking for him. (That was another thing Maze had said: that his eyes were wild. He laughed it off but when he caught his reflection in the mirror behind the bar he noticed that his pupils did have a larger aspect than normal and that he was blinking with an unusual rapidity that he couldn't control.) When the performance began, he would have his suspect, but it would be imprudent to jump onstage and make the arrest in front of a packed house. Better to wait until the set was finished and shuttle him out of the club before his absence was noted by the mob. Best of all, however, would be to arrest the killer before the show began.

Bill slid between the crowded tables, careful to avoid nudging the waiters with their trays overburdened by martinis and highballs, scanning the crowd for a clue. Instinct had brought him this far and it would have to bring him the rest of the way home. He scrutinized each brown face, questioning the men in his mind and questioning his own questioning. It wasn't easy—there were a lot of brown faces. The Cosmopolitan, in a gesture of fair-mindedness or whimsy, had made tickets for its jazz night available to Negroes at a twenty-cent markup. But all Bill could detect in their faces was the anxious merriment that preceded a momentous public happening. It was more complex than good cheer. In their faces danced something as heavy and as light as hope.

"Sir?" A hand gripped Bill's forearm. The man wore a double-breasted red velvet jacket with twin columns of brass buttons shining down its length; on the lapel the name of the club was written in gold string. "May I show you to your table?"

"I don't know that I have a table." Bill wondered if it was the suit. Could the maître d' tell that it was only a twenty-dollar Styleplus?

"I'm afraid we're booked. I'd offer you a place at the bar, but as you can see—"

"Is there no option for standing? With a drink, of course."

"The show is fully reserved. The first two acts have already played. Perhaps we'll hold another jazz night next week. There is demand, apparently."

The lights fluttered. Should he show his badge? Impossible. Tell a lie? Already four Negro men at a nearby table had noticed the confrontation and pretended not to watch. At a more distant table sat William Drain, Art Hegney, John Legall, Jr., and other members of the 69th Regiment—not quite dead but not quite alive either. No seats were left at their table. Bill had to figure some way to remain through the rest of the show. It was no good to wait on the street, when Zeno might leave through the back. And if Bill waited in the back—but he was being led by his elbow out of the club.

"Detective?"

A man in a top hat by the door was waving. The maître d'hôtel halted.

"I guess you don't recognize me without my monkey suit," said Captain Capo.

He shared a table with three women, none of them his wife, and an enormous man. The giant looked familiar but Bill could not immediately place him. His total recall, his greatest talent, was failing him. The giant reminded him of Leonard Perl. They didn't look anything alike physically, for this man was nearly twice Perl's size. Still something in his face or behind his face was familiar, ghoulish.

"I didn't realize you were a jazzist, Cap," Bill heard himself say, as if from across the room.

"I like hot music as much as the next toit. Where's the lovely Maisie?"

"I was leaving, actually." Bill gestured to the maître d'. "Forgot to make a reservation."

Captain Capo screwed up his mouth. "That's absurd. Join us! We have an uneven number anyway." He winked. The women were obviously prostitutes. Expensive ones, you could tell from the tulle and velvet gowns. Nobody wore those materials since the war except sporting women.

"I'm afraid every chair in the house is claimed, Captain," said the maître d'.

"Bring that one," said the giant heavily. He pointed to a chair one table away that had been occupied seconds earlier by a Negro patron who was on his way to the restroom. The maître d' nodded several times and did as he was told. Two of the smiling women, eyes brimming with invitation, made space between them.

Bill wiped his brow with his handkerchief, then his temples and neck. The cloth came away damp and gray. The throbbing in his head told him that Capo was onto him. Had Capo seen the bulge under Bill's jacket? Had he organized this evening to entrap Bill? But Capo soon ignored him and his anxiety lightened. They drank Pernod frappés; Capo already had two empty glasses before him. His eyes were on the brunette sitting beside him. She playfully fondled his purple liver spot. His hand was in her lap.

The giant was also distracted. But not by a woman. He appeared to be one of those new white jazz fanatics. He stared longingly at the stage, waiting for the final band to come on. Bill had given up any hope of apprehending the murderer before the show but at least now he would be able to follow Zeno off the stage. For once, he thought, his headache subsiding, he had come into luck.

A waiter brought another round. Bill ordered a rye. Pernod muddied the brain; rye had clarifying properties. Maze said that he wasn't thinking clearly and maybe she was right but his mind was clear enough to know that it wasn't clear enough. A finger or two of rye might really do the trick.

"You're not thinking right," she'd said. "I regain my sanity, you lose yours."

He knew he was supposed to be honest with her and he wanted to be honest with her but how could he explain what he was doing?

"I know that you don't care one way or another whether I capture this ax maniac."

"The only maniac I care about is you."

"We won't be safe unless this man is caught or dead."

"I thought he doesn't know who you are. How could you be in danger?"

"Not that kind of danger. He does not know me. But I know him and if I let the killing continue, I won't forgive myself."

"You mean for what happened with Perl?"

"What happened with Perl cannot be undone."

"I forgive you," she said. "Isn't that enough?"

"That's a lot. But it's not everything."

There was no explaining to Maze, not in words. Perl said he had seen Maze in the river. Now Maze was out of the river and on dry land. If the Axman continued to kill, she would fall back into the river and he would follow her there and they would drown together.

"On the top level," he'd said, "I'm conducting a police investigation. But there is a level underneath that."

"I'm completely lost."

He thought, Lost in a Maze. "Let me try again. On the underneath level there is an evil that has unbalanced everything—unbalanced me and unbalanced the city and maybe thrown the whole business into unbalance."

"The whole business?"

"The whole rotten business. If I don't stop that evil then really I am part of it."

"Slow down, Bill."

Lost in a blaze of word haze. "Captain Cap doesn't understand it. Mooney is incapable. I'm the only one who can stop it."

Maze began rifling through the bag that contained the pills and papers she had been given when she checked out of the hospital.

He could not quite explain to her that it was on the underneath level where, if he stopped the Axman, he would drown the part of himself that in the Forest of Purroy had climbed over his comrades and out of the hole in the ground when he thought only of saving his own life. He would drown that part of himself not in the Mississippi River where Perl had drowned on the top level, but in the underground river that had no tributary or outlet. *There are forests buried under forests,* Perl had said. *There are towns within towns. There are rivers that run down and run back up too.*

"You could say I'm trying to reverse the flow of the river. I thought that Perl's death would do it. But that only made the river flow faster."

She produced a thermometer. "Darling? Put this in your mouth."

Lost in a dazed blaze with Maze. Crazed and malaised. He chuckled.

"What is it?"

"I don't think you're listening." But he couldn't elaborate because the cold glass stem was clinking against his teeth and squirming like an anole on his tongue.

"Hold it one minute. One minute, Billy."

The show had already begun. He didn't have a minute. He plucked the thermometer from his mouth.

"Bill!"

"It will end tonight," he said. "Give me this night and we can go back to how things were."

"I don't want to go back to that!"

"You're right." He put his hand on her shoulder. "We'll go forward. Together."

"You look strange," she said. "Your eyes are wild."

They were dancing in circles: a crazy polonaise. He laughed again. "You're supposed to be in bed. Remember what the doctor said."

"I had visions too, when I was coming down with it. But that's all they are: visions."

"I love you, Maze." Unfazed Maze.

"You're stretched out too thin. You're going to snap."

Bastrop couldn't help himself: he snapped his fingers.

"Don't think you're doing this for us," said Maze.

"I don't. It's for me."

Lost in a daze of Maze, on a hazy crazy malaisey Friday.

She made a move to block the door but she was slow and uncoordinated from her week in bed. He was easily past her and outside, running down Tchoupitoulas toward the Vieux Carré.

Bill had tried to put Maze out of his head, but it was impossible once he noticed that Leonard Perl had joined Captain Capo's table at the Cosmopolitan Club. Bill had a strong sense that Perl had been sitting there for some time, two seats away, and he was disappointed with himself that he had not made the observation sooner. The sight of Perl induced in him a great and sudden fatigue, a reminder of a grim duty that with great effort he had managed to put out of mind. Perl was engaged in earnest conversation with one of the whores. She listened with a patient smile. She seemed not to notice the gash in his neck and the purple bruises on his face, or she was being polite and feigning indifference. It was clever of Perl to pretend to be so deeply engaged in conversation with the prostitute but Bill knew that Perl was secretly watching him. Perl didn't need to have his eyes on Bill to watch him. He was watching on the underneath level where human eyes had no use. A movement on the stage distracted Bill and when he looked back, Perl was gone. He had been replaced by the giant, who had picked up the conversation with the prostitute. It was clever of Perl, to appear and disappear like that, though Bill would not be intimidated by Perl tonight. He was there for the Axman and would not be deterred.

The atmosphere inside the club was undergoing a transformation. The ceiling fans whirled more quickly and Bill became cold. The sweat went clammy on his neck and under his arms. The chandeliers again dimmed but this time he was certain it wasn't his imagination because the sound in the room abruptly diminished. Voices dearticulated into excited whispers: the show was about to start. In the dim ruby light he realized why he recognized the giant man. He recognized him from the Axman investigation, he was certain, but could not immediately place how. The man was not Mr. Schneider of Hibernia Bank, nor the grocers Recknagel or LeBoeuf, nor the barber Andrew Maggio, who said that in New Orleans there were towns within towns. Nor was he a laborer at the Industrial Canal. But he *had* been at the canal anyway, Bill was sure of it.

It came to him. He wasn't sure if it was the colder air or the rye or the dimming lights that brought him clarity, but it came to him. The Vizzini boy. Of course: the overseer of the dig and Beatrice Vizzini's son. But Bill couldn't let himself get distracted because now Slim Izzy, the Axman himself, was striding onto the stage.

MARCH 28, 1919—THE FRENCH QUARTER—THE INDUSTRIAL CANAL

They were wrong to call it the devil's music. It didn't come from below but from above—at least the way he played it. Sure there was deep feeling in it, subterranean fears and hopes that could only be voiced through wordless music, but when Isadore played he felt himself reaching higher, beyond the planet and even the heavens, into outer space. He would write a "Black Moon Blues," a "Saturn Stomp," a "Red Planet Rag." He would be pied piper to the empyrean. He was close too. The Van Benthuysen Mansion show was one thing, but playing at the Cosmopolitan was playing in front of all New Orleans. Once the people heard his music, they would follow him, honking and singing, dancing the Extra-Terrestrial Trot and the Interstellar Itch, to the end of the galaxy.

The club itself had a Martian quality, the maroon plush and tobacco smoke and golden chandelier light and the unusual intermingling of whites and Creoles and Negroes conspiring to create an otherworldly atmosphere. It was said that on Mars all races lived and toiled beside each other in peace. Did they also dance together to the sounds of the stars? For tonight in the Cosmopolitan Club they were.

"That is some funny stuff," said a white man seated at one of the front tables, after Isadore's first solo. "Funny it up some more, will ya?"

Their set was the same but his playing was different. In "Chicken Dog" he made the horn squawk like a rooster and bark like a terrier.

"That man is dangerous!" someone screamed.

During "Make Me a Pallet on the Floor" he improvised a conversation between a crying woman and a fractious man with a deep baritone. In "Ole Miss" his cornet growled like a bear, hissed like a snake, and sang like a meadowlark.

"Play it, mister. Play that thing."

He went soft to draw the audience close, then played the chorus loud, driving them into fits of giddy dancing. He slurred and growled and klaxoned. He called out all his props, bending notes, executing long, breathless runs, applying a series of mutes, glasses, even a bucket.

"Damn the world. Damn the heavens. Damn my eyes."

He played the happy parts melancholy and the melancholy parts happy, the raw parts polished and the polished parts raw. He did all this without ever losing the melody. But it was all just a buildup for "The Whore's Gone Crazy."

"Slaughter me dead!"

Through his horn he shouted, *Love me! Hear me! Want me!* The crowd shouted back.

Frank Bailey had been right all along. He was right about the Axman and right about the importance of giving the audience something new—something tricky that made the saliva flow. That was the only way to become king. Like Oliver with his showmanship, Bolden with his volume, Ory with his tailgate trombone, Isadore had his own trick: a horn that impersonated animal and human voices, seduced women, emboldened men, discovered alien tones and colors and languages.

Even Orleania, sitting at the end of the bar, looked surprised. After nearly a week of caring for Isadora without interruption, Orly left the baby with Miss Daisy so that she could watch the Slim Izzy Quartet play the most important show of their lives. Not even she had heard Isadore play this way before. Nobody had. Only now, during the second encore, could he appreciate what he had done, before members of Uptown and downtown society, musicians young and old. Buddie Petit and Honoré Dutrey, who had played an earlier set, stood by the bar, mouths open tall enough to catch flies. Johnny Dodds and Lee Collins stared with expressions of wonder and scrutiny from a distant table and Isadore recognized other musicians too, not to mention every advance man in town. And it had all happened because of Orly. She had insisted that he play the show—not just for himself, but for her too. She was proud. The pride filled her to the brim.

There was something else too, if he were to be honest with himself. If there was one place in New Orleans where he could feel safe from an ax-wielding maniac, it was at the Cosmopolitan Club in front of a large crowd.

But when he stepped off the stage into the ravenous applause he saw that the pride in Orly's eyes had been replaced by a clammy terror that he had seen just once before, on the night of the Axman's jazz, when he returned from the Van Benthuysen party to find her weeping with fear after having been visited by a strange white man bigger than big.

"He's here," she said, through clenched teeth. "The man from Tartarus. Angry eyes."

She was interrupted by a white stranger. He placed an arm roughly around Isadore's shoulder, grinning as if he were an old friend come to congratulate Isadore on a fine performance. But his voice was cheerless and urgent.

"Detective William Bastrop," he whispered wetly into Isadore's ear. "New Orleans Police. Walk to avoid trouble."

Over the man's shoulder Isadore looked at Orly. From her surprise he could tell that this was not the man she had warned about. The detective was not bigger than big, after all. He was a couple inches shorter than Isadore, with thin arms, a pale, unshaven, cadaverous face, and recessed eyes. He looked unhealthy and ravenous. He had a damp, wheezing cough. His cheap suit was baggy and wrinkled, as if he'd slept in it or stolen it from somebody who had.

"In ten seconds," said Bastrop, "it gets bad."

"He wants me to go," said Isadore.

"Leave," said Orly. "Go with him. *Now.*"

The weight of Bastrop's arm guided him away from the throng of well-wishers that waited by the bar. Bastrop pushed him back onto the stage and across it, to the dressing room, where Sore Dick reclined on a chair, cherishing a cigar.

"I never seen you storm like that before, Iz."

"Say something," said Bastrop into Isadore's ear.

"Just going to have a conversation with this man here."

Sore Dick raised his eyebrows. "Which establishment do you work for, sir?"

"All of them."

Bill pushed Isadore through the back door, into a dark long hallway.

"Pick it up," said Bastrop.

"What is this anyway?"

"You know what it is."

Isadore considered his options. He could run and get shot. Or he could continue walking away from the club, down the dark, mildewed hallway, escorted by the detective to some unknown future. It wasn't promising, exactly, but better than certain death. Better than waiting in the Cosmopolitan Club for the bigger-than-big man.

Bastrop pushed Isadore through another door and they stumbled into the Cosmopolitan's newer annex, which had its own lobby and was less formal than the original hotel. It fronted Bourbon Street and was busy with drunk tourists and their loud laughter. Bastrop's hand pressed more tightly around Isadore's shoulder. The lobby's electric brightness accentuated Bastrop's features unsympathetically: his nervous mouth, small ears, sweat-dripping brow, the bluish hollows in his cheeks. When he coughed, the explosive force seemed to catch him by surprise. It attracted the attention of a porter, who seemed perplexed by the sight of the white man walking in a semi-embrace with the Creole jazz musician. The porter was too well trained to intercede, however, and they made it to Bourbon Street without obstruction. A police car waited at the curb.

"We're going to the station," said Isadore.

"Nah," said Bastrop. "We're going to the canal."

It was a black night, the moon hid behind clouds. Beyond the white-burning cones of the headlamps the world was empty. Bastrop had the energy of a newt, twisting and fidgeting and looking everywhere except at the street ahead of them. Pedestrians emerged from the gloom just in time to leap away from the oncoming automobile, shouting in terror or outrage as they did. As a concession Bastrop began honking the horn every few seconds to alert the onrushing night.

"I don't think I am who you think I am."

"What?" Bastrop looked pained. The engine was too loud for conversation.

"Can you go slower?"

Bastrop honked four times.

"Who do you think I am?"

Bastrop ignored him. He was too busy glancing this way and that, his pupils scrambling like mosquitoes. Isadore held tightly to the strap above the passenger's window. Bastrop turned up Esplanade, nearly knocking over a horse feeding from a bucket. He turned downriver on Burgundy and after five blocks pulled over. Darkness had eliminated the street behind them. He cut the headlamps. The engine sputtered, the chassis heaving, out of breath. Isadore touched the door handle. If Bastrop tried anything, he'd dive out of the car and run. But if Bastrop was going to try something, why had he stopped the car in the middle of a residential street full of potential witnesses, leaving the door unlocked? Why had he marched Isadore out of a club before a crowd of more than two hundred people? The adrenaline of the performance had morphed into an anxiety approaching panic.

"You wrote the letter." Bastrop kept his eye on the rearview mirror.

"I didn't kill anyone. The letter was a gag. I didn't realize—"

"I know that. But I only figured it a few minutes ago."

"How?"

"An old friend told me."

"Who told you?"

"You don't know him. A buddy from the war."

"What are we doing here, then?"

"Waiting."

"For what?"

"For the actual killer."

"He lives here?" Isadore looked at the street: a row of spavined shotguns, lit from within by frail dancing candlelight.

"He's coming."

"Why do you need me? I have nothing to do with the man."

"You're bait."

The man from Tartarus, Orly had said. *With the angry eyes.*

"I am not a musical expert." Bastrop turned his searching, blank eyes to Isadore. "But I never heard noises like that."

Isadore realized he'd left the cornet backstage. Would Dick know to take it for him? Would Orly? It took Isadore the space of a heartbeat to remember that the fate of his horn would be irrelevant if he was slaughtered in the middle of this dark Marigny street.

"How did you learn to play like that?"

"It's difficult to concentrate," said Isadore. "Given the situation."

"Don't worry about the situation. Leave the situation to me."

Isadore nodded. He looked for shapes in the darkness but only saw darkness. "I learned all the other ways to play. But none of them sounded right to me."

Bastrop looked at him very seriously for a while. "I know what you mean."

A white light pierced the rear windshield. Bastrop flipped the ignition. "That's him."

"How do you know?"

"He's driving too fast."

Bastrop hit the headlamps. The chassis grumbled into motion. The second car followed them a block behind. Isadore thought he could make out the driver's gigantic shape, like a black bear hunched over the steering wheel. Bastrop resumed his steady honking and accelerated. He coughed between honks and the coughs were almost as loud inside the car as the horn. They must have been going nearly twenty-five miles an hour. Burgundy was the only paved street between the Vieux Carré and the Industrial Canal, two miles downriver, but it was frequently interrupted by potholes and cracked pavement stones. Isadore held tightly to the strap with both hands to avoid knocking his head on the ceiling.

"What am I supposed to do? Just hope you kill him first?"

"What?" yelled Bastrop, between honks, glancing through the rearview.

"Who is he, anyway? The killer."

Bastrop honked crazily.

Ahead a bicyclist fell and ran to the curb to avoid a collision. Bastrop swerved to avoid the bicycle. Several seconds later the headlamps behind them repeated the swerve. The neighborhood grew sparser as they advanced downriver. They passed a block with only five houses, a block with two houses. Then they were amid overgrown fields and horse pastures. A cow raised its head at the sound of the approaching automobile and stared into the headlamps. Its eyes were embers.

The second car did not attempt to close the distance but remained about one block behind. Everything felt choreographed: the way the detective had swept him out of the Cosmopolitan, the police car waiting at the curb, Bastrop's confidence that the Axman would follow, the measured progression downriver, the acceleration—and now came another wonder. As the bascule bridge that led over the Industrial Canal came into view, Isadore recalled that its construction had not yet been completed. He tried to explain that a wooden barricade was blocking their path and if they hit it they would not survive the collision, but there was no time. He braced for the collision, sinking into his seat, flinging his arms over his head to block the cascading glass shards.

There was a jolt, but it was only the hum of the tires as they jumped onto the steel grating of the bridge. Isadore glanced back in time to see the discarded barricade in the headlamps of the trailing automobile. It had been moved to the shoulder, clearing the way. Bastrop had never even decelerated.

Bastrop spun the wheel sharply at the end of the bridge. The car pivoted, the tires skidding, and sped left, toward the lake. Where there had once been pastures and luxuriant long-limbed live oaks was a sere wasteland. The headlamps only created varying shades of blackness. The blackest shade marked the point where the earth ended, at the bank of the man-made river.

"What the hell is going on, man? Are you trying to kill us?"

Bastrop cursed loudly but not in response to Isadore. He saw something in the rearview mirror. Isadore turned. The dust kicked up by the tires gave them a vague and twinkly wake, the dust glittering like mica in the headlamps of the Axman's car. It followed them along the canal, weaving slightly in the loose dirt. Isadore saw the source of Bastrop's irritation. A third car had joined the procession. It crossed the bridge.

Bastrop spun the wheel and with it Isadore's insides. They came to rest, facing the direction from which they had come. Dirt sleeted the windshield. Isadore prepared for another collision. But the Axman braked and the two cars faced each other, lamps glaring, the dust mushrooming between them. The Axman cut his engine. Bastrop cut his engine. The chassis relaxed, as if lowering itself slowly to a seated position.

"Listen close," said Bastrop. The hot white light of the pursuing headlamps grimly illuminated his rheumy eyes, his sallow cheeks. "I have a plan!"

"Why the hell should I trust your plan?"

"If you follow it, we'll both live."

"If not?"

"I'll kill you myself."

Bastrop reached inside his suit and showed Isadore his service revolver. "Don't worry," he said. "I'm your friend in this."

"What choice do I have?"

"I'll prove it. Do you know how to shoot a gun?"

He had held Bailey's Webley & Scott plenty of times—had aimed it plenty—but never shot it. "I'm not exactly a professional."

"It doesn't matter." Bailey removed a pistol from beneath his seat. "Hold it as if you know what to do."

It could not be a good idea to accept a pistol from a cop.

"Just take it." Bastrop forced it into Isadore's hand. "When we get out, you point it at the driver of the other car. I'll do the same."

"That's the plan?"

"He can't shoot the both of us."

"Why not?"

"Two against one."

"Let me get this right. We both aim at the guy and hope you shoot him before he shoots both of us?"

"It's not much," Bastrop conceded. "I figured out as far as getting us here. I figured if he followed—"

They were interrupted by the sound of a car door opening. A leg stomped heavily onto the ground. Ribbons of dust plumed around it.

"No more talk," said Bastrop. "Get out."

"I don't want to get out of the car. No, sir. I do not want to get out of this car."

The other leg, about the circumference of an oak stump, emerged from the driver's seat.

"If I go out," said Bastrop, "how do I know you will follow?"

"I tell you plainly that I will not follow."

"If he sees me, and he doesn't see you, he might leave. The whole business will be squandered. He'll be on the run again and we might never catch up."

Isadore did not believe for a moment that the detective would shoot him. He recognized now, in the white headlamp glare, a familiar look on the detective's face. He'd seen it on his own face before—in the mold-covered mirror in Virginia's bedroom, when the navies arrived; in the mirror at Sis Pinky's, when he thought he'd have to give up music and rely on crime to support his family; in the window at Charity hospital, when Orly in her birthing frenzy chanted an old Creole chanson and it seemed the baby would never come. Yes, he saw it plainly in the detective's incandesced face: Bastrop was terrified. He coughed loudly, a deep bronchial cough that ended in a wheeze. His face was slippery with mucus and sweat.

Bastrop clutched his revolver and, with a violent grimace, opened the door. "Perl," he said, addressing neither Isadore nor himself, but something in the night. *"Perl."*

Bastrop lurched out of the car. Using the door as a shield, he aimed his pistol out the open window. The dust thinned to reveal the Axman standing beside his car. His arms hung from his sides like meat hooks. The head had the weight and authority of a Roman bust; it was too big even for his gigantic body, a stately, ridiculous head, a head like two heads merged into one. He hunched forward, as if overwhelmed by its weight. His mouth was arranged in a sickly grin. Isadore recognized him at once: Giorgio Vizzini, who used to supervise the dig, chewing ice and blasting the laborers with the power hose. He had always struck Isadore as a sadistic bully. He wouldn't have believed the man capable of a series of calculated murders but it was impossible to know what a man was capable of until he was pushed.

Isadore shrank into his seat, bracing for another collision. He did not sink so low that he couldn't watch the action, however. He squeezed the door handle as if it were Orly's open hand. If someone started shooting, he could roll out of the car, using the door as cover, and run to the precipice of the canal. From the steep high wall, he would plunge to the bottom. But a few broken bones would beat a bullet.

"New Orleans Police—" Bastrop was interrupted by his own violent cough.

Vizzini appeared amused by the detective's presentation. Bastrop might have been trying to order a wild, carnivorous animal hunched over a carcass to stop eating.

"Hi there, navy. You hiding the jazz-playing nigger in there?"

"New Orleans Police Department. Drop your weapon."

Vizzini's response was drowned out by a sudden roar. The third automobile, a Peerless Model 56, skidded to a stop alongside his car.

Vizzini appeared disturbed by the development. "Raymond?"

The man in the driver's seat, a Negro wearing a black hat, gave an awkward smile. The passenger door opened and an urn-shaped woman gingerly stepped out. Isadore sat up straighter in his seat. He recognized her from the dig too. Though sturdy of build, she had none of her son's gigantism. The only things outsize about her appearance were the gold rings that adorned the fingers of both hands. In the white brightness of the headlamps the rings sparkled like pixie dust.

"Mamma?"

"Officer, there has been a terrible misunderstanding."

Bastrop looked between mother and son, the revolver rattling in his hands. Vizzini, dazzled by the sight of his mother, appeared to have forgotten about the cop. He took a pair of clumsy steps and passed in front of his automobile. He held no gun. His hands were empty. *Empty* was the wrong word, though; his fists were weapons on the order of boulders or jackhammers. Still Bastrop had a point-blank shot. Beatrice Vizzini seemed to appreciate this. She flashed Bastrop a strong, urging glare. If Isadore hadn't known that she was Vizzini's own mother, he would have concluded that she wanted Bastrop to fire. Bastrop, however, was frozen. He appeared to be dreaming and blind to the world.

"I'm sick, Mamma."

"Let's go home, Giugi. There has been a big confusion."

"Mamma, it's hard for me to breathe." Vizzini tried to walk but stumbled and had to steady himself on the hood of his car. He paused there for a moment, eclipsing one of the headlamps. His mother glanced again at Bastrop, who responded with another violent convulsion of coughing. Vizzini was even closer now, less than ten feet away from the barrel of Bastrop's revolver.

"*Shoot*," whispered Isadore, but it was no use. Bastrop retched, shaking.

"Mamma, I think those oysters were bad."

Mrs. Vizzini shook her head. "I'm sorry to see you like this."

"It's getting worse."

"I don't know what to say." Her voice was distant, impersonal.

"Why are you talking like that?"

"Like what?"

"Like I'm not your son."

"It's late. Let's go home."

Vizzini paused, shaking his head. He spat. "Why did you follow me here?"

"You seemed unwell."

Vizzini considered this. "I think I know why you came."

"I was concerned about you."

"You were concerned I would live."

"Giugi! You're ill."

"You *poisoned* me." The word seemed to revitalize Vizzini. With great effort he rose to his feet. "Just like you did Poppa."

Mrs. Vizzini again glared urgingly at Bastrop but it was useless. He had fallen to his knee.

"You killed me," said Vizzini, marveling. Though his gait was jerky, he moved with determination toward his mother. Mrs. Vizzini seemed to consider returning to her automobile, before realizing that it would be useless. Her son was fully capable of yanking the door off its hinges, of smashing his fist through the glass.

"Shoot, why don't you?" she shouted, her gaze slashing at Bastrop. "There's your Axman! Shoot!"

Vizzini closed fast. His mother backed away from the vehicle. When Vizzini paused in front of the Model 56, she turned to her driver.

"Now, Raymond! Drive!"

Vizzini's instincts, however impaired, were quicker than Raymond's. Vizzini pivoted and reached his hand through the open window. He squeezed the driver's throat. Raymond's head fell limply on the wheel and the car began slowly to jog away from the canal. Mrs. Vizzini turned and ran. In a few paces she escaped the penumbra of the police car's headlamps and disappeared into the blackness.

Bastrop finally rose to his feet. "I know now. I saw him on May twenty-sixth, 1918."

"Get your head together," said Isadore. "He's coming for us next."

"On the corner of Baronne and Thalia. Long trench coat. Dark homburg—"

Bastrop fired his revolver. The Model 56's windshield exploded. Vizzini looked up—not in alarm so much as curiosity, as one might respond to an unexpected rap on the front door. He was surprised to be reminded of Bastrop's presence. He paused, debating whether to address Bastrop or his mother first. He chose his mother. But his motor system was misaligned. He ran awkwardly. He was fighting some internal force that pushed him right though he wanted to run left.

"Mamma?" His voice had an edge. "Wait a minute, Mamma."

"Help me!" she yelled from the darkness. "Officer!"

Bastrop fired again. Isadore wondered if he had imagined the sound because Bastrop made no movement but a thick column of smoke rose from the barrel. The bullet appeared to go nowhere near Vizzini. The giant continued to hobble in his manic, uneven manner, like a lamed ruminant. Some twenty yards distant, Mrs. Vizzini reappeared at the fringe of the nimbus of light cast by Bastrop's headlamps. The light might have dazzled her, or perhaps it drew her from the darkness as it would a cloud of termites. Or perhaps she was drawn by the pitiful sight of her dying son. After a moment's hesitation, Mrs. Vizzini began to run again—toward the canal.

"We can't lose him," said Bastrop. The gunshots had restored him.

Isadore saw in his head Orly and Miss Daisy and tiny Isadora, an earthworm dazzled by daylight, writhing and sobbing. "I'm not going anywhere."

"Stay here then." Bastrop walked into the white light of Vizzini's headlamps, revolver extended, his figure abstracting into a silhouette. Then Isadore was outside the car. He followed Bastrop into the light.

It was easier to see once he'd passed behind the headlamps. Mrs. Vizzini had again vanished but up ahead, by the lip of the canal, her son fell to his knees.

"I only wanted to help." He spoke softly. "But you made me sick."

Isadore realized, too late, that he had left in the car the pistol that Bastrop had handed him. He listened for Mrs. Vizzini but could not hear anything apart from Bastrop's wheeze and Vizzini's strangled breathing.

"I think I'm dying." Vizzini's tone was matter-of-fact. "I *am* dying." The words energized him. He lurched back to his feet. "Mamma? Mamma! I'm *dy*-ing."

Bastrop lowered the gun—not out of strategy, it seemed, but physical weakness. Isadore felt it too, the weakness. It came upon him in a wave, a miasma rising from the muddy canal.

"I'm dying, Mamma." Vizzini stumbled again, rose halfway up, tilted sidewise, fell again. "Don't hide. Don't you want to say goodbye?"

The silence was interrupted by Bastrop's cough, muffled in his sleeve.

Vizzini rose with difficulty to his feet. He couldn't straighten himself. Hunched over, his torso nearly parallel to the ground, he advanced toward the edge of the canal. Isadore and Bastrop followed quietly, taking tentative steps. Vizzini appeared oblivious of them. When he resumed, his voice was bright and taunting.

"I'm dying, Mamma." In a quieter, confiding voice, he confided to himself, "I'm really dying." He palpated his stomach, his head, his throat, as if trying to determine where the poison was doing its work. With a lurch he straightened his trunk and screamed, triumphant, "I'm dying! I'm dying! I'm dying!"

A low sick thumping noise came from the darkness. Another followed, and several more in rapid succession. Vizzini cocked his head, listening.

"Mamma?"

He scrambled with strange stomps and uncontrolled gesticulations, to the canal. The quarter moon sliced through the clouds and gave Vizzini's wet face a nickel-plated glow. He bent and stared over the edge. Bastrop and Isadore stared over the edge too. A shapeless mass lay huddled at the bottom of the canal, some thirty feet below. In the moonlight Isadore saw the pale skin of an arm, and at the end of it, a concatenation of gold flickering like an eternal flame.

Bastrop coughed loudly and Vizzini whirled around. His eyes were crazy. Isadore felt his organs plunge in his thorax. Bastrop doubled over, his gun hanging limply from his hand. Vizzini charged like a bull—a bull that had been pierced several times by a lance—limbs flailing, head bowed. Isadore reached for the detective's gun. He did not remove it from Bastrop's hand but raised the hand so that it trained on the giant's dark, galloping form.

"Pull!" said Isadore. "Quick!"

The gun exploded. The force of the bullet stopped Vizzini but failed to knock him over. He looked with childlike wonder at his shoulder, where a corolla of blood was blooming. He prodded it and removed his fingers to contemplate their stickiness.

"I'm dying." Vizzini turned to the two men and contorted his face into something resembling a smile. He held up his blood-smeared fingers. "I can do anything."

"Pull it," yelled Isadore into Bastrop's ear, but it was too late. Vizzini covered the remaining distance between them in a single bound and knocked them both to the dirt. The revolver skidded out of sight, somewhere below the reach of the headlamps. Isadore rolled away from the others and there was a sickening sound of deflation as Vizzini threw his full weight on top of Bastrop. But the fall depleted Vizzini. A violent shuddering overtook him; his legs went limp and his arms curled in on themselves. Still the force of his weight alone would be enough to crush a normal man. Beneath the giant Bastrop went limp.

At the edge of Isadore's vision a glinting came through the darkness. He crawled toward it.

"I have enough left for both of you," said Vizzini, between

convulsive breaths. He raised an engorged fist above his head and brought it down on Bastrop's face. With his full strength the attack would have killed the detective, even decapitated him. But Vizzini was frail and had relied on gravity to give his blow any force. "You killed my mother." He lowered his fist again onto Bastrop's head. A convulsion shot through Vizzini, tensing his spine, rolling his eyes back.

Isadore suspected three bullets were left in Bastrop's revolver, maybe two. At this range he only needed one. If he missed, it would not matter how sick Vizzini was, or how close to death; he'd summon enough strength to kill. What was the alternative? Run home and hope that Vizzini didn't survive his poisoning? Wait for another knock on the door?

The giant turned to Isadore. "It's a beautiful canal. When I'm done with him, I'll bury you in it."

"It's not your canal," said Isadore.

"'Course it is. I made it."

"No, you didn't. I did."

Isadore fired. The heat bit his knuckles and he dropped the revolver. Vizzini did not budge. Isadore looked down; the gun was halfway between them. But Vizzini didn't appear to notice it. Sitting astride Bastrop, he stared in amazement—not at Isadore so much as through him, toward the canal and his mother who lay at the bottom of it.

A strangled gurgle came from beneath Vizzini. Bastrop was trying to speak. With tremendous effort, through a bloodied mouth and broken teeth, and a diaphragm concaved by the weight of a giant, he tried again.

"*Offa* me."

"What?" whispered Isadore, as quietly as possible, so as to avoid interrupting Vizzini's reverie.

"Get 'im *offa* me!"

Isadore took two steps closer. Vizzini did not react. Isadore took another step and dove for the revolver. He rose from the ground, gun aimed, but Vizzini remained frozen.

Bastrop groaned.

Isadore cocked the gun and advanced again. When he came within a few feet he saw that Vizzini's eyes had rolled back in his head. His chest was matted with blood. Isadore nudged his shoulder with the barrel of the revolver and backed quickly away. Vizzini didn't move. Isadore pushed Vizzini's shoulder, hard.

Bastrop groaned.

Isadore leaned into Vizzini with his own shoulder. It was like knocking over a tree stump, and like a stump Vizzini at last fell stiffly to his side. Bastrop gasped as the weight lifted. He tried to take a deep breath but the pain of it made him whimper.

"Let me help you into the car," said Isadore.

"Don't," said Bastrop. "They're coming."

"They? Who's they?"

A pair of headlamps lit up the bascule bridge.

"Sit here," said Bastrop. "I'll protect you."

Isadore almost laughed. If anyone needed protection it was the bruised, flu-ravaged detective. Isadore sat beside him. For the first time he noticed the lights of the city in the distance beyond the infernal abyss. Somewhere out there Orly and Isadora waited for him. Out there the word of his performance at the Cosmopolitan Club was spreading from Uptown to the Garden District to the Tenderloin and the Back of Town. From there—who knew? Maybe it would travel on the riverboats up the Mississippi, or as far as Los Angeles and Chicago and New York.

"You hurt?" said Bastrop.

"I don't know."

"This canal." Bastrop said it like a curse. "Man has no business making rivers. Digging up the past."

It might have been a product of the detective's delirium but Isadore suspected he was onto something. The purpose of a canal, as far as he could understand it, was to link things together—a lake to a river. But really it divided, cleaving a city in two, separating not only land but communities, families, lovers. In that way it was the opposite of song, which joined people together. Music flowed from city to city, generation to generation, growing deeper as it went, each singer modulating it with his own human strangeness, the song growing richer and weirder and bigger, flowing forever to the end of the universe.

Isadore knew he had lost himself in these thoughts because he did not notice the arrival of the second cop car until its front bumper came to rest several feet from his head. A woman burst out of the passenger seat and ran to Bastrop. A paunchy white man emerged from the driver's seat. He approached warily, gun raised.

"He didn't do nothing, Charlie," said Bastrop. "Just saved my life."

The big boy nodded and after a glance at Vizzini's corpse to make certain he was dead, turned his attention to the detective.

"Oh God," said the woman. "We need an ambulance."

"I drive faster than any ambulance," said Charlie. "Stay calm."

The woman, crying, palpated Bastrop's body, seeking the damage. "It's over. Isn't it?"

"It's over," said Bastrop.

It was beginning. Isadore thought of the other musicians at the Cosmopolitan tonight: Buddie, Honoré, Dodds, Collins. They had seen what he did and they had seen the response. They knew Isadore would never leave New Orleans; undoubtedly they would take his tricks on the road. Maybe they would give him credit or maybe they would pick from his style what they liked and pass it off as their own. The idea would have bothered him only days earlier but now he accepted it in a spirit neither happy nor sad. The song was his only for a little while. Then it was everyone's. If it was a good song—a real, honest song—and it had a swing, it would be sung forever.

The paunchy cop finished settling Bastrop in the backseat of the patrol car. The detective's wife got in beside him. She held his hand.

The cop approached Isadore. "I'll need to ask you some questions," he said, "but not tonight."

"I understand."

"I can't give you a ride back."

"I'll walk."

"The body squad will be out soon. I'll tell one of them to take you."

"There are three bodies. One's at the bottom of the canal. The other is in an automobile that drove off that way somewhere."

The officer walked to the precipice and gazed down. "Yah. I see that one. It's sparkling." He looked at Isadore for a moment like he wanted to add something. Then he got into his car and started the engine.

As much as Isadore wanted to reassure Orly that he was safe, that the bigger-than-big man was dead, he wasn't ready to leave the canal. There was too much to think about. He wanted to remain in the darkness long enough to let it sink into him. His mind had gone out to the ends of the universe but now it went down, to the mud at the bottom of the canal that was already devouring Beatrice Vizzini and, below that, to the buried primeval forests, where once there had stood colossal trees and wildflowers and spreading vines. Those lost forests had sheltered mastodons, glyptodonts, and giant sloths but also countless small creatures now lost to the world—obscure lizards and insects and burrowing rodents. His brain was full of them, the slithering, conniving animals, sometimes burrowing in the mud and sometimes climbing to the crowns of the trees, famished for life, each confident in its strange heart that its life was the only one to be lived, each full of joy and terror, each singing in its own funny way at the moon, just as loud and as pretty as it knew how.